ROCK OF AGES

ROCK
OF AGES

A Junior Bender Mystery

TIMOTHY HALLINAN

Published by Soho Press, Inc.
227 W 17th Street
New York, NY 10011

Library of Congress Cataloging-in-Publication Data

Names: Hallinan, Timothy, author.
Title: Rock of ages : a Junior Bender mystery / Timothy Hallinan.
Description: New York, NY : Soho Crime, [2022]
Series: The Junior Bender mysteries ; 8
Identifiers: LCCN 2021055443

ISBN 978-1-64129-459-1
eISBN 978-1-64129-219-1

Subjects: GSAFD: Mystery fiction. | Suspense fiction.
Classification: LCC PS3558.A3923 R63 2022 | DDC 813'.54—dc23
LC record available at https://lccn.loc.gov/2021055443

Interior design by Janine Agro, Soho Press, Inc.

Printed in the United States of America

10 9 8 7 6 5 4 3 2 1

This is for:
my brother Mike, who is now painting the stars;
Peter Sanderson, making sure they're doing everything right in heaven;
Laren Bright, whose default switch is generosity;
and Munyin Choy: now more than ever, the light in the room.

No rock bands were
killed or injured
during the writing of this novel.

Part One

Dud November

1

Maybe a Hat?

Friday Night

The drum solo had gone on so long that it seemed to be taking place in geological time, and there was no indication that it was nearing an end. On the contrary, every time my hopes rose, someone in the sparse audience screamed something like "Faaaaar *OUT*" or "Go, *Boomboom*," and the message seemed to get through the wall of noise because the drummer—who went by the name of Boomboom Black, although (as I had recently learned) he'd been born Morton Fefferman—did the impossible and played even louder.

And then he did it again.

Still, whenever I was gripped by a really compelling need to flee the theater, I looked at the guy holding the sticks—Morton or Boomboom—and felt a grudging admiration for his willpower and his stamina, while withholding the laurel wreath for taste. With the sparse, stringy, shoulder-length gray hair, the seemingly frail arms, and the ropy neck, he looked like he was moments away from having a special soft-food breakfast delivered on a tray in a place with a name like Perpetual Acres or Sunset Highway. Instead, he had embarked on a solo that, from my perspective, threatened to outlive him.

The evening had begun on a note of discord and had grown more cacophonous ever since, a bad joke that had slowly turned into a worse one. When there were butts in the relatively few seats that had been sold, the lights had gone to half and the absolutely massive speakers that had been hung over the stage erupted with the enormous chords of Strauss's "Thus Spoke Zarathustra," better known to the generation—some of whose members had (in part, at least) embraced this band—as "the *2001* music." A follow spot lit up, pointed at no one, and then, after a jiggle or two, jerked spasmodically to our left, to the area downstage where a silver-haired little guy, who might have been five feet two inches tall and maybe seventy years old, was standing, mike in hand, looking out at us.

"Good evening, good evening," he'd said in a voice simultaneously sweet and ragged, like a flute being played through a wet dishcloth. "I'm Oscar Fiddles—" and from behind us, a guy who obviously gargled with rocks yelled, "So what does Oscar fiddle?" and someone else shouted, "Can you play 'Melancholy Baby'?" Oscar Fiddles nodded wearily a couple of times, cupped a hand to one ear, raised his eyebrows, waited to see if they were finished, and then said, "Boys will be boys. With friends like mine, who needs enemies? But seriously, folks, we're all glad you're here, and I hope you're not packed in too tight." A little wave of laughter sputtered over the seating area, indicating the presence of the easily amused and the extremely polite. "That's better," Oscar Fiddles said. "This is the last time we'll be doing this show, but don't forget, we got two completely *different* shows coming up tomorrow night and Sunday. Tonight, though—tonight's a *monster*—"

"*Speaking of a monster*," shouted someone, probably one of the midlevel thugs whose damp idea the concert tour had been, "get a load of that nose. You could park your car under it." Someone else contributed, "Or sit under it so you shouldn't get sunburned."

A feathery ripple of laughter was the result, but Fiddles wasn't having it. "Glad you folks think that's funny, but I gotta tell you, twelve weeks, three times a week, and you know what? You guys can go fuck yourselves, or maybe each other, why should tonight be any different?" And he dropped his microphone on the floor with a remarkably loud bang and stalked off the stage.

One of the guys who'd been harassing Fiddles shouted, "Oscar's gone to fiddle around with himself, folks, so let's get this thing started. Here's a band I *know* you all remember. Let's hear it for *Goat Motor and the Cranks*."

A tepid sprinkling of applause, no more enthusiastic than the beginning of a drizzle that's not fated to swell into anything like actual rain, started and then faded away as nothing happened, and then a stagehand darted out to recover Oscar's dropped mike. He waved to the crowd as though his mother was in it, getting a few sarcastic cheers in response, and then, as he ducked offstage, the ancient LA DJ, who was supposed to announce the bands when he wasn't up packing his nose in the men's room, said, "Booooyyyyyssss and GIRLS! Welcome to Rock of Ages, and let's hear a big Los Angeles welcome for a band you all love, *Goat Motor and the Cranks*!" And the center-stage curtain rose to reveal four harassed-looking musicians who were hurriedly plugging in. The audience was clapping in impatient unison by then, and after a good three minutes that felt like a quarter of an hour, Goat Motor kicked off with the riff that announced "Chainsaw through the Heart," one of its sparse little cluster of hits.

The business of the evening was finally underway.

Goat Motor's set stretched over several generations and the rise and fall of great civilizations. Their standard for being called back for an encore was, in my experience, uniquely modest. Still, eventually they yielded the stage to Rat Bite, and any expectation we had that the evening would get better flew south in seconds. The theme of the performance was the apparent loathing between the drummer, Boomboom, and the lead guitarist. They'd been stepping on each other's toes for what felt like an eon when Boomboom embarked on The Solo That Would Not End.

Three times already, the lead guitarist, who obviously sensed time's wingèd chariot hurrying near, had launched into the rag-gedy six-note riff that had briefly owned much of AM radio, back when the heavy chains around the drummer's neck had been de rigueur, which is to say when my parents were in high school. Under traditional circumstances, the decades-old riff, the song, and the band that played it would be half-remembered curiosities for a few people tottering on the edge of geezerhood, long replaced by newer, and often better, music. But rock and roll ignored the rules and refused to fade away as virtually all earlier forms of popular musical had. Rock was, after all, both the choice and the creation of the largest and richest generation in history. So here we were, fifty-some years later, watching the drummer swivel to turn his back on his bandmates and bang away even more loudly, exploring as-yet-unused features of his kit, which was bigger than some people's apartments. This time, he went for a long line of cowbells, each of which, pre-sumably, had its own unique sound and meaning, at least, to a cow. Looming all the way to the left, just beyond the cowbells, big and black and ominous, was the famous Ultra Boom®, a massive amplifier that was, apparently, being saved for the Big Finish, if any of us lived long enough to hear it.

George Santayana once defined a *fanatic* as someone who doubles his effort when he's forgotten his aim, and the drummer was well into Santayana territory. The guitarist, whose skintight black pants bulged over something that looked suspiciously like a large blackjack, gave it another despairing try, a scream-ing series of minor chords, complete with an attempt at a Pete Townshend arm-windmill that suggested impending rotator cuff surgery. The drummer responded by moving one step closer to the Ultra Boom®, stopping at some tall burnished-wood African drums that had once probably summoned far-flung children to meals across the rippling infinity of the veld. The drummer and the guitarist, as I already mentioned, had hated each other since FM radio was still something most people picked up on their fillings.

An elbow nudge from the right made me aware that someone was trying to say something, and I cupped a hand to my ear and leaned over. My daughter, Rina, shouted, "How long can this *possibly* go on?"

"It's a tradition," I yelled. "There were three prices for every Rat Bite concert: those who were under eighteen, those who were over eighteen, and those who turned eighteen during the drum solo."

"You made that up."

Someone behind me tapped me rather forcefully on the shoulder, and I turned to see a man in either late middle age or early old age. He wore a mustache that curled up at the ends as sharply as a fishhook and then degenerated into a pointy little goatee straight out of Frans Hals. This display was framed by a set of hair parentheses—sideburns thicker and bushier than the Forest Primeval, all of it topping off the first Nehru jacket I'd ever actually seen on a person who wasn't Nehru. The jacket's high collar suggested that the sideburns might actually extend down to the tops of his shoulders and possibly keep going across the backs of his hands.

"Some of us want to *listen to the music*," he said. He wasn't shouting, but he had a remarkably loud voice.

"Oh, *I'm* sorry," Rina yelled. "If I'd known it was *music*, I wouldn't have dreamed of—"

"Wow," Nehru said, poking me again with a thick index finger. "She's got a mouth on her, doesn't she?"

Brushing at the spot he'd poked, I said, "Sometimes it feels like she has several."

To my surprise, Nehru laughed. He said to Rina, "I'd probably be trying to chew my way through the floor if they were playing *your* music."

"I'm sorry," Rina shouted. "I was rude."

"Aaaahhh," Nehru said, waving it away and cupping his hands to his mouth. "I remember wanting to back a car over my parents when they played the stuff they *loved*. The music you grow up with is like your first boyfriend or girlfriend, you know? It takes you *years* to figure out why nobody understood what you saw in them."

A shrill, glass-endangering scream of outrage from the direction of the stage yanked me around just in time to see the guitarist swing his gleaming black Stratocaster at the drummer's head. He struck with the kind of accuracy that comes only with years of practice and/or extremely vivid wishful thinking. It was a seriously solid impact that sounded like someone slamming a car door; the drummer's head, if it hadn't been attached to the rest of him, would have probably flown over the edge of the stage and ended up in a lap in the third row. But, since it *was* attached, his body simply followed it stage right at a remarkable speed, dragging his torso and his thin black-clad limbs—he seemed like the kind of guy who, as Baby Morton, had probably insisted on black diapers—straight across the exotic part of his drum kit, knocking over the cowbells and the African drums and the Indonesian rain stick, and into the nightmare hulk of Ultra Boom®, which emitted a sound so low and so loud that the concrete floor beneath my feet actually shivered. As the room continued to shudder and the African drums toppled in all directions, the keyboard player, who up to now had been essentially scenery, abandoned his instrument, wrapped his arm around the guitarist's neck, and wrestled him to the floor. The low vibration from Ultra Boom® increased, only to be augmented by the still-amplified guitar, which had clearly shorted out, emitting a deafening, unwavering squeal that felt like a wire inserted into one ear and shoved straight out through the other, and then tugged back and forth. With knots in it.

By the time I got my hands over my ears the stage was swarming with beefy roadies in plaid shirts and—wearing a skintight T-shirt—a serious bodybuilder I'd met, not very happily, the previous evening. Lots of roadies are big guys, but the bodybuilder dwarfed them all; he looked like the Mr. Universe finalist from the planet Steroid, and he brought a measure of primitive, blunt-force order to the scene by kicking the keyboard player's legs out from under him, grabbing him by the back of his belt, hoisting him one-handed into the air, and carrying him, kicking and shouting, arms and legs flailing toward all points of the compass, into the wings and out of the audience's sight. I'd learned that the weightlifter's name was Bluto when I first met him, and seeing him in action made the moniker seem even more appropriate. In his absence, the plaid-shirted crew, who apparently drew their fashion inspiration from the halcyon days of early nineties Seattle, joined the other band members in milling around and shouting at each other. The bassist took a few half-hearted swings at the person nearest him, but nobody noticed. Nobody ever notices bassists.

"Come on," I shouted to Rina as I stood up. "Let's go meet the guys."

She said, "You're shitting me," but she got up and joined me in the aisle.

The guy in the Nehru shirt cupped his hands to his mouth and shouted, "Hey, where you going? It's just getting good."

We'd come a little early and had been honored with seats in the seventh row, much too close to the stage for my taste, and so, walking up the aisle, I got my first real look at the band's surviving fan base: heavily male, many of them so battered they looked deep-fried. Some of them might have arrived on cobwebbed antique motorbikes after three or four amphetamine-fueled decades on the road with the Hell's Angels or some lesser group, crisscrossing deserts at high noon, boldly swiping bags of Cheetos from convenience stores, and improvising other inspirational feats to burnish their legend. They wore cracked and peeling leather jackets over much-worn bug-spotted T-shirts, their eyes were haloed by pale raccoon imprints, courtesy of a lifetime's worth of sunglasses, and they sported an improbable ratio of walrus mustaches, perhaps to compensate for receding hairlines.

The biker guys and their dates shared the rows of seats with an assortment of rail-thin possible former crack enthusiasts, superannuated hippies, and, here and there, a sprinkling of men, and a few women, whose grooming and attitude suggested that at some point in their lives it had occurred to them that they might eventually get older, prompting them to seek out the narrow road to the middle class. They seemed keenly aware that they'd dressed wrong, even though some of them gamely sported heavy earrings that must have required some painful reopening of the piercings of yesteryear.

From my brief survey I estimated that the place was about 70 percent male and 30 percent empty. I'd been told that most of the tour's twelve earlier stops had been, if not always sellouts, still pretty solid and occasionally packed to the rafters, but that LA was an exception. LA was supposed to be the big finish, but things were clearly winding down with a whimper.

Behind us, down near the stage, some optimistic fans set up a rhythmic clap that spread across the audience like oil on water. It was then amplified by foot-stomping and, here and there, cries for more.

Rina shouted, "They've *got* to be kidding."

"It's been a long time," I said. "Fifty or so years ago, they loved those guys."

"I thought music from back then was all rainbows and unicorns," Rina said, practically yelling into my ear. "Pacifists smoking pot and growing flowers in their hair. Meals of vegan broth around ecological campfires."

"That's tomorrow's show," I said. We had almost reached the door. "It's a three-day tour, different music, different audiences. Gristle and heavy metal tonight, beads and incense on Saturday, Brits and nervous, skinny-necktie rock, quasi–new wave on Sunday."

"These guys don't sound like heavy metal."

"Yeah, well, they might have been more dangerous when they had their teeth."

The crowd began to chant: "RAT BITE! RAT BITE! RAT BITE!" The chant was in time with the claps and the stomps, and was audible even over the feedback. The floor of the theater was actually shaking.

"Kind of a cool name, though," Rina said.

"I'm just sorry you're not going to get to hear Wet Spot and Teeth of the Nameless."

"You made those up."

"Afraid not." I got my hand on the door to the lobby, eager to put it between me and the shrill guitar feedback. Before I could push it open, I was frozen by an ear-scraping chorus of screams, one of which belong to Rina. I wheeled around just in time to see a roughly built set wall that suggested the interior of an old Midwestern farmhouse—complete with a red gingham curtain over its only window—knife down from the flies, where it had been hanging the preceding day when I first explored the theater. It landed, like an enormous and somehow homey guillotine, on the unconscious drummer. One of his legs flew into the air, a spasm of some kind, but before he could do anything else—if he was capable of doing anything else—the wall tilted toward the audience and, slowly and majestically, its red curtain fluttering, fell forward onto the stage, spewing a thick cloud of dust that rolled out over the audience.

Santayana also said that those who fail to understand the past are condemned to repeat it. If the melee on the stage was any evidence, it looked like old George was right again.

When we got outside, we discovered that it had started to drizzle, the moisture creating halos the precise color of breath on glass around the streetlights and lending a kind of temporary charm to a neighborhood of right angles executed in aging concrete. Like all good Californians, we paused instinctively beneath the theater's brightly lighted canopy, waiting for the almost-rain to lighten. God forbid we should get damp.

Rina said, with a little wobble in her voice, "Do you think he's dead?"

"Yeah. And if he's not he'll probably wish he were. That thing must have turned about a foot of his spine to powder."

"Is it bad karma to be kind of grateful that we get to go home?"

A car splashed by in what would usually be the parking lane, and we stepped back. The middle lanes were taken up on both sides of the street by a gaping black hole almost half a block long, turning the parking lanes into splash territory.

"It's not just bad karma," I said, "it's also impossible. The minute I can figure out what to do with you, I've got to get backstage."

"What to *do* with me? How quaint. And anyway, why in the world would you go back—"

"I guess you'll have to come with me," I said. I took her hand and dragged her into the drizzle and around a corner of the theater into a little alley about as wide as two small cars side by side. We had the theater wall on our left, and ahead of us, at the end, stood a small two-story stucco office building that I believed to be the source, geographically at least, of all the trouble. I said, "Maybe Lavender will take care of you."

"Lavender? You know someone named *Lavender*? And since when do I need—no, no, wrong question. What in the world is going on?"

"Tell you later," I said, breaking into a trot toward the door that opened onto the stage. "Listen, if we don't find Lavender, stay close to me, and I mean close enough to touch. You hear me?"

"Yes, Daddy," she said in a high little-girl voice. "Whatever you say, Daddy."

I broke a rule about not swearing in Rina's company and said, "Oh, shit."

Rina said, "What?" and then added, "*Oh*. No kidding."

Bluto, the bodybuilder I'd glimpsed on the stage, bulled his way out through the hangar door, pushing through the welter of people, some fleeing the stage area despite the drizzle, some barreling out of the little office building and heading for the noise. At that precise moment, the feedback squeal, which was bouncing around between the walls of the alley, was cut off. Bluto stepped in front of us, his massive arms spread wide.

"Who's the chicklet?" he said in his oddly wispy voice. "Too young for you, Jack. And no, she can't go in. Only people who—"

"You are out of your weight class," I said. "Whoever your bosses want in there, you steroidal vacancy, I'm guaranteed to be one of them. Or do you want to talk to Cappy about it?"

I'd thought that Cappy's name would get his attention, but he wasn't even listening. Rina had stepped right past me to stand in front of him. "Wow," she said, looking him up and down with a hand on one hip. "You've done a *lot* of work."

"You gotta take it serious," Bluto said.

"And *these* ones?" she asked, her voice higher and younger, sounding like she had at twelve or thirteen. She reached up and touched the top of his left shoulder. "These ones, right *here?*"

He did something to make them look even bigger and said, "The traps, sweetie. The trapezius."

"The *trapezius*," she said, as though he'd just quoted her favorite sonnet. People were still running past us in both directions, and one of the guys fleeing the stage turned up the alley and lost his dinner against the theater wall.

"That's right, Chicklet," he said, "the trap—"

"Well, I mean," she said over him, "I've never seen them this . . . this *huge* before. But, I mean, when you get them just, you know, wayyyy *big* like this . . ."

"Yeah," he said, and this time he inflated them one at a time.

"Well," Rina said, "when they get this big, they make your head look really *weensy.*"

He backed up a step. "Whaddya mean, they make—"

"I mean, I'm sure some girls really *like* a small head, probably means less competition or maybe they think it'll be easy to hold up their end of the conversation, but it's not an automatic sell for most of us. Still, it's good on you, you know? It *suits* you." She reached back, took my hand, stepped around him, and led me, as though she were the parent, into the backstage area. Over her shoulder, she said to him, "Maybe a hat?"

2
One-Way Ticket to a Broken Heart

When you're in an audience, looking at the stage that's in use, you're not really seeing the stage at all. Despite its size and its cumbersome mechanics and the fact that it's the space to which all eyes are drawn, the stage should no more draw attention to itself than a picture frame does. The stage's job is to disappear and become whatever is being presented: a gathering of people beneath open umbrellas in low light becomes a New England funeral; a follow spot on one musician, such as the one that had been directed at Boomboom when the wall fell, makes you forget everyone else onstage. You're in a realm where time and space seem to be malleable.

But under work lights, with the act curtain lowered—that's the big one between the stage and the audience—a stage has all the mystery and allure of an auto repair shop; it's just a wide, largely empty rectangle with a much, *much* higher ceiling than we're used to seeing—the *flies*, in theater jargon—from which can be hung huge set pieces called *flats*, such as the Midwestern farmhouse wall that had floored the drummer. That and the other flats, so-called because they're mainly painted canvas framed in wood, hang well above the audience's sight line, waiting for the cue that will lower them into position, usually while the curtain is down or the audience is looking elsewhere. As I led Rina in, I glanced up at the other flats hanging there, identifying the ones I'd seen the previous day: the Yellow Brick Road, dwindling in perspective as it bisected the lush landscape of Oz; the high green towers of the Emerald City, their spires shrouded in clouds; and the densely decorated interior walls of the Wizard's palace, its details lifted from the classic movie.

On the stage floor downstage right, where a slice of a Kansas farmhouse had fallen on Boomboom, I saw the current drama: around the fallen drummer a little knot of men had gathered, tight as a flexed muscle. It included some of the roadies, a few musicians in their outmoded stage outfits, and two or three apparently curious stagehands. The energy, though, flowed from a tense little coterie made up of three dark-suited guys in their sixties and seventies who were definitely not rock musicians and were deferentially orbiting the man who called himself Sparks: the men in the dark suits were, in fact, three of the four thugs who had put the tour together. They were walking the fine line between being right at hand for whatever Sparks might suggest while also maintaining a safe distance from him, even though one or all of them had surely hired him. Staying out of his way required a certain amount of choreography because he was pacing back and forth with a cell phone pressed to one ear, apparently taking orders, which he relayed to everyone within shouting distance. The red zigzag of lightning on his briefcase shone all the way across the stage, a sort of portable *beware* beacon.

As if on cue, a bubble of chatter rose from the knot of men, and one of the suits—Jack Gold, if I correctly remembered the photos Irwin Dressler had showed me—whirled and ran toward us, heading for the door. I stepped in front of him and he stopped; he'd seen me the previous day with Sparks, and he had no way of knowing what our relationship was.

I said, "What just happened?"

"He moved his legs," Gold said, shifting from foot to foot like someone who desperately needed directions to the men's room. Big and beefy as he was, he had the tight, panicky eyes that identified most of the people who spend any time around Sparks, and a pointy little face that looked like it might have been pushed briefly into a giant pencil sharpener. "Well, he moved *one* leg," he said. "Sparks says that means his back isn't broken."

"And that means what?"

"Sparks says *it means that his back isn't broken*," Gold repeated, louder. He started to step around me, but I put a hand on his arm.

I said, "And *that* means?"

"That we can *move* him," he said, actually miming picking something up and putting it down again. "Get him the fuck out of the *way*, you know? Get the show on the road. Where are the *bands* s'posed to play? You want they should dance around him? Sheesh." He feinted to his left and then went right, and I resisted the impulse to put out a foot and bring him down, just for fun.

In response to some command I'd missed, stagehands swarmed onto the set and began to wheel Rat Bite's piano upstage and into the stage left wings. From the other direction, two guys who had been pried away from gaping at Boomboom shoved an electronic keyboard toward center stage. Opposite us, a couple of roadies were breaking down Boomboom's enormous drum kit at hyperspeed, and over the PA system I heard the cigarette rasp of Robert W. Natural, the ancient classic rock DJ who'd made me want to clear my throat for decades and who was doing the between-acts patter. He was a guy who had stuck faithfully with amphetamines for forty years, refusing to be seduced away from them by the stronger and more lethal uppers that came and went, often taking their users with them. His hands shook like personal seismic zones and he had eyes like fried eggs, but he was still alive.

"Don't worry about Boomboom, boys and girls," he said, sounding like the world's biggest match being struck. "He's up and laughing it off." From where I stood, if Boomboom was laughing it off, he was doing it while he was being hoisted none too gently onto a stretcher, his head flopping back and forth bonelessly and one arm hanging off the edge, limp as a windless sail. The DJ, who had never known when to shut up, said, "Hold the vibe, folks, we've just begun to rock out. Coming up—the one, the only . . . *Wet Spot*."

Rina said, "They're not really just going to keep *playing*, are they?"

"The show must go on," I said, "unless they're planning to hand out refunds, and that's not going to happen. See the guy with the briefcase over there, the one with the lightning bolt on it? He's essentially the not-so-secret weapon of the four old mugs who financed this thing, and he has never heard of a persuasive reason not to just *maim* anybody who gives him an argument, so, yeah, I'd say they're just going to keep playing."

"That's disgusting," she said. "I mean, he wasn't very good, but still . . ."

As the guys carrying the stretcher started toward us, I realized who was missing. I snagged a passing anorexic, whose skintight pants, dead-black hair, and thick pancake makeup marked him as a performer.

"Where's Doc Bellman?" I asked. "I saw him in the audience."

"They want a *real* doctor, don't they?" the anorexic said in a British accent. Beneath the makeup he was working on a museum-quality collection of wrinkles. "Old Doc Belly was fine for the tour, you know? He could put ice on things, you know? But he was on the bus *mainly* because he had a prescription pad, you know? He could write us up for everything short of the big sniff, and the fans always had that, bless their souls. Anyway, Belly's a fookin' *veterinarian*, isn't he? Boomboom seems to need someone who's familiar with, you know, *people*."

"You don't sound very upset," Rina said.

"Well, *hi*, sweetie, where'd you come from?" With the

exception of a landmark-crooked set of British National Health teeth, dyed a vivid smoker's yellow, he had fine, even features that must have provoked their share of screams back in the day. "No, I'm not upset. Boomboom got floored a couple of times already on the tour, although this is the first time a house fell on him, but that's showbiz, innit? I mean, he's been getting coldcocked on the stage by old Franky for bloody decades. Practically in the script, you could say. *And* he's a shit drummer. What's your name?"

"Charles," Rina said. "This new makeup is *fabulous*."

"Well, Charles," the Brit said, "you're close enough for me. Most of the girls I've met on this tour were only girls in the sense that a bunch of bones in a museum is a Tyrannosaurus rex. What are you doing after the—"

A woman behind me said, "Pay him no attention, darling," and I looked up to see Lavender, wrapped in a dress that seemed to be made entirely of pink bows and that was held up at one shoulder by a clasp in the form of a large, rhinestone-studded alligator. "You're talking to a man who dyes his pubic hair."

"And you'd know how?" the Brit said.

"Oh, *please*," Lavender said. "It was in *Rolling Stone*."

A bit sullenly, the Brit said, "I had a *lot* more fun when I was young."

Lavender extended a finely groomed index finger and touched him gently, even affectionately, on the tip of his nose. "You certainly did," she said. "And I was there for some of it. Twice, I think. Not that *you'd* remember, of course. What's your name again, darling?"

"Nigel," the Brit said. "You've forgotten my bloody—"

"Oh, no, how *could* I? It's burned into my soul. The Holiday Inn, in Phoenix, an unlikely location for paradise, sometime in March of 1974. But actually, the name I was asking for belongs to this lovely young lady, the one you were leering at."

"I don't *leer*," Nigel said, sounding genuinely hurt. "I don't need to. Do you *really* remember—"

"Of course I do," Lavender said. "How could I forget?"

"Well," Nigel said, standing a little taller, "I've got a show to get ready for. Ta, love." He patted Lavender's cheek, winked at Rina, said, "If you change your mind," cocked a thumb toward the dressing rooms stage left, and then headed toward them.

"That's what makes lead singers so irresistible," Lavender said. "That combination of egomania and insecurity."

"Lavender," I said, "this is my daughter, Rina."

"*You're* Lavender," Rina said. "He's already mentioned you to me. He said you could protect me."

"Darling," Lavender said, "you don't seem to need any help."

Rina gave me a take-a-bite-out-of-*that* glance and said, "Ahem," pronouncing it exactly as it's spelled.

"But on the other hand, he's *supposed* to worry about you," Lavender said. "It's his job."

"Yeah, but you know, he acts like I've been in a freezer since I was eleven."

"To him you're always going to be a little girl, the same way, I suppose, that Nigel, to me, is always going to be twenty-two years old, fresh as warm bread, and just off the boat from Blighty. Until I did my first British band, I had no idea rock and rollers could have manners."

Rina said, "Your first British *band?*"

"One at a time, of course, darling. What do you take me for?"

"Well," Rina said, and then they were both laughing.

"Glad you guys have hit it off," I said. "But keep it fit for family listening, okay? No hat racks."

Rina said, "Hat racks?" and Lavender said, "So you're saying that I probably shouldn't tell her that most drummers, including poor Boomboom, are hung like butterflies?"

"That's *exactly* the kind of thing you shouldn't tell her."

To me, Rina said, "Where are *you* going?"

"I have to do some snooping, and there are some people,

probably on this very stage, who won't like the fact that I'm doing it. I don't want more people than necessary to associate you with me."

"There are times," Rina said, "that I wish I had a regular father."

"Please, honey, be grateful," Lavender said. "Regular anythings are boring. Come with me, and I'll tell you about Keith Richards."

"Keith who?"

"Oh, no," Lavender said. "I've outlived my interest value. Do you have a boyfriend?"

"Do I ever."

"Well, if you promise not to tell him, I'll show you a peephole into the dressing room that Child of Man are using. They're not quite as withered as most of these guys."

I said, "I have a better, if somewhat duller, idea. Why don't you take her out of here and into the office for a while?"

"Wow," Rina said, "an *office*? I've *always* wanted to see an—"

"It's the patriarchy, sweetie," Lavender said. "Over hundreds of thousands of years, they've evolved an infallible alarm system to alert them to the possibility of female fun."

"Beat it," I said. "Both of you. The patriarchy has spoken."

"Oh, my poor heart, how it *pounds*," Lavender said, but she took Rina's arm and led her toward the door to the alley. "If you know where to look," I heard her say, "there are a *lot* of things most people don't know about offices."

Bluto was still guarding the hangar door to the alley, and I watched until Rina and Lavender had gotten past him—he actually turned his back to them—and then I decided to do something that, broadly speaking, was probably part of my ill-defined job. I began to cross the stage toward the point, downstage right, where Boomboom had become the first person since the Wicked Witch of the East to have Dorothy Gale's house fall on him, but I had to hold up as the members of Wet Spot assembled onstage. They stood there as still as statues of royalty, radiating impatience while roadies did the menial task of plugging in their instruments.

At that point, the audience went quiet, so suddenly that a door might have been closed on them, and I guessed someone had dimmed the house lights to half. After a little feedback-squeal during tuning, I realized the big curtain, the act curtain, was about to go up, and I headed rapidly for what I now thought of as *Boomboom's wing*, downstage right. As I got there, the DJ shouted, "Ladies and gentlemen, boys and girls: let's hear it for WET SPOT." The stage lights came up partway, the bass began a familiar rhythmic figure, and the keyboard guy began a staggered three-chord one-TWO-three-four riff. He kept it up as the curtain rose all the way and the lights blazed up to full, when the drummer kicked in like thunder and the keyboard player sang, "Bought a one-way ticket, a one-way ticket, bought a one-way ticket to a broken heart," and I realized that I knew the song and even *liked* it, and for just a moment, I knew why all those people were sitting out there, and rock and roll was okay after all.

What with all the movement of the stagehands and the band's own roadies, who were responsible, among other things, for protecting the musical and electric gear, the little knot of crooks had moved upstage to clear the way. I took advantage of this temporary lapse of attention to go take a closer look at the wall that had ended Boomboom's solo and, probably, his career.

It was a big, heavy wall, as its loud and disastrous landing had suggested. Its weight had probably discouraged the crew from carrying it any farther than the few feet required to tilt it against the wall downstage right. The stagehands had stored it topside up, so it took just a few seconds to get a look at the thick rope from which the flat had been hanging and locate the bit in the middle where the rope had been—what? Cut? Frayed?

And, in fact, it seemed to have been both cut *and* frayed, a fact that changed this contentious, misconceived ego festival into something I hadn't bargained on: the scene of an attempted murder.

I was backing away from the wall, reluctant to turn my back on it, when I looked up and caught a glimpse of Sparks glaring at me; and suddenly I regretted even *more* deeply the decision to bring Rina with me.

3
He Wants to See You

Friday Night/Thursday

One of the problems with being a crook is that you have to lie a lot.

It was bad enough to have dragged Rina, inadvertently, into a potentially perilous situation, but my sense of guilt was compounded by the fact that I didn't feel—even at that juncture—that it was possible to explain it to her. Being honest with her would not only have opened a discussion of an area of my life she and I had never discussed, it would also have required mention of the He Who Must Not Be Named of Los Angeles organized crime. And one simply didn't do that with a light heart.

Even a brief explanation of why I was there and who had asked me to show up would have inescapably led to a barrel of questions about someone who should not be discussed by anyone who wants to remain eligible for life insurance. Placating a curious teenage girl—even if she was my daughter—was not one of the reasons.

The fact that I'm a professional burglar had been aired thoroughly and often loudly in my arguments with my former wife, Kathy, during the stormy months that ended with me being ejected from the house that she and I once thought we would share until we doddered off into the sunset, holding hands. Through those spirited discussions, Rina had kept her ear pressed to the door of her room and absorbed the essence of the way Kathy saw my life, which she had boiled down during one especially heated exchange to the memorable phrase *thief in the night*. Like any dutiful daughter who's curious about the details of what Daddy does, Rina had tucked that snippet away in her memory and, when her mother was safely out of earshot, had tried to persuade me to elaborate on it. By and large, although I'd managed to sidestep the specifics, it was pretty clear that she knew that I occasionally visit people's houses without an invitation and that I sometimes remove from those houses things that catch my highly trained eye.

Lately, though, she'd been demonstrating an unsettling *enthusiasm* for that part of my life. She'd brought it up repeatedly, sometimes quite bluntly, in the past few months. She'd read several books about it, including *In and Out with the Goods*, the self-serving autobiography by Frankie Fingers (a nom de plume, obviously). From my perspective, it was a sketchy, ham-fisted memoir by a third-rate second-story man with a first-class agent, but according to Kathy, Rina had talked about it for days. She had also ransacked the internet for info about burglars. At one point not so long ago, she had startled me with a question about someone I had actually known, a guy named Whispers Wallace who specialized in Art Deco and Art Moderne and who could smell a really good piece through a foot-thick concrete wall. Unfortunately, Whispers's nose had been sharper than his ears, with the result that he's no longer with us. But the lurid details of his death—he was thrown through a third-story window and took a bad bounce onto a busy street—didn't seem to have diminished her interest. Now, what with Kathy's temporary absence and the fact that she had placed Rina in my care for several days, I was trying to sidestep the topic of my profession. Still, I could feel it there, lurking just below the surface of our relationship, waiting, like the Loch Ness Monster, to poke its big, ugly head up at the very moment that we realized we were too far from shore to turn around.

I was also kicking myself for having brought her to the concert at all. I should have known better, and in one part of my mind—the sober, responsible part I so often ignore—I *did* know better. But she had wanted to go, and she had accompanied the request with the big, mournful Margaret and Walter Keane eyes she had mastered by the age of four. Like a complete doddering schlub I hadn't thought there was any chance of danger. *All those people just sitting there*, I thought. *Eyewitnesses everywhere*, I thought. *What could go wrong?* I should know by now that when I ask myself that question, the answer is invariably "everything." Even now, I couldn't tell her *why* we were there. I couldn't talk about the phone call or the guy who made it. You just don't ever tell *anybody* about the guy who made the call, at least not unless you're *much* more confident in your judgment than I am.

The call had come in only a day earlier, while I was happily planning all the things I would do with Rina over the four days she'd be spending with me and my extremely significant other, Ronnie Bigelow. Kathy was somewhere in the Midwest, "getting to know," as she put it, the guy she was currently auditioning to be my replacement. I fell in love with Kathy when we were in eighth grade. The love had lasted through high school, college, marriage, childbirth, and early parenthood. Ultimately, though, I'd been given a clear choice: either follow my dream, as people like to say—although their dream probably isn't high-end burglary—or follow *Kathy's* dream, which involved me putting in a solid forty-hour week in her father's insurance agency. As someone who had decided before I graduated from high school to become the kind of guy people buy insurance *against*, I found the leap to be just too great. A man's got to stand for something.

But Kathy and I had not only loved each other, we had also *liked* each other, and she had been generous in letting me share in Rina's life, although it was understood on both sides that our togetherness was not to include father-daughter burglaries.

When, several years later, I met and fell in love with Ronnie, Kathy had instantly befriended her. And it had lasted.

From time to time, Kathy developed an enthusiasm for one of the men who looked at her and talked to her and thought, *thank you, Jesus*, or something similar. She'd gone out with some of them and brought a couple of them home with her, but this was the first time she'd traveled with one, and the first time I'd been offered full, if temporary, custody of Rina. Ronnie and I had spent a week turning the guest bedroom in my enormous ninety-year-old secret apartment into a teenage fever dream. I'd cleared my calendar, so to speak, by declining a perfectly fine burglary target—the currently empty Malibu house of an operatically rotten zillionaire who had spent years enthusiastically plagiarizing the work of midlevel crime writers and turning it into shit television with no acknowledgment of, or payment for, the source material.

I'd been steered toward the job by my fence, Stinky Tetweiler, who kept one ear pressed twenty-four hours a day to a sort of criminal party line. It was widely known in Hollywood that the producer had spent really substantial chunks of his loot on the finer products of human inspiration, the kind of artwork and books that create the impression that their owner is something more than a pumped-up, plagiarizing, bottom-sucking vulgarian, someone who eats the steak without killing the steer.

Like most Hollywood art wannabees, the producer had a collection that leaned heavily in the direction of the Buddha—who would weep to learn how many Hollywood vampires have placed his selfless likeness in brightly illuminated display cases as the precise decorative touch for the rooms in which they compose their daily to-do list of creative violence. I know of one famously foulmouthed agent, an Olympic-quality double crosser, who has practically papered his walls with old and relatively inexpert, but genuine, paintings of the Crucifixion. This is a man who was sued for throwing a cup of boiling water at an assistant who had lowered the wrong teabag into it. He's quoted as having said to one set of friends that Christ's face as he yields up the ghost reminds him that forbearance is essential in this imperfect world, and to another set of friends that it's hard to find really *interesting* vertical compositions. It's widely believed that he has a wall safe containing an eighteenth-century crown of thorns, studded with amethysts, which he wears when he's on the phone with certain studio heads.

The general rule is, the worse the guy or gal, the better the art. The owner of the empty beach house had amassed an eclectic collection of first-rate pieces I could have carried out single-handed with no effort at all and passed directly to Stinky, pocketing a Bible-thick wad of hundreds in exchange. It was made for me, but it was not to be.

The moment Kathy said I could have Rina for a few days, I handed the burglary off to a colleague, and Ronnie and I spent a string of feverish days preparing for Rina's arrival. The actual moment when everything looked *perfect*—just as the two of us inhaled deeply, nodded at our handiwork, and smiled at each other—the phone rang, and when I picked it up, I heard five one-syllable words spoken by the guy on the other end, who went by the name of Tuffy.

Tuffy said, "He wants to see you."

And that meant I had to see him.

The world is lousy with superstars: in sports, the arts, finance, even politics. They're enshrined for their accomplishments, useless as some of them seem to be, and most of them seem to enjoy their fame. In my field, for reasons I hope are obvious, we keep our superstars to ourselves. Not many people know about Benny "French Dip" DuBois, who won a hundred-thousand-dollar bet by picking the pocket of a former vice president of the United States. Or Elena Marcucci, whose Monet and John Singer Sargent canvases hang proudly in midlevel museums on three continents. Or Wilhem "Thousand-carat" Haffner, who, in 1937, used a shotgun to salt a barren African hillside with a few thousand dollars' worth of rough diamonds, and then sold it to the De Beers monopoly for almost forty million. In cash. In 1937 cash. I could go on, but what would be the point? You've never heard of any of them, just as you've never heard of the greatest of them all (in my opinion): Irwin Dressler.

To see him now, balding and shrunken and diminished in the aftermath of a surgery to remove what he described as "a little something near my pancreas," you'd think he was one of the lonely old duffers who daily fill a communal table or ten at Nate 'n Al's delicatessen in Beverly Hills. Nothing about him at this sad stage of his life would tell you that he had crumpled up and discarded every aspect of himself that wasn't absolutely essential to who he was. Many people seem to me to be a collision of mismatched individuals, but every atom of Irwin Dressler, at this point of his life, anyway, was Irwin Dressler.

And he wanted to see me.

Back in the mid-1930s, when the Purple Gang and other Jewish crime syndicates in the Midwest, especially Chicago and Detroit, got tired of being shot by the Italians who owned those cities and the cops the Italians controlled, the Jews began to look for cities of their own, as far as possible from the Guidos. And there, glistening like a giant rhinestone at the edge of the Pacific, was the plumpest, ripest, lowest-hanging fruit on the tree: the City of Angels.

By then, though, the Italians had sent an advance party under the thuggish leadership of a blunt-force weapon named Jack Dragna, who had established somewhat shaky control over the more obvious wrong-side-of-the-law enterprises, such as prostitution, numbers, and smuggling. But when the Detroit and Chicago guys came to town, they sent businessmen and accountants instead of ground-level crooks, and they sidestepped the Italians' entry points: they focused instead on the land market, which was booming, the nascent labor unions, including the ones being formed in the motion picture industry, and a Hollywood obsession of the period, horse racing, which gave them their access point into gambling. Their domination of Los Angeles gambling is why Las Vegas, just a hop and a skip from California, was founded by Jews rather than Italians.

When the big boys back in the Midwest decided to expand the franchise, so to speak, to take charge of pretty much everything LA had to offer, they realized they needed a deeper long-term strategy and someone capable of fabricating one. So, in 1948, they sent their smartest kid, an eighteen-year-old prodigy who still holds the distinction of being the youngest person in American history to attain a law degree. His name was Irwin Dressler.

For the first few years of the Dressler regime, brains were the weapon of choice, but the Italians, as their sovereignty eroded, began to see a well-placed bullet as preferable to a snappy comeback or a warning note. That's when Dressler's name became synonymous with *sudden death*. The rule was simple: three murders to repay one. During one memorable period, Dressler ordered hits with such frequency that he once said *Larry* instead of *Harry* and accidentally dispatched someone to take out his tailor, the only guy in California who got lapels the way Dressler liked them. It's hard to feel sorry for a hit man, but the story goes that the one who shot Larry fainted dead away when he learned what he'd done. Dressler—whose menials were waiting for him to order a pair of them to haul the unconscious man into the chaparral above Beverly Hills and put a couple between his eyes—instead called for two glasses of ice water. He poured one on the hit man, waited until the guy had come, spluttering and terrified, back to consciousness, and then leaned down, patted the hitter affectionately on the cheek, and poured the second glass over his own head, although he took off his jacket first. It was one of Larry's. "One consonant," he'd said to me once, when he was in a rare nostalgic mode, "one consonant and eleven years of bad lapels. And lapels are something I *know* about."

During the years after the shooting died down, Dressler remained behind the scenes as he extended his gang's influence and gradually realized his long-term plan: he turned most of the gang's activities *legal*, in the process shaping and bettering Los Angeles in ways that mayors and city council members were happy to claim as their own. He had been a power behind the scenes for decades.

So Irwin Dressler was not someone I—or anyone who wanted to keep his arms and legs attached to his torso—took lightly. He wanted to see me. I went.

4

Birthday Cake

"Not so good," Tuffy said as I climbed out of my old white Toyota, the closest thing to an invisible car, as far as LA cops are concerned. Tuffy had apparently come on the run from the kitchen—the location of the buzzer unit he'd been closest to when I rang from the gate—and he was obviously hoping to chat for a moment out of earshot from Dressler, whose hearing was subject to precipitous lapses and miraculous recoveries.

Tuffy was panting slightly; it can be tiring, running on tiptoe to avoid being detected by someone who spent much of his adult life keeping track of who was behind him. Tuffy's weightlifters' biceps emerged from a frilly blue apron; something yellow ran in a ruler-straight diagonal down the skirt.

He caught me looking at it and said, "Lemon frosting. Almost the only thing he'll eat these days is cake. Birthday cake. I've been baking for weeks."

"Any *good* news?"

"Well, we've finally run out of candles, and I've learned how to make *fabulous* frosting florets. I could probably bake for Marie Antoinette. And that thing near, or on, his pancreas doesn't seem to be getting bigger, although the doc says it will unless he goes back for radiation. At least, with all this cake, he's gaining some weight. I hate to think what it's doing to his teeth."

"His teeth are the least of his worries."

"Let's hear you say that to *him*. Lately—I mean, since the surgery—he's been saying things like, 'Still got all my choppers.' It's like they're a consolation prize."

I said, "You're a good guy, Tuffy."

Tuffy said, "Ahhhhh." He glanced over his shoulder at the enormous house, clad in stone of such a deep gray that the place turned black when it rained. I knew he was checking the picture window in the living room, even though it was certain that Dressler wouldn't be peering at us through it. Dressler had been leery of that window ever since, only a couple of months after he arrived in Los Angeles, pink-cheeked and sweet-looking and just out of law school, he introduced himself by ordering a hit on a high-ranking Guido. The guy took two through the head while sitting on his living room couch, right in front of his picture window. Dressler, who was always more careful than he acted, moved all of his own living-room furniture away from the windows. In the dining room he yanked out a quarter of an acre of clear, beautiful windows and replaced it with opaque stained glass. More than seventy years later, a large fish tank filled the picture window in the living room. It had no fish in it.

"If it was anyone else, I'd say he's *scared*," Tuffy said. "He's up in the middle of the night, wandering around the house in his robe. Barefoot, no less, with forty pairs of slippers to choose from. Three in the morning, I hear talking. I come out, he's all alone in the living room, arguing with himself."

"About what?"

"Who knows? Sometimes he looks up at me and doesn't see me, just keeps talking or nodding like he agrees with whatever he just said. Babe—and you know he doesn't get nervous easily—and I . . . well, we're worried as hell." Tuffy looked back over his shoulder as though he thought Dressler might have materialized there. "Come on, let's go in. He'll know we were talking about him, and it'll piss him off. It's like a big hole in the side of a boat that no one on board is allowed to mention."

The first thing I noticed as the front door closed behind me was that the heat was on and pumping at full blast, putting out that acrid dust-and-lint smell that usually means the furnace hasn't been used for years. Beneath the sneeze-inducing output of the heater, I picked up a sharp edge of charred wood, the probable aftermath of an unskillful attempt to put the fireplace to work.

The smells momentarily kept me from seeing that the entry hall, always immaculately empty, was now littered with mail, including at least two weeks' worth of supermarket shopping ads and a bunch of thick, important-looking envelopes. I kicked one of them aside as we rounded the corner into the living room.

"Have a nice chat?" Dressler, wearing a brown cardigan sweater and a wool scarf wrapped almost up to his ears, was sitting in a blood-red leather armchair next to the fireplace, rather than his usual place on the couch against the room's front wall. The fireplace, at which he had been glaring when we came in, was nursing an asthmatic little fire, two good-size pieces of wood that seemed to be debating the pros and cons of going all out. This marked the first time I'd seen the fireplace used for its natural purpose. Normally, it was so pristine that Dressler stacked books and dried flowers in it.

"Tuffy," he said, without looking at us, "if you're all talked out, maybe you could bring in some wood and take another pass at getting this thing going? So," he said to me, "you get all the medical bulletins?"

"Actually, he was giving me the secret of a really light lemon cake," I said. "One of mine would sink a cruise ship."

"Really," he said, his eyes flicking to Tuffy, who hadn't budged. "One of the advantages, one of the *few* advantages, of being old and, I guess you'd call it, *sick*, is that I can't get fat." He turned back to Tuffy. "Tuffy," he said, "you're maybe waiting for a tree to sprout in the fireplace?"

"No, no," Tuffy said. "I'm on it."

"Well, you'd be *more* on it if you went to where it is."

"It's just . . ." He swallowed so loudly I could hear him. "I didn't have the, uh, the chimney swept out. I know you told me to, but then—" He swallowed again.

"But then?" Dressler was speaking quite softly, which was a lot more intimidating than a shout would have been.

"But then you wanted, you wanted that—that cake your mother used to make, and it was a *Bundt* cake and I didn't know how to make one, and then I found out it needed a pan, and we didn't have a pan, so I had to—"

"Tuffy," Dressler said, raising one hand an inch or two from his lap and letting it fall again. "Subside, okay? You're among friends. The cake was good. All your cakes are good. Could I please get some fucking firewood before I freeze in this position and you have to carry me to bed like furniture? Is that too much to ask? If we cough from the smoke, we'll cough from the smoke. Maybe for a change I'd like some company when I'm coughing."

"I'm on it," Tuffy said again, and then he was actually jogging to the front door. I heard it open and close, but I couldn't stop looking at Dressler.

"He's on it," Dressler said, closing his eyes and slowly shaking his head. "He's so on it he forgot the door locks automatically behind him, and he'll be back here with the wood, enough wood to heat the White House, although the goniff who lived there last should be cold all the days of his life, if you ask me. That *hair* of his, I haven't seen hair like that since Mamie Van Doren. And then when he comes back—Tuffy I mean—with his arms full of wood, he'll have to put it all down and ring the bell, and he'll be worried I'm mad at him because he forgot about the lock. So, please go open the door. It squeaks a little, so do it slowly. I don't want him to hear it and know you had to do it for him. You wouldn't know it, looking at him, how sensitive he is."

I said, "He loves you."

"What is this?" Dressler said, "Valentine's Day?" He let out a sigh. "I suppose you want to sit on the couch."

"Well, I mean, we usually—"

"Violets," he said. "I'm surrounded by violets." He grasped the arms of the chair, preparing to stand, and I stood there, jiggling like a bowl of aspic, wondering if he'd get mad if I went to help. "Most sensitive guy I ever knew was a hitter," he said, shifting his weight forward. "Cried at Shirley Temple movies. We called him Boo Hoo, but not when he was in the room, you understand? You called him Boo Hoo to his face, you'd have so many holes in you that you could stand between me and the lamp and I'd still have enough light to read by. I read a lot in those days. But boy, when I was in college . . ." he said, and then he stopped talking.

I dealt with the silence by saying brightly, "I'll get the door," and heading for the entryway, trying not to hear the groan as Dressler brought himself to his feet.

"Just an inch," he called out. "Leave it wide open, and he'll know we've been picking up after him and he'll blush. Guy with muscles like that, he blushes in neon. And then you have to pretend not to see it or he begins to stutter. Got a stutter like a nail gun. The *things* I put up with."

I pulled the door open an inch or so and waited. I didn't want to watch him cross the room.

"You don't like the cake?" Dressler asked. "It's good cake, got all the right stuff in it. You know, *cake* stuff."

I said, "It's great." I had left a couple of small bites' worth on the plate and hoped he wouldn't notice. Of course, he was Irwin Dressler, and there was nothing he didn't notice.

"'*It's great*,' you say, looking down at it like if you stick the fork into it, there might be a bear trap down there. *Eat* something. I told you, he's sensitive."

I ate the cake. It was sweet enough to gag a honeybee. Dressler leaned forward slightly to watch me, as though he suspected I might slip some of it up my sleeve.

When my mouth was completely full, he said, "As long as you're chewing, I might as well tell you what I want. You're young enough, you know the rock and roll?"

I swallowed. "I know the rock and roll," I said, just for the pleasure of using the definite article. It earned me a sharp look, so I said, "Yeah, yeah, sure, the rock and roll."

"Awful stuff," Dressler said. "Where's the melody? Not Cole Porter or Rodgers and Hammerstein, not even Kitty Kallen or Jerry Vale, just *boom boom boom* and yelling and dirty words and hair, but you know, there's money in it." He took a breath, but I could tell there was more coming. "You know Kitty Kallen?"

"Not that I'm aware of."

"What're you, a senator? You afraid that saying something you don't mean *today* might contradict something you didn't mean a couple days ago?"

"No, it's just that I don't remember—"

"Talk about guts," he said. "Parents were Russian refugees, Jews staying a few steps ahead of the Cossacks, sometime in the late teens, early twenties. You know, when the welcome mat was still out in this country, when the lady in the harbor was still saying to the people on the boats, *Come in, come in, we got plenty of everything and we won't take your kids away and lock them up*. Came here without a kopeck, her parents did, which if you don't know, is one hundredth of a ruble. Not enough to buy a laugh in a tickle factory, but they got their feet under them, worked their asses off, had a bunch of kids—talk about *heroes*—and kept the family together. And one of the girls, Katie, she had a voice like an angel."

I said, "That's very—"

"You got no sense of story," he said. "Wait for the good part before you clap. So Katie turned herself into Kitty Kallen, one of the girls who sang the boys home from World War II, and then, when she was on top, when she probably coulda sold a record of hiccups, she went to London to sing at that big fancy Palladium they got over there, and up on that stage, in front of all those lords and ladies, she lost her voice."

He looked at me, eyebrows raised, and I said, "Huh."

"*Huh*, he says. Suppose you lost your *taste*."

I said, "I don't really eat for—"

"Hush," he said. "Don't ruin what's left of the respect I used to have for you. Your *taste*, you know, the thing, when you're in somebody's house, that tells you to take *this* thing, but not—"

"Oh," I said, "*taste*."

"What, I was talking in a foreign language? Your *taste*, you wouldn't want to lose it, because without it, where would you be, probably prying open parking meters. Anyway, *she lost her voice*. Opened her mouth, what came out, it sounded like a chicken fight."

"Well," I said, because he had stopped talking, "sounds like that would be . . ." I trailed off. I'd been so certain he'd interrupt me that I hadn't thought it through.

"Would be," he prompted. "Would be . . ."

"Well, probably nothing that would keep her on the charts."

"I knew you'd get to it. No, not good enough at all. So you know what she did? She worked her ass off for a year and a half, sitting in a room all alone and trying to sing, and when she figured she could do it a little, she started booking little crap clubs under different names. Lilly Looper, I don't know, just not Kitty Kallen. Most people didn't know what she looked like, not so much TV back then. And so she played these little jerkwater joints until she knew she'd got it back, and then she started cutting records again. One hit after another, better than ever. Beytsim, you know?"

I opened my mouth, but he waved me off. "No, you wouldn't know. *Balls*, it means balls. Lady had balls. Some ladies got more balls than most men."

"I'm not sure that a lot of women these days would see that as—"

Tuffy came in, saving me from completing the sentence.

Working very hard to look as though he hadn't been listening, he stopped in the middle of the room, cocked his head to one side, and gave the fireplace a diagnostic once-over. It had come to life, even crackling a little for the last few minutes, and no one was coughing and we could all still see one another through the smoke, and Tuffy said, "Maybe some bigger chunks, what do you think?"

"I don't have to think," Dressler said. "I got you for that. Great cake, Tuffy." To me, he said, "Tell the man you like his—"

"Amazing," I said. "Best cake since my wedding."

"Really?" Tuffy said, his face lighting up. "Babe helped with it." He turned to Dressler. "He wants to know what you'd like for dinner."

"Cake. Plus, just to shut you up, chicken soup, but not the chunky kind I gotta chew." He turned to me. "You staying for dinner?"

"Well, gee," I said, "I mean, it sounds great and all that, but I—"

"But you can probably get real food at home. Anyway, there's someplace I want you to go tonight, before dinner, which doesn't give you much time. Go, Tuffy, we're talking."

Tuffy went. As he turned the corner into the hallway, he called out, "More wood in a minute."

Dressler smiled but then he felt my eyes on him and tucked it away for future use. "So, the rock and roll," he said. "You know, at the beginning, some of it wasn't so bad. I kind of liked that Frankie Avalon. Good hair, wore a suit, smiled a lot. Songs were okay, I mean not 'Stardust' or 'Moonlight in Vermont,' but okay. Lot of bounce, you know bounce? Kid looked clean. Bouncy and clean. He was a Philly wop—sorry, Italian—of course, but they can sing, I got to give them that. Look at opera."

"Sure thing," I said, for lack of anything better. He seemed to be waiting for more, so I said, "Yeah, opera."

"Hello? You getting any sleep? So, like I was saying, he was from Philly, bunch of them were from Philly, and at the end of the fifties, Philly was—still is—the Italians' town, so they moved in on it, the Italians did, pretty fast, and we started to pay attention. *Lot* of money was coming in, and not just in Philly, *lot* of money. And I mean, my guys, they go where the money is."

I said, "I've actually heard something about that."

"You don't really need to start talking every time I run out of breath. What you heard, whatever it was, is probably wrong. But, you know, it *was* one of the veins in the mine that my guys were working. I mean, you can't leave it all to the Guidos. This was like a big new pot of money, barely had a lid on it. And in those days, everybody who mattered, everybody whose face or voice or songs sold records, they were all amateurs. *Sixth* graders. Nobody actually knows how many copies a record really sells. Who you gonna ask? It's not like there's somebody out there on the highway, counting as they go by. And most of these musicians were just dopes, kids who thought long division was some kind of math that took a while to do, and that a thousand bucks was most of the money in the neighborhood. They'd never *heard* of things like foreign rights or residuals or building a catalog. And I mean, *publishing*—which is where a lot of the money is—might have been in Esperanto. So the Guidos saw all this and they got in pretty good, at least in Philly."

"But," I said, and got an upraised hand.

"But we all know the Guidos aren't so good with money. Their idea of long-term planning is making a dental appointment, so we shoehorned ourselves right in. I mean, *they* did, these guys in our, ummm, group. Me, I wouldn't have done it if the records had frolicked around my knees and followed me from room to room, telling me I was handsome. But they, my guys, made a *lot* of money off it, so I was wrong." He sat back on the couch and looked down, perhaps at his spotted, heavily veined hands. "Or maybe I was just too old. Even then."

"Or just not a fan."

"Fan, shman. It was money. And as you maybe don't know, Jews have always been the people behind American popular music, starting with Irving Berlin and 'God Bless America,' even 'White Christmas,' the song Irving wrote to give Christmas to the rest of us. And Broadway—I mean, who on Broadway isn't Jewish?—all the way through the Brill Building and some good songwriters, even in the rock and roll. Carole King, Neil Diamond. That guy—Paul Simon. And, you know, the record labels and the management companies were just sitting there, waiting for somebody with some brains. So some of my guys stepped in."

"Got it," I said. "And this somehow involves me?"

"Only old people are patient," he said.

I said, "Well, I have to admit that I'm sort of tapping my foot to find out what you're getting me into. Dealing with your 'guys,' as you call them, is rarely a low-risk proposition."

"Ahhh, anybody who can break into the house of a thug like Rabbits Stennet, the guy who feeds people to his Rottweilers whenever there's nothing on TV, what should you be afraid of? Bunch of old gangsters with bifocals whose hands shake? Some guys with long hair and mascara, pretending they're still young? Worst that can happen, you'll have to listen to some dreck, too many drums, not enough brains. More cake?"

I cut into the cake, as luck would have it, just as Tuffy came in with more wood. He gave me a smile that brightened the room, which, in fact, was getting dark. During the deepening gloom of the next half hour, lighted only by the fireplace, I had the unique experience of being *pitched*, rather than commanded, by Irwin Dressler. As he told it, four old guys—by whom he meant four of the killers, extortionists, leg-breakers, kidnappers, armed robbers, and threat specialists who made up his former social circle—had put together a concert tour. Among them, they had for decades controlled the careers of a few dozen second- and third-tier acts, bands that would have been past their sell-by date even if they'd spent the last thirty or forty years in vacuum jars. But, nostalgia being one of the few things that gets stronger as people get older, they figured that an audience could be scraped together by taking a whole *bunch* of acts into third-tier markets, the ones that never got any closer to Earth, Wind, and Fire than Ear, Nose, and Throat.

The basic hope was that absence really *did* make the heart grow fonder, and that they could squeeze some final nickels out of that fondness by creating a sort of mega-tour of minor talent—twelve bands in all, to be presented in three consecutive nights' worth of concerts in thirteen different markets. Each of the three evenings would have a *theme*—somewhat loose since, from what Dressler said, it wasn't easy to assign a category to some of the bands. It was to be a sort of grand farewell, a final attempt to strike fire from matches that were decades old, and give the one-time kids—both in the audience and on the stage—a parting taste of what it had been like a few decades back, when the world was young. They were calling the thing ROCK OF AGES, a name I felt might have been given a little more thought. Miraculously, after a shaky start, it had more or less worked. The bands hated each other, some of them were rusty, some needed cue cards for their lyrics, and three guys had shown up in wheelchairs. There was a *lot* of fighting about the order in which they played. The first couple of stops lost money—not much, but some—and then, as things smoothed out, the houses filled up—better radio ads, Dressler said, and on the right stations. But then there were new problems: Turned out that someone was apparently siphoning off some of the proceeds. Turned out that someone had possibly tried to kill two of the musicians on the tour.

"In the same band?" I asked.

"I should know? How can you tell them apart? One of them, he stepped into a hole cut into the stage, for, I don't know, magic or something."

"He couldn't see the hole?"

"Cardboard. Someone put a piece of cardboard over it. And another one, he came out of his second-story motel room in Denver early one morning to get on the bus, probably sleepwalking,

and stepped on a bunch of ice cubes someone left on the top
step. Ass over elbow all the way down."

"Could he still play?"

"They were lucky. Or maybe not, the way he plays. But most
of the cities went pretty smooth, and now they're here. Last
stop of the tour."

I said, "Where?"

"Little theater on Wilshire, the Lafayette. Started out as a
temple a hundred years ago."

"I know the place," I said. "Not exactly top of the line.
When?"

"Starts tomorrow. I want you to go over there tonight."

"Shit," I said. "My daughter is coming."

"From where? I thought she lived in Encino. You make it
sound like Peru."

"Yeah, but her mother—" I broke it off. His face had dropped.
When someone has done what Dressler had done for the past
seven decades, he or she learns to manage facial expressions. I
blinked a couple of times and said, "I'll work it out. Somehow."

"In a couple minutes I'll tell you why this matters to me," Dressler
said. "You know, I wouldn't do that for most people." We had
moved into the dining room, a journey that seemed to take most
of a leap year and that provoked some anxious hand-wringing
as Babe and Tuffy watched from the kitchen. Spotting them,
Dressler had said, "Don't just stand there. *Bake* something,"
and the two of them backed into the kitchen and the door swung
closed.

We'd taken two chairs at one end of a brilliantly buffed
mahogany table big enough to feed the United Nations, and
after he caught his breath, Dressler had called out for Babe to
go up to his bedroom and get the big manila envelope that had
Schmendricks written on it.

I was looking at the big table and trying to figure out who
had once occupied all those chairs: Crooked politicians? The

family that had pulled up stakes and abandoned him all those years ago? Friends? He rapped his knuckles on the polished wood to get my attention, and I looked at the envelope that had just been laid in front of him.

I said, "Schmendricks?"

"Dummies, clowns. Comes from an old play called *Schmendrick, or the Comical Wedding* by a guy named Abraham Goldfaden, sort of the first Neil Simon back in 1880. It ran like forever in the Yiddish theaters in Europe and New York. A schmendrick is a doofus, a dimwit, a schnorrer, except that a schnorrer is a thief, so it's right that I should call them that, too, because back in the day these guys stole every penny they could get their hands on. The bands still made *some* money, but it was leftovers by the time it went through my guys' car wash. Nickels on the dollar. That's one of the reasons I asked you to come here."

"What, you're worried about some old rockers getting light paychecks?"

He looked down at his hands, folded in front of him on the table. He had lost so much weight his knuckles looked like marbles. "No," he said. "I'm worried about *me*. I'm worried because I loaned the guys some money and I don't think I'm going to get it back."

"How much money?"

It took him a moment. First he had to chew on his upper lip and when he'd worn that out, he had to pull his seat closer to the table. When *that* was done, he suggested I have some more cake, and I sat there, willing my jaw not to drop. It was like watching a century-old oak tree quiver in a light breeze; I'd never expected to see it, and I knew I'd never forget it.

He swallowed a couple of times and said, "Quarter of a million bucks. And it's not really a loan, it's an *investment*. I called it that because I was trying to make nice, trying not to make it seem like I was giving them charity, like I didn't think the project was a stiff from A to Z." He smacked the envelope with his index finger, hard enough to make me think it must have hurt.

For lack of anything better, I said, "Ahhh."

"But it's not really about the money, or at least it's not *only* about the money, it's the *principle*. And if that sounds too noble, the principle, I mean, is the one that says *thou shalt not fucking rip me off*."

"And do you think they will?"

"I think they already have. For one thing, they haven't told me that a certain amount of money just *disappeared* on the road."

I said, "How do you know that?"

"Obviously, one of the four of them told me. About three weeks ago. And don't ask which one it was. First, I don't want you to treat him any different because the other guys would probably spot it, and second, for all I know, it's not even true. It could be all of them, pretending to sneak me some information as, like, a first move to prepare me for when they claim down the road that the whole thing lost money. But . . ."

I waited. Then I cleared my throat.

"Yeah, yeah, yeah. This isn't easy to say. I think it's about making me look old and weak. I think it's a setup."

I said, "For what?"

He shook his head. "Forget it. For your purposes, it doesn't matter. One way or another, *whatever* is wrong, it all starts with *these* assholes."

He put the fingertips of both hands on the envelope and slid it back and forth a couple of inches in each direction, pressing down hard enough to turn his swollen knuckles white. It felt like the beginning of a somewhat menacing magic trick; suddenly the envelope would no longer be there, and I'd be looking at the faces of the men whose pictures were presumably inside it, and then they'd *smile* at me.

"So," he said, "just to be clear, which is the least I can do, considering what I'm going to ask you to do for me: it's not just that they're not paying me back or answering my phone calls and maybe planning to divide up my share, although I gotta tell you that would have been very dangerous for them ten, even five years ago. There could be other reasons, of course, perfectly logical explanations, but I learned decades ago to expect the worst, and here's the thing, here's the thing I wasn't going to say."

He stared down at the table. He was actually grinding his teeth. "The thing is that now, at my age and, let's face it, *sick*, I *can't be seen as someone a bunch of midlevel assholes can rip off.*" He sat back and drew a couple of shallow, slightly shaky breaths. "That would be the death of me, and that's not just a figure of speech. There would be vultures coming from all directions."

He tore off the top of the envelope, fanned the four faces as expertly as a Vegas dealer, and sat back as though he thought one of them might spit at him.

I leaned over. One of them was gray in a grandfatherly way, two were standard muscle, past their prime but still menacing, and the fourth was something of a surprise. I put my finger on his picture. "Chinese? Korean?"

"Japanese on his mother's side, but her genes had the muscles. Yoshi Perlman, a guy who put up with a *lot* when he first got active. His nickname was 'Egg Foo Young' even though he wasn't Chinese, and then it got changed to 'Hirohito.' He took it all with a smile and a slap on the back, and years later, some of those folks disappeared. He's smart and smooth, and he's the angriest of the bunch. And he's the *youngest*, which means that the bands he managed are probably the least likely to die onstage. I actually thought about that, back when they first asked me to kick in. Some of the acts are pretty damn old. If one of them popped off during a show it might dampen the audience's enthusiasm."

"Be a hard act to follow, anyway." I touched the next picture, an old guy with shoulders that looked as wide as the mud guard on a tractor and the face of a boxer who never learned to keep his hands up. "And him?"

"Jack Gold. A punisher, a no-finesse pug not good for much except pointing him at people and saying, 'Kill.' He did okay in the music racket because he could apparently pick the bands that would sell. Sort of a double skill, music and murder. Go figure. He likes to slap people around."

"Moving along," I said. "Number three?"

He snapped the next picture with his index finger: a guy with military-short hair and a nose so bent that it looked like it had been used for batting practice. "Eddie Prince, not his real name. An enforcer, no one you want to bump into by accident. He pretty much does what Yoshi tells him to do. It would probably be a good idea to keep in mind what people always say when their dog bites somebody: 'Gee, he never did *that* before.' And you shouldn't want him mad at you. He's got what they call these days *anger management* issues."

"And this one," I said, indicating the grandfatherly one. "Who the hell *is* that, Kris Kringle?" He seemed to be in his late seventies, with the sad eyes of a basset hound and cheeks so full he could have been shoplifting apples, topped by a tangle of tightly curled white hair that made him look a little like something you might use to scrub a frying pan.

"That's Oscar Fiddles, and, yes, there's a story behind the name, and, yes, he'll tell it to you first time you pause to take a breath. He's the whaddyacallit, the card that can be anything—sorry, the wild card, the *joker*. There's days my memory is like dandruff, it's flaking away. Him you can turn your back on most of the time, although you might want to keep your hip pocket buttoned. And he *never* shuts up."

"Who's the most dangerous?"

"Mentally? Yoshi because he only ever thinks about what he wants, and he's the smartest. Physically? Sort of a tie between Gold and Prince, maybe an edge to Prince. Oscar, probably the biggest danger is he could bore you to death." Dressler leaned back and looked at the line of pictures. "What a bunch of mamzers."

"And you think they're cheating you."

"I think they intend to. And it's not just for money, it's for status; they'll be the guys who prove that Dressler has lost it." He leaned back in his chair, rocked forward, and leaned back again. He ran through the sequence three or four times, the chair squeaking beneath his shifting weight, and then he leaned forward and scooped up the pictures. "Want these?"

"No. I'll remember them."

"Fine," he said, and he tore the pictures in half and then in quarters. "So. If I haven't already gone over this, the reasons I think they're fucking me. First, they were supposed to pay back half of it while they were on the road, out of box office receipts. They owed money to some other suckers, but it was crystal clear that I was supposed to be paid first. So far, gornisht. Bubkes. Nothing. And when I call them to ask where it is, they pass me from one to the other and everybody says, no problem. One thing you learn in my business is that when people say there's no problem, there's a problem. And sure enough, someone tells me about a suitcase full of money that vanished while they were on the road. This was never going to be a big-profit tour, not with the acts they got and the costs of moving them around. I figure what was in the mysteriously missing suitcase was most of the profit that was supposed to pay me back."

I said, "Who told you?"

"One of the four, but, as I already said, I don't wanna say. Don't want you to think one of them is on our side. I want you to look at them like they're all guilty. For one thing, they may be, and for another, I don't want you thinking that one of them, the one who broke the news about the missing money, is less dangerous than the other three. Don't want you to be comfortable turning your back on any of them. Got me?"

"Got you."

"So here's the short version. Tomorrow they do the first of the three final shows in that theater, the whatever it is. Friday, Saturday, Sunday, here in LA. After that, game over, everybody just drifts. What I don't want is for them to drift with my money. And even more than that, I don't want anybody *talking* about it. You know, we've been trying to keep this thing with my, my whatever it is—"

"Your pancreas," I said, and fought off an impulse to punch myself in the mouth.

"Yes, *thank* you, what *would* I do without you. My pancreas. Things leak, everybody knows things you don't think they know. And I'm thinking just maybe they hit me for the money in the first place because they figured if they could just delay payment long enough, my pancreas would solve the problem, cancel the debt. I gotta tell you . . ." He tapered off.

"You've got to tell me what?"

"Right, right, I was just wondering whether to say it out loud. If you'd asked me, say, a week ago, whether at this point in my life there was anything anyone could do that would still really piss me off, I probably would have said no. And I would have been wrong."

"Got it," I said.

"So I'm asking you to go down there and figure out what's going on and get my money back—or at least learn where the hell it is—before Sunday night, when they all get on planes to anywhere." He backhanded the stack of torn photographs, sending them skittering across the table, random eyes and noses and mouths. It looked a lot more violent than it sounds. "You think you can do that?"

I wanted no part of it, but when I looked at him, I said, "I can try." Then I said, "Shit."

"What?"

"My daughter," I said. "I have to figure out what to do with her this weekend."

He sat silent for a moment, and then he said, "Ah." He put both hands on the table, pushed himself to his feet, and stretched out a hand for the pieces of the pictures, which were a yard or so away. He couldn't bend at the waist enough to reach them.

His hand was shaking.

"I'll work it out," I said.

"Good," he said. He was still looking at the table. "One way or the other, I'll owe you a favor. With some people, that still counts for something."

5
Lavender

Thursday Night

Every few years Mother Nature gets pissed off, probably at Hollywood, and deals Los Angeles a dud November. A dud November is like the whole winter has been boiled down into what fancy chefs like to call a *reduction*, which is then poured, slowly and at great length, over the city—a cosmic unhappiness sauce, drizzling down from the sky until suicides hit a high point for the year. It's the meteorological equivalent of a sinus headache, but it's bigger and it lasts longer: a nonstop preview of the fact that the worst weather of the year, with all its bleak and baleful weight, is hovering just offshore, planning to tiptoe in, bringing with it entirely new forms of discomfort.

Needless to say, a dud November isn't the Los Angeles that people probably picture in, say, Duluth, if they picture us at all: no elementary school kid's lemon-yellow sun beaming down on tilting houses, no Crayola sparkle on the water. Instead, it's a procession of gray days beneath skies as gray as a dead tooth. A dud November is, essentially, a Mahler-length symphony in gray; and nowhere is it more gray in all directions than in midtown on Wilshire Boulevard, the neighborhood to which Dressler had dispatched me.

My spirits were not lifted by the gaping black hole in the center of the boulevard, a blemish that had been moving slowly west, the street behind it closing as the street in front of it opened, like one of those infuriating gaps in the middle of a zipper. Big trucks of various kinds—what I don't know about trucks would fill a doctoral dissertation—idled noisily, spewing fumes into the gray air. Important-looking guys with hard hats and clipboards swarmed the perimeter of the excavation as traffic, reduced to one narrow lane in each direction on each side of the hole, inched past. Some drivers lowered a window to share their feelings, but the guys with the clipboards were immune: they'd totally screwed with these people's drives, and in LA, that's a power that almost qualifies as regal.

I was looking at the construction as I ducked out of the mostly imaginary drizzle to take psychological shelter beneath the marquee of the Lafayette Theater, an old gray shambles that had been degenerating for decades, a sort of solo slum. When I'd first noticed it, years ago, I had guessed that it had begun life as a temple, and Dressler had confirmed it. But that was all I'd known, so, on my way from Dressler's sprawling, empty, sad house, I had pulled over, taken out my phone, and brought up the modern burglar's most indispensable tool: the internet. I prefer not to go into a building that I don't know several ways out of.

The temple's clean, streamlined architecture marked it as having been built in the twenties, the age of Art Deco. During the thirties, many of those who worshiped there had moved farther west—along with much of the city's money—toward areas like the one in which Dressler lived. The building stood deserted through the end of the Depression and the beginning of World War II; and about the time America entered the war it was being passed from hand to hand, serving the motley and sometimes undignified purposes that realtors summarize as *multiple uses*. In 1948, riding the national swell of optimism that followed the war, it was transformed into a theater.

Western theater has its deepest roots in houses of worship, so it was probably a reasonably effortless conversion; the building already had, at one end, a relatively small raised area for the bringers of the Word and, at the other, a much larger seating area for the faithful. I had no way of knowing whether the Lafayette had ever been a successful concern, although if it had been, it would have been an exception; live theater in Los Angeles has long been a loss leader. During the years since I moved into the secret apartment in Koreatown, I'd driven past the Lafayette occasionally, and it was always dark or housing some kind of low-rent attraction: touring companies of minor Broadway musicals, invitational screenings of possible Oscar-nominated documentaries, vanity productions of plays written by people with important relatives, and so forth. Mostly, it had been empty. The last time I'd seen anything at all on the marquee had been at least three months ago. It had read, BACK BY POPULAR DEMAND: ARTIE MACK'S ALL-PUPPET ORCHESTRA; not an "A" ticket in anybody's book.

But tonight the marquee was doing its best to dispel the atmosphere of gloom. What must have been a truckload of new lights threw their cheer onto gargantuan capital letters that said, YO! HEAVY DOWN!!! HERE AT LAST!! THREE NIGHTS ONLY!!! ROCK OF AGES!!!

Below the giant letters, in the marquee equivalent of twelve-point type, were a bunch of names I hadn't seen or heard for years and years. A couple of the names I remembered with a wince, and some not at all. But here they were, in the presumably deteriorating flesh, a final chance, in all likelihood, for their surviving fans to connect with them.

At the bottom of the marquee, in letters the size of the legal disclaimer on a package of earphones, were the words COMING DECEMBER 15: ALL LIVE! THE WIZARD OF OZ. And I realized that I'd seen that before, probably four or five times as I'd driven by. It was presumably their seasonal standby.

Through the locked double doors I heard a guitar note, high enough to peel an artichoke at five hundred yards, followed by someone screaming into a microphone, using words I'd never heard until I was in my teens. I took a deep breath and set out for the little alley at the right side of the theater, in which Dressler had warned me not to park.

I had a feeling it was going to be a very long three nights. And what *was* I going to say to Ronnie and Rina? If it had been anyone but Dressler, I would have turned around and gone home.

"Yeah, bub?" The guy who was so effortlessly blocking the door to the office building was about six-six, with muscles that looked like he bench-pressed the entire gym as a time-saver. His forehead was perilously low, with a brow ridge so pronounced that tiny organisms could have used it for diving practice, aiming for the pendulous, wet-looking lower lip that provided shade for his receding chin. His gray eyes were a match for the day, but not as lively, and his buzz cut looked like it had been done at Camp Pendleton. He wore skintight jeans three sizes too small, just in case anyone had missed the point. Other than that, he was a total wow.

I said, "*Bub?*"

His eyebrows moved closer together, and I could almost hear the muscles creak. He said, "What, you didn't hear me?"

"Listen," I said, "I'd love to chat, but it's already November, so if you could haul the beef a couple feet to your left, I'd like to come in."

"To see who?"

I said, just because he pissed me off, "Whom."

"Yeah," he said. "Him, too."

With every foot-dragging moment I was growing more certain that the sane thing to do was to turn and run. I had a bad feeling about everything, from the music to the theater to the twenty-year supply of lox blocking the door. It would have been a deep pleasure to turn around and go back the way I had come. Home to Ronnie, home to anticipate Rina's arrival, home to the elaborate air castles I'd constructed about how we'd use the time together.

But.

But Irwin Dressler had looked, as impossible as it was for me to admit it to myself, almost *desperate*. So I said, as pleasantly as possible, "Let me talk to your superior. Surely you have many."

The giant took a step toward me, which made him look a lot bigger. "Name?"

"Junior Bender."

"Never heard of him."

"Ahh," I said, "you wanted the name of the person I'm here to see."

"Well, *yeah*." He held up two helpful fingers. "Got to do it in the right order, bub. First I need to know the name of the person you want to see"—he folded his index finger, leaving the rude one dancing a solo in the air—"and then *your* name"—he folded the remaining finger—"so's he'll know who he's gonna tell me to kick all the way to the street."

I said, "I don't remember his—"

"You don't—"

"No, but he sits up there and he's in charge of the musicians." I ventured a guess based on what I knew about the workings of rock and roll. "He's like the tour manager."

He closed his eyes and I admired the definition in the muscles around his eyelids. Then he said, "Got it. Cappy," and opened them again. "I'm going up *there*," he said, with a thumb over his shoulder, "and you'll stay out *here*. Got it? Swear to God, you come in, you put even one foot on this carpet, and I'll crush you like a potato chip."

"Fair enough," I said, but he'd already turned and walked away. I saw that he'd pumped up the muscles on either side of his chest with such enthusiasm that his arms hung away from his body in that sort of relaxed-ballerina angle that keeps them from wrinkling their tutus.

At the last moment, I caught the closing door with one hand and waited until the door to the stairs had clicked shut behind him, and then I put a toe through the doorway and touched the carpet with it. *There*, I thought fearlessly, *take that*. Flushed with revenge, I withdrew my foot, leaned forward, and took a slow look inside, left to right, just devoting a few moments to the burglar's instinctive survey, hoping to confirm what I'd learned online.

Someone to my right laughed, the kind of brittle, tinkling laugh I associate with ice fairies. It was a female laugh, and it sounded neither derisive nor unsympathetic. In fact, it sounded friendly. Without touching the carpet again, I leaned farther through the open doorway, looked to my right, and sort of hung there, gazing at her: a slender, high-boned, very attractive woman, probably in her seventies, with an elbow-length mane of fine silver hair that flowed down over what appeared to be six or seven layered T-shirts. Each shirt was emblazoned with the name of an old band. She had chosen shirts that had names printed in different places, and she had simply cut through each shirt to bare the name of the band on the one directly beneath, which meant that the outermost shirts were, almost literally, hanging by a thread. Even at this distance, some of the band names gave me an impulse to make the sign of the cross and throw myself beneath a speeding train. Below the shirts was an ankle-length gown in a kind of weary purple that was a lot prettier than it sounds.

She said, "Watch out for the guillotine."

I said, "The . . ."

"Guillotine." She pointed at the top of the door frame. "Comes straight down, lops off your head without even slowing down, and then old Bluto, whom you've just met, picks it up by the hair so he won't get his hands dirty, drops it into a plastic sack, and takes it to a bowling alley over on Crenshaw where they let him knock down the pins in exchange for him not killing everyone in the place."

I said, "He's going to bowl with my head?"

She shrugged and said, "If he likes you." She was seated on a folded metal chair but somehow she inhabited it in a way that suggested it should be made of gold. "You might be a little old for him."

"And if I am? If he doesn't like me?"

"He uses your head as a paperweight."

"He doesn't look like a guy who goes through much paper."

"Toilet paper."

"Oh," I said. "Still, that's better than being bowled with."

"Snob," she said. "Many people with perfectly normal intelligence, or approaching it but perhaps missing a few essential cogs, find bowling to be a healthy and enjoyable form of recreation."

"Do you?"

"Oh, honey," she said. "*Please*. It's probably the only thing in the world that I wouldn't choose as an alternative to being buried alive. 'Bowling? No, thank you, Mister Undertaker, just tell me where to lie down.'" She extended a long-fingered hand, tipped with violet nails, a color that complemented the skirt. "Just mime the handshake," she said. "Do it from over there. You really *don't* want him to come down and find you in here. I'm Lavender."

"I'm Junior," I said, "and that's my actual name."

"Lazy parents, huh? Poor baby," she said, shaking her head. "And what in the world is someone of your generation doing here?"

"Well," I said, "it's a long story."

"I'd ask you to come over here and tell it to me, but I think I hear the light, airy step of—"

The door to the stairs flew open hard enough to bang against the wall, and Bluto said, "Come on, I haven't got all day."

6

A Crack in the Light to Let the Dark In

The moment I stepped into the stairwell behind Bluto, I smelled it: that throat-clamping, long-closed-old-building smell, rich in damp, dust, and mold, that suggests roof leaks and a fortune in deferred maintenance. I also smelled—offsetting the general desolation in a cheery and reassuring way—*popcorn*. I allowed it to lift my spirits because, really, what was the alternative?

But I couldn't get carried away; I had to watch my step. The building had been crammed into the end of the little alley, which meant that the stairway was steeper than usual and the steps so narrow they practically demanded to be taken on tiptoe. I was taking some pleasure in watching Mr. Muscle mince his way up until I realized I looked just as silly as he did.

He held the door for me at the top and then, while I was still on the next-to-last step, he leaned down and said, in a peppermint whisper, "If you know what's good for you, you won't smart off in there. Guy in there, he'd as soon kill you as wave at you."

"Won't be the first time in my life," I said.

"Yeah," he said, "well." And having completed his thought, he stepped back and trotted down a musty hold-your-elbows-in hallway, lighted erratically by the occasional dim fluorescent tube. He halted at the third or fourth door on the right and pushed it open with one overdeveloped arm. He backed away as it opened so that nothing but his unmistakable arm was visible to anyone inside; it reminded me of a little kid hiding by closing his eyes. When I had stepped in, he let the door swing closed behind me. I heard him jog pretty quickly down the hall.

As the door bumped against my outstretched foot, I saw in a far corner of the room the man who, according to Mr. Universe, would just as soon kill me as say hi, and, even in a town as big as LA, it was hard to think of anyone much worse. I decided on the spur of the moment to ignore him, to focus instead on the guy Dressler had mentioned in his lecture: the broad-shouldered, bearded older dude wearing the wool plaid shirt. He was sitting at a scarred wooden desk, one that might have been used for decades by teachers in some long-closed junior high school. The desk was shoved up against the wall on the far side of the room, under a single window so dirty it was almost opaque. He wore a faded Pendleton shirt, the first I'd seen in decades, and sewed on it was what I assumed to be his nickname: *Cappy*. Just in case someone missed it, the name was repeated in shaky handed but indelible black marker on the baseball cap he had pulled low on his forehead.

I have a tiered set of prejudices against grown men who wear baseball caps and are not baseball players, beginning, at the least objectionable end, with joggers and real pale guys who might be dodging skin cancer, up through golfer-looking dandies whose caps match their shirts or slacks, and then—worst of all—guys who *still* think it's cool to wear them backward. Cappy didn't fall into any of these categories. Beneath the cap and the blizzard of hair he was solid and grizzled and his blue eyes were charged with energy, and the smile he gave me seemed to be not only genuine but also relieved; he, or rather, *they*, had been *waiting*, and some people wait more graciously than others. The word that came to mind to describe Cappy was *avuncular*, although I sensed that the twinkle masked something harder and more complicated. Still, I figured we could get along.

Unfortunately for me, Cappy, in terms of clout and influence, was almost certainly the number two man in the room. The number one man was something else entirely, and, although I'd never actually met him before, he was a member of a very, very small club: people I just purely hated. I recognized him because he'd been pointed out to me from across a street by a friend, a guy who, several years after the fact, still wore the scars, both physical and emotional, of their one and only encounter. He would wear them until he died, which he did by his own hand; and I held the other man in the room personally responsible for my friend's death. If I could have shot him in the face right there and then and walked out without worrying about the legal consequences, I would have done it without a moment's thought.

He had no idea I knew what he had done.

In his carnivorous middle-fifties and as thin as an abandoned hope, he gave off chilly waves of disdain. He was smoking with the aggressive negligence of someone who lit one off another all day long and much of the night. He had tucked himself and his brimming ashtray into a scarred leather armchair wedged diagonally into a corner, as though that eliminated two potential directions of attack.

He was a symphony in shine: a black suit, shiny at the knees; black sharp-toed shoes, so reflective they had to be patent leather; a black satin shirt sporting obsidian cufflinks the size of hamsters; and a narrow red tie. Above the funereal duds gleamed an intensively polished bald head that looked like an ad for SHINE-O furniture polish. He had a bone-thin face, with lips sharp enough to turn a kiss into a paper cut, and the downward-drawn edges of his mouth were bordered by deep and apparently permanent wrinkles. He had cut himself shaving, which, given that rocky facial landscape, was no surprise, and he either didn't know or didn't care that he still had two little wads of toilet paper, even at this late hour, sticking to his face like teensy snow-capped mountains. His teeth, as I saw when he gave me a welcoming sneer, were a rich amber.

Even if I hadn't recognized him, even if every detail of his appearance hadn't been burned into the DNA of every crook who'd ever met him, there was still the custom-made black leather briefcase in his lap, as unmistakable as the sign that identifies a McDonald's. The bold red lightning bolts printed on both sides were intended to remind you of what was inside the case, and they certainly did, if you already knew. If you *didn't* know, and if you were a comic book fan, you probably looked at it and thought, *Shazam*, because it was pretty much a straight swipe off Captain Marvel's outfit. Children, I'd been told, sometimes shouted, *Look, Mommy*, and pointed at it in the street. If mommy was a crook, odds were she grabbed the kid and ran. The man with the briefcase, who was called Sparks for a very good reason, was said to be a little *touchy* about what had clearly been intended as a terrifying logo. He had sworn many times that he'd never even *heard* of Captain Marvel. The very small number of people who felt safe from him apparently teased him about it. From a few yards away.

I was not a member of that group. I *definitely* wasn't safe from him. I *did* know what was inside the case—the hardware he'd invented, the innovation that earned him his nickname. I was not unfortunate enough to have actually *seen* the infernal machine, but it had been described to me by the guy I mentioned earlier, a car thief named Leadfoot Perkins, who could visualize—who couldn't *stop* visualizing—every obscure detail, down to the number of horrifying projectiles set into its shiny gray surface, and would remember it, quite literally, until he killed himself to get away from the memory.

I had liked Leadfoot, and what he described to me was unthinkable.

"Took your fucking time," Sparks said. He had the soft rasp of someone who hadn't had to speak up in quite a while.

"Well," I said, "as you so generously suggest, it *was* my time." I turned my back on him, pulled up one of the room's six or eight folding chairs, and plunked it down in front of Cappy's desk, taking my jacket off and draping it over the chair's back. "I'm Junior Bender," I said. "I think you've been told I'd be stopping in."

"Yup," Cappy said. "Got a call from one of the dark lords."

"Sorry?"

"Said he was one of the mugs who put up the money for this thing, but not one I'd met. Said you'd be coming around and that I should talk to you. He also said the other guys would know you were coming and that they weren't really knocked out by the prospect. Then he hung up."

"But you didn't talk to them."

"No. For one thing, it's only been about twenty minutes since our chat."

I said, "If he didn't give you his name, I won't say it either, but I can tell you that he's on a completely different level than the other guys. Six or seven years ago, before he decided to slow down a little, they'd have been emptying the ashtrays at his parties, and that's only a small exaggeration."

Sparks hissed.

Cappy gave him a weary glance.

"So," I said, "let me ask you two questions. First, do you know something that the other guys wouldn't want you to tell me, and second, do they know you know it?"

"Yes, and maybe yes. I know something some of them wouldn't want me to tell you, and maybe some of them don't know I know it. Depends on how much attention they were paying, and there were a lot of rough spots and diversions on the tour. Like every rock tour in history, it was pretty much *all* rough spots and diversions."

"Okay. Let's get back to basics. Can you give me an overview of the whole thing from your perspective, starting with—I hope this doesn't offend you—who you are and what you do? I need to get caught up."

From Sparks I heard a noise that sounded like a preparation to spit, and when he was finished, he crossed his legs.

"Wait, wait," I said to Cappy. "Does he *have* to be here? Doesn't he have some children to threaten or something?"

"They sent him up. But if you want him to go, by all means, you go right ahead and tell him so. I'll stay where I am while you do it, if that's okay with you."

"Right," I said. "Sorry to have interrupted. You were just getting started."

"Who I am, who I am," Cappy said slowly, as though bringing himself up to speed on his identity. "My parents named me Duane Philbrick, but everyone calls me Cappy. If I've got a title, I suppose it's *band wrangler*. I get them on the bus, get them off the bus, make sure they're ready and willing to go onstage and that they *do* go onstage even if they're not willing, which happened a lot on this particular tour. If they get a case of the bunkhouse sulks, I flatter them back to what passes for normal. If they OD in some motel, I throw them into a cold shower and get the tour doc. And I keep it quiet. If they stub their egos, I apply salve and reassurance. If they trash a hotel room, I settle the bill and make a note to deduct it from their final payment." He looked over my head and drew a long breath.

"*And* I serve as an after-show filter through which no under-age girls or, in some cases, boys, can pass. Not that that's a problem with most of these guys at this point in their lives, although there are still a few who'd screw the crack of dawn if it held still long enough. I've spent almost forty years as the road manager for some of the worst-tempered bands on earth, and that's saying a lot. It's kind of like feeding giant pythons—you gotta know where both ends are if you want to serve lunch but not *be* it. Some of these guys, they got egos from here to the next resurrection. They got egos like the universe: they expand at the speed of light."

"How does that happen? I mean, they're just musicians, they didn't cure typhus. I know a couple of cellists and a harmonica player, and they're pretty much like you and me."

Cappy scratched his nose, then took a deep breath and blew

it out, looking like someone who's been making the same speech
for decades. "Okay," he said, "as an example, just because I was
there when it started for them, let's take the Flubs."

I said, "The Flubs."

"Well, *sure*," he said, sounding like someone at the UN
whose simultaneous translator has just had a nervous break-
down. "You telling me you don't remember the *Flubs*?"

"Of course I do," I said, packing it with conviction, "but I
thought they were all dead."

A disappointed shake of the head. "Most of them are still
alive. Alive enough to be on this tour, anyway. And *Quincy's*
still alive, which is all that matters."

Primarily because no matter how long I lived, I would never
get another chance to do it, I said, "Quincy Flub?"

"*Yeah*, the lead guitarist, you know? The only lead guitarist in
the world who stands way upstage in the dark, where the bassist
usually stands. Hey, you know the story about the groupie who
killed herself because she accidentally fucked the bassist?"

"I do."

"Yeah, well," Cappy said, clearly disappointed, "don't tell it
to a bassist."

"Who *gives* a fuck, you don't understand how they turn into
buttholes?" Sparks's voice reminded me of a swarm of wasps.

I could feel my heart banging in my ears. "*I'm* sorry," I said.
"I wasn't aware I'd addressed you. But, just to be polite, thanks
for the interruption, asshole."

Cappy inhaled as sharply as someone who's just had a handful of ice slipped down his shirt, but when I turned to Sparks,
all I got was a one-millimeter widening of the eyes, followed by
the kind of tight smile I'd last seen on the face of a kid whom I'd
made a fool of in sixth grade and who spread me on the pavement like peanut butter about six minutes after school let out.

"Yeah, well," Cappy said with a quick glance at Sparks. He
located his left ear in all that hair and tugged on it. "So. The
Flubs. Just like an example, okay? I've seen this a hundred times

but that doesn't make it any easier to believe if you haven't been *there*. You gotta let Quincy—you gotta let *all* these guys—be who they are. It's the only way you'll get along with them. They haven't been anyone except who they are *right now* since the first time, maybe forty years ago, when—" He held up a hand. "Wait a minute, wait a minute. Let me take one more step back, 'kay? *Why does Quincy—why do a lot of the guys like Quincy—have a guitar?* Because junior high school, for a lot of kids, is the ninth level of hell. They're maybe not good-looking, which Quincy certainly isn't, or athletic, or clever—good at making jokes or redirecting scorn, 'cause there's a lot of scorn in junior high, the place *runs* on scorn—so he, Quincy, he was like fodder for the popular kids. They just fed on him. Boring day? Make Quincy bleed. And he bleeds. But then, one inspired day, he gets himself a cheap used guitar and figures that learning to play it might be a good alternative to suicide. And six, eight months later some *other* dweeb stops him in the hall one day and says he can play the bass, and *another* six months later they've got a band. In Quincy's case it was called the Loose Ends. And they do little gigs, usually for free, and the girls notice and start to say "Hi" in the halls, and they get better, and maybe one of them—in this case, it was Quincy—writes a song and then another song, and guess what? They get a better drummer—*everybody* needs a better drummer—and they make a record and against all the odds, it goes someplace.

"And then it happens. They change their name to something cooler and the record's making some noise and they're doing a gig, probably in some crap town, and the kids there have heard the record. Quincy is all of eighteen and still shy, playing way the hell upstage in the dark 'cause he's most comfortable where nobody's staring at him, there, and maybe he's looking down at his guitar, maybe it's a tricky piece of fingering, and his hair maybe gets in the way and he leans back and shakes his head to get the hair out of his eyes, and some chick sees it and screams. A really good ear-shredding high school scream that prompts a few screams from other girls, like a reflex, and *bang*! It happens. You ever seen that ultra-fast footage of ice crystals spreading across a window? That's what it's like, only it happens a *lot* faster and it's not just on the surface. Goes all the way through.

"So you got Quincy Wiggins, that's his real name, from like Putzville, some dimple in the asphalt just outside of Lompoc or Cow Patty. He's just one year out of the concentration camp of high school, and he hears that scream? He's frozen *right there*. The old Quincy falls apart, breaks into a million pieces, and that nice, shy kid is gone. You know, all you need is a crack in the light to let the dark in, and once it's in, it's in for life. From that moment on, what steps onto the stage is gonna be Quincy the Rock Star, the lead guitarist in the Flubs, and he gets more stuck in that shell every time there's another scream. It's who he'll be for the rest of his life—even now, when the Flubs are like a joke on the internet. Quincy Wiggins is as dead as aftershave." He shot a quick, apprehensive glance at Sparks. "If you were strangling him and you said, 'Want me to stop, Mr. Wiggins?' he'd choke either till he croaked or until you called him by his rock and roll name. Quincy Flub, it's who he is now, and you know what? He *can't help it*." Cappy sat back and tucked a disobedient snowdrift of hair into his cap. "Still, imagine twelve bands full of them, which is to say almost fifty of them, jammed together on a bus. *That's* why I was hired."

"So what do you do? Carry a chair and a whip?"

"Nah. They knew who I am—knew who I *was*—most of them, anyway, by the time we all got into that bus. And that was a little touchy, 'cause we weren't operating at the standard to which they had become accustomed, as my wives' lawyers all said at one point or another. Nice tour bus, but not top of the line, and, ummm, crowded. No flying, which means no first class. Not Motel de la Roach, but not Le Méridien, either, and no big suites."

"They're lucky to be working," the swarm of wasps said from his armchair.

"That's not a productive attitude," Cappy said, giving me a glimpse of his diplomatic skills. "They *meant* something to the people who loved them, back in the day. To the fans who are above ground, they still do. They're not so bad. They just had too much too soon, followed by too little too late. They feel like, you know, the world spun right past them."

I said, "And I don't suppose any of them ever got anywhere near the box office takings."

Cappy leaned back in his chair, which squealed in protest. "No, and the take was surprisingly good until we got to LA. People are so *spoiled*. If you bump into Taylor Swift in the goddamn hardware store, why you gonna pay eighty, a hundred bucks for a ticket for some fading memories? Hell, my wife and me, we saw Sidney Poitier in *Costco*.

"So when we planned LA we got stuck with this teeny little house, smallest one on the tour. Sixteen hundred seats and four hundred in the balcony that we're not even trying to sell, and the way tickets are moving, most of the ones we do try to sell will be empty. But that wasn't your question. No, the money from the gigs, the box office take, was kept in custom-made suitcases with two, three locks each, and they shrilled like banshees if anyone fooled with them or, for all I know, even just picked them up without entering the code first."

"The, um, the receipts from—"

"Am I not being clear? Like I said, special suitcases. Locks like the Tower of London."

"I'm feeling a little slow here," I said. "The receipts from the gigs were in *cash*?"

He filled his cheeks with air and blew it out. "Hundred percent. That's the root of the problem. It was arranged in advance with the venues. They got a premium of three percent to pay us in cash, which got counted three times and checked against the sales records, which we got e-copies of in real time. Even so, the guys walked the aisles to count the house every night and went in with their own numbers the minute the gig ended.

These guys"—he reached up with one finger and bent his nose to the left, a once-universal sign for *gangster* that's retained its meaning over the decades in some circles—"they deal in cash; they don't want a lot of inconvenient paper that might end up at the IRS."

I said, "How much?"

In the corner, the wasps hissed. "Not your area, buster."

"Well, I hate to surprise you because you don't seem like a guy who deals well with surprise, but that's *precisely* my area."

"You? You're a fucking petty thief."

"And you're a low-rent psycho."

Sparks was pushing himself up from his big plush chair, literally shivering with rage. "You don't . . ." he said, "you don't . . ."

Softly, almost singing it, Cappy surprised me deeply by saying, "Irwin Dressler."

"Who the fuck cares?" Sparks said. He took a step toward me, tottering slightly. "Goddamn antique, and I hear he's got the big rot running through him like wildflowers."

I said, "Wildfire is probably what you mean, if you mean anything. And Dressler is more of a man when he's sick than you are in your wettest dream."

Sparks did something wordless with his voice that was almost too high to hear, but it was eradicated by a deafening *bang*, and I whirled around to see Cappy holding a heavy-looking black revolver, a six-shooter straight out of an old John Ford western, pointed straight at the ceiling. He was being snowed on gently, a fine dust of white plaster sifting from the bullet hole directly above his head.

When I'd been staring at him long enough to put a big period at the end of my conversation with Sparks, Cappy pushed his chair back, slipped the gun into something beneath his loose plaid shirt, and said to me, "Come on, I'll show you the scene of the crime."

7

Just Donuts

"Sorry about him," Cappy said as soon as the door had closed behind us, leaving Sparks audibly seething in his corner.

"That strain of humanity should have been wiped out when it first showed itself," I said, "back when people were squabbling over which cave had the best view. It's a grudge I hold against the Cro-Magnons. If they could make those gorgeous cave paintings, they could recognize raw evil."

"Problem is, there have always been people who have a *use* for guys like that," Cappy said. "Hard to think of a period of history where there was high unemployment among sadists."

"Well," I said, "thanks for the briefing." He opened the door to the stairway and started down. "Mr. Dressler, whose name I guess you've known all along, gave me the basics about the tour, but rock and roll isn't really his thing."

"Well, about Dressler, it was just a guess." He stopped and looked up at me. "Everyone made *shhhhh* noises whenever his name came up, *What would Dressler think? What about Dressler?* In a couple of cities it was obvious that we could sell more tickets than we had seats, but the question was, if we managed to sneak in extra shows, did Dressler have to know about them? And then here, of course, in blasé old Los Angeles, we wound up having to pay off our contract with a much bigger house and booking this dump. Could we inflate the loss? Every one of those decisions provoked a lot of mouth flapping about Dressler. Sometimes, being the masters of subtlety that they are, they whispered his name, just to make sure everyone knew it was important." He started down again. "They're not all dumb, but Prince and Gold pull the average down. And as for rock and roll not being his thing, Dressler's thing, everybody acts like it's different than selling donuts."

Cappy shouldered open the door at the bottom of the stairs. The muscle man, whom I was still thinking of as Bluto, had been leaning against the wall next to the front door. When he heard Cappy's voice he whirled at the sound, probably hoping for someone to flex at, but when he saw who it was, he turned and went back to admiring his extended forearm, moving his hand up and down to bring different muscles into play.

I said to him, "More than six hundred and fifty muscles in the body. How many have you worked on?"

"All the ones that matter," he said without looking up.

"It's so rare these days to meet a man with *focus*," Lavender said, still in her chair. She was holding a book I recognized as *Eve's Hollywood* by Eve Babitz, one of the best-known LA scenesters of the 1960s and '70s, a Hollywood High School graduate who was Igor Stravinsky's goddaughter, who posed naked playing chess with a fully clothed Marcel Duchamp soon after her high school graduation, and who went on to have several meaningful relationships with a who's who of LA rock. Eventually she designed record jackets for some classic bands. When her long moment in the sun was mostly over, she drew a deep breath and started writing about it.

"How do you like the book?" I asked.

"Gee, I don't know. How did Billy Graham feel about the New Testament?" She looked past me at Cappy. "How you getting through the final twenty yards, Cappy?"

"Let's see," he said. He began to cross himself. "Yup, got my spectacles, testicles, watch, and wallet. Looks like everything I need for the final act. I can depart this life *intact*."

"Never doubted it. Are the boys all tucked in for the night?"

"God only knows, and I doubt he cares. Bunch of them live in LA, so I don't have to babysit them, and at least the hotel bills will drop."

"Is it true," Lavender said, with the air of someone who's finally getting down to it, "what I hear about that dickhead Lionel?"

"No comment. Even if it *is* true, you know how, ummm, complicated he is."

"Complicated, my ass. He thinks everyplace he's ever gone should be named after him: Lionelville, Lionel Junction, Lionel-by-the-Sea, the Duchy of Lionel. So, you're working on him, trying to get him to go for it, right? I mean, if he does, and if you could get the word out in time, some people might actually *show up* on Saturday night. Imagine that."

"Like I said, no comment."

"Butts in the seats," Lavender said. "And without *her*, Lionel is the dud of the Western world."

"You're thinking logically. This is *Lionel* we're talking about, and please *don't* talk about it. Keep it zipped."

"Sparks himself couldn't get it out of me," she said. "At least, not for a couple of seconds."

"Counting on you to keep it confidential," Cappy said, pulling open the front door. To Bluto, who was lost in the intricacies of his forearm, Cappy said, "No, really, don't bother. I'll get it."

I said, "Lionel?" as we stepped out into a chilly dud-November drizzle, but he shook his head and said, "Later." I followed him toward a door that led to the backstage area. It was right beside the big hangar door, still closed, that undoubtedly opened wide to admit whole touring companies: costumes, props, and sets, up to and including, for all I knew, the helicopter for *Miss Saigon*. The drizzle was coming down at a diagonal.

"As I was saying," he said, "everybody thinks it's . . . rock and roll, I mean, everybody thinks it's magic or something, but it's just another kind of donuts. With a donut shop, you build it where the customers are and wait for them to come to you. With a rock tour, you do the same thing, but it's portable: you *take* it to wherever the customers are."

"As far as I know, donuts don't have egos. And they have a sell-by date."

"Yeah," Cappy said, pulling open the door to the stage to reveal a deep gray nothing, and stepping aside to let me pass. "But to challenge the metaphor, not many people fall in love with someone to the sound of a donut. And unlike a donut, the sell-by date is *elastic* because rock is stamped all over people's favorite moments. And *that's* because—let's face it—adulthood is mostly one long disappointment. Lot of people keep the door to their heart open to the music that made them feel good when they were still satisfied with themselves."

I said, "Not as many, though, as the guys who put this thing together hoped there'd be. Or, at least, not as many as they've been reporting to you-know-who."

"Actually, it was nowhere near as bad as you might think, or as some people might be claiming it was. That topic is *wayyy* above my rank. Hey, tell you a secret." He waved me through the door and followed me in. Lowering his voice so reverently we might have entered a church, he said, "Gangsters are as soft-hearted about their old music as everyone else is. They wanted to *hear* this buncha clowns—although that's not fair, some of them used to be good and a few still are. But one way or the other, the hoods wanted to hear them again, wanted to give them another chance to play. And, yeah, pick up a few shekels while they were at it."

I said, "But just because they got a little misty, that doesn't mean they're going to go all honest and scrupulous about split-ting the take."

We were standing in relative darkness, facing a huge floor-to-ceiling hanging backdrop, obviously lighted on the other side, that obscured my view of the playing area of the stage. Every now and then a shadow would move across the backdrop, and there were some faint, metallic rhythmic sounds I couldn't identify. The place had the mummified stuffiness that comes from having been shut up for months. I fought an impulse to fan the air, try to dispel the sharp edge of mildew.

"No," Cappy said. "They're not gonna go all Eagle Scout. They've done something from the bottom of their hearts, most of them for probably the first time since they were about eight and they slid a valentine onto some little girl's desk, but that doesn't mean they're not looking at the take and thinking, *Huh, I can rake off a bunch of that.* And two or three of them are feeling personally betrayed. See, what no one will tell you is that, while they've probably always been planning on stiffing your friend to some extent with a sort of Four Musketeers solidarity, all four of them have been doing the occasional fancy step to siphon off a chunk for themselves. They may be united against your friend, but they've had their hands in each other's back pockets since the show hit the road. I mean, come on, they're *crooks.*" He tugged on my sleeve like I was a kid and said, "Watch your step, there's gear everywhere."

I tagged behind him as we moved toward the relative brightness on the other side of the backdrop, picking our way through a miscellany of things—electronic equipment, musical instruments, suitcases, both open and closed. "Step on this stuff, your ass is grass."

When we cleared the backdrop, we found ourselves in the downstage area where the musicians would work whatever remained of their magic. The floor, which was painted a dreary, light-eating gray, had been divided into roughly equal thirds by invisible lines. In each third stood a four- or five-guy band, all wearing major earphones; each group member held the eyes of his bandmates, studiously ignoring the other bands. All three bands seemed to be playing their hearts out in semi-silence. I heard the strings being picked, tinny and barely audible without amplification, the squeak of fingers over frets, and the occasional grunt or hummed fragment of a tune. The drummers were playing as though their lives depended on it, but their sticks barely touched the skins or the rims. Everyone seemed to be perspiring. Every few seconds, someone would say something like "*Yeah!*"

"Gotta give them credit," Cappy said. "It's the last stop, they've been playing these tunes for decades, they've been on this fucking tour for what must seem like most of their lives, and they know this last stand will be mostly empty seats, but they're out here, working. Not *all* of them, but these three bands, and a couple others who have the space reserved for later. Always working on it, trying to find ways to keep it fresh."

"You said this was the scene of the crime."

"Well, from my perspective, it is. As you've already guessed, some money got stolen and more will be, and guess whose piece it's most likely to come out of?"

"Right, I'm keeping all that in mind, and so is Dressler. Listen, the guy who stepped on the ice cubes. In Denver, right?"

"The *guy* was Quincy. I was just talking about him, back in the office. Nasty fucking thing to do. Motel room opened onto an outdoor balcony that ran all the way around the building, stairs were high and steep and concrete. And, you know, he's a *rock star*; in the morning, he can barely count his feet. Could have broken his neck."

"What time was it?"

"Pretty early. Me and my crew had just phoned everybody to get them onto the bus."

"Denver can be cold this time of year."

"Sure can. *Oh*, right, I see. It was low thirties and there was a lot of ice. Could have been put there maybe an hour, two hours earlier, since the night was so cold. I actually worked through that timeline on the bus, once we got going. It was a nice short time span, you know? But even if it had been eighty degrees and the ice had melted in ten minutes, it probably wouldn't have mattered from a, you know, evidence perspective. All the guys had their own rooms, so nobody was bunking with anybody, nobody was keeping track. How do you know about the ice?"

"Dressler."

"You've really met him, huh?"

"I have."

"And he likes you."

"I have no idea. I'm not sure he thinks in those terms."

"So someone told him about all that, the sabotage or whatever it was."

"So it appears."

"Have you wondered why?"

"Repeatedly."

"You've got some pressure on you."

"You might say that. Does this stage have one of those openings in the floor, like the one the other guy fell through?"

"A trapdoor? Yeah. They did some opera here for a while, which sooner or later means *Don Giovanni*, and *that* means the ghost, the, uhh, the Commander, Commendatore, whatever the hell he's called. Biggest bit in the show. The trapdoor lets him appear in a puff of smoke or behind some people who are standing around being uninteresting while everyone's looking at the other side of the stage—however the hell they want to do it. Stage manager here says they'll be using it in *The Wizard of Oz* for the Wicked Witch of whichever direction it is when she melts. And I already thought of it. He's got it locked and sealed, and he says he'll check it every night. 'Course, it was supposed to be locked last time, too."

"So," I said, "the ice cubes were most likely someone on the tour, but the trapdoor might have been someone on staff at the theater you were playing."

"You mean, like they made a mistake?"

"No, I don't mean that at all. Was it a union house?"

"No, it was a waiver house, same as this one. You know, a couple union supervisors who, like, drop by and say hi maybe once, maybe twice, so the guys running the local chapter can say they did their job. Everybody else was . . ." He stopped and said, "Shit."

"Yeah. If it was nonunion staff, it was somebody who was getting paid maybe a hundred bucks, easy to tempt. A union guy wouldn't dare. I think you need to have somebody keep an eye on that trapdoor all three nights."

"Done. Thanks." He looked at his feet for a moment. "I gotta tell you, though, both these, the ice cubes and the trapdoor, they both could have been just shit luck. I mean, someone drinking late and leaving his cup and the ice cubes outside? Nothing there that seems inconsistent with a bunch of rock and roll musicians. An open trapdoor in an old theater? I'm not sure we'd even be thinking about it, about either of them, if someone wasn't claiming that a bunch of money was missing. I mean, that theater was older than this one and it had been closed for a long time." He looked around the auditorium. "Same league as this one, only bigger and maybe a little junkier."

"You think they both could have been accidents."

"You know, when you got a bunch of guys who drink and dope too much and sleep in a different place every week so they can't find their way around in the dark, stuff is going to happen."

I said, "You're the expert. I'll make a note," and waved my hand at the dark rows of seats. "This place can hold sixteen hundred people?"

"Minus eight for the damn sound system, which will sit about halfway up in the center section. We also lose the six seats behind it." He pointed into the audience area. "Up there, that dark space, that's a balcony, seats four hundred more, but it hasn't been used in so long it's almost scary up there. There are smaller venues here in LA, but this was the one that was dark." He stared out at the dim house. "Not exactly what these guys thought they were going to get, but you know, a small house that's half-full is better than a big one where it's just you and the echoes."

"Do you have any worries about, I don't know, trouble from the audience?"

"No one's gonna rush the stage for these guys nowadays, or if they did, they'd do it very slowly." He broke off and said, "Was that the kind of trouble you were wondering about?"

"Not exactly."

"No, we haven't had anything negative from the audience so far except a few boos for Lionel. Some women, God bless them, think the act is an insult."

"Well," I said, "you've got two entry points, one for each aisle. I'm pretty sure I could get Dressler to float a couple of metal detectors. Wouldn't slow things down much."

"Really? You could do that? *That* kind of trouble? You think we might need it?"

"I have no idea, but this being the end of the road, the last gig, the one where one hundred percent of the money has come in, if anyone is planning some kind of really big snatch, this is the time. I think Dressler would go for it. I don't know whether your guys are worried or desperate or what, but they *are* crooks, and I wouldn't put it past them to come up with some kind of diversion that might explain a big chunk of missing money. I mean, it's now or never, right?"

Cappy waved the back of his hand at me and said, "Make it so. Shit, I've waited a lifetime to say that."

On the far side of the stage, the band that had been working there—four guys who, all together, probably didn't weigh 450 pounds—stripped off their headphones and started yelling at each other. I said, "Who are they?"

"Rasputum," he said. "Punk rock. They wear Russian robes and spit at each other."

I said, "They're kind of young to be punk."

"They got the news late. They were a country cover band in Bakersfield and they dressed like Buck Owens, all those boots and fancy shirts. Then some post-post-punk band on its last legs came to town and these guys looked at each other and thought, 'Hey, we've got clothes like that at home,' and they hung up the spurs. Little later they thought of the robes and made 'em out of blankets. They had a great producer who gave them a name to go with the robes and a couple, three hits. They go second on the last night because they threw a fit about being called "post-punk" and claimed they were *so* post-punk that they were really new wave." He shrugged. "Musician logic."

"I'll arrange to be elsewhere."

"Far be it from me to discourage you. The ones in the middle? That's Anthrax and Moonbeams, kind of punk romantics, good singer, and the band closest to us, that's Wet Spot. Them, I like. Hell, I like all of them to some extent personally, if you don't count Lionel. It's just that you might not be a fan of the kind of music they make."

"How well do you know the guys who put up the money for this thing?"

"About as well as a manicurist knows her four o'clock. I met with them, I think, three times before we went on the road, usually two or three at a time, and there were always two with us on the road—don't get your hopes up, not always the same two. But at no point did any of them take me home to meet the missus or invite me to go fishing. Mostly they gave me the old steely eye and grunted. And then, probably helped themselves to some of the receipts."

"How much is missing?"

"It's hard to say, but in a motel with thin walls in, I don't know, maybe Wyoming, I heard two hundred and seven thousand bucks getting shouted into the wee hours, lost, or maybe pocketed, somewhere along the way. There had been other fights earlier, although I can't be sure they were all about money. These guys are long on aggression and they bump heads a lot."

I said, "For some of them, the head is probably the safest thing to bump. People don't hire these guys as a source of ideas. The money, though, that's probably something to keep in mind."

Cappy and I talked for another twenty minutes or so as the members of Rasputum squabbled at the edge of the stage and the other bands worked on their inaudible (to us) music. Toward the end of our chat, Anthrax and Moonbeams folded its tents. The last drummer on the stage, the one with Wet Spot, celebrated with a full-volume solo that, to my ears, owed a legally arguable debt to Dave Grohl, and then the rest of the band turned the volume up to eleven and went to work.

I followed Cappy into the audience section, going down a little six-step stairway stage left and hiking up the aisle to the back of the house, under the overhang of the balcony. Once there, he pulled from his hip pocket the programs for each of the three nights and walked me through the bands: which ones were the big draws, relatively speaking, which ones I might actually like, which ones were feuding with other bands, and which ones had serious hate affairs going on among their members. Then there was a hollow *boom* that we could hear even over Wet Spot, and Cappy said, "About fucking time." He took off at a trot with me at his heels, back up the steps to the stage and then across it, past Wet Spot, all the way to the big door in the theater's rear wall, which had just been banged open. A big truck was idling there, emitting a profound diesel pong, and three guys in jeans and light jackets were milling around it, shouting instructions to each other.

"The sets," Cappy said. "One for each night, plus the sound system, which is a behemoth. Gonna be a pain in the ass to get it into place, and like I said, it's costing us some seats, too, not that we're likely to need them. We done here for now?"

I said that we were, but that he should grab his phone and call me if he thought of anything else. I gave him my fanciest business card, the one that identifies me accurately as a *Removal Specialist* and has both my phones on it. We shook hands, and even before he'd let go of mine, he was yelling at the guys to start doing the things they were already doing.

The drizzle on my shoulders reminded me that I'd left my jacket in the room where I'd met Cappy and Sparks. I trotted up the driveway, which was now wet and shining, and knocked on the door to the office building. When Bluto opened it, I said, "Working late," and headed to the stairs.

"Hurry it up," he called. "I gotta get to the gym."

At the top of the stairs, I realized that all I'd done the first time I'd gone up was follow him, without paying attention to where we were going. The corridor was damp-smelling and as blank as a lost thought: there was nothing hanging on the walls, no names or numbers on the doors. The only thing it had going for it was that it was short.

Four doors in all. The one at the near end of the hall bristled with padlocks, many of them shiny, new, and recently installed, as though someone had been profoundly dissatisfied with the original security. I made a note to pop the locks sometime relatively soon. I squinted down the hall, trying to figure out which door it had been, and guessed door number three. When I opened it, it solved one small mystery: the popcorn smell came from a commercial-size popper that had clearly been lugged up from the lobby. It was turned on, warming more popcorn than I could eat in a week, and I love popcorn. Either someone on the permanent staff here—if there was a permanent staff—had serious popcorn issues and wanted the popper *right here*, or Cappy had decided that popcorn was too wussy for a serious big-time rock concert.

I made a mental note to ask him to put the machine back. It might slow the audience members down, give me an extra few seconds to look at them. Not that I had any idea what I'd be looking for.

I got lucky with my next try and opened the door to Cappy's office. I did it quietly, just in case Sparks, who seemed like the wrong kind of guy to surprise, was still seething away in his corner, doing mental victim replays to pass the time. All that remained of him, though, was the stink of his cigarettes and a mound of butts in the ashtray. My jacket wasn't hanging from the chair where I'd left it. Instead, it was wadded up on the floor, with its arms tied in a knot. I slapped the right rear pocket of my jeans and felt the reassuring rectangle of my wallet. Even if someone had eased it out of my pocket and then slipped it back in, which I thought wasn't likely, it contained virtually no accurate information. Even the address on my driver's license was a letter drop—a real house in a nondescript neighborhood, empty most of the time except for a caretaker who cleaned out the mailboxes every other day and tidied up the front yard each week. Every two weeks or so a young, attractive, nicely matched pair of plausibles—con artists—earned a couple hundred bucks each for spending the night there, waving at the neighbors and saying they "traveled a lot."

By the time I'd finished unknotting my jacket, my phone said it was almost ten. Guessing that Cappy would be busy with the unloading for a while, I pulled out the chair at his desk and sat there, opening and closing the single drawer, which was apparently empty except for a nice leather pouch that bulged with very potent-smelling pot. I sat there, looking at it for a long and somewhat stupid minute, and then, resisting the urge to slap my forehead, I pulled it all the way out, and there, shoved all the way in and flush with the back of the drawer, was a small and notably grimy notebook, about five inches by four.

It fell open—apparently from sheer force—to the first of several pages that listed towns I recognized as places where shows had been performed. Beside most of the towns' names Cappy had penciled in one or more female first names—or nicknames or, in several cases, both. Beside most of the names was a phone number and a number of crudely drawn stars, one at the lowest and four at the highest. Just a vivid if not particularly cryptic reminder for an old rocker on the road and keeping score. Two of the four-star ratings were accompanied by exclamation points. It was, in all, so chilly a way of evaluating people that it felt like looking through a window into a freezer.

The next page was decorated with two more wobbly hand-drawn columns: same dates, same towns, but this time, instead of a Guide to the Groupies, the third column simply contained a number from one to four, except for three markets that were numbered *one* and *three*. I didn't know what it meant, but I copied it down on an unused page that I tore out so I could pocket it. I passed on the groupies.

Otherwise, *nada*. I said, "Well, shit," and slid the drawer back into place. Then I picked up my phone again and called the apartment.

"I was wondering what happened to you," Ronnie said. "I thought maybe you'd decided to run away with some band."

"And I might have," I said, "except that none of them is going anywhere. Tell me how much you miss me."

"Well, I've been sitting all alone and gazing at a portrait of you and sighing from time to time. Staying away from the kitchen knives."

"Which picture?"

"The one when you were eleven, in the cowboy shirt with the little arrow pockets. Be *still*, my heart."

"My mother still has that shirt. Along with everything else I ever touched or wore or breathed on."

"Lucky you. My mother barely remembers my name."

Idly, I opened Cappy's drawer again. Nothing had changed, which was kind of a relief; I wanted to believe he was on the up-and-up and it was good not to be contradicted the first time

I checked. "Listen," I said, "I'm about done, by which I mean everybody here seems to be done with me, for tonight, anyway."

"And? When you pause like that, it means you're trying to figure out how to tell me something I don't want to hear."

"I'm sorry," I said, "but we have a problem, a big one. I have to be back here pretty much all the time during the next three days and nights."

"Ah," Ronnie said, and there was an edge to it. "The very nights that Rina will be with us. Or, I guess I should say, with *me*."

I said, "You have no idea—"

"How upset you are? Of course I do, and it makes me feel terrible. And *she's* going to be even more disappointed than I am. Tell you what. We'll change all the clocks, get up about four in the morning, and you can spend quality time with her until the sun comes up. On the other hand—" She broke off.

"What?"

"Maybe she'd like to go *with* you. She likes music, doesn't she? I mean, every kid loves music."

I said, "It's, um, it's a good idea, but I'm not sure she'll thank me for taking her to these particular shows."

"She'd be with *you*."

"Tell you what," I said, "I'll be home pretty soon, and we can talk about it then, okay?"

"I guess so. Drive carefully."

"I always drive carefully."

"I know," she said, "but I have to say something."

And she hung up. We'd been together for more than two years, and despite the occasional collision over nothing, I couldn't remember her ever hanging up on me without saying goodbye.

So I sat there, a monument to divided attention, thinking about the fact that she'd hung up on me, worrying about how to handle the situation with Rina, and asking myself if there wasn't some way I could walk away from this thing without letting Dressler down. I came up zero on all three issues, so I got up, sighed, pulled on my jacket, and went down the stairs and through the now Bluto-free lobby.

"You're leaving?" Lavender was putting what looked like a lifetime's accumulation of possessions into a huge canvas tote.

"Into the teeth of the storm," I said, and I turned up my collar and headed through the drizzle, past the knot of guys who were offloading the truck, and angled right on Wilshire toward my car, which was parked around the corner.

And when I got there, I saw a note on the windshield that said DONT COME BACK and found that both front tires were flat, and not just flat, but *slashed* flat; people talk about slashing tires as though one could do it one-handed with an old bread knife while gargling mouthwash and reciting French poetry, but in fact, tires are made specifically to *resist* being slashed, even by sharp objects struck at high speed. Someone had used a lot of muscle and a very sharp blade. I'd be able to identify him easily, I thought, by the muscles and the fact that somewhere on him, he had an unused apostrophe.

I stood there thinking, which seemed to be a more creative option than screaming and waving my arms. Then I pulled out the phone again and dialed.

"I'm sorry," Louie the Lost said, "but all our operators are busy. Please leave a message after the beep, and we'll get back to you during our extremely reasonable business hours, which do not include whatever the hell time it is now. And *thank* you for your patronage."

I waited as I looked at the right front tire, which was slashed to a depth that would have required a substantial complement of excess beef. The same old candidate came to mind.

Finally, Louie said, "Okay. *Beep.*"

I said, "I need either a new car or two new front tires for the Toyota, plus someone to put them on the car, in the mid-Wilshire district, like ten minutes ago."

He said, "Nice to talk to you, too. What, you haven't got Auto Club?"

"What I've got," I said, "are friends who are tried and true, friends who are always eager to help out a guy in need, friends who don't log every call they make and share the log with the cops at the slightest hint of interest."

"Yeah, okay, but it's gonna take some time, 'cause it'll have to be *me* since my vast staff are all on vacation in Cabo San Lucas *and* I don't got any tires just lying around so I'll have to swing by the storage unit."

"I'll owe you."

"And you'll pay me, too. Address?"

I gave it to him and told him to call when he was in the neighborhood. Then I put the phone away and stood glaring at the butchered tires.

Louie was the closest thing to a friend I had, among crooks at any rate. He was one of the few people I'd ever met who'd always known what he wanted to do: from the time he was five or six he'd seen himself as the world's premier getaway driver, waiting calmly at the wheel of some highly buffed speedster just outside a bank, cool as Puget Sound, while inside his associates were sweating bullets, waving guns around and emptying cash drawers. Then, as they raced across the sidewalk, he'd pop the trunk open, calling out, "Toss it in back, boys. Money is dirty, you never know where it's been," and then, the minute they were all inside the car, he'd peel away from the curb, the rest of the gang jammed together in the back seat, speechless with admiration as he wove a pattern as delicate as Chantilly lace through traffic-clogged arteries and sleepy residential blocks until they arrived—traveling at a sedate speed by then, nothing to arouse the interest of the cops—at their hideout. The guys would climb out of the car, slapping him on the back and calling him *Wheels*. "Great job, Wheels," they'd say. Or, "You can count on Wheels," and "There's nobody like old Wheels."

But it was not to be.

After two jobs—one involving a two-miles-per-hour chase through rush hour traffic and the other ending with the guys in the back seat holding up matches to read the maps unfolded across their laps as Louie circled a nameless block in Pacoima—the calls stopped coming. For most of an endless, deeply depressed year he sat beside the phone like last year's starlet, waiting for Hollywood to call. Eventually, though, he was forced to come to terms with the hard, unyielding truth: a getaway driver with no sense of direction is not a hot property.

But he was great as long as he wasn't driving; he was a good listener, and crooks, like everyone else, rarely find anyone who's actually interested in what they have to say. So he dug in, perfected a listener's encouraging nod and learned all sorts of memory tricks so he wouldn't have to take notes—he'd discovered early on that the tone of the conversation changed abruptly when he pulled out a notebook—and he widened his circle of friends. When he realized there was more going on than any single set of ears could ever hope to hear, he began to run a string of informants; crooks (and this should surprise no one) get screwed over a lot, and they're not shy about getting even if an opportunity presents itself. After a year, he found himself selling information to the people from whom he'd been stealing it. Even in the first flush of success in his new enterprise, in his heart he was still Wheels, and soothed that wound by starting a profitable parallel career acquiring and renting out untraceable getaway cars for other people to drive.

And he had a talent for friendship. He was the kind of guy you could call up in the middle of the night to slap a couple of tires on your car.

I kicked the right front tire just to feel like I was doing something, and then hiked back into the alley and past the open stage door and the truck, now mostly empty of its cargo, to the front door, which was propped open with a copy of *Eve's Hollywood.*

9

Three-Foot Tongue

Lavender slid into the other side of the slick semi-leather booth—a queasy shade of pumpkin—shoving her big canvas tote in front of her. We were across the street and a short block west of the theater, in one of the last remaining "family restaurants" of a once-mighty chain of eating places that opened each morning with pancakes and bacon and closed late at night with burgers and tough steaks. Of course, that was when families ate with each other rather than with their phones, and before pinpoint demographic research did away with categories as vague as "family." The demographers' quest for precise targeting having been successful, and this being the middle of the night, the place was almost empty.

"Been eating here since I was younger than you," she said. "It's not very good, but it's consistently mediocre. Have you noticed that lately, things that are good aren't very consistent and things that are consistent aren't very good?"

I said, "Not really, but I could probably develop it into an essay if you'd like."

"That's okay. It's worth coming in just to see Dorrie, the waitress who's staring at us over there, trying to figure out what someone as good-looking as you is doing with someone as old as me. The burgers are okay."

"You're not so old."

"Keep it up," she said, "although I notice you didn't deny being good-looking."

She was way ahead of me conversationally, so I opened what I figured was probably one of her main subjects. "What was the first record you loved?"

She shook her head. "You probably never heard of it. 'Yakety Yak,' by the Coasters. In 1959—a very good year—when I was thirteen, the song came out of the car radio one day, bit me on the thigh, and turned my world upside down. We, by which I mean my family, were whiter than Christmas, and I thought I was so *daring*, so *avant-garde*, liking Black music, until someone told me that the song was written by two middle-class white guys from LA who were hanging out in the Black clubs down on Central Avenue. They wrote 'Hound Dog,' too, for Big Mama Thornton, although you-know-who had the hit. I remember my parents being horrified that I was playing music by African Americans. A little later I discovered Ray Charles and Chuck Berry and Little Richard. My parents never got past Nat King Cole. Almost no one in their generation did, but they all felt pretty liberal about it." She fanned herself with her menu, which was so big you could use it to flag down a train. "*Listen* to me."

"I know 'Yakety Yak,'" I said. "It's a classic."

"To you, it's a classic. To me, it's summer in a convertible and my father getting pissed off."

"Bet you didn't know that Nat King Cole was Chuck Berry's favorite singer."

She turned her head slightly aside and looked at me from the corners of her eyes, and it came home to me what a heart-stopper she must have been. She said, "Where did you hear *that*?"

"I read it, in *both* of his two autobiographies. They don't always agree with each other, but Nat King Cole's in both of them."

"My, my," she said. "A savant."

I said, feeling vaguely guilty, "I read a lot."

"People like you should be forced to wear glasses so people

like me could be careful. But, hey, did you know that Little Richard's guitarist for a while was Jimi Hendrix?"

"I did not," I said. "Talk about a couple of originals."

"Little Richard was the onliest person on the planet. And James Marshall Hendrix, just a kid, got out of the army, which he joined after he stole a car and got offered military service as an alternative to jail. So first thing he did when he was free again was get a job playing with the Isley Brothers, who were just fucking great, and then he joined up with Little Richard. Maybe 1965. I was on my second convertible by then. Had a *much* better radio."

"My first car ever was a convertible," I said. "My mother bought it for me after my father split, sort of a consolation prize. It leaked."

"They all leak." She put the menu down. "I have no idea why I'm looking at this, I always have the same thing. Did it console you?"

"The car? No. Tell you the truth, I didn't need much consoling. My dad was a putz. I'll have a dish of chocolate ice cream, plus whatever you're having. Thirty-eight years old, and I still plan dessert first."

She waved for the waitress, a severe-looking woman with seriously ambitious hair—a long tangle of braids as complicated as the knots Boy Scouts learn to win badges.

"Hey, Lav," the waitress said, not taking out her pad. "Same old?"

"Times two, Dorrie, plus a double chocolate ice cream for my grandson here."

The waitress said, "Puleeeeze," and turned away. Over her shoulder she said, "Coffee coming up. Looks like you brought your own sweetener."

"They know me," Lavender said. "Maybe too well. In fact, she's the only person I allow to call me *Lav*, since it's Brit slang for toilet, as a member of the Moody Blues once informed me. Do you remember what the father's threat was? In 'Yakety Yak'?"

"The *threat*?"

"Yeah, this poor little chick is, maybe, fourteen or fifteen but she's already got it going on, and she's getting this endless list of chores from her old man, and at one point he says if she doesn't scrub that kitchen floor, she's grounded—no more rock and roll." She sat back, shaking her head. "Talk about a *line in the sand*. There it was, the whole generation gap, in a jokey song. Old Dad there, he spotted why his daughter was changing. You know, kids in my day didn't have money, we didn't have clout, we didn't have cars—most of us, anyway—we didn't have places we could call our own. We could fight wars, or at least the boys could, but we couldn't vote against them. We fucked in drive-ins or up on Mulholland Drive, or anyway, I did. What we *had* was rock and roll, and all the way back in the fifties, writing this harmless-sounding joke song, Leiber and Stoller give us this big butthole father threatening to take away his daughter's music. He recognizes the peril: no more 'Yes, Daddy,' no more *Father Knows Best* on TV. I'm telling you, everything that happened in the sixties and seventies and eighties, the whole generation gap thing, it starts right there. And look where all the prophets we followed came from. They came to us over the radio. They came from rock and roll."

"I'm not arguing."

"And it *kept* changing things for two or three generations. Longer than any other style of music, ever. All that stuff in the early fifties about how rock and roll will never die, well it was whistling in the wind, but it turned out to be almost true. I've been around since they paved the Garden of Eden, and it wasn't until fifteen, twenty years ago that rock began to fade. And what's funny about that was that rock was about the *powerless*, which is to say kids, and rap and hip-hop are about another segment of the population that never got its propers. I mean, I'm not crazy about the hit parade these days, but at least pop music, whatever the hell it is, is still subversive to some extent." She glanced around the restaurant, which was empty except for

Lavender and me and, in a booth across the room, a couple in their fifties. They were so focused on their food that they might as well have been alone—so far, neither of them had said a word—and suddenly I remembered the silent meals before my father slammed the door behind himself for the last time. "Hello?" Lavender was waving at me. "So," she said, leaning forward and resting her chin on her hand. "What kind of crook are you?"

"I didn't think it showed."

"It doesn't. You look like the kind of boy my mother always wanted me to bring home, only *interesting*. But you went upstairs across the street, you met Cappy, you must have seen Sparks. This whole thing is like a bad musical, a version of *Jail-house Rock* without Elvis, where all the crooks are so ugly they look like their wanted posters were rejected by the post office."

"You were on the road with the tour?"

She sat back and lowered her chin to her chest as she raked her fingers through the silver hair, doing tangle patrol. When she was finished, she said, "I was in four—no, five—towns. I came and went. Cappy wanted me along for old times' sake; we know each other from way back, but it was just too depressing. Most of these guys, they were second- and third-rate when they were hot. And now a few of them, they're so bad they should be paying the audience for their time. 'Course, I'm from LA, where we had the best of the bands playing in our local clubs, not to mention the big tours. This was *not* that kind of tour; some of the towns these guys played, they probably would have paid to see the Muppets lip-synching. Not that *all* these guys suck, but I'll tell you, some of them make me feel really, really old." She regarded me for a moment and then smiled. "You pass. If you'd said something dutifully gallant, I would have made you pay for my dinner."

"So you were, umm, active in the sixties."

"I was, and that's such a *sweet* way to put it."

"As a . . . a . . ."

"Just come out with it, honey. A groupie. And a relatively famous one, too, at least in some circles. It was a different world then, of course."

"In what way?"

"Well, biologically speaking, for one thing. Back then you could be, as they used to say, *free with your favors*, without catching anything that would kill you. The clap, syph, herpes— unattractive, but not fatal. Or chlamydia. I've always thought *chlamydia* sounded like a character in a Greek play: *The Tragedy of Chlamydia, Queen of Athens*. It was *all* different, in a lot of ways more innocent."

"Were you—I mean, did you ever meet—the Plaster Casters?"

"God," she said, sounding weary. "People come and go, nations rise and fall, but a really bad idea lives forever. First, though, no, I wasn't one of them. Did I *know* some of them? Sure. We were chasing the same guys. But, you know, the idea of making little statues, like tutelary gods for my mantel, out of some bassist's dick didn't much appeal to me." She picked up her coffee, which had just arrived. "And don't think I didn't notice that you ducked *my* question about what you do."

"I'm a burglar," I said.

An eyebrow went up. I've never been able to do that. "That's pretty far down the tree."

"I'm a highly specialized burglar."

She was blowing on her coffee. "In what way?"

"If you were a museum director with a low budget and a board of directors who wanted a major expansion the day after tomorrow, I'm the burglar you'd hire to fill in the blanks. I can, as they say in my trade, tell the stuff from the duff."

"A connoisseur's crook."

"I steal from the rich and sell to the richer."

"And *I* was a connoisseur's groupie. The Plaster Casters—I mean, they had fun, but not the kind of fun I—hey, hey, you know Lionel Lyon, Lionel and the Pussycats? Remember them?"

"Barely. I've put years into trying to forget them."

"Snob. The big hit was 'Three-Foot Tongue.' You do *too* remember that." She sipped the coffee and gave it a betrayed scowl.

"The Pussycats must be older than Philadelphia by now."

"Not a chance. Lionel replaces them like ballpoint pens, first wrinkle they get, they're on the sidewalk and some fresh pastry takes their place. So, no job security and he pays them minimum wage, but hey, you know, it's *showbiz*. Lionel, of course, being a man, never gets old. He just gets *seasoned*. All three hundred pounds of him."

"You were talking about him in the lobby, right? With Cappy. Some kind of problem?"

"You want to know about that, or you want to know my Plaster Casters story?"

I said, "Why is it always *either/or*?"

"In heaven, I'm told, it's *and*. Although burglars rarely make it through the gates. Which one will it be?"

"In that case, the Plaster Casters."

"Okay." She lifted the cup to her lips, thought better of it, and waved it in the air. "Actually," she said, "since I'm in festive spirits this evening, I'll give you both. As luck would have it, they overlap." To the waitress, who had just materialized, she said, "Do you think I could *possibly* get some of this that was made in this decade?"

"It's younger than *he* is," the waitress said, "but since you're an old friend, what the hell." To me, she said, "How's yours?"

"I'll take her word," I said, pushing the cup over to her. "In fact, I'd like a Diet Coke."

"It's your stomach," the waitress said. She picked up my coffee, turned away, and called out, "New brew for the princess!"

Lavender pulled her big purse closer and tilted it to the right to lean on it, swiping back a strand of silver hair that had floated down over one eye. "So. First, I know this is *true* because I heard it from one of the girls who was there. Lionel was briefly hot, professionally, I mean. Before he went on the fried chicken and milkshake diet, he was pretty cute. Skin-deep and from a distance, anyway. So one of the Casters, a girl named Bordeaux, decided to go after him. You following me?"

"Lionel. Bordeaux. Plaster Casters."

"You get a gold star." She pursed her lips and looked past me for a moment, gathering her thoughts. "Couple of the Casters had tried to nail Lionel before, because back when he was a normal-size human being, he had seemed to possess a really remarkable set, if the landscape in his stage pants was any indication. Looked like he carried his own personal fire hose and maybe a couple of softballs so he could practice juggling in between sets. But they couldn't get him to go for it no matter what they promised him, and when he got laid, he got laid in the dark. So Lionel's junk remained, if you know your Shakespeare, 'the undiscovered country from whose bourn no traveler returns.'"

"That was death, wasn't it?"

"Every life is studded with small deaths, darling, as practice for the big one. So, like I was saying, the Casters had turned him into big game, like the one who got him could have next crack at Roger Daltrey, and one night at the Chateau Marmont, a girl named Ferrari dumped half a dozen ludes—" She stopped and blinked a couple of times. "Do you remember ludes?"

"Not really."

"I love when people say that. It's like they think 'no' would be admitting ignorance but 'not really' puts them above the humdrum world of facts. Your generation has no sense of history. Ludes, or quaaludes, were sleeping pills that were also supposed to be an aphrodisiac, like you could boink somebody and catch a few Zs at the same time. So anyway, back to Ferrari, and thank you for not asking if that was her real name, she dropped a handful of them into his red wine. *Lionel's* red wine, in case your attention has wandered. From the Casters' point of view, the ludes were a brilliant solution, because he'd be (a) out cold *and* (b) flying the flag at the same time. And if you were going to do a *cast*, you obviously had to have something to wrap the mold around. Did you actually just raise your hand?"

"Yes, ma'am. I was wondering how it worked. I mean how did they get the plaster off without amputating his—" Words, as they say, failed me. "Or, at the very least pulling all his pubes out."

"I admire people who can admit their ignorance," Lavender said. "They didn't dip it into plaster, you twit. What were they going to do, sit there playing mahjong until it dried and then break it open with a hammer? People always underestimate groupies. It was actually quite elegant, even *soigné*. After Lionel finally passed out, they went to work. I'm told that some of the girls had to put on their glasses to spot it. One of them told me she couldn't believe the level of *detail*. It was like one of those miniature cities built inside an eggshell. Anyway, when they'd stopped marveling over it, they greased it up and then submerged it in a martini shaker full of dental gel, the stuff your dentist uses to take an impression for a new tooth. When the gel was set, they eased the martini shaker off it and then they used butter knives to cut the mold in half the long way so they could pull it free without damaging the, uuuh, individual details in the impression. Then they sponged wee willie off and tucked it back into his pants. When he was all tidy again, they tiptoed out, leaving him with a goodbye note and a series of Polaroid close-ups detailing the process. Next day, probably, they put the two halves back together, poured the plaster into the mold, let it set, and then dissolved the mold. *Voilà*—Lionel, what there was of him, preserved for posterity, exposed to anyone with good eyesight or a magnifying glass. The first Plaster Caster miniature."

"They were actually in some museum, right? MoMA or something."

"Yes, MoMA it was. Imagine being the person who had to get the releases for that? *Hey, remember that night you let those girls ice your Johnson? We'd like to put it in a museum.* You know who the first real star to say yes was? Jimi."

"Big catch," I said.

"In more ways than one."

"So," I said, "you're no fan of Lionel's."

"I can think of more vehement ways to put it."

"The Pussycats, as I remember, had cute, soft little paws that they'd lick and then use to groom their faces, and then they'd all groom Lionel. While he sang."

"You *do* remember."

"Well, it's not for lack of trying to forget."

"Those things on their hands were called *Kitten Mittens*, and they were part of the merchandise sold at the concerts. I'm told some were actually bought, a few by women and the others by some of the odder men."

"Oh, well," I said. "People eat eggplant, too."

She interwove her fingers, like someone about to pray. "Here's the last Lionel story. Shalimar Stardust, whom I had once known as Sadie Motley, was in the plaster game early, so she wound up with almost a full set of the little plaster stiffies. A decade or so later she got tired of picking them up and dusting them or something, so she went out and bought a big pole and glued them to it. Turned them into a hat rack."

I said, "A hat—"

"Sure. You know, they all angled upward, more or less. Perfect to hang a hat on, if you're not squeamish. And after a while, when the novelty had worn off and she was thinking about moving it to the garage, she had an idea. She began to throw what she called *hat parties*. Everyone who showed up had to put twenty bucks into a hat, naturally, and then everybody would drink or indulge in the drug of their choice until they were all stupid enough for the main attraction, which was a contest. So, when people were *really* ripe—"

Dorrie, the waitress, materialized with a plate in each hand, and said, "Chapter two. Make a little room for the main course, such as it is."

"And the coffee?" Lavender asked.

"Coming up." She slid the plates into position. "Had to teach the busboy how to make it from scratch."

"Fine, I guess," Lavender said. Dorrie stayed where she was. Lavender said, "Don't you have anything to do?"

"*Look* at this place. If you see any customers except for that couple who hate each other, I'd like to borrow your glasses. Your conversation looks more interesting than the busboy's. He's talking about dog racing, and after somebody says, *See, there are these dogs and they race*, there's not really anywhere to take it. What kind of contest?"

Lavender slid farther in. "Have a seat."

"Oh, I couldn't possibly," Dorrie said, sitting down.

"Exposition, first," Lavender said. "We're talking about the Plaster Casters and an interesting use one of them found for the little pickled dicks when the thrill of owning them had worn off."

"Can't imagine that it ever would," Dorrie said. "All those potent symbols of—"

"You want to tell it, or should I?"

"Sorry." Dorrie leaned back, moved a few inches to her left, and settled in.

Lavender brought Dorrie up to speed and then picked up the thread. "So Sadie—sorry, Shalimar—had a long, narrow living room. She put the hat rack at one end and everyone stood at the other end, right at the edge of the carpet. If you stepped on the rug, you were disqualified, although you *were* allowed to fall face down on it, which happened from time to time, especially among the downer contingent."

"Got it," I said.

"Everybody had to use the same hat—a nice snap-brim that Shalimar stole from Leonard Cohen. They got three throws apiece at three bucks a toss, although that went up to five if there were any agents because everyone wanted to see agents lose money, and Shalimar rotated the hat rack a third of the way around after each throw so everybody got an equal chance.

You won five bucks if you hit a dick and your hat stayed on it, although it was only two bucks if it was Jimi Hendrix because he was so hard to miss. The jackpot, all the money that no one had won, was given to anyone who could hang the hat off Lionel's dick. If no one did, Shalimar kept the prize money. She had these parties for *years*, and I'm telling you, they practically supported her. Nobody ever hung one on Lionel. Far as I know, nobody even managed to hit it."

"Hung like a gopher, huh?" Dorrie said.

"He is to plaster dicks," Lavender said, "what Monaco is to nations."

"What the pinky is to fingers," Dorrie volunteered. "What a mosquito bite is to the first minute of *Jaws*."

I said, "What's the big secret issue with Lionel that you and Cappy were talking about?"

"Jennifer Summers," Lavender said.

"Ooohhh," Dorrie said. "I used to love her. In fact, I still love her. That *Heartprints* album, I played it until it was white on both sides."

"I sort of remember that," I said. "I think. What's she got to do with old dimple dick?"

"She was in the third or fourth set of Pussycats. He fired her because she went public to say he'd stolen a song she wrote." Lavender stared over my head until something apparently came into focus. "'Three Strikes,' it was called. Remember?" She beat time on the table. "'One strike and your heart aches—'" She moved her glass so the busboy could put down our burgers.

"'Two strikes and it breaks,'" Dorrie sang. She had a nice whiskey alto.

"'Three strikes,'" the two of them sang, with Dorrie finding a nice harmony, "'and it cuts like a knife; and you're picking up pieces for the rest of your life.'" Lavender mimed applause for Dorrie, and Dorrie said, "No, really, you're kind, really, thank you, thank you, but I can't possibly . . ."

"I heard him sing it once, in performance," Lavender said.

"Maybe the only time before he got shut down. Later that same week she sued to keep him from singing it at all." She picked up her burger, took a bite, and glared at Dorrie.

"Hey, honey," Dorrie said. "It's what we got in the kitchen."

"So anyway," Lavender said, putting the burger down. She glanced up at the window. "Does he belong to you?"

"In a manner of speaking," I said. "That's Louie." I waved him in, and he waved back with a tire-blackened hand.

"He's got that grease monkey thing going," Dorrie said. "I like grease monkeys. They're sensible and practical and they know how things work. And in the morning they can fix your car."

"So, if I may, to back things up," Lavender said. "She, by whom I mean Jennifer, takes this song she wrote to Lionel, like a complete dweeb, and asks if she can sing it in the show. Lionel tells her to sing it two or three times so he can remember it all, asks what key it's in, and says, essentially, 'Nice tune, sweetheart, but not our style.' And a couple weeks later he's in the studio doing the next LP, and he cuts it. Without telling her, of course. And with his name on it as the writer, naturally."

I said, "But they were all recording it. Didn't she—Hey, Louie." I moved over to make room for him, and especially for his left hand, which looked like he'd just struck oil.

"The Pussycats were never allowed anywhere near the studio." Lavender looked at Louie and said, "You'd be Louie," and then plunged back in. "He always hired backup singers. Lionel didn't hire the Pussycats for their voices, he used to say, he hired them for their lungs, ha ha ha. Anyway, he cut the song and made it the title of the album, 'cause the simp never figured that a chick, and a *Pussycat* at that, could take him down. But she did."

"Lionel who?" Louie asked.

"Lionel Lyon."

"Ooohhh," Louie said. "I hate that guy."

"You have good taste," Lavender said. "You hungry? Our waitress is sitting right here."

"I noticed that," Louie said. "Nah, I'm good. Although I wouldn't mind—"

"So Lionel begins to work up an arrangement of the song for the live shows, and Jenny—'Jenny' being Jennifer Summers," Lavender said to Louie. "Jenny says something like, 'Hey, that's my song, and old Lionel is all, Read your contract, sugar, anything you write with me is mine, and anyway, how the hell you gonna prove you wrote it? I've already copyrighted it.' And Jennifer—"

"What a louse," Louie says. "I used to love Jennifer—"

"We all did," Dorrie said. "Do you want anything?"

"My whole life," Louie said, "my whole life I've wanted things."

"Well, to narrow it down—" Dorrie said.

"Can I finish this fucking story?" Lavender said. "Sorry, Louie."

"No problem," Louie said. "I get a lot of that at home."

"So turns out that Jenny has a dub of the song, something they used to call an *acetate* back in the day, just a cheap forty-five cut in soft plastic that wasn't air quality. In fact, it was only good for three or four plays before the needle wrecked it, and that was intentional so no one could steal it, dupe it, slap his name on it, and start sending it out to radio stations. She cut it in some dinky little studio wherever she came from—Airbag, Arizona, someplace like that. So she's got the demo and the studio has the master tape *and* the dated log that shows when she cut it, which is like a year and a half earlier, and she walks into the office of the A and R guy at Lionel's record company and when they ask her why she's there, she holds up the demo and says she wants to save them a big lawsuit and a lot of humiliation. Guy says, 'You're saying *you* wrote the tune?' and Jenny waves the demo around and says, 'Got someplace you can play this?' and the guy listens and writes down the dates and the name of the studio and he calls the studio, and then he says, very casually, 'So who's the singer?' and Jenny says,

'*C'est moi*,' only probably not in French, and fifteen minutes later she's got a contract offer to show the lawyer of her choice, and the record company, which was Lunar Music—long dead by now—is having a quickie meeting. Upshot is, they pull the song off Lionel's album, refuse to let him record a replacement, which means the LP is one cut short, and they also retitle the album and refuse to make a new four-color jacket, just slap a cheap piece of paper over the old one, and they give it the title of one of the songs Lionel *did* write, a total stiff called 'Thief in the Night.' Then, probably, they all sat back and had a good laugh."

"Poetic justice," Louie said. "What *is* it with these people, anyways? They got everything in the world, they're paid better than the president, and you read about them, you hear about them, and they're *awful*—they act like nobody's hugged them since they were born."

"It's not just them," Lavender said. "Musicians are just more conspicuous than other people. I've been thinking about this since Kurt Cobain killed himself. He wasn't my vintage, but I loved him, and it started me wondering. I think some people just don't have a talent for happiness. They never expected to experience it and they don't know what to do with it. It frightens them. They can't take credit for it; they feel like impostors who are going to be found out just any old minute. It's like when something—fate or their talent or whatever—picks them up, hauls them into the light, puts them on a—a kind of hill, some new altitude, they think it's there just to give them something to fall off of."

"Jeez," Louie said. We sat in silence for a moment, and he asked Dorrie, "Hey, can someone get me a glass of milk?"

"That would be me," Dorrie said, getting up. "Don't you want to wash your hands first?"

"These?" Louie said, holding them up. "Nah. That's why they make jeans dark blue." He rubbed his palms on his thighs, held them up, and said, "Good enough for rock and roll."

"Darling," Dorrie said, leaning across the table. "Where have you *been* all my life?"

I said, "You made a conquest." We were crossing a largely empty Wilshire Boulevard midblock, a flagrant violation of the law. There was a time, long, long ago, when that infinitesimal infraction would have thrilled my rebellious teenage soul.

"She's something," Louie said. "It's a good thing Alice wasn't around." Louie's wife somehow looks at him, shaped like a large snowball, five feet, four inches tall, with two of the inches being a genuinely architectural comb-over, and sees Brad Pitt. It was the thing I liked best about Alice. "And the other one," he said. "*Sheesh*."

"When we've got a week to kill," I said, "I'll fill you in on her."

We hit the curb and angled left, heading for the huge dark hole in the road. Louie said, "So I got the tires on, but I was wondering if you read the note."

I put my hand to my shirt pocket and felt the square of paper I'd put there. I said, "A note? Where was it?"

"Right on the windshield, tucked under the wiper. Hard to miss."

"Sounds impossible to miss. What did it say?"

Louie didn't even have to take it out of his pocket. "It says, *You don't get warned twice.*"

Part Two

The Burglar's Handbook

10

Downstage Right

Friday Night

Once I'd gotten into the lobby of the little office building, the door to which was unlocked and unguarded, I punched in Rina's number.

"It's my dad," she said to someone, presumably Lavender. "He worries." To me, she said, "So?"

"So where are you?"

"We're in the room of infinite popcorn, gorging ourselves. Where are *you?*"

"Is the door locked?"

"Hey, Lav," she said. "Is the door locked?" Then she said, "Lav says it is."

"I didn't hear her say anything."

"Do me a favor," Rina said. "Just bear with me a second. Now put your chin down near your chest and then lift it up until your head is slightly tilted back. Then do it again a couple of times. What does that mean?"

"Yes?"

"I knew you could do it."

"She's letting you call her 'Lav,' huh? She must like you."

"Oh," she said, "the *stories* she can tell."

"That's exactly what I was afraid of."

"Yes," Rina said, "and she speaks well of you, too."

"Stay there," I said. "And keep the door locked. I think we'll be able to leave in a little while. I'll come and get you."

"Do you want to do a secret knock or something?"

"Yeah, I'll do the *two bits* and you do the *shave and a haircut.*"

"So, um, you don't think that anyone else in the world might just knock twice, like for 'two bits'? I mean, that's sort of the default, isn't it? *I* always knock—"

"This is what happens when I get too clever. I'll just say, 'Hey, Rina,' okay?"

"Can't you just hang up on him?" Lavender asked in the background. "I'm not going to live forever."

"I love her," Rina said. "Bye, Dad."

She loved her. I'd had my daughter for less than one day, and she'd seen an attempted murder, spotted one of the most terrifying crazies since the Spanish Inquisition, and fallen in love with a groupie from the 1960s. This was probably not what Kathy had in mind.

I said, "Why was Boomboom where he was?"

Cappy tilted back in his chair and rocked a little, like some extra in a western, waiting outside the saloon for the trouble to start. He looked at me for a good ten seconds before he said anything. "That's where he is every night. It's where he's been for decades. It's even specified on the layout they give the crew to use when they're setting up the stage."

"Have you ever seen a drummer downstage right before?"

He said, "Not often," and waited.

"And why not?"

He said, "Why does this interest you?"

"Because," I said, "it will interest Irwin Dressler."

"*Well*, question asked and answered." He wasn't so avuncular at the moment. He looked over my shoulder for so long I had to fight the impulse to turn and look over it myself. Then he lowered his head and fiddled with his drawer, opening it a few inches and closing it again, and I felt a teeny pang of guilt for having taken a furtive peek at the notebook. When he'd exhausted the possibilities of the drawer, he pushed it closed, hard enough for it to make a little bang. "It's in his contract." Right on cue, I heard the siren of what had to be an ambulance.

I said, "Is there any other band that has their, I don't know what you'd call it, their stage positions in their contract?"

"Damn near every one of them." He held up his hand and looked at his nails, or something in the vicinity of his nails, for a moment. "They've all got a few big heavy pieces, right? Keyboards and drums, for example, stuff that doesn't move around, or didn't before some showboat decided to fly the whole kit, drummer and all, not that any of *our* bands could afford the machinery to do that. See, we need the blueprint or schematic or whatever you want to call it because, you know, at a certain level rock musicians become *way* too important to be bothered with anything as bottom-level as setup, so we get our marching orders in the form of a diagram. Where the pieces should go, relative to each other and the geography of the stage, how much distance should be between them, exactly where the mikes should be, and so forth."

"So where are those pieces, usually?"

"The keyboard and the drums? Most of the time, they're upstage more or less center, with the drummer back farther than anyone else because he's usually up on a riser, so he's visible even when someone is in front of him."

"Upstage center," I said.

"Yes," he said, and the stress on the word was intended to make me aware that he was being patient with me. "Upstage center. Singers and lead guitarists like to think of downstage as their exclusive real estate, to wander around and show off in, especially now that there are wireless microphones. Also, if they're downstage they're easier to hit with a follow spot, which a lot of them *also* have in their contract."

"Any other drummers insist on being downstage right?"

He didn't even have to think about it. "None I've ever worked with. Sometimes, if the lead singer is at the keyboards, they'll put *that* downstage, too. Elton John, for example. And then there are drummers who sing—Dave Grohl, Don Henley some of the time, Phil Collins—but even so they stay upstage a little so people can move around and the stage isn't all static. What's your point?"

I said, "We read from left to right. Most people, when they come into a space with a choice of two doors leading to the same place, will go left. They don't think about it, they just do. When a curtain rises and the lights come up, people's eyes tend to go to their left, which is, of course, stage right."

"Sure. Go to any touring production of a Broadway play that's got one star in it, usually slightly on the fade, and he or she will pretty much have a lease on downstage right. That's where they'll be when the curtain goes up, if they're onstage at that moment, and if they're not, that's where they'll make their entrance. That and downstage center are the strongest positions there are."

"And yet, Boomboom was there."

"It might be hard to see, now that he's a geezer, but he was the band's real star, back in their limited day. He made it onto a lot of 'best drummer' lists, usually in fifth or sixth place, but, you know, there's a ton-load of fucking drummers, and fifth, sixth, that's pretty damn good for someone in a B-minus group. Led to bad feelings in the band. Franky, the lead guitarist, he just flat-out hated—I guess I should say *hates*—Boomboom. Band broke up every fifteen minutes."

The siren, which had stopped, started up again, presumably heading for a hospital.

"And," I said, when I figured he could hear me, "the drummer, since, as you say, he's got this big, heavy kit, isn't going to wander around. He's going to stay put."

"Ahh," he said. "I see."

"And the other thing is—I mean, if I'm right—when there's

no drum kit there, the people who *do* move around, the singer, the guitarist, whoever, they're in and out of that position for short, unpredictable lengths of time."

"Right, right. But how could anybody know that the flat would—" He'd been tilted back, and now he leaned forward and the front legs of his chair hit the floor with a bang. "You're saying—"

"The rope was feathered, but it had been cut, too. You saw it—it was a big thick rope that stretched from one of the top flat's corners to the other. It had been worn almost to nothing, like someone took a rasp to it, but the last, say, a little less than half of it had been sliced right through."

He said, "I need to think."

"Fine, but in the meantime, I think the guy who cut it went up there on the walkway, or whatever it's called, in the afternoon, maybe when no one was on the stage. Then he lay down so he couldn't be seen from below, and waited. When he was ready, or maybe at a cue from someone, he took a really sharp knife and cut the last couple of fibers on the flat's stage left corner so it would come down sharp-edged instead of horizontally, and land on Boomboom with its full weight."

"Which is what? It's just canvas framed in wood. Fifty, sixty pounds at most."

"And all of it concentrated into the lowest corner, which is about two inches wide. I've read that a woman of average weight can exert a pressure of two hundred forty pounds per square inch at the tip of a stiletto heel. And the thing had been falling for ten or twelve feet. Accelerating with every inch."

Cappy said, "Fuck me. I should call the cops."

I said, "I doubt your employers would give you any medals if you do."

"Shit," he said. He was drumming his fingers on the desk. "Are *you* going to do anything?"

"Well," I said, "first thing tomorrow I'll tell Dressler about it."

Cappy said, "Why does that not reassure me?"

11

Where People Park Participles on the Lawn

The silence had probably stretched for four or five seconds. In mid-sentence I'd glanced over at Rina, her silhouette framed against the raindrop spangle of the passenger window. In the tilt of her neck, the line of her jaw, I'd seen Kathy as she'd looked when I met her; and then I'd seen the *rest* of it as time simply collapsed, and it felt like my heart was exploding. I'd known Rina looked like her mother, but somehow I'd missed the fact that the resemblance bordered on the supernatural. I completely lost my train of thought.

She glanced over at me. "And?"

I said, "And what?"

"Well, never mind," she said. "Tell you the truth, it wasn't a very interesting conversation. I'd rather talk about Lavender."

"I'm sure you would." The evening's dud sprinkle was well into its transformation into a dud rain, and I hate to drive in the rain. It's not just the slick streets, either. Like most Californians, I treat my windshield wipers like something I won't need until the Great Trumpet sounds and we all line up for Judgment. I actually see better in the rain with the wipers off.

"She's *fabulous*," Rina said. "Lavender, I mean. She gives me hope about getting old."

"I thought I did that."

"No. Well, sure, but you're not old. Not *really* old. I mean, she saw the *Beatles*."

"She didn't tell me that."

"At the Hollywood Bowl. Said she couldn't hear a word, just one long scream."

"Sounds unpleasant."

"She had to change her undies twice."

I looked at her again.

"Eyes on the road, remember? *Baby on Board* and all that stuff."

"She did *not* tell you that."

"The line to the ladies' room was so long a bunch of girls took over the men's. Marched in waving spare undies like the proud flag of womanhood."

I said, "It won't be strictly necessary for you to share this with your mother."

"Give me a break." She looked out the window and played a little rhythmic figure on the glass with her nails, which drew yet another quick glance from me. She'd stopped biting her nails? She was a dead ringer for her mother? What the hell *else* had I missed?

"You know," she said, "I always thought the Beatles were really stupid-looking until Mom got that movie, and we watched it twice and they just got cuter and cuter. You know what? I'm hungry."

"It's pretty late."

"Well, *yeah*," she said. "That's why I'm hungry. Korean, okay? You've got all these great Korean restaurants all over the place, practically under your bed, and what have we got, out in the Valley? The Cheesecake Factory." She sat back and bounced against the seat back a couple of times. Then she said, "That show tonight, I mean, I know I only heard one band and a minute or two of another one, but is it *all* going to be like this?"

"Not intentionally, anyway," I said.

"It was all pretty white, huh?" she said. "Glad Tyrone didn't come." Rina was in fully reciprocated love with a beautiful Black kid named Tyrone. It had gone on for an improbable length of time for someone her age.

"That's pretty much how it was back then. Even radio was sort of segregated. Mostly. And even when *radio* got more integrated, live performances weren't, at least not so much. Not until the big festivals. People forget how wide the dividing line was between white and Black. In the 1950s, in parts of Saint Louis, Missouri, any mixed-race couple the cops saw was bundled into a squad car, taken to the station, and forced to get a shot for venereal disease."

"*No*," she said.

"Yes."

"Wow." She was fanning herself. "Is *that* salty."

"Sorry?"

"Terrible. Bitter. Awful. Wonder if Tyrone knows it." She bounced against the seat back a few more times. The evening had energized her. "But tonight wasn't just white, it was all really *old*, too. Nothing from anytime since I was born."

"No. The guys behind the tour—the ones who ran the careers of the bands you saw—they kind of went out of the business around the turn of the century."

"Who are they?"

And there we were, right at the nub, the very place I hadn't wanted to be. "They're . . . well, they're gangsters. A couple of big national gangs were in the music business from the late fifties on."

"So you went there why?" she said. "I mean, wait, *wait*. You're doing whatever you're doing because some, some *mob guy* told you to? Are they paying you?"

"No. It wasn't an order, it's a *favor*. It's a favor for someone I can't talk about."

"There's a lot we can't talk about, isn't there?"

My windshield wipers, which make their erratic passes at the rain pretty much whenever they feel like it, took a tardy swipe to further muddy the view. We could have been in a giant carwash, except that there was oncoming traffic and we weren't getting the free wax. The rain darkened the visible world and shrank it into a narrowing vista of gleaming streets and colored lights, all somehow increasing the delicacy of the fact that I was, for the first time in quite a while, alone with my daughter.

With, as she'd said, a lot of things we couldn't talk about.

After most of a dank block had sloshed by, she sighed in what sounded like surrender and gave me a break. "Almost nobody showed up tonight. Empty seats everywhere. I mean, that poor guy could have died in front of a half-empty theater. Okay, okay, I know that's mean. It was awful, but it's kind of sad, too, isn't it? Poor old geezer. Oh, wait. Is he alive?"

"Time is rarely kind," I said, "except maybe to Lavender. I don't know whether he's alive. But they apparently took him to a hospital, not the morgue." I swung left, beneath a colorful bouquet of wet-looking traffic lights, and onto Olympic, which is especially rich in good Korean restaurants.

"Mom says stuff like that thing you said, that thing about time, over and over. It's like her mantra. That and 'Jesus, *look* at me' anytime she passes a mirror."

"You're kidding," I said. "She's gorgeous."

"She says she feels like a beach. A little more washes away every day, and what's left is rocks. Getting into *hag territory*, she says." She fiddled with the circular concert program in her lap, which was embossed with the tour's rough-surfaced ROCK-ASAURUS logo. The whole thing looked a little like an irregular stone pancake that some idiot had drawn on. "God, this is so low-budget."

"She can't really feel like that," I said. "I mean, look, she's still beautiful and there's a suitor for her hand, so to speak. And he's swooped down and carried her off to—to where, Detroit?"

"Cleveland."

"The *other* Detroit," I said.

She turned and gave me the *no bullshit* gaze, which she'd developed by the time she was eight or nine, probably in response to the avalanches of misinformation I'd dumped on her and her mother when we were all living together. God knows

Kathy was truthful; if Diogenes had bumped into her, he would have stopped midstride and sold his lantern. I could feel Rina's eyes warming the side of my face. She said, "Are you really not even the *tiniest* bit jealous?"

"I might be," I said, "if it weren't, on the one hand, for Ronnie, and, on the other, for the fact that his last name is Fudge."

"I know," she said. "It sounds like the beginning of a limerick. But it's not his fault. And he really *is* nice."

"He'd better be."

"Hoo hooo hoooo, my father the criminal surfaces at last."

"I wasn't threatening him."

She shrugged. "That's kind of disappointing." She ran her fingertips over the embossed figure on the program. "She doesn't love him the way she loved you."

"What can I say to that?"

"*I* don't know. I suppose you could tell me how you feel about—you know, that there's someone else she might be going for?"

"It's complicated. I want her to be happy, but I think about you, too, and all I have to say is that he'd better be the right guy."

She did the rattling nails thing again. "Or . . ."

"Just or."

"Brrrr," she said. "That's good to hear. I like your apartment. It's sort of a palace."

"Well, we'd both love it if you could spend more time with us."

"I could spend a week just in that chair in your book room. You didn't have books like that when you lived with us."

"Yes, I did, but they were in storage. I wanted to build shelves in your room, but your mother wouldn't let me put you up for adoption. Which one caught your eye?"

"Banana Yoshimoto."

"I've got three or four—"

"*Kitchen.*"

"Why that one?"

"Because I started it at home and forgot to bring it."

"I envy you."

"Why? You've read it."

"In a perfect world," I said, "there would be some books you could read at least twice for the first time. Do me a favor and phone Ronnie to ask if she'd like to meet us at Kang Ho-Dong. She won't, but at least we'll have tried."

"That's the one on Sixth?"

"It is." While she pulled out her phone, I mulled over what I needed to do on the following day. It seemed like another visit to Dressler was in order.

And then I thought—

"She's not hungry."

I waved off the craziest idea I'd had in months and hit the turn signal for a left. "Well, we'll have to take her something or she'll sulk for a week."

A block blinked by, badly matched blips of haloed neon, as I listened to the wheels turning in Rina's head.

"Were you armed tonight?"

I let the silence fill the car. She was looking out the window. I said, "No."

"Why not?"

"I'm almost never armed."

"Why not?"

In for a penny, as the Brits say, in for a pound. "Because that way, I'm much less likely to shoot someone. Shooting someone usually creates needless friction."

"The thing that happened to that guy tonight, that was on purpose, wasn't it?"

"Well." I drew a deep breath. "Yes."

"So that means . . ."

"Yes, it does."

"And you won't be armed *tomorrow* night?"

"Who says I'm going back?"

"What were you doing while I was with Lavender?"

"In order? I was thinking, I was watching some guys, I was checking out a hunch, and I was talking to someone."

"Who?"

"Whom."

"Oh, don't be silly."

"If you use *who*, it tells people that you grew up in a grammatical slum where they park participles on the lawn and prepositions are what sentences end with, and, yes, I did that on purpose. *Who* tells us that the actual question you've framed in your mind, even if you've spared us the agony of actually *hearing* it, is that fabulous old dud, 'Who were you talking to?'"

She said, "And?"

"Eeek," I said.

"Okay, who were—pardon me, *to whom were you talking*?" It was the worst British accent I'd ever heard, like a teenager from Guatemala doing her first pass at Maggie Smith.

I said, "Guy named Cappy."

"What an *interesting* name."

"He wears a cap."

"Well, think of that. Wears a cap, calls himself Cappy. It's like school. What was the hunch?"

"Look," I said. "There's the restaurant."

"And it's right where it was last time. Let's go around the block."

I tried to come up with an artful dodge and failed. Instead, I said, "You don't want to eat Korean food that late."

"Okay, let's skip the food and just talk."

I said, "Suppose *I'm* hungry," but I made the right to go around the block.

"Well," she said, "you could talk with your mouth too full for me to understand you, or you could go all firewall on me, or you could just change the subject. As usual. Or you could, maybe for the first time ever, treat me like an adult and tell me the truth."

"You just want me to indulge you."

"What a condescending thing to say."

"Yes, it was," I said. "The hunch was that the rope holding up that wall had been messed with."

"And had it—oh, wait. That's how you know that—"

I was impressed with her speed, but it didn't seem like a fatherly thing to praise, so I just kept my mouth closed.

"Do you know who did it?"

"Do we *have* to talk about—"

"Only if, for once in my life, you want to stop *coddling* me."

I tried to look like I was concentrating on my driving.

"So," she said, "*this* is the kind of thing—"

"No, it isn't," I said. But I knew that wasn't going to put the discussion to bed. We'd gotten to the point at which it was *sooner or later*, and *later* just felt like too much work. "Okay," I said, slowing. "We're here."

She looked around: just a middle-class street, mostly rapidly appreciating single-unit dwellings from the forties and fifties, the majority of them dark. "What do you mean, we're here? What's here?"

I pulled to the curb and said, "Use your imagination, and watch what I'm doing. I'm turning off the headlights, putting the car into *park*, and taking my foot off the brake pedal. Why do you suppose I'm doing that?"

A pause, but not much of one. A slow release of breath. "To attract less attention?"

"Good. As you've already deduced, if your library withdrawals are any indication, I'm a burglar. That means I *pay attention to things*. A car idling with its lights on or with intermittent brake light activity—that draws eyes and, occasionally, a call to the cops. And for cops, nothing is more fun than pulling up beside a parked car and blinding whoever is inside with their special atomic flashlights." I looked over at her, and she shut her mouth, which had literally been hanging open. "This conversation is obviously not intended to be shared with anyone, especially your mom. What *didn't* I do when we stopped the car?"

She chewed on her thumbnail, realized what she was doing, and yanked it away as though it were hot. "Turn off the engine?"

"And why—"

"Because . . . because you weren't sure whether to stay or go?"

"Good. Why else?

A pause. "Because you noticed that someone was looking at us? Through a window or something. If the engine is running, you don't have to—"

"One hundred percent. But, you know, maybe that person wasn't actually looking at us at all. Maybe she noticed something on the inside of her window, a smudge or something, and was wiping it off. Maybe she's waiting for someone who's late, and she's peeking out from time to time because she's worried. Might have nothing at all to do with us. Probably doesn't. But I leave *right then and there*. Leaving too early may be boring, it may be unprofitable, but it's absolutely *always* better than leaving too late. One of the things about being a burglar, although the job might seem kind of, I don't know, adventurous, is that we all *want to avoid as much adventure as possible*. The duller the job, the better we like it. And getting noticed when we're not even *on* a job is just bottom-rung stupidity."

She was studying the windows of the houses on either side. "Makes sense. So . . ." I got the little drumroll of nails on the window again.

I said, "So?"

"How did you decide to do this?"

"Like almost everything else that really matters in a person's life, it was a combination of accident and luck."

"What kind of an accident? What kind of luck? I mean . . . um—" She leaned forward.

"Um, what?"

"The light went off in that house. Down there, on the left."

"Nice catch. The Spanish house?"

"I guess so." She squinted and tilted her head to the right. "Yeah, I guess that's Spanish."

"And which light?"

"The outdoor one, the one over the—the what is it, the porch."

"Mmmm," I said. "What time is it?"

She checked her phone. "Eleven-thirty."

"Ninety percent chance it's a timer. People, for some impenetrable reason, set their timers for either the hour or the half hour. Sometimes they'll throw caution to the winds, live dangerously, and go for quarter after or quarter to. If it had gone off at, I don't know, eleven twenty-two and I was working, I'd be out of here so fast you wouldn't be able to see me go. As it is, I'm *still* going to move the car."

"So at night, when I was growing up, you, um, you did stuff like this."

I signaled and pulled away from the curb. "Not much. Most of the time, when I was living with you guys, I wasn't working. I'd hit a couple of big ones when I was filling up the bank account I figured we'd need after you were born, and we got by on that. Mostly. I did a few daylight jobs because your mother has always believed that burglars only work in the dark. Overall, though, I took it easy. Your mom got very upset when she knew I'd done a job."

"Because she worried about you."

"That's certainly one of the reasons."

"What are the others?"

"You."

Rina said, "Oh." For a moment, we rode in silence, and then she said, "But you need to pull over again. We're not finished."

"We're not?"

We went half of a slow, wet block in silence, and then I said, "All right, all right."

Instantly, she poked my arm, hard. "There's a space."

"Look again."

"Oh. Fire hydrant."

I steered past it but kept my eye open for other spaces. "I had a friend once, guy nicknamed Steeltoe, who—"

"Steeltoe? What kind of name is that?"

"It's the nickname of a guy who was keenly aware that anyone who commits a burglary strapped—sorry, carrying a gun—is automatically charged with a felony, as opposed to misdemeanor breaking and entering, even if all he took was a handful of pencil erasers. Felonies, not to go into detail, are much, *much* more serious, *prison* serious. But the nickname: at some point in his past he'd been married to a woman who taught flamenco, and he learned it from her. I never saw him dance, but he developed *extremely* fast feet. Wore boots with, well, as you've probably guessed, steel toes. Even if he got caught with a pocketful of someone else's diamonds, boots don't count as a weapon. But I'll tell you, let him get close enough and he might as well have had a .38. Once, I'm told, he took down a guy he was doing a job with—a dimwit named Willie Klim, who was every bit as interesting as he sounds. Klim had been driving and had parked in front of a fire hydrant. When they came out, Steeltoe spotted the hydrant, got a little crazy, and decided some punitive action was called for right there and then. Problem was, Klim already had his gun out. Not a bookie in the world would have taken a bet against him, but later when the two of them had kissed and made up, Klim said he couldn't even see Steeltoe's feet move. One minute Klim's got him dead to rights, and a second later Steetltoe is backing away with Klim's gun in his hand and Klim is curled up on the ground, singing soprano. He walked folded like a paper clip for days."

She didn't reply, so I glanced over at her and saw the pursed mouth that, on her mother, meant either that she suspected that what she'd just heard might not have been completely true, or that she hoped it wasn't.

I pulled up to the curb and went through the drill again. She was looking at the houses, but what she said was, "Wow. I guess."

"Well, you started it. Crooks aren't as interesting as they sound. Get a dozen of them around a dinner table and start a conversation, and I can guarantee it won't be enough to keep the blood flowing to the brain."

"I can get stupid conversation at school. Can't be much worse than that."

"I don't know. I could put you in a room with two getaway drivers who will argue for hours about the superiority of one street you've never heard of, over another street you've never heard of. Literally for *hours*, and their interest will never flag."

"You're not going to distract me. What did you mean when you said it was a combination of accident and luck? You deciding to be a burglar."

"Okay," I said, and I turned the engine off. "We're back in the straight world, not casing houses anymore. Nothing to worry about. Even if the cherry lights go on behind us, there's nothing in the trunk or the back seat that shouldn't be there. We're together, we have ID that proves you're my daughter, and we're having a father-daughter chat. Once the cops see the ID, they'll leave us alone. They've got problems with their kids, too."

"This is a problem?" she said. "Some fathers would be flattered, their daughter wanting to know all, or even *anything*, about their job. What do you mean, accident?"

"I was fourteen," I said. "We lived in Encino, next door to an old fart who hated dogs. So naturally, we had a dog, a big dumb mutt who ate my father's shoes every chance he got and who barked unendingly at birds, apparently hoping to talk them down to a place where he could eat them. The guy next door liked to open our gate, let the dog out, and then call animal control."

"Asshole," she said. Then she said, "Sorry."

"Not at all. We've moved onto a conversational plane on which that's a perfectly appropriate response. He *was* an asshole. The third or fourth time he did it, I waited until he went to work and then went into his house through an open window. He lived alone and he worked all day, so I knew I had some time. I wore my mother's dishwashing gloves because I was thinking about fingerprints. I was barely in my teens, this was the first time I'd ever been in the house of someone who didn't know I was there, but I was already thinking about fingerprints."

"What did you take?"

"Nothing. I *left* him something. I had a big tube of super-glue with me. I started by gluing down everything on his living room table, including his book, his ashtray, his pack of ciga-rettes, his lighter, and his TV remote. I glued the controls on the remote, too, but before I did that I glued the TV's plug into the outlet and tuned it to a channel that was mostly fun-damentalist preachers demanding money in various regional accents. Then I glued shut all the cabinets in his kitchen and then I had an inspiration and glued down the seats and the lids on both his toilets. I figured that would get urgent pretty fast. Then I went back into the kitchen and glued his refrigera-tor closed, and squirted glue into the latch of every door in the house and closed them, although I left the kitchen and the bath-room doors open. And just before I left I glued the stopper into the sink in the master bedroom and turned on the water. This was about eleven in the morning, and he didn't get back until six or seven, so I figured he'd come home to an indoor pool. He had teams of people working there for a couple of weeks, but even after that I'd occasionally hear a scream of fury in the middle of the night. He knew it was me, but he couldn't prove anything."

"How did you know? That he figured out that it was you?"

"The dog was never set loose again."

"Um," she said, and paused. For a moment I hoped she'd drop it. But instead, she said, "How did it feel to be in his house?"

I said, "That's the right question, and I should answer it dis-honestly, but I won't. It felt fantastic."

"What kind of fantastic?"

"Powerful."

"So after that, you knew? I mean, that was all it took?"

"I thought you were hungry."

"They stay open late."

"Ronnie will get worried."

"That's what phones are for."

"Wow," I said. "It's like arguing with me."

"God, I hope not."

"Okay, I'll give this five or ten minutes more, and then we're done. If you still have more questions, and if I feel like answering them, we can do it tomorrow."

"Thank you," she said.

"Don't do that," I said, starting the car. "I'm off-balance enough as it is."

12

Kissquito

"I can't *believe* we're talking about this," Rina said as I worked my way into a third parking space, which was a little snug. My stomach was grumbling. The rain had let up, solely to make way for fog. "For years it's felt like a red-hot floor, and I knew I couldn't cross it." She settled back, turned away from me, and said to her closed window, "And I kept wondering if it would have been different if I was a boy."

"If I *were* a boy."

"Oh, *thank* you," she said. "You've saved me from a lifetime of humiliation."

"Here's some more police management. Put your ID on the dash. When you're not doing anything wrong, go out of your way to make the cops happy. Even with you in the car, at this time of night no cop's going to want us putting our hands out of his sight, digging away in our pockets for ID. This way you can say, 'It's right there, officer,' and smile at him."

"Or her."

"Smile at whoever it is. So anyway, the dog was the accident. Here's the luck."

"You're *enjoying* this."

"Maybe, a little bit. So, okay, in my early teens I began to play a kind of game. When I was sure my mother was asleep— my father had packed up and left us by then—I'd go out through my bedroom window and walk for hours, just looking at houses, guessing which rooms were which, what kinds of things were in them, who lived there and what kind of stuff they had, looking for alarm systems, spotting ways in and out—that kind of thing. And then one night about a year later, when I had a car and could get a safe distance away from my own neighborhood, I was standing in some bushes around one in the morning and actually thinking about breaking into a big house up in the hills, and somebody behind me cleared his throat and said, 'Forget it, kid. It's mine.'"

"Oh my God, I would have gone twenty feet in the air. What did you do?"

"I put up my hands. He had a gun."

"But you just said guns were—"

"It was a squirt gun. He carried it so that if a house he thought was empty turned out to have someone in it, he'd have something to persuade them to let him get the hell out of there. But it was still a risk. There are cops who, if they'd caught him, would have taken the gun, looked at it, shot him on the spot, dropped the gun next to him, and claimed he drew it on them, they had no way of knowing, *et cetera*." I glanced over at her. Her eyes were enormous.

"That's not true. Is it?"

"It is. This is not a game; not for us, not for the cops."

Even with all the stops, we'd gone three-quarters of the way around the block by then, and I hit the turn signal for a right on Sixth. I pulled into the restaurant's parking lot, almost empty, turned off the lights, set the brake, and waited. But not for long.

"Why was he important to you? The guy with the squirt gun?"

"He changed my life," I said. "There I was, a sort of burglar fan boy, and there *he* was, an actual living burglar. He looked me over and saw something, I have no idea what, and right there and then, he sort of adopted me. He gave me fifty bucks and asked me to sit in my car at the entrance to the circle the house was on, and blow my horn, a couple of short ones, if a car entered the circle."

"He—" she said, and then she stopped.

"He what?"

"He gave you the money *first*? I mean, how did he know you wouldn't just pocket it and drive away?"

"He didn't. It was a test. He was looking for someone he could teach, someone to whom he could pass along everything he'd learned, a lifetime of skills. Like a son, I guess. He didn't have a family. So I became his pupil, whatever you want to call it. Over the course of four or five years I learned most of what I know, and not just about burglary, from him. Eventually there were four of us, one of them a woman."

"Really. He mentored a woman."

"She was already a pro, she just wasn't very good. But he changed that."

"Where is she now?"

"Someone murdered her," I said. I opened the door. "Coming?"

She had turned away and was looking out her window. "No."

I was in and out fast, just asked for what they'd made up in advance and hadn't sold, and when I got back to the car she was still facing away from me, although I couldn't see anything interesting through the passenger window. I tapped her shoulder and waved the bag around, but all she did was take it and put it in her lap. I said, "Careful, it's greasy."

"Grease on my *jeans*?" she said. "I'm terrified. It'll *never* wash out." She chewed on her lower lip and said, "What happened to—the guy who taught you?"

"Someone murdered him, too."

She said, "Oh." I heard her swallow, and she said, "Is that why your apartment is a secret?"

"It is. When you're a crook, you tend to come up against other crooks. And crooks, much more frequently than other kinds of folks, kill people."

I waited, but that seemed to be the end of the conversation, so I pulled out onto Sixth, which was black, empty, and gleaming. As far as I could see, we were the sole beneficiaries of a fine, sparse drizzle, and I only had to let my wipers do a single back-and-forth tour once or twice per block. I was focusing on how much I loved driving in LA at night when she cleared her throat. It was an editorial throat-clearing, one with purpose behind it: to make me shut up and listen.

She said, "Do you remember the Kissquito? Every now and then when you and Mom were arguing and it got a little loud, I'd hear you coming toward my room, like you were worried I might be awake and listening and, I don't know, scared or something. I'd scrunch down and squeeze my eyes really, really shut, and then you'd open the door so quietly I couldn't believe it because it always squeaked for me and—"

"You have to lift up on the—"

"Thanks, we'll get back to that, if that's okay. And you'd peek in for a minute and then, if you figured I was awake, you'd make this high little *humming* sound, like a giant mosquito but really quiet so it wouldn't wake me up if I was asleep. If I was awake, and it felt like you *always* knew when I was awake, you'd come all the way in, still humming, and you'd say in a big deep monster voice, 'It's *Kissquito*, and he's come a hundred miles to bite any little girl who's still awake,' and I'd say, trying to sound like a baby, 'Oh, no, help me, help me, *help me*,' and you'd say, in this *muu-haa-haa-haa* voice, 'Too late, little girl. Like it or not, here it comes,' and you'd lean down and kiss me on the forehead. Then you'd hum or buzz or whatever it was a little bit more, and tiptoe out as though I'd gone to sleep."

I was completely at a loss. All I could think of to say was, "You knew it was me, huh?"

"Even at that age I could tell my father from a mosquito. The reason I thought of it was that you made up the Kissquito to keep me from learning any of this—"

"You were a *baby*."

"And now I'm not." She looked over at me. "It always frightened me when you and Mom got into fights, but I really loved the Kissquito. And now we don't need him anymore. Okay, a lot of what you said is kind of scary, but it doesn't change anything. This isn't vocational training. I'm not looking for a *tutor*, I'm not going to buy a mask and a squirt gun and embark on a reign of terror. I'll probably never steal anything more valuable than a ballpoint pen, even if I live to be a hundred. But you're my *father* and this is *your world*. I can either go on imagining it and worrying about it and probably getting it all wrong for the next few years, until I just give up and move on, or you can give me some kind of feeling for what it's like, where you go, who you know. What you're doing. Don't you understand? I *worry* about you."

It took me a few seconds to replay what she'd said and to kick myself, and when I was finished, I said, "I see."

"You *see*," she said. "You know, I can count on the fingers of one hand the times I remember when we've been alone with each other for any length of time. Where we can, you know, *talk*? And then, when I *do* see you, I'm on tiptoe all the time. There's a big part of your life that's classified information, and when I raise it, I get pabulum, nothing that means anything. Not tonight, but always before. It just flat-out scares me. *And* it pisses me off."

And there I was: face-to-face *again* with the craziest idea I'd had in months. I said, "I hear you, and I'm working on it. I promise." And we splashed through the last mile as though we were in different cars. When I got home I gave the bag of food to Ronnie, who had already set three places. Rina grabbed a bowl of rice and drifted into the book room, Ronnie began to rub the wooden chopsticks together—she had a terror of swallowing a splinter—and I went into Ronnie's and my bedroom, crossed my fingers, and made a call.

And, to my shock, got an answer that could have been abbreviated as *why the hell not?* Now all I had to do was live through it.

13

Gâteau Is Just a Fancy Way to Say Cake

As the gates groaned open, Rina leaned forward, eyes wide, wide open, and said, "He lives in *Manderley*?"

And in fact, the morning's hangover of drizzle had turned the house's gray stone to a gleaming coal-black, making it look like a place that might very well be home to a small convention of literary madwomen . . . I said, "You've read *Rebecca*?"

"No, silly," she said, "I saw the movie." I started to pull in, slowly, because Dressler's gates took their usual sweet time to open—the house's way of saying, *You might not be welcome.* In the old days, uninvited guys with guns would have been a constant issue.

"Mom's got me watching a bunch of oldies on YouTube, but they're mostly pretty good. Mrs. Danvers just creeped me—" We rounded the curve past the dense scrim of protective shrubbery and she said, "Wow, they came out to *meet* us?" She studied the little group in front of the door with her mouth open, and I found myself closing mine; in all the times I'd been here I'd never had a formal reception. I wouldn't have been more surprised if we'd been met by the Queen of Hearts and the Dormouse.

"*Look* at this place," she said. "I guess crime *does* pay. Who's the midget in the middle?"

"That's your host," I said, "and he's only little on the outside." I needed to squint to make sure I was seeing what I thought I was seeing, and when I confirmed it, it made me swallow a couple of times.

Babe and Tuffy had retired their shorts and bakers' aprons and the fluffy fur slippers they used to polish the house's eighty-year-old Brazilian hardwood floors while gliding to Viennese waltzes. Those daily duds had been replaced by identical jaundice-yellow sport coats and white slacks that made them look like a *very* white soft-rock band from the fifties who sang about high school proms and teenage queens and Catalina Island, and had a name like the Yearbooks.

But the real shocker was the tiny figure between the two lemony sport coats. Dressler looked like someone who had escaped from one of those miniature towns that come with really expensive model train sets. Standing defiantly unsupported, Dressler was wearing dark slacks and a tweed jacket with scholarly looking elbow patches. It was two sizes too big for him, although it had probably fit to the hundredth of an inch before he'd gotten sick. Wrapped around his throat was something that suggested a friendly green reptile. He raised a hand to wave, wobbled a little, and grasped Tuffy's sleeve. On the third squint I identified the thing around his neck as an ascot.

An *ascot?* His days as a dandy had ended long before I met him. In all the time I'd known him, I'd never seen any evidence of Dressler even being aware of what he was wearing, much less decking himself out in some kind of *ensemble.* He owned an apparently infinite collection of loud, eye-scratching old-duffer golf slacks that, paired with clashing polo shirts, seemed to satisfy him just fine, however the rest of us felt about it. But today he'd *dressed up* for us, and the bright green ascot was such a jaunty, misguided touch that, for a moment, I thought I might weep.

Rina said, "I asked you—"

"I told you, he's your host," I said, clearing my throat as I pulled to the right to park the car in one of the six jumbo-size spaces. "And he's probably the biggest man you'll ever meet."

She said, "Really," craning around to look back at the welcoming party. "And the Mr. America candidates?"

"They're his help. Babe and Tuffy. And although they can be amazingly sweet, they're not people you'd ever want mad at you. In fact, all three of them are giving you a very unusual welcome, and it would be productive if you were on best behavior."

"I'm always on—"

She broke off because both of the car's front doors had opened simultaneously, and I found myself staring at the yellow buttons on Tuffy's sport coat. They were straining against some recent poundage, perhaps an effect of living on Dressler's current diet of flour and sugar. Tuffy leaned down and said, "Not a *word* about the ascot. He's been off and on about it all morning."

"I'm touched," I said.

"You fucking should be," Tuffy said. "He tried on three outfits before he settled on that one." He leaned down and stared across me at Rina. "Good God," he said to her. "Your mother must be a knockout. You surely didn't get it from *him*."

"He's okay-looking, for his age," she said, and to Babe, who had opened her door and given her a tiny bow, she said, "*Thank you, kind sir.*"

"Got class, too," Tuffy said. "Who'd have thought?"

I was accustomed to the baronial grandeur of the entryway, with its fourteen-foot arched ceiling and the line of small ruby-glass windows set high in the left wall to catch the sun, but the sheer scale of the place obviously caught Rina off guard because she slipped her hand into mine and kept it there for all of five seconds, something she hadn't done in three or four years. And here came the memory of my mother, baffling me when I was twelve or thirteen by saying that nobody paid enough attention to their children until the children were too old to want it. Suddenly, I knew exactly what she'd meant, and I had an urge to put an arm around my daughter's shoulder. Before I could do it, though, we turned the corner to the living room. Rina stopped in her tracks and reached over to grab my sleeve as Tuffy chuckled behind us.

It stopped me, too. Dressler's living room, half the size of an

Olympic pool, was pretty eye-popping even on a normal day, but today it looked as though clouds of winged fairies with advanced degrees in interior decoration had woven spells over it all night long. The couch was back in front of the picture window for the first time, probably, since Dressler went *mano a mano* with the Italians, and it had been tormented with leather polish until it gave out a reluctant gleam. An enormous Persian rug, in black and tan with feathery accents of a deep, deep red, claimed the center of the room, setting off the warm wood of the flooring. The rug had been vacuumed so vehemently it was striped lengthwise. But the real heartbreaker had been pulled up to the couch: a long, large, low, deeply carved Chinese table from, I guessed, the Qing dynasty. The Qing was one of the longer-lasting of the modern dynasties, so there was a lot of room for chronological error, but I dated the table around the very early 1800s. It was made from a highly reflective rosewood with four inset squares of translucent pinkish marble to mark the spots where hot dishes could be set down without marring the wood's regal finish. The whole thing vibrated with the genteel murmur of absolute authenticity, giving me what I think of as the *burglar's pang*, a sudden desire to come back with a truck when everyone is asleep. I was so focused on the table that it took me several seconds to register what was on it, centered on three of the four marble insets. The fourth was taken up with a little stack of plates. Rina beat me to the big picture, saying, "Oh, my God, whose birthday is it?"

"Well, my dear," Dressler said, and it took me a moment to recognize from his tone that he was *teasing* her. "We all know it isn't *ours*, and as much as I like your father, at least, on a good day, I can't see myself staying up all night to bake cakes for *him*, so I suppose we'll have to pretend it's yours. You *do* like cake?"

This was as unexpected as, say, The Rock walking into the room wearing a grass skirt. Dressler's tone wasn't even close to the voice I'd grown accustomed to in the years I'd known him. He'd scrubbed away the rough Midwestern edges, tabled the

Yiddish slang, and softened his tone until he sounded like some well-born midlevel diplomat. It took a moment for me to realize that this was probably the voice he had used in all those wearying daylong Senate and House subcommittee hearings where they'd never been able to lay a glove on him and had invariably closed the session by thanking him for his cooperation.

And it was a gift to me. I could literally hear a buzzing in my ears.

"But," Rina said. She was still standing in the hallway, one step up from the living room, and she showed no inclination to step down. "I mean, you don't even *know* me."

"I know your father," Dressler said. "Guys, how do we feel about Junior?"

"We like him okay," Babe said. "Even though he's got a dog's taste in clothes."

I said, "Hey," and Babe, who was standing beside Dressler at the table with a knife in his hand, said, "*Look* at that *jacket.*"

I said, "There's nothing wrong with this—" but I had to stop because Rina was saying, "I know, he dresses like a discount furniture salesman. My mother kept buying him nice stuff, and he'd wear it once and we'd never see it again."

"Yeah, well, your mother wasn't the one who had to wear it," I said. I saw the little spark in her eyes and changed tack. "Moths ate it. The San Fernando Valley, it *swarms* with—"

Dressler lifted both hands, his palms toward us, until he noticed that they were shaking. He glared at them and clasped them behind his back. "My dear," he said, "there's nothing we can do about his taste, this late in life; it's been set for years. But the *present* day is calling for attention, as it so frequently does when you're my age." He extended a hand, palm out and fingers together, like someone on an old quiz show whose job was to demonstrate the prizes in a way that would provoke envious *aaaahhhhs* from the audience, and moved it over the cakes. I half expected a little rain of glitter. "These beautiful cakes? Tuffy and Babe made them just for you."

"You helped," Babe said gallantly.

Rina said, "For me? But—" and I said over her, "What am *I*, chopped liver?"

"Of course not," Dressler said. "But compared to her, you're old news, you're like the schlub who takes a movie star to a party and stands around wondering why no one is paying attention to him. So please, my dear, come a bit closer and choose one. To start with, I mean. No one here would even *dream* of cutting into one of—"

"Yeah, right," Tuffy said, still standing next to me. "No one in this house would *dream* of cutting into—"

"All right, *all right*," Dressler said, making an uncharacteristic effort to be fair, and blinking fast at the sheer strain of it. "I will admit that I, from *time to time*—"

"A time like *breakfast*," Tuffy said, "a time like *lunch*, a time like three-fifteen in the morning—"

"And just for the record," I intervened, "I've *also* seen you eating—"

"You're here by invitation," Dressler said, "but we could always send you out to sit in the car like some Airedale while we chat with your daughter."

Rina cleared her throat and I smiled at her, expecting some kind of daughterly defense, but what she said was, "I'm Rina."

"Beautiful name. Oh, well," Dressler said to me, "you've driven all this way *and* you brought the guest of honor. Please, please, for heaven's sake, both of you come the rest of the way in and give these cakes the attention they deserve." He was waving her in with the fingers of his right hand. To me, he said, "You, too, of course, don't play hard to get. *This* one is angel food cake, which some people, mostly provincial Gentiles, seem to enjoy, but then some people vote Republican, too, don't they, and we didn't know your preferences, but we figured we'd hit home with at least one of these. The frosting is orange, a nice improvisation that Tuffy came up with at about four this morning when he realized we were out of lemons and I said no, rather decisively, to the notion of powdered lemonade mix. He also grated a little orange peel into it, which, if you're a minimalist, might be overkill. This dark one is a Black Forest *gâteau*, chocolate layered with cherries and whipped cream—*gâteau* is just a fancy way to say *cake*, since the French can't be bothered to talk like the rest of us."

Rina, who had beaten me to the table, said, "Oh my God."

"And *this* one, the one with the somewhat arterial coloring, is a transplant from Dixie called red velvet cake. I'm not overly fond of the red velvet, but Babe grew up in the land of cotton, and it apparently brings back aspects of his childhood that he enjoys recalling. Which will it be?"

"Um," she said.

"A slice of each?" Dressler said. "Of *course*. Tuffy, could you—"

"I don't want to be a pig," Rina said. She shot me a look that said, *Laugh and you're dead*.

"I don't know why not," Dressler said. "It's not often anyone gets an opportunity like this one, with no wrong choices. In the old stories, when the hero or heroine is offered a few alternatives, there's usually one that's fatal, isn't there? This path leads to grandma's, and this one takes you directly to the wolf. *This* magic word opens the enchanted door, and *that* one turns you to sauerkraut. Tell me, my dear," he said, fingering the ascot around his neck, "do you like this thing?"

"You mean, really?" Rina said.

"When you know me better," Dressler said, "you'll learn that I don't ask idle questions." He swiped the icing on the angel food cake with his index finger, put it into his mouth, and made the betrayed face of someone who expected a cherry but bit down on an olive.

"I'll start with the chocolate one, please," Rina said. "The scarf? No. It looks, ummm, silly."

"I thought it looked nice," Tuffy said, outing himself as the person who had dug out the scarf, probably from some closet that hadn't seen the light of day since Truman was president.

Dressler said, "In what way, silly?"

"Like—like gift wrap. Like something that's supposed to be nice-looking but all it really does is get in between me and the surprise. Or—or it's like pouring honey on a chocolate bar."

"And so it is," Dressler said, pulling it off, wiping his fingers with it, and dropping it to the floor. "The only person in the world who could wear one without looking like a ponce who dressed in the dark was George Sanders."

"What's a ponce?"

"Someone who puts on a tie to open a can."

Rina said, "You're funny."

"Well," Dressler said, "that'll be our secret, okay?"

"My mom and I just saw *All About Eve*," Rina said. "George Sanders was great. A little of the red velvet, too, please."

"Yee *haw*," Tuffy said as Babe sunk the knife into it. "The South *shall* rise again, if we can get enough ammo."

"Not *that* big," Dressler said to Babe. "She might eventually want to try the angel food, for some reason." To Rina, he said, "George was not the happiest man in the world. Killed himself, you know."

Rina, who had stretched an impatient hand toward the plate, pulled it back and said, "He *did*?"

"Left the only good suicide note I know of." Dressler was looking at the huge slices Tuffy had cut for Rina. "Short and devoid of self-pity: he was bored. No plea for sympathy, no striving for *style*. So many of us want to make a good impression when we won't even be around to see it. Emotionally, I think most people never get out of junior high school. George, of course, was not only an adult, but he'd also survived being married to Zsa Zsa, and after that, most things probably seemed weary, stale, flat, and unprofitable. Well, weary, at any rate. But, of course, you have no idea who Zsa Zsa was."

"Thank you," Rina said to Tuffy, taking the plateful of cake. "What if I spill on this beautiful table?"

"We'll throw it away and bring in the spare," Dressler said.

She gave him a quick glance but saw nothing in his face. "You don't—" she began, but then she stopped, shook her head, and said, "I think I've heard of Zsa Zsa. Spelled funny, right? Hard name to forget." She attacked the Black Forest cake with her fork, gouging out a quantity that would have brought a *tsk tsk tsk* from her mother. "Oh my God," she said with her mouth full. "This is *perfect*. Did you *know* those people? Personally, I mean?"

"Oh, yes," Dressler said. "That's not the same as saying I liked them. On the whole, I prefer crooks to actors. They're more honest."

"How did you get to know them?"

"Ahh. Well." He shot me a look, and I shrugged. "I represented most of them at one time or another."

She managed to get about half of the cake on her fork into her mouth, and said around it, "Represented them how? You mean, like an agent?"

"*Please*," Dressler said. "You don't know me well enough to insult me. No, like a lawyer."

"A *lawyer*? But I thought you were a gang—I mean, a, a ummm, I mean . . ." She broke off, eyes so wide I could see the whites all the way around the irises, and started to clap her right hand over her mouth, but she was holding the fork with the cake on it, and she froze and the moment stretched out until I could almost hear it creak. And it struck me like a bolt of lightning that if something like this had happened during the first few months *I'd* known Dressler, I wouldn't have been surprised to see a couple of guys bull their way out of the kitchen, armed with tommy guns and hard-boiled one-liners.

And then I heard a desiccated rasping sound, like someone trying to clear a pound of gravel from his throat, and I looked over and saw Dressler's shoulders shaking. Babe and Tuffy were watching him, so slack-jawed he might have been walking toward them on the surface of the sea, and neither of them moved a muscle, even when he said, "My whole *life* I've wanted to do this," and reached across the table, scooped up a big, sticky handful of angel food, thick with frosting, and threw it at Babe.

It caught Babe on the right cheek in an almost silent explosion of sticky white glop, studded with vivid bits of orange peel from the improvised frosting, and Babe froze, staring at Dressler as the stuff slid down his cheek, and then he said, "All *right*," and reached for the Black Forest cake.

"The *angel food*, you schlemiel," Dressler growled, a tone of command with decades of weight behind it, and Babe changed course in midstretch, plunged a wide-open hand into the center of the angel food, and brought up four fingers of goop, which he rubbed, quite deliberately, into Tuffy's hair. I was so enthralled by the sight that I took my eyes off of Dressler just long enough to get plastered dead center with what felt like frosting and smelled like my mother's vanilla Christmas cookies.

"You disappoint me," Dressler said to me, wiping his hands on his previously immaculate slacks. "You're supposed to have *instincts*. If you can't even keep your eye on the most dangerous person in the—"

A substantial piece of angel food cake, thrown frosting-first, blossomed in the center of his chest, and he stared down at it in obvious disbelief. "There," Rina said. "Members of *our* family defend each other."

Dressler looked at Rina long enough to make her blink twice, then nodded as though confirming a remark no one else had heard, and said, "You may be my new favorite person, although I should warn you that it doesn't usually last. Tuffy, can we get a bunch of small towels?" To Rina, he said, "Was the word you abandoned so abruptly *gangster*?"

With a quick glance at me, she said, "I guess."

"Well, thank God *that's* out in the open," he said, sitting on the couch. "After a lifetime of desperate pretense I can relax at last." He touched a finger to the mess on his chest and tasted it. "Not as nasty as I thought the first time. But, my dear, you'd probably be *amazed* at how many crooks are lawyers, and vice versa."

"On TV, they're usually on opposite sides."

"No one has ever accused the television industry of abandoning a good, solid stereotype that doesn't require the audience to think. *Consider* it." We could hear Tuffy opening and closing drawers in the kitchen. "What does a lawyer most need? Wait, wait, wait," he said, patting the couch, "please, come sit." After a quick glance in my direction, Rina sat beside him. "They need a *client*, which is to say, quite a bit of the time, a gangster. And what does a gangster most need?"

"A lawyer?"

"Babe, could you please go help Tuffy before this stuff hardens and we have to use a chisel?" He waited until Babe was out of the room and then he leaned toward her and said, "Can you think of any reason someone shouldn't be both?"

"Now that you bring it up, no."

"Your father—like me, but on a different level—is a superior crook for two reasons. First, he's never been arrested, and second, he has a working, if somewhat flexible, moral code. He'd probably deny that, but it was one of the things that first interested me in him. Do you think your father is an honest man?"

"Well." Her eyes were down, darting back and forth like someone who knows she's about to step on a booby trap but can't figure out with which foot. "Yes," she finally said. "In areas that matter."

Dressler gave a slow nod of approval. "So you've already figured out that people are complicated."

"*Interesting* people are," she said.

"From the mouths of babes," Dressler said. "And here's Tuffy with the towels. Ladies first, Tuffy."

"Even *I* know that," Tuffy said. "But we'll have to wait a second to use them. Babe's bringing the wet ones."

"So, the movie stars . . ." Dressler said and then tapered off, watching Tuffy critically, as though anticipating a lapse in the long-established etiquette of handing towels to people who have been in a cake fight. I took advantage of the moment to sit, uninvited, on the couch. Tuffy, without asking, cut a piece of the Black Forest for Dressler and the velvet for me. When we both had cake and forks, Dressler cleared his throat and picked up the thread. "The movie business, like everything else, is essentially about money: who gets it, when they get it, and how much they get. The studios take in—and, to a lesser degree, pay out—buckets of money, whether we're talking about theaters or DVDs or the new universe of streaming and rentals. Some things are cast in stone; as in any other industry, there's the eternal schism about how the money should be divided between the company, on one side, and the workers, on the other. Therefore, both groups need lawyers. At one point, after we ousted the oafs from the mob who had moved in while we were busy elsewhere, I represented both sides: on one hand, the labor, which is a drab way of describing the actors and some of the major behind-the-scenes people, and on the *other* hand, the studios."

"But," she said, and stopped, clearly doing a mental replay of what he'd said. "But wouldn't that be illegal? I mean, I know that's a stupid question, but—and *what* mob?"

"Not stupid at all. Of *course*, it was illegal. Totally, glaringly, one hundred percent. Conflict of interest everywhere you look. But on the other hand, it was *manageable*. Someone had to *step in*. The studios, to which we'd been lending money for decades, had been overrun by low-ranking members of that ever-feuding collection of deviants and dimwits known as the Mafia. They were putting muscle on the creatives—actors, mostly, but also some of the better-paid directors and camera operators—promising much bigger contracts. And they were getting them, too, but the mob, being the mob, was pocketing a substantial chunk of the increase." He pointed a frosting-dappled index finger at us. "Let me tell you, ninety-nine percent of the time, the difference between smart and stupid is greed. So the folks in the talent pool were paying higher taxes because their IRS returns showed bigger salaries, but because of the depth of the mob's cut they weren't actually *getting* much of the increase, which meant they were coming up *double-short*: smaller-than-expected raise, bigger-than-expected tax bite. And from the studios' perspective, *they* were paying more to the talent than ever before but not seeing any improvement in their *relationships* with the talent, so *they* were coming up double-short, too. So, you tell me: Not counting the mob, who was happy?" He looked, eyebrows raised, at Rina, whose plate was now empty.

"Um," she said, as Babe came in with a stack of medium-size, surgically clean dishtowels that had been spattered with water. When Rina had hers, she used it on her hands, since no one had tossed anything at her. "Who was *happy*?" she said. "Ummm, nobody?"

"Bullseye. Nobody. Double-short is a dope's game. If you don't make the marks happier than they were before, why do they need you? Of course, the studios aren't the bravest people on earth and there was a . . . predictable amount of *risk* in telling the mob to take a hike, but the studios and the talent knew that we—by which I mean my people—that we would step in to defend them until the mob either realized the game was over or grew alarmed at their mortality rate, which is nothing we need to talk about. So then we had a period of time when I essentially just represented everybody. So, yes, I was a person of some interest to the stars."

Rina had shot me a couple of disbelieving glances while Dressler was unspooling his narrative, and his pause, which seemed to deserve some sort of reply, took her off guard. "Who, ummm, who were the ones you liked best?"

"I'm assuming you mean the actors, not the mob idiots. One mob idiot is pretty much like another, and, for that matter, so are most actors." She looked disappointed at that. "But the ones who made the strongest impression on me, although these names might not mean much to you, were Jimmy Stewart and Barbara Stanwyck. They were both real people. Katharine Hepburn was another. George Sanders, too, since you brought him up. He could be amusing, although knowing George was not necessarily the same as liking him."

He stuck his index finger into the angel food, tasted again, and shrugged. "I met most of these people late in their careers, since even *I'm* not old enough to have known them when they were young, so they'd been getting the star treatment for years and years, and they'd come through it intact. Most stars . . . well, most stars are a mess. There was a reason so many of the Roman emperors went nuts. When the whole world kneels for you, it's easy to begin to *expect* it. When a publicity department is spinning absolute air palaces about where you came from and what kind of person you are, and when people who are not in the industry lose their minds at the sight of you, you begin to believe it. It doesn't help that so many actors and actresses start out with low self-esteem, that the reason they go onstage in the first place is that they're looking for a little applause that will make them feel better about themselves. And when someone like that is *getting* that applause twenty-four hours a day from a studio that tells them that they're brilliant, that they're beautiful, that they poop perfume—I mean, they start to believe it. It's probably not their fault, but that doesn't make them any more pleasant to be around." He sat back, glanced down, and sponged a little more cake off his shirt. "And I've gone on at some length because you seemed to want me to, but this surely isn't what you came to talk to me about—a bunch of old movie stars whose names you barely know. That's not why you wanted to meet me, is it?"

She said, "You've got a little more, up near your left shoulder."

Without breaking eye contact with Rina, Dressler said, "Babe," and held out the cloth he'd been mopping himself up with, and Babe practically bounced across the room to get at it. For a moment, Babe was between Dressler and Rina, but the second he stepped aside, Dressler said, "*Is* it?"

"No," she said. "But, I mean, are we in a hurry or something?"

Babe froze. There was a moment of absolute silence, and then Dressler started to laugh. I could hear Tuffy swallow, an uneasy sound.

"Why should the young hurry?" Dressler said, wiping his eyes. "But to those of us who probably have less time in front of us than you have behind you, yes, minutes do matter. So, as much as I'm enjoying your company, let's pretend I'm in a hurry. Why did you want to come? Or perhaps I should ask, why did your *father* want you to come?"

Rina glanced at me and drew a deep, slightly shaky breath, and I shrugged and left it to her to shape the discussion. She'd done pretty well so far. She chewed her lower lip for a moment and said, "He wanted me to . . . I mean, I'm thinking about . . . well, not really *thinking* about, but sort of *considering*, and, you know, last night we were talking about . . . I mean, I don't know what *he* hoped you'd do, but I . . ."

Dressler held up a hand that didn't shake at all. "But you want to go into the business."

"*Maybe*, I don't know anyone who, who . . . *does* this . . . except my father, I mean, so I guess, it's . . . it's, uhh, I . . . Why did *you decide* to go into this, this business? What made you want to? How old were you?" She sat back and released what sounded like enough air to inflate a tire.

For the first time in my acquaintance with him, Dressler punted. He looked at me, absolutely expressionless, and waited for the call.

I said, "I'd kind of like to hear that myself."

"Me, too," Tuffy said. From the kitchen, where Babe had taken the towels, he called out, "All ears out here."

"Oh, *well*," Dressler said. "That settles it." He cut a little slice of the red velvet, saying, "I'll regret this." Then he pushed one of the clean forks into it and said, "I was ten."

Rina said, "Jeez. What could you do at *ten*?"

"I could add and subtract and multiply and divide. I was something of a prodigy with numbers." He tasted the cake and gave Tuffy a brusque nod of approval. "It's a bit of a story, I'm afraid." He glanced at me. "Do we have time for this?"

I said, "Are you kidding?"

He pulled his shirt and coat out and looked down at them, presumably searching for stains—another first. I'd never seen him stall before. "I was living in Detroit. My father was a tailor. He and my mother and I came over from Germany late in the 1930s, and when I wasn't in school I was in the shop, because I could speak English to the customers, mostly, but what I ended *up* doing were the accounts. The accounts were . . . complicated. It was the Depression, and no one had much money, so there was a lot of deferred payment, a lot of the installment plan, and there was interest that had to be figured out as the periods of payment stretched on. And blah blah blah, detail, detail." He glanced at me almost imploringly, as though he hoped I'd get him off the hook.

I said, "It *sounds* complicated."

"I'll remember this," he said. "So, my father. My father made very *sharp* clothes, a little sharper than most people wanted in those days. Had a lot of what they used to call *dash*, mostly in the way things were cut. He used to say, 'A lapel should look like you could slice your finger on it.' This was a time when most men, it was like they dressed to disappear, and here's this little German tailor with a shop on a corner where nobody ever goes, doing really snappy stuff, putting a little flare in the leg, lining a jacket or a suit with a fabric, had a *design* on it, even though lining was just something to make the fucking thing *drape* better. You should excuse the language, this is taking me back."

He broke off, looking down at his lap for a moment.

"Adding and subtracting," Rina prompted, and Tuffy drew a sharp breath that sounded like a drop of water hitting a hot iron.

"Kid's got guts," Dressler said to the room at large. "Nobody's given me a shove like that in years. So here's the thing, okay? Mostly my father's taste, it was a little on the *racy* side. Not stuff you'd expect to see on your dentist or your stockbroker, but there it was, in the windows in front of the store seven days a week, and certain kinds of guys saw it and began to come into the shop, guys who didn't *want* to look like a dentist, guys with wads of cash, no layaway involved. And there was my father, making the exact clothes they didn't even know they'd been dreaming of, clothes people would see twenty years later in gangster movies. And there I was in the corner day and night, doing the books in my head, just glancing at a string of numbers for a second and writing down the sum." He gave Rina a look and said, "The numbers racket, you know anything about the numbers racket?"

"Um, no."

"It's a hundred million dollars, a dime at a time. To make the story short, my father's new customers were what was left of the Purple Gang. You never heard of them, they were a Jewish bunch in the twenties and thirties, operated out of Detroit and a few other towns. Mean as snakes and too smart for the competition—which is to say the Italian gangs and the cops—to put up with. In the end those two groups, which had a lot in common, teamed up to put the Purple Gang away, push them out of illegal booze and smuggling, which was where the big money was. So the Italians and the cops, they killed a bunch of the Purples and locked up some more, and when the harvest was over, the guys who were left, they were sort of junior league. But they needed something they could have to themselves, something too small to get the big guys' attention. So they went into numbers, the world's cheapest vice, a dime to play, thirty cents to play three times. You're going to focus on tiny bets because your target is mostly poor people, so you got to find a way to get a *lot* of bets. So they scraped their way through the local losers, looking for suckers who could act as touts."

"What's a tout?" Rina asked.

"A tout is someone who's dumb enough to break the law for peanuts by taking bets. Lots and lots of bets. All the touts had a book in which they wrote down every bet they accepted. For a dime the sucker picked any number between 000 and 999. Anything—001, 692, 988, any three digits. They could pick multiple numbers for multiple dimes if they were desperate or feeling lucky, and the tout wrote each set of numbers in his book, with the date and the bettor's name. Then he tore off another page, one he'd written the bet on, so the mark could show up the next day and collect if the numbers hit."

Rina was squinting into the middle distance. "So the odds were . . . what, like a thousand to one?"

He looked at me, almost but not quite smiling. "That's pretty much it, for the jackpot, anyway. So the suckers are betting a dime, or three dimes, or ten dimes at terrible odds, but they can tell themselves, *It's only a dime.* If the sucker got all three digits right, in the right order, they won like six hundred dollars, a great return on a dime. If they got the three digits right but the order wrong, they got a hundred dollars. If they got two out of three, they won gornisht, zip, nothing. And before you ask, the numbers we used were the last three digits of the number of shares traded in the New York Stock Exchange, which was always in the business section of the paper the next day, so no one could fix it. This is how profitable it was: by the fourth month the gang had almost seven hundred touts in every imaginable place, from bars to barbershops to public parks, from buses and church picnics to whorehouses and racetracks, and they were taking something like fifteen thousand bets a day, which eventually would top out, long after I was gone, thank God, at about four hundred thousand a day."

Rina, who had her eyes closed, sat still for a moment, then nodded and looked at him. "And what did *you* do?"

"Beginning around three in the afternoon, the touts' bet books would start to come in with all the bets in them. We got the stock exchange numbers about six at night, about an hour after the exchange shut down for the day."

"But . . ." Rina said, and stopped.

Dressler eyed her for a moment and said, "Bright as your mind is, honey, it's not bright enough for me to read it."

"So people were supposed to stop betting before whatever time it was, but what about the whatever you called the, um, touts?"

"Jackpot," Dressler said, "and you figured it out faster than some of us did. The touts. And don't think we weren't nervous. I mean, suppose they got the number early and rigged two or three phony bets. And, in fact, just when we began to worry about it, one tout got three jackpot winners in a single day. They shot him through the head. When they realized they were wrong, that in fact he'd turned his book in early and there was no way he could have rigged it, they gave his wife ten thousand bucks. So from then on, all the books had to be in by a minute or two before the markets closed, so the numbers couldn't be leaked, or they wouldn't be accepted."

"And you had to go through all of them," Rina said.

"They started getting the books to me around noon or one, but there wasn't anything I could do until a guy named Silky would bring me the winning numbers around six-thirty. I'd work in the store until it closed and then in the car going home, and then in my room. I just fanned through the touts' books because I could scan a whole page of numbers and spot any winners—jackpots *or* runners-up—in three, four seconds per page, and I just folded a top corner for a jackpot and a bottom corner for a runner-up, and there we were: no one could rig it, and the next day, when a winner showed up at the pay site with his receipt and the name of the tout he gave his money to, they could look at the flagged pages in that tout's book and the customer could get paid off in just a few minutes. So I was getting paid pretty good and my father was selling suits right and left, and after a while we had enough in the bank that he wanted me to quit and focus on school. Is this boring you?"

"God, no," Rina said. "I wish I could take notes."

"You don't need notes," he said. "I can tell by the way you

listen." He sighed and glanced at me again, and I cupped my fingers to my ears. "So, my dad was pressuring me. And I was already three grades ahead of where I should have been. Someone high up in the gang thought it would be nice if they had their own lawyer, so I kept doing the numbers for them and they pulled some strings, and two years after that, at the age of just barely sixteen, I'm in a good law school, and when I graduate, I'm maybe the youngest kid in the country with a law degree. They got me a job with a mob lawyer named Manny Brenner, probably the funniest and most profane man I ever knew. And Manny, who was always thinking about the future, was looking very hard at LA, which was sort of loosely held by some fifth-rate Italians, the kinda guys who, in the real world, woulda been in New Jersey, hijacking the wrong trucks. So I came out here with a dozen boys who were suddenly unemployed because the Italians had finally figured out how the numbers worked and they were shooting our guys right and left.

"People back in the thirties—before I was active, obviously—they used to say that in LA the fruit, it just fell into your hand, and the trees practically chased you to give you some. Well, they didn't quite, at least not when I got here, but taking over the pieces of the action we wanted was something, coulda been done by a bunch of Cub Scouts." He shrugged. "And all these years later, here I am. Like the dame in the Sondheim song, I'm still here."

In the kitchen, Babe burst into applause.

Dressler sat back, glanced at me, and rubbed his palms on the beautifully tailored trousers, working a little more white frosting into the creases. "Was that what you came for?" He sniffed his palms and said, "Probably not *completely* indelible."

Rina said, "It's sort of basic, don't you think?"

He gave her a long, silent assessment, and she sat up straighter, but then he said, "It's kind of like Jimmy Stewart. There was a lot of complication tucked away under all that simplicity."

It took a second, but Rina laughed, and then he joined her,

and I laughed along, trying not to look like someone whose underarms were sopping wet.

"I never heard all that before," Tuffy said. "About the numbers and all."

"And now I gotta kill you," Dressler said. "But who cares? I'm history now. Mostly."

"And now?" Rina said. "How do you feel about all of it now? I mean, people know where you live, right? Do you, you know, worry that somebody might—"

"Tuffy," Dressler said, "show her," and Tuffy unbuttoned his pale yellow sport coat to show her the shoulder holster with the dull black automatic in it.

"I see," Rina said. She looked slightly dazzled. "But having to live like this and all the rest of it, I mean, do you think you made the right choices, or, or—"

"I *know* what you mean," Dressler said. He sat back and clasped his hands between his knees, an unusually self-defensive position. "You know," he said, "when you've lived in the same house for a long time, you stop looking at your street. You're asking me to look at my street."

"I didn't mean to—"

"Don't back down now. So what's it like on my street?" He leaned forward far enough to get a good view of the rug, and when he started to talk, the words came so quickly, with so few pauses, that they might have been woven into the fine old rug.

"So today, what have I got? That's what you're really asking. Okay, I got a zillion dollars I'll never get to spend. I've got a wife, for the past thirty years she's been living in a post office box that forwards a big fat check every month to wherever the hell really she is. I've got two kids whose own kids I've never met; I hear from them, maybe, on my birthday or the high holidays, might be a five-minute phone call or a commercial greeting card, but whatever it is it'll certainly be a request for money. I got the shreds of power still hanging off me, a sort of spotty authority over a bunch of aging schmendricks who still defer to me, who still run bits and pieces of what used to be a much bigger organization, who are getting too old to stay on top of things and are mostly being brushed aside—like lint off the shoulder of one of my father's racy suit coats—by younger and meaner guys with bosses I've never met who think of me as a dinosaur that hasn't gotten the word that it's extinct. And I'm farting around—because my guys wanted me to—with this fucking rock and roll tour that probably made them feel younger for a few weeks before it all started to go south." He looked around the room without a lot of conspicuous fondness. "I got this house, which is getting older at the same rate as me, and is now mostly big rooms that nobody goes into, full of stuff like this Chinese table that nobody ever looks at, and it's got stairways that are steeper and longer every week that I have to climb them. And I share it with Babe and Tuffy, bless them, a couple of enforcers with good aim and sweet sides, who make cakes and schlep me to doctors and tell me everything's going to be fine with my health when more and more that's a bet I wouldn't take even for a dime, and also I'm getting to the point where I don't much *care* whether I'll be fine. And none of this is about anyone feeling *sorry* for me. I had my good times, I fell in love, I sang, I danced—"

"What kind of dancing?"

He sat back, as though the question had come at him too fast, and then he smiled just a little, more like someone who's *thinking* about smiling. "Nothing you would do. I waltzed, that's the one where you actually hold your partner in your arms, I did the foxtrot. Very sporty dance. You ever do the foxtrot?" He waved the question away. "Of course not. So there were good times in my life—there still are—and it's the life I made, and I'll live it all the way through, and be grateful for stuff that doesn't even have anything to do with me, like the fact that no one has shot your father in the face in a dark house that he thought was empty, because the fact is that nobody gets shot in the face more often than burglars. Which is something you might want to think about."

The phone rang, and Tuffy jumped up and went into the hall

to answer it. Rina watched him go because, I felt, she absolutely *had* to take her eyes off of Dressler.

"I'm not looking for sympathy here," Dressler said. "You asked, and you're Junior's daughter, so I didn't bullshit you. Seems to me that no one who lives to be my age is completely happy with the deals he made with himself along the way. One of God's little jokes is that the future is like a map that shows you the destinations that you might want to go to and the ones you wouldn't wish on you worst enemy, but it doesn't tell you which streets you should take to get to one or the other."

Rina said, "My turn?"

"You want a turn? Take it."

"I loved my party," she said. "Thank you for talking to me. My father won't but—"

"He's got his—"

"I'm sorry," Rina said. "I know it's rude to interrupt, but I wanted to thank you for the party and say that I loved my cake, and most of all, I wanted to tell you that you can't live on cake."

"I can live on—"

"I know you like it. I like it, too. They make wonderful cake, your guys do. But they're worried about you, my *father* is worried about you, and now that I know you, *I'm* worried about you. And the cake, I know it makes things better while you're eating it, but it's not helping. Please, for all of us, go back to the doctor. Find out what's happening. And don't try to live on cake. Now that I've met you, I don't want to have to miss you."

I was aware of Tuffy, standing like a statue in the entryway with the phone, an antique Princess model from maybe 1960 in a glaucoma-threatening shade of pink with an enormously long cord, in his hand. He was blinking fast enough to cool the room.

"Your father is a lucky man," Dressler said. "He ever treats you wrong, give me a call. Bring it *in*, Tuffy, bring it in."

Tuffy trotted in and held the phone out to me. Even before he was halfway across the room, I could hear screaming on the other end. Tuffy said, "Guy named Cappy. Wants to talk to you."

14

SPECIAL GU

"You're being mean," Rina said. She was expressing her resentment by pressing herself against the passenger door so tightly it made me nervous, but I wasn't going to show it.

"Are you kidding me? Look, I just set you up for an *hour and a half* with the guy who more or less shaped this city for decades, and he gave you more attention and more information than he gave the Senate Subcommittee on Racketeering. Okay, so he didn't buy you a mask and a gun and break a bottle over your head to launch you into a life of crime, but half the cops in LA would give up a promotion to hear what you heard today."

"It was mostly about Detroit."

"Well, excuse me all to hell," I said, "but you were the one who was asking the questions. And, by the way, you're welcome."

"They were the questions he wanted," she said, and I couldn't argue that. Dressler had actually seemed to enjoy the morning.

I made a sharp right, perhaps a little faster than I should have, but it peeled her off the door and tilted her in my direction for a moment. I said, "Will you *please* make sure that door is locked?"

"It's exactly as locked as it was when you asked me three minutes ago. Are you *really* taking me home?"

"Where do you think?"

"It's not fair," she said. "After all I've learned and . . . and, I mean, I mean, listen, I *like* Ronnie and all, but—but this is—"

"What this *is* is *over* as of right now. Your mother would boil me in sheep fat if she knew anything at *all* about—" My phone rang, and, still straightening the wheel from the sharp turn, I said, "Shit" and clawed at my shirt.

"Other pocket," she said. "Want me to take the wheel?"

"No," I said, grabbing at the phone, "no, I do *not* want you to take the—" I swerved to avoid hitting a low-slung zillion-dollar urine-yellow testosterone aberration that had just drifted airily into my lane. I flicked the button on the phone as I shouted, "Look where you're going, you fucking idiot!" As I passed him, I said into the phone, "*What?*"

"Why the hell aren't you *here* yet?" a man said, and I recognized Cappy's voice. Behind him I could hear shouting, an apparent face-off between two operatic basso profundos who sounded pissed enough to take bites out of each other.

"Laws of physics," I said. The yellow aberration roared past, all affronted carbon monoxide, cut in front of me, and hit the brakes by way of expressing appreciation. "You see," I said to Cappy, "it's all math; Vehicle *A*, traveling forty-five miles per hour, will need—"

"Well, fucking goose it," Cappy said. "We're drawing a fucking *crowd* here, and the damn cops are probably already on their—"

"Cappy," I said. "You're a big strong guy. Find a way to placate the beasts for about ten minutes."

"Make it five," Cappy said. "We're in broken-neck territory here."

"If I get arrested you're bailing me out." I blew out enough air to fog the windshield, dropped the phone on the seat, and accelerated just enough to put my headlights in the aberration's rearview mirror. I flicked them on, hit the horn, and swerved right to get around him, floating an upraised middle finger at him by way of saying *fare thee well* as we passed, and Rina said,

"What Mom says is true, isn't it? Men never *do* grow up. And wow, looks like there's no time to get me home, huh?" She settled happily into her seat, chewed on the nail of her right index finger for a moment, and said, "Shot in the *face*?"

I couldn't come up with anything, so I just zipped it up.

As I made a too-fast, slightly wobbly turn into the theater's forbidden driveway, I registered that the top line of the theater's marquee read, in trillion-point letters, SPECIAL GU, and that there seemed to be a fight to the death going on just below it, where a thickset, enormously tall bearded guy was doing his best to topple the ladder to which a much smaller man, about twenty feet up, was desperately clinging. A handful of others, including a couple of wispy, pallid guys who had to be band members, were trying to yank the big guy away from the ladder, a plan that demonstrated limited forethought because he would have taken the ladder, and the guy hanging on for dear life on top of it, with him. As I ran toward them I heard a shout from up the alley and turned to see Bluto lumbering toward me in a skintight muscle-rippled T-back shirt that said ALPHA DUDE on the front. He was bristling with righteous satisfaction and waving me to back the car out, but I kept running, and pushed my way through a little knot of passive onlookers until I got directly behind the bearded guy and yelled at him to stop. When he didn't even glance at me, I pulled the gun I had grabbed that morning when I realized there was no way Rina was going to go home after the visit with Dressler, positioned it about eight inches from the big guy's left ear, and pulled the trigger.

The giant threw up both hands, cupping them to his ears and backing away, and the ladder began a majestic, slo-mo topple to my right, with the man on it demonstrating a surprising falsetto. Three guys, including two ninety-pound rockers, stopped its motion *somehow* and pushed it upright, and the guy on it celebrated his safety by side-arming several sharp-looking marquee letters, probably weighing three or four pounds each, at the big bearded guy. One of them, a many-cornered uppercase *E*, caught him just above the left eye, an area that houses one of the major intersections of the body's circulatory system, and within a second he was running in blind circles with his hands covering his eyes, trying to staunch an emphatic flow of blood and roaring like a lion with a paw in a trap, when he tripped and fell on his face, sending a gush of blood from his nose as well.

Lion. Of *course*, that's who it was. When we stabilized the ladder, the guy on it slid down expertly, slowing his descent by tightening his feet over the outside of the rails, and took a couple of aggressive steps in the direction of the bleeding hairball, who was now leaning against the glass front door, bellowing for a doctor. Before the sign guy could go after him, though, one of the band wisps put out a foot and delicately snagged Sign Guy's ankle, and Sign Guy went down face-first on the sidewalk, surrounded by what looked like a spill of some giant's alphabet soup. The musician, whom I recognized as one of the members of Rasputum, paler than death in the daylight, thoughtfully sat on Sign Guy's back.

"You, too." I waved a couple of the other lightweights over, surprised by how eagerly they leapt to the task, but then I realized I was still holding the gun. I slipped it back into the holster that was covered by my jacket—one of several that are two sizes too big—and surveyed the little panorama: the cryptic scramble of letters on the marquee, the sign guy struggling not very convincingly against a skirmish of rock and roll featherweights, and Lionel, who showed no sign of wanting to peel himself off the theater's glass door and to wreak mayhem on anyone. In fact, he was whimpering. Then someone new materialized and kicked Sign Guy's thigh, just missing the lead singer, if that's the proper term, of Rasputum, and I recognized Cappy, who had come down from his office so fast he'd lost his cap.

"You," he said to Sign Guy, "shut up. And *you*," he said to one of the broad-shouldered stagehands who had arrived with him, "get Lionel into the fucking office and take him to the doc, who's eating popcorn in my office. Go through the front door, for Christ's sake, can't you see it's open? And don't let him bleed on my floor." To me, he said, "I suppose you're the asshole who fired the gun."

"You suppose correctly." I was looking past him for Rina. "You couldn't handle *this*? What the hell are you *for*?"

Cappy said, "The real problem is inside." Sign Guy was yelling to be let up, and I shouted for him to button it, which, to my surprise, he did. I stood over him, the seated band members looking up at me for their cue, and then I said, "Are you ready to get your ass back to work?"

"Sure," Sign Guy said, but he was sulking. "Just keep fatso over there away from my ladder."

"He'll be inside," I said, "being stitched without an anesthetic. Does that make you happy?"

"I'm just here to put the fucking letters up, Jack," he said. "Can you get these poofters off me?"

"You going to get on your ladder?"

"Sure, whadya think, I'm getting combat pay here? You need to get my *E* away from that fuzzball over there."

I recognized the guy sitting on Sign Guy's chest—*Nigel*, that had been his name—as the Brit who had attempted to chat up Rina the previous evening, and said to him, "Would you please get off our friend here, Nigel, and go get that letter?" Someone was hauling Lionel through the glass doors, and the letter was leaning against the front of the building.

"Sure thing, mate," Nigel said, getting up. "Where's herself, the little lovely?"

"She's coming," Cappy said, "but she's obviously already got a date."

I turned to see Rina coming toward me with a *boy-do-you-owe-me* expression on her face and Bluto trotting beside her, whispering undoubtedly monosyllabic sweet nothings in her ear. I was amazed that she hadn't just hauled off and kicked him, but then I saw my car keys gleaming in his right hand.

"Looks like you've got a new son-in-law," Cappy said. "I need you to come inside the—"

"Here you go, pops," Bluto said, pitching the keys at me. "Hey, Lana and me, we—"

I said, "Lana?" and Rina crossed her eyes so forcefully they nearly collided on the bridge of her nose. "Oh," I said, "*Lana*. Well, yeah, I mean, married or not, Lana can spot a choice hunk of beef at five hundred feet."

Bluto said, "Married?"

Nigel said, "Married?"

"For a dog's age," I said. "Young as she looks, she's tied the knot. Teddy, that's the hubby, was going to come with us today, but at the last moment he had to go to Woodland Hills to do a hit. At the Motion Picture Retirement Home. Old comedian, sweet, funny old guy, made millions of people laugh, but he told one joke too many about the wrong person. If it were me, I'd tip him a wink and give him a head start, but not Teddy. Teddy's merciless. And no sense of humor. Hasn't laughed since the day the barber's daughter swallowed the soap."

Bluto's forehead muscles wrinkled in puzzlement. "Barber's daughter?"

"Teddy's mom," I said. "Poor thing. She was singing in the shower. Teddy could have saved her, but he wanted to finish buffing his nails."

"Oh," Bluto said. "I get it." He looked down and scuffed his toe on the pavement, his lower lip protruding even more than usual. "Well, you can't park there." Nigel was drifting toward the glass doors, shaking his head at the news, bereavement written all over him.

"I know, believe me, I know, no one in the *world* can park there. It's a sacred—"

"*You* move the fucking car," Cappy said to Bluto.

"I'm not gonna—" Bluto said, but Cappy said, "You're going to do what you're told, you over-marinated meathead, or you'll be back teaching ten-year-olds how to bench press twenty pounds, so fast you won't have time to say *triceps*."

"Park it carefully," I said, tossing the keys back at him. "I had it waxed two, three months ago."

"Asshole," Bluto said, but he turned toward the car.

I looked back up. The marquee now said SPECIAL GUES. "Hey," I said, "who's the guest?"

Cappy said, "Well, that's why Lionel is falling apart." He pointed a thumb back over his shoulder, and I looked past him and, for the first time—admittedly, I'd been busy—I saw the line. An actual line. Waiting to *buy tickets* for this thing. The box office was still dark, but there were 70 or 80 people already standing in a neat, orderly line, in ones, twos, and occasional threes. *More* than 80, then; maybe 120, 130. Some of them looked relieved that the sign drama was over and done with, and some looked disappointed that it hadn't gone further; television has destroyed empathy. I saw more of them heading down the block toward us from both directions, and another eight or ten waiting obediently for the Walk sign to tell them it was okay to cross Wilshire.

All of them were women.

Cappy said, "Three one-minute radio spots—on three, count 'em three—oldies stations. They ran every half-hour for the past eight, nine hours. Had to get 'em on fast, so I just read them over the phone to the radio stations, and they just taped them, trimmed them, and put them on. See? It's like donuts. You just need to talk to the people who want donuts."

I looked up at the marquee again. It said SPECIAL GUEST JENNI. I said, "Jennifer *Summers*?"

"So, yeah," he said, pushing his hand up to adjust the bill of his cap, which wasn't there. He passed his hand over his hair just to make sure, shook his head in obvious annoyance, and said, "Shit." Then he tugged his bangs down to cover, at least in some small part, a high forehead that had obviously been getting higher for years. "You *remember* her?"

"Someone just reminded me of her. Couple of nights ago."

"That *Heartprints* album?" Rina said.

Cappy said, "*You* can't remember that? You were still potential energy, a tiny bright spot, a white moth fluttering around in the dim future."

"*Listen* to him," Rina said. "My mom has it. She loves it. Got a really good song, *Three* something, on it."

"'Three Strikes,'" Cappy said. "That was our song, me and the only girl I was ever really serious about. Well, *one* of the only girls. And it was more her song than mine."

"What was *your* song?" I asked.

"'Fifty Ways to Leave Your Lover,'" Cappy said.

"Guys are *awful*," Rina said, watching more women get in line. "Shouldn't the box office be open by now?"

"Yes, it should," Cappy said with a glance at his watch. "It should have been open at nine-thirty. But until about two hours ago, demand for tickets had been what you could have called, with no fear of contradiction, *light*. Guy who should be sitting there selling tickets is upstairs at the Xerox, making some."

"Well, there aren't a lot of female artists on the tour." I was watching the sign guy, who had shinnied down his ladder again, moved it to the right, and climbed back up to finish Jennifer's first name.

"Well, we got the Razorettes," Cappy said. "Their big one was 'I Cut Out Your Heart to Make a Valentine for My Girlfriend.' They were big in the East Village. Credited with a minor uptick in the sale of plaid shirts. They wrote another one that got them kicked off the radio, even FM, 'God's Name Is Bud.' They rhymed it with spud, dud, thud, and Elmer Fudd."

"Still," I said, "kind of a limited appeal."

Cappy was shaking his head before I got all the way through *limited*. "Lot of pissed-off women in the world, and why wouldn't there be? They gotta put up with us, and, as your daughter just reminded us, we're awful. They, the Razorettes, I mean, they also did a concept album called *Saint Valerie*, a rock and roll mass, if there is such a thing, for Valerie Solanas, the chick who shot Andy Warhol to ribbons back in the whenever it was. Lead singer calls herself Vera Virago. Nice girl, when you get to know her, although that can take a while. Smokes like Pittsburgh."

He backed up a couple of steps and glanced into the alley. "Listen, I could stand here chatting and watching these paying customers line up all day long, but you and me, we need to talk. Bad as things are with Lionel, that's not why I called you. Let's get inside. Hey, sweetie," he said to Rina, "you want some popcorn? Just made ten pounds of it, fresh." He drifted toward the driveway with us tagging behind.

"I had enough popcorn last night to hold me the rest of my life," Rina said to his back. "I want to know what my dad's gotten himself into."

"Up to you," Cappy said, but he said it to me.

"I'm back over here," Rina said.

"You gotta meet Vera, honey," Cappy said. He checked his watch again.

"As long as we're walking," I said to Cappy, "tell me how you guys can get away with forcing Lionel—as big a schmuck as he is—to accept having Jennifer Summers on the bill."

"Not just a quick little three-song set, either," Cappy said. "Look at that billing, *special guest star*. You probably don't know she was a Pussycat a million years ago, and things between her and Lionel aren't what you might call *warm*. She wants to go onstage for a couple of numbers *with* him and the Pussycats—with her own little follow spot, thank you very much—and then, after Lionel trots off the stage to go cut his wrists, she's gonna follow with a solo turn. Just to dispose, once and for all, with any question about who the star is."

"Really rubbing his nose in it," Rina said. "I'd like to meet her."

I said, "But how can you guys make him let her actually take the stage during his own act? Doesn't he have a contract?

Obviously, he can't do anything about her being hired for a solo turn, but his band is his band, right?"

"Not tonight, it isn't, and it's all Lionel's fault," Cappy said. Before he could continue, I heard my car start behind me and get cranked to about twelve million RPM, and I turned to see it rocket backward at roughly thirty-five miles an hour onto Wilshire. There was a screech of brakes but no impact, and then Bluto laid rubber out of sight. "He's a good driver, believe it or not," Cappy said. "He won't even ding it. Maybe. Anyway, it doesn't matter what's in Lionel's contract because he screwed himself proper last week. Just didn't show for the next-to-last gig, which was in Phoenix. Said he'd sprained a vocal cord or something, got half a chicken lodged in his windpipe. One way or the other, he just packed up and went to San Francisco, where he lives. It was *wayyy* too late to change all the radio and newspaper ads, but one of my guys, he went to Google and looked up 'Lionel Lyon and the Pussycats tribute bands.'"

I said, "There *wasn't*."

"There was, and they weren't that far away, either, in Nogales. I guess there's no weed so ugly that someone won't plant it."

Cappy had gotten to the stage door, but he stopped and waited until we were close enough that he wouldn't have to raise his voice. "So the guy, the Lionel impersonator, he came up to Phoenix, weighed about four hundred pounds, but, you know, Lionel is no spring breeze himself, and the guy had the cat suit and the big whiskers and the claws and his own Pussycats, all of them Native American and cute as hell, and they really knew the stuff. So we put the real Pussycats onstage with them, and they *killed* it. Best night of the tour, if you ask me. And here's the kind of guy Lionel is: when he learned about it, he said if he wasn't paid his appearance fee for the date—fifteen K, thank you very much—he'd sue us for both the pay *and* false advertising because we had 'profited by use of his name.'"

"I hope you told him to hang it out the window and chop it off. I would have loaned him a knife."

"Naw, we paid him. The Pussycats are the best thing in the second show, the one we're doing tonight. I mean, they sing in tune and even with that pill upstaging them, they seem to be having fun. You can *look* at them. But here's the thing. In all the craziness about trying to get the substitute on the stage in Phoenix, nobody looked at Lionel's contract. And when someone *did*, just yesterday, it turns out that old Lionel has a no-show provision because, apparently, he's pulled this shit before, and when our lawyers wrote his contract they put in a seventy-five-thousand-dollar no-show penalty. Didn't tell *us* about it, which would have been helpful in Phoenix, but then again, I suppose they thought someone would read it. Anyway, it's down in black and white, signed and witnessed and everything. So when Jennifer called last night out of nowhere, while the show was actually going on, to suggest that she turn up and do a set, the so-called producers took a vote in about ninety seconds and decided to offer Lionel a choice: either roll out the old welcome mat or hand them the seventy-five K. He howled and screamed and did the full King-Lear-on-the-heath number, but I don't think it really sank in until this morning, when someone told him there was a guy out here changing the marquee, and he went batshit."

I said, "There's something about rock and roll and emotional maturity that are just mutually exclusive."

"Well, it's all boys," Rina said.

"*And,*" Cappy said to me, "don't forget what I told you about those first screams from the girls and what they do to these guys. Even with Lionel, it's not *all* his fault." He wrapped his fingers around the handle of the stage door, opened it a few inches, and stopped it with his foot. "You sure about that popcorn, honey?"

Rina said, "*What* first screams? And I'm not going to be bought off with popcorn."

Cappy looked at me, and I shrugged. "Okay," he said, and he closed the door again and led us a few steps away from it. Lowering his voice almost to a whisper, he said to Rina, "Tell you about the first screams later. You were here last night, when the big flat fell on Boomboom."

Rina said, "We both were."

"Right, right." Cappy looked at the closed stage door and then past me at the door to the office building, and then he turned all the way around as though to make sure Bluto wasn't coming back through the alley with my keys. Lowering his voice almost to a whisper, he said, "I got a phone call an hour, hour and a half ago. Boomboom died this morning."

I said, "Oh, no. I was hoping . . . *damn*. He had more energy at his age than most people have in their teens."

"Yeah," Cappy said. "Not a bad guy, as long as you weren't in the same band with him."

Rina brought us back to business. "Who called?"

"The cops. Wanted to know exactly what happened. I told them that, to the best of my knowledge, a house fell on him, and they said they'd send somebody over to take a look." He glanced at his watch. "So anyway, I went to take a look at what *they* were going to take a look at, and thought I should call you."

"Because."

"Because, obviously, something has *happened*." He opened the door to the stage again. "I don't know who's in there right now, but I want you to keep your reactions to yourselves, okay? I mean it. No gasps or slapping your forehead or anything. I'm glad you got here as fast as you did, though. I wanted you to see this before the cops arrived. Are we all in agreement?"

"We are," I said. "I mean, assuming that Rina—"

"Oh, stop," she said.

He stepped in and held the door for us, and we went in.

The place smelled even dustier than it had the previous night and was pretty dim overall, although some rehearsal lights directly over the performance area picked out the members of a band I didn't recognize: four standard-issue skinny guys and one who apparently hadn't put his fork down since the day the hits stopped coming, all of them with hair down to the middle of their backs. They were rehearsing, but the volume had been turned down to *endurable*, and I thought I recognized the song. I said to Cappy, "Something about karma, right?"

"Not bad. 'Karmic Overdose.' The band is Ounce of Stems, which was a pretty mild joke back in the day when the first thing every doper in America did when they scored was to open the bag and spend a long, relatively happy half hour picking out the stems."

"Oh, right," I said to Rina. "This is Incense and Campfire Night, something like that."

The heavy guy stepped forward and began to attack his guitar. He had the longest hair in the band, and although the effect lost some of its potency because he was wearing a spangled hairnet, he played like the spawn of Satan on speed; even at this merciful volume, I could tell he was tying his guitar in knots. I said, "My, *my*."

"That's Orlando Ortega," Cappy said. "The problem with this band—and they've all got problems—is that the lead vocalist, the unhappy-looking guy in the orange hot pants, was the founder of the band and wrote all three of its hits *and* sang lead on two of them, but out of the whole band, only Orlando is still working. The other guys are sitting around watching the royalty checks dwindle to small change, and Orlando's making a fortune doing sessions. He's one of the A-list sidemen for most of the major LA record producers. Does four, five sessions a day, pulls in more than half a million a year just for that. And you know, he's doing *this* tour as a favor to the other guys, but that doesn't mean that he's not bitching nonstop about how much it's costing him." He shrugged. "Every unhappy family is unhappy in a different way."

We followed as he picked his way across the floor, which was once again littered with equipment and as gritty underfoot as a beach. The path he chose kept us upstage of the band that was playing, and once we were well past them, he led us to the area downstage right where everything had happened. There it was, still propped against the stage right wall, exactly where it had been when I last saw it the previous evening: the big interior wall of Dorothy's house that made that premature descent and wrote *finis* to Boomboom. Across the way, on the far side of the stage, the members of an intense little huddle were glaring at me: Sparks, cheerful as ever, and the four antique crooks who, according to Dressler, had grandfathered the tour. Seeing all four of them in the flesh was actually somewhat reassuring because, by and large, time had pushed them around as they deserved. Not only did most of them look considerably older than their photos, but the two punishers—Jack Gold and Eddie Prince—were hauling maybe seventy additional pounds between them, and their silhouettes made them look like a mismatched pair of shoes. It took me very little time to confirm that I'd still do whatever it took to avoid being trapped in a room with either or both of them. The brilliant white hair to the right, of course, belonged to Fiddles, whom I'd seen briefly the previous night as he attempted to get the show rolling. He projected an air of frailty that the others lacked, the dubiousness of someone who always got the news last, knew it, and had decided not to argue about it. I realized that he was at least four or five steps from the others, and I thought, *Hmmmmm*, and tucked it away.

That left the enigma and the bad news. The bad news, of course, was Sparks, who was attempting to glare me to death. I've been glared at by the best of them, so I just blew him a kiss. That produced a spasm of fury and a quick step toward me, but Yoshi Perlman put a couple of fingers on Sparks's shoulder, and Sparks froze in place.

I heard Cappy release a long and somewhat shaky sigh.

"It's a little late for this advice," Cappy said, "but ignore them. And look at this thing without being all obvious about it. Tell you what, I'll stand in front of you, but make it fast." He put an arm around Rina's shoulder and moved her downstage, between me and the thugs, pointing out into the house and saying, "See that big ugly thing in the center of the house? That's the sound system that permanently impaired your hearing last night." Then he said something else, but I missed it because I was looking at the big rectangle leaning against the wall.

The difference was glaring. The rope from which the piece of Dorothy's house had been hanging—which had been frayed most of the way through and then cut a decisive little bit on the previous evening—had been replaced with one that was simply frayed all the way through, ragged and torn.

I took Rina's arm, smiled at her, and said to Cappy, "I want those four guys, minus Sparks, up in your office in ten minutes."

"Why do you think they'll come?"

"Tell them Dressler wants them to talk to me." I took another look at the big flat and its fraudulent, frayed rope. Nothing had changed. "Let's go," I said. "Let's go *now*."

The chat had to be faced sooner or later, and I was running out of *later*, what with the second evening's concert approaching. Even if I'd had a *week* between performances, though, I would still have wanted desperately to get out of that building, preferably before I had to listen to any more music and before what was supposed to be my weekend with Rina was over and lost forever. So even though I didn't actually feel prepared to take them on, my rationalization was, essentially, *what the hell, let's piss them off, make them nervous, make them distrust each other even more than they do already, see who shoves whom.* With such limited hopes, this time seemed as good as any other.

It took me a little more than three minutes to get Cappy's office set up the way I wanted it: four chairs in a row, facing the front of the room, schoolhouse style, with the desk pulled front and center, right where the teacher would be. The effect was heightened by how *teacherly* the desk was. I had everything but a whiteboard and an eraser.

I wasn't as successful with Rina, who cinched her case by saying she'd go to the popcorn room if I insisted, but that she'd wait seven minutes and then come back into Cappy's office and take a seat.

In the end, I assigned her to the armchair Sparks had occupied the first time I'd been here. I told her that if she got up or interrupted or sneezed or cleared her throat or did anything *at all* that drew their attention, I'd call the whole thing off and take her straight home. The best thing about the armchair was its position; once I'd lined up the chairs the guys were going to sit on, they'd literally have to crane 180 degrees to look at her.

"What are you going to do?" Rina asked, settling into her assigned seat.

"This is just one of the reasons I prefer to work alone," I said. "There's no one to ask me questions I can't answer."

She wrinkled her nose. "This chair smells like it smokes a pack a day. But you must have *some* idea what you're after."

"Normally by now," I said, "I would have asked at least a few questions of everyone who has anything, even remotely, to do with this thing. But they're all crooks, and crooks tend to be good liars, and they're *also* more likely than members of the population at large, so to speak, to tell me to go fuck myself, sorry about the language. Or shoot me. But we're at the tipping point, I think."

"What does that mean?"

"I was kind of hoping you wouldn't ask. There's a show tonight, and this place is absolutely rancid with resentment. It would be nice if nobody else got killed."

"Oh," she said. "But, I mean, actually *killed* . . ."

"You saw Boomboom. You saw the rope. You have to trust me that when I saw it last night it had been cut with a very sharp knife. And in my expert judgment, we've reached the point at which even a futile gesture in the direction of shaking things up might unnerve somebody, maybe tickle the self-preservation reflex, make him think twice. Maybe even motivate one of them to tell me what's going on, so he won't be where the hammer falls. These guys don't take Dressler lightly. Problem is, it'll be dangerous. Whenever you light a fire, no matter how careful you are, you run the risk of burning yourself. So this is sort of an attempt to strike a match, but safely, hoping the only thing I light is somebody's fuse. And when this meeting is over, I'm taking you home."

The door opened and I swiveled so fast it made me momentarily dizzy, so perhaps I was just a *weensy* bit overwrought, but Rina said, "*Hi,*" and when the room stopped spinning I saw that it was Lavender. Today she was wearing a long-sleeved flowing ankle-length *something* that had been tie-dyed in every possible shade of purple. Years ago, when I was trying to figure out which precious and semiprecious stones were really worth stealing, I'd learned that amethysts—which had for centuries been owned so exclusively by royalty that princes and princesses were said to be "to the purple born"—had hit the global skids when they were suddenly discovered just sort of lying around in various places, in almost vulgar quantities. Then, adding insult to injury, they were identified as nothing more than a fancy-shmancy kind of *quartz*, the most proletarian of all gemstones, the catcher, so to speak, on the team. But if you're absolutely *committed* to bagging amethysts, the thing you want to look at is the *depth of the color*; you want the deepest and the purest. There are, it turns out, something like fifty shades of purple, ranging from pale African violet to deep, deep—almost black—plum; amethysts can be found in almost all of them, but Lavender's dress, near as I could see, had been dyed with every single one.

"Oh my *God,*" Rina said, her voice so high she might have been breathing helium, "where did you *get* that?"

"Four geological strata down in my closet," Lavender said, "just above the clay from the Cetacean era, before the first ugly little life forms dragged themselves out of the sea." She came the rest of the way in, let the door close behind her, and did a modest twirl that did wonders for the dress. "Silk," she confided. "If you're going to twirl, honey, you want to be wearing silk. This is a lot older than you are. Hell, it's older than your *father*. I don't even remember who was president when I bought it."

"Can I come over sometime?" Rina said. "I just want to touch everything."

"You can play gimme if you want. I've got to get rid of some of this stuff while I'm still on this side of adult diapers." She sniffed the air, looked at me, and said, "What's that on your lapel?"

"Um," I said. "Vanilla frosting?"

"Where did you—" She broke it off, came over to me, and rubbed her index finger over the stain, sniffed, and then licked her fingertip. "*Well*," she said, "it's good to know that the party is still going on *somewhere*, even if I'm no longer invited."

There was a single rap at the door. We all turned to watch it open toward us a few cautious inches, and then I saw a sort of silvery Brillo pad that turned out to have Oscar Fiddles's face below it. "Hey, *whoa*," he said, spotting Rina and opening the door a few additional inches for a better look. "Whose lollipop?"

Rina said, "I'll bet you say that to all the girls, and I'll bet—the girls who'd go with you—I'll bet they're just *fine* with it."

"Prickly, prickly," Oscar said, wagging his finger at her. "I *like* prickles. What would a rose be without them? *Word*, Lavender."

"Word, Oscar, and thanks. People who cling to antique slang make me feel young."

"Maybe that'll get me to heaven," Oscar said, wiggling his substantial eyebrows at Rina. "Probably nothing else wi—" He let out a little yip, lurched to his left, and disappeared. We heard some stumbling and a thump followed by an *uuuummphhh*, and a bunch of coins skittering across the floor, so he'd obviously gone all the way down. Then the door banged against the wall, revealing Sparks.

"Are we fucking going *in* there or are we standing around with our fingers up our butts?" Sparks stood there breathing heavily at us, briefcase logo displayed for the benefit of the forgetful. The others, minus Oscar, peeked bravely over Sparks's narrow shoulders at me. "We haven't got all day."

"Well," I said, "this is a bit delicate, but *you* actually *do* have all day, so you can put your finger anyplace that's comfortable, and I'll bet your butt is familiar territory." The producers, who—other than Oscar, who was just wobbling his way back into the picture—had taken a cautious step or two back, now took another one. "You're not invited, you're not coming in. Yes, *you*," I said to Sparks by way of clarification. "This is not a meeting for flunkies."

For a fraction of a second Sparks's eyes met Yoshi Perlman's. It had been Dressler's guess that Yoshi was the one who had seen a need for Sparks, and although Dressler was almost always right, it was nice to have some confirmation. Perlman shook his head about a quarter of an inch, and I said to Sparks, "So you can take your cute little Captain Marvel kit and get it *and* your ass out of here. Go find a masochist to play with." I watched Sparks's face drain to a chalk white that would have challenged even the most skillful mortician, and he began to move toward me, saying, "*You fucking little—*" but before he could get to the creative part of the sentence, sheer, icy rage overwhelmed me. I set my feet, grabbed the open door in my left hand, and slammed it directly into his face.

Through the closed door I heard a shaky "Oh, Lordy" from Cappy and, from behind me, a little decorous applause, probably from Lavender. I unholstered my gun, stuck it into my trousers at the small of my back, caught a glimpse of Rina, her mouth so wide open I could see her wisdom teeth, and then pulled the door back toward me. Sparks was sitting on the floor with a hand pressed to his forehead, blood streaming in a rewarding fashion from both nose and hairline, his eyes wide and unbelieving.

"Doc's downstairs," I said, "probably still looking at the fuzz-ball, the one who thinks he's a lion, but that's been going on for a while, so you shouldn't have much of a wait. Why don't you just take your little kit and trot on down. I hear he used to be a veteri-narian, so you should feel right—"

Sparks reached for his right pocket but before he got to it, I was leaning over him with my gun touching the center of his forehead. "Oh, *please*," I said, seeing everyone else scatter in my peripheral vision. My heart was thundering in my ears. "Please, just give me a chance, with all these lovely *witnesses*. You know how when you kill someone, there's usually this little *twinge* just before you pull

the trigger—you know what I'm talking about? You can't, or, at
least, *I* can't, help asking myself, *is this death* really *deserved*? Is
this maybe someone who is kind to *children*, who pets carefully
chosen dogs, who tosses a quarter into the bucket for the Salvation
Army once a year, who is the sole support of an aging mother, and
you know? Just at that *final moment* the gun feels a little *heavier*
than it should, like a sort of merciful last-minute reminder that I
might ultimately *regret* doing what I'm about to do—putting out,
so to speak, a light that can't be relit. Well, right now *this* gun feels
like I could open my hand and it would float to the ceiling. So
please, *please*, give me a fucking reason."

He looked at the floor.

"I'll take that as a *no*. Oscar, if I may call you that, could you
please slide that big bulky automatic out of his pocket? Be careful. It's undoubtedly loaded, and we wouldn't want to shoot him
accidentally, would we?" No one said anything, so I said, "Or
would we?"

Behind me, Rina said, "No," and in the hall, Yoshi Perlman,
who was glaring down at Sparks, said, "Not accidentally, anyway." He kicked Sparks's outstretched leg.

Oscar Fiddles, who had snatched his hand away from Sparks's
pocket when Perlman got his kick in, returned to his chore, working the gun loose and beginning to slip it into his belt as he stood.
I said, "Ah-ah-*ah*," and he slapped it, a bit resentfully, into my free
hand. Since I was holding it, I pointed *it* at Sparks, half hoping it
had a hair trigger. "Okay, you can get up, Sparky, and find your
way downstairs to get your boo-boo looked at, and the rest of you
can come in, if that fits into your plans."

Everybody kept quiet, a couple of them staring at their feet
or stepping back as Sparks pulled himself upright. There was no
competition to lend him a hand. As he trudged down the hallway,
Yoshi Perlman said, in a light, pleasant voice, "You know, he *will*
kill you if he gets a chance."

16
Just Think of Them as Chairs

I waited until the door at the top of the stairs closed behind Sparks, and then I stepped aside, indicated the row of chairs, and said, "Please? I know how busy you all are. Have a seat." Cappy slipped past them and into the room, and Fiddles eased in to take a post just beside the door. It might have been a security routine, a bit of prudence in case of a booby trap, or just an acceptance of the reality that he was expected to stand by until the bigger animals had chosen their chairs.

"How tidy," Perlman said, eyeing the room as he came in. Up until now I'd seen them in person only at a distance—usually across the stage—and also in Dressler's old photographs, which had shown me younger and slimmer versions of all of them except Perlman, who didn't seem to have gained an ounce. Gold and Prince had draped their bulky bodies and prizefighters' shoulders in whatever-comes-to-hand clothes, mostly a size too small. To me they looked like they might have been separated at birth only to find each other decades later, happily sharing the *thug* end of the criminal spectrum. Fiddles, his tightly curled silver hair gleaming in the fluorescent light, looked like an aging elf, airy and insubstantial, despite his spherical, hard-looking little belly. He blinked oddly, in quick twos and threes, as though he saw something flying toward his face.

Perlman, clad head to toe in black, was tall and slim and

elegant, but up close it was the surface elegance of a Vegas dealer: too many rings, a shirt made of bogus satin. His jet-black hair, which undoubtedly got some help from a colorist, was receding on either side of a widow's peak that was on the verge of becoming a peninsula. I'd already seen him smoothing it apprehensively a couple of times. Like the others, he must have been in his seventies, but his distinctive features—courtesy, no doubt, of his Japanese mother—made him look a decade or more younger.

He glanced up, catching me in midstare, and said, "Do you have a seating chart in mind?" His voice had the almost super-naturally relaxed quality of a late-night DJ on a jazz station, someone with a name like Frankie Cool.

"I thought I'd let you sort that out."

"You can learn quite a lot from an exercise like that," Perl-man said, obviously enjoying the sound of his voice. "Who's dominant, who's recessive, who's confident enough to come right in and grab the first chair, who waits until everyone else is already sitting, who's comfortable stuck between two others, who doesn't worry about sitting in front of an open door."

"I pretty much know all that already," I said. "Just think of them as chairs. Far as I know, none of them has a tack on it. I'll be checking for gum, though, when we're done." I heard a squeal behind me and turned to see Cappy dragging a leftover chair to the spot where his desk usually stood.

"Sorry," he said. He sat with his fingers interlaced in his lap, looking like he felt exposed without his desk.

Perlman took the chair farthest from the door after putting his hand on the seat back and jiggling it to test its sturdiness. Before he sat, he swiveled to give the room a neutral glance, just mapping it out. He slowed to nod to Lavender and, apparently, memorize Rina. The other three, all of whom looked every day of their age, filed in and sat without seeming to think about it. Eddie Prince—who packed on an extra forty pounds in the jowls and around the middle and had the disappointed expression of someone who's spent his life looking for four-leaf clovers and finding poison ivy—sat heavily next to Perlman and said to me, "I wouldn't turn my back to that door if I was you." Jack Gold sat next to Prince, and Oscar Fiddles took the seat closest to the exit, glancing uneasily at Perlman as though he half expected to be told to remain standing. Gold unbuttoned his sport coat to give his belly some breathing room, revealing the butt of a stubby automatic, and said, "I fucking hated school."

"*Such* a surprise," Oscar Fiddles piped. When he wasn't being all suave and professional with a microphone, he had the kind of voice I always figured a hummingbird might have, high-pitched and paper-thin, something you could make holes in with a wet finger. Other than the halo of silver hair, the feature people probably remembered about him was a truly remarkable nose that seemed to have been stolen from a much larger face and badly damaged in the process, so that it did a sudden dogleg to the left that made his face look like we were seeing it through a piece of rippled glass. "You hated *school*?" He gave Prince the kind of smile I save for someone I haven't seen in weeks and didn't miss at all, and said, "School saved my life."

"We *know*, Oscar," Yoshi Perlman said, sounding weary. "We know. The blessed Mrs. Ridgley, that damn violin."

"Best thing—" Fiddles began, but Prince interrupted in a rasp like a striking match to say, "*We've heard*, Oscar, for Chrissake. I even remember the number of the room the fucking class was in."

The one who seemed least interested in contributing to the mini-squabble Gold had started was Eddie Prince, who looked like everybody's third-favorite plumber, a guy you could meet a hundred times and forget in seconds. The most striking thing about him was the discouraged slope of his shoulders, which gave him the well-whipped posture of someone for whom the world has been just one disappointment and double-cross after another. On the ring finger of his right hand he wore a polished piece of agate the size of a small tortoise. If he was right-handed, it would have been dead-center in every punch he threw.

Once the chatter died down, Prince sighed deeply, looked over at Perlman, and said, "Somebody get this thing started. We still gotta settle old Lionel down before he kills somebody." Behind him, Rina got up in response to Lavender's tug on her sleeve. Her chair creaked, and Jack Gold turned around and registered both of them for, apparently, the first time. "Hey, look who's here. Who's your little friend?"

"Hey, Jack," Lavender said, without much enthusiasm. To Rina, she said, "Let's get moving."

"Going where?" Gold asked.

"Tallahassee." Lavender headed for the door, keeping Rina in front of her.

"Yeah? Why there?"

"Because I just learned how to spell it." She poked Rina in the back. All four men were looking at them. "*Hit* it, Cindy."

"Cin—oh, right, *Cindy*."

"God," Oscar Fiddles said, watching them go. "It's like the two ends of the alphabet finally got to meet each other, and they're both *fine*."

Lavender said something, but the closing of the door cut her off. A second later, we could all hear the two of them burst into laughter.

"Wow," Prince said, "Lavender's got a trainee?"

"So," Jack Gold said to me, with the air of someone just barely suppressing a yawn. "You may have nothing to do, but we've got a show to manage."

I leaned back, teacher-style, against the desk. Like dogs hearing a whistle, Prince and Oscar sat forward. "Well," I said, "I know you have busy schedules, but before we get to the stuff that *really* matters, I'd like to have your version of how this whole thing started. I've got Dressler's version but I'd like to hear yours."

Eddie Prince said, apparently to the room at large, "Somebody tell me again why we're talking to this clown."

"It's an act of courtesy to Irwin," Oscar Fiddles said. "Isn't that right, Yoshi?"

"Yeah, yeah, yeah," Prince said. "Poor old guy. All alone in that big house with nothing to do."

"I'll pay you five thousand bucks to say that to *him*," Yoshi Perlman said.

"Since you guys have wandered so far afield," Oscar Fiddles said, "I'll pick up the cue." He watched them all a little anxiously, like he was afraid he'd spoken out of turn. "Over the past twenty, thirty years, we've all talked from time to time about the wonderful bands—" Someone made a farting noise. "The *wonderful bands*," Fiddles said, putting some teeth into it, "that we used to represent and record, back in the day." He sat back and fanned himself with his right hand.

With exaggerated vibrato, Gold sang, "*Memories . . . all alone on the junk heap—*"

"Stifle the wit, Jack." That was Yoshi Perlman.

"So okay, okay," Fiddles said, "a few of the bands weren't so wonderful. But you know, it was an interesting time. We were young then. *They* were young then."

"We were young *together*," said Gold, sawing away on an imaginary violin. "The *world* was young."

"Well," Fiddles said, sounding like he'd said it a thousand times and was tired of having to bring it up, "we *were*. And I don't personally give a rat's ass what you guys think now. But back then—and you gotta remember I was *there*—most of you seemed to be having a pretty good time. I mean, it wasn't *all* about money."

"My dick still worked," Gold said. "Sometimes twice in one night. What was not to like?"

"You *fake*," Fiddles said. "First night of the tour, wherever the hell it was, when Wet Spot started playing 'One-Way Ticket,' you were bawling like a baby."

"Had something in my eye," Gold said. "And you be careful how you talk to me, you fucking—"

"*Jack*," Perlman said, and it was raw with menace.

"Yeah," Fiddles said. "But still, big tough guy, boo-hoo boo-hoo boo—"

Gold said, "I'm telling you, Oscar—" but Perlman leaned across Prince to put a restraining hand on Gold's arm and said, "Okay, okay, *okay*. We *all* got a little sentimental." He sat back and, with the air of someone spreading oil on troubled water, he said, "Just cool down and think about Heather."

"I'm *always* thinking about Heather," Prince said. "I been thinking about Heather since the first night. You could cut me into a hundred pieces and use me for seeds, and every plant that came up would be thinking about Heather. If you used me for bait, the *fish* you caught would be thinking—"

"Got it," Perlman said. "I rest my case."

"So, let's cop to it. This tour was for money, but it was for memories, too."

"The money was a by-product," Oscar Fiddles said. "What it was *about* was being young again. And for the bands, too. These were kids we poured our hearts—"

As if on cue, we all heard a *screech* that could have husked an ear of corn a thousand yards away, followed by a *bang* that might have come from heavy artillery, and Cappy was on his feet, saying "That goddamn Thunderfoot, I'll break his fucking knee," and he was out through the door. He was kind enough to pull it closed behind him, but by then we all had our fingers in our ears.

Everyone sat for a minute or two with their fingers jammed in their ears. I eased one out, jammed it back in, eased it out again, and said, "Better."

No one seemed to trust me. They all watched me for a minute as though they thought I might disintegrate. Then, one at a time, each of them took out one finger, waited another moment or two, and then removed the other. Fiddles was the last to come around. "Jeez," he said. "Guy's been deaf as a turnip for, like, forever, but his roadies are supposed to watch the goddamn volume and make him wear his phones."

"Fucking rock star *assholes*," Gold said.

"So," I said, "this whole thing was essentially a sentimental journey. Is that what you're selling me?"

"We don't got to sell you shit," Prince said.

"Hold it, hold it," Oscar Fiddles said. He had both hands in the air, like someone being robbed at gunpoint. He held the pose for a moment, looking around at his co-conspirators, and then he turned to me. "It's like high school," he said. "Almost nobody *really* had a good time in high school. But twenty, thirty years later, when you look back on it, it looks different. The bullshit kind of fades, and what you remember is—"

"Heather," Perlman said, drawing the first laugh of the meeting.

"Yeah," Oscar Fiddles said, "and being young."

"Going on the road with all these guys all those years ago?" Jack Gold said. "Loud music followed by ace ass every fucking night. Meet 'em, say hi, take them to the hotel, and first thing in the morning, change your zip code. *Paradise*."

I said, "Lavender told me some stuff about all that, but obviously from a different perspective."

"Lavender," Oscar Fiddles said, shaking his head affectionately. "You know, she coulda been rich if she'd wanted to, coulda been a rich lady. Couple guys, and I mean *big* guys, they woulda married her in a shot. One of them, he was—you remember Pop Tart?"

"Vaguely, maybe. Two drummers, right?"

"No, that was Double Cross. Or maybe Palooka Uppercut, there were a few of them. Pop Tart was the only band in history with two bassists. Well, so they didn't make *your* kind of music, but they sold like they were giving it away free, and their lead singer, he also wrote the songs, so he could have heated his house with hundred-dollar bills. Pete Grey was his name, *Grey* spelled Brit-style, with an *E*, because he thought it looked classier. Gotta be the smallest name change in the history of showbiz, but anyways, he hired a skywriter guy, and the guy wrote over the hotel they were at, *Marry me, Lavender*, and he dragged her out to see it. She said no because David Bowie was coming to town later that week. Pissed a few girls off so bad they never talked to her again. Like she'd disgraced the profession."

"For a *while*," Perlman said. "They didn't talk to her for a while."

"Yeah," Fiddles said. "They were pissed, but they came back. As shitty as the business was most of the time, people can't stay away, not even the girls. Sooner or later, everybody comes back. Hell, look at us."

Another brief silence. Everyone seemed to be studying either his lap or the floor.

"So," I said, "in addition to all this warm and fuzzy nostalgia, all the stroll-down-memory-lane stuff, there's a money side. Dressler floated you guys a loan, enough to keep things moving."

"A *loan*? Are you trying to be funny?" For the first time since he came into the room, Yoshi Perlman sounded really, as opposed to strategically, upset. "He didn't lend us a *nickel*. He made an investment—he'll get twenty-five percent and that comes out of our end, which means he's getting more than any of us. I don't want to hear his fucking boo-hoos. No going on the road, no sleeping in chain hotels, no limp, greasy bacon and weak coffee for breakfast, no babysitting a bunch of burned-out prima donnas. All he has to do is send people like you to get in our hair while he sits in that big house with his chorus boys, Lala and Fluffy, or whatever their names are—"

"Stop right there," I said.

"Ooohh," he said, blinking up at me. "Hit a nerve?"

"Either of those guys could stamp you flatter than a Mercator projection without even putting down his spatula. And if you want to take half-assed potshots at Dressler when he's not here to defend himself, that's your privilege, although it tells me a hell of a lot more about you than it does about him."

"Okay, okay, *okay*." Perlman held up a hand. "So you're not just a lapdog, you're a *faithful* lapdog, a true believer. But you know, if you ever watch those, those nature shows, animal shows, on TV—I *like* animal shows, they can tell you a lot about human beings." He sat forward and rested his palms on his thighs. "If you watched them you'd know that there's a reason why, when the time comes, the lions in a pride stop giving the oldest male first shot at the kill. Sooner or later they stop backing off and waiting patiently until he's stuffed himself. Sooner or later they start to keep him at bay while *they* chow down, and leave him to fight with the hyenas for the leftovers. If there are any."

"And they do it to his face," I said.

"You wanna debate morality, you could probably pick a better bunch of guys. I'm willing to say that old Irwin has a right to check up on his investment, which is my best bet about what you're doing here, although he could have just phoned me."

"You don't seem to pick up very often."

"I got a lot to do. I don't know what *he* does with his time. Probably sits around with Fa-Fa and Peewee, looking at picture albums of people he called hits on, back when he still had clout." He stopped, seemed to listen to what he'd just said, and nodded in agreement with himself. "And I'll tell you, I've given you all the time I've got for you. So you can hang around and call in your little reports until you get in my way, and then you'll be gone." He got up. "Come on, you guys. The fucking clock hasn't stopped, and we've got a real live audience tonight, not another zombie reunion."

"What's the head count?" Oscar Fiddles asked.

"We've gone clean, even counting the balconies. Almost ninety percent for tomorrow, too, if it hasn't filled up already."

"We've got her tomorrow, too?" Oscar said. "I thought it was just—"

"Old Cappy," Perlman said over him, "who's more awake than the rest of you put together, looked at the lines this morning and figured, what the hell, and called her, and she said, sure, she'd do both shows, today *and* tomorrow, if she can go on last. Gave us a discount even, thirty K for two shows. The closer was supposed to be See Spot Run, but I'm going to pay them off. They'll be going home early."

"Damn," Gold said. "Shoulda had her for the whole thing instead of old fatso."

"We would have lost the Pussycats," Oscar said. "And none of us ever worked with her, remember? This is a tour of people we—"

I said, "Just for the record, when do you plan to pay him? Irwin, I mean."

Perlman threw me a look that I think was meant to give me pause. "When we're done, when we've got a clear sense of how much we made or lost."

"Lost, my ass," I said. "What a guy. Take money from a sick man, and hope that you never have to pay—"

"It's called hardball," Perlman said. He got up and turned to go, and the others leapt to their feet. "What's he gonna do with it, sit around and count it with Fifi and Buster?"

I said, "Well, gee golly, what about all the money that disappeared on the road? How you going to explain that?"

Perlman stopped. In front of him, Prince walked into Gold's back. They both swiveled to face me, but Oscar kept heading for the door.

Gold said, "How the fuck do you—" and over him, Perlman said, "*What* money?"

"If I were in your shoes," I said, "I'd probably be worried about that, too. There are really only two things it could be, right? Theft or incompetence. If it's really even missing, I mean. Maybe you just *plan* for it to be missing when it's time to divide it up." My phone rang as Cappy came back in, practically sniffing the air, and retreated to his chair.

"Gotta take this," I said. I put it to my ear, and Rina said, "Hey, Dad. Lavender and me are at a restaurant across the street."

I said, "Great timing, Irwin. We were just getting to—"

She said, "Irwin?"

"Yes, and I agree. Seems to be pretty much what you thought, except maybe a little dumber."

"Oh, ho hoooo. Hey, Lavender, Nigel. The gangsters are still there."

"That's right," I said, "they're right here. Want me to say hi?"

"Blow them a kiss for me."

I said, "I don't think they'd appreciate that. They say you never call, you never write—"

"They're just not my type. They look like they've got hair between their toes."

"They undoubtedly do," I said. I glanced up at Perlman and found him trying to stare a hole in me. I finger-waved good-bye and turned my back on him—which was more difficult than it sounds—and walked toward Cappy, who watched me come toward him with the wide eyes of someone who's just realized he's in the line of fire. "No," I said, "not completely, but there's nothing to worry about. Nothing you haven't already got your finger on."

"Can I go over to Lavender's house? She's going to let me paw through her stuff."

"Absolutely," I said. "I was going to suggest something like that, but I'm a little restricted in what I can say here, what with this audience."

"Oh, fuck you," Perlman said, "and stay the hell out of my way." He shoved Prince, who shoved Gold, who turned to shove Oscar, but Oscar was already standing behind the door, holding it open with both hands.

"Bye, guys," I said. "Thanks for the chat."

"Blow them a kiss for me," Rina said. "If you think that would be appropriate. So it's okay to go to Lavender's?"

"I suppose so," I said.

The door clicked shut behind them. It seemed to me that Fiddles had given me a last look, one that might have had some panic in it, but he was gone now. "So," I said, "go ahead, you and Lavender. But I want you to call me before you go anywhere else *at all.* I don't care if it's to In-N-Out, you don't go without telling me. And you do *not* come back here until we've talked. Is that clear?"

"Girl Scout Oath. Bye."

"Wait, listen, if she's really giving stuff away and you see anything Ronnie might like, you grab it, okay?"

"I would have done that."

"Oh, well," I said. "I'm supposed to say this stuff."

Rina said, "And *you'll* be careful, too, right?"

"Sure," I said.

"I'll be *burglar* careful," Rina said. "Like you showed me." And she disconnected.

Cappy said, "What was that meeting about?"

"If I knew one hundred percent that you and I were on the same side, I'd tell you that it was to make things look a little less solid to them. They can slag Dressler as much as they want, but they know he could still, even now, probably blot them all out with a single phone call. But they also know that he doesn't have many of those phone calls left before the guys on the other end stop picking up. They're walking a fine line and gambling on Perlman's assessment of the situation. This is the kind of atmosphere in which people have arguments, and right now arguments are something we want to encourage. I'm telling you this because I think I'm a good judge of character and because, if you really want to know, it doesn't make any difference if you go to them in ten minutes and report everything I just said. I personally think that all of them except Perlman would vote to give Dressler his money back with a big ribbon tied around it and maybe a little extra interest to show goodwill. But Perlman is the meanest dog in the pack and I think he's looking forward to a time when he'll be the guy who stood off Irwin Dressler. Gonna be a big shakeup here and elsewhere when Dressler dies or folds his hand, and I think old Yoshi is putting himself in a position to inherit, to be the young lion who starved out the old one."

"Sounds to me like you *do* know that I'm with you. And I appreciate the trust."

"Don't be too grateful. Dishing out a whole bunch of stories is just too confusing."

He looked at me for a few seconds and then he grinned. "I like you, too," he said. Then he turned away, obviously listening to something, and a beat later, I heard it, too: a sort of mob cheer, seemingly all female, and the *thunk* of a really substantial car door swinging shut like it meant business. He waved his hand out the window, as exaggerated as a little kid in a home movie. "She's here," he said over his shoulder. "Our new headliner. Let's go rescue her from the mob."

17
Surrounded in a Cul-de-sac

After the concentrated testosterone of the past day and a half, this felt like an estrogen riot: crowded and humming with energy, but a kind of energy that was softer-edged and even polite, almost *perfumed*, compared to the lethally sulfurous bouquet I'd been breathing. While I was upstairs, talking to crooks and at least one murderer, a peaceful, expectant crowd had been gathering below. A lot of the women who'd come out to buy tickets had obviously decided to wait around on the assumption, I guessed, that Jennifer Summers would show up early—to rehearse a little, get to know the stage, and do whatever else musicians do before a show. Their commitment had borne fruit, and now they were thickly bunched, eighty or ninety of them, in the alley that led to the stage door, a tight, mannerly, expectant knot surrounding a long gunmetal-gray limousine that, from the smell of things, was still running. The driver stood at the rear curbside door, obviously waiting for his cue to pop it open.

"The passenger side, where the dude is," Cappy said, leading me into the alley and toward the side of the car farther from the stage. We were already close together, sidestepping as much of the crowd as possible. Over their heads I saw more women coming from both directions. "She always used to sit in the right rear seat so she could call ahead to have someone manning the door, and she'd just let the limo slow at the curb and then jump out and dart straight into the venue before the people realized who she was. My guess is that some idiot told her to have her driver pull in here so no one would spot her, so here she is, surrounded in a *cul-de-sac.*"

"And I bet I know who the idiot is," I said as we edged around the group of women. "Is she gonna be pissed?"

"No, she'll probably be pleased that so many people have shown up, but she's got a little claustrophobia thing going. Excuse me, excuse me." He was slipping, as gently as possible, through the crowd toward the limo.

"Wait your turn," a woman said to us.

"Just doing my job," he said. "Believe me, she'll sign for everyone before she goes in. Excuse me? Excuse me?" The crowd opened in front of him with a minimum of hostility, and I couldn't help imagining how a cluster of males would have reacted. When we were only about halfway in, the passenger door opened and a woman, presumably Jennifer Summers, cried out, "Cappy! How great to see you. Let him through, ladies, he's the guy who's going to make me look good, like I know what I'm doing tonight."

"You look good right now," a woman called. "What do you do for your *skin*?"

"I keep it in a can overnight, and thanks for the compliment," Summers said, "but Cappy can work miracles. He'll make me look not like an old bat, but a *young* bat, the bat of a boy bat's dreams. A *mature* boy bat. Hello, sweetie." She opened her arms to him and they hugged, and a woman behind me asked me, "Who *is* he?"

I said, "Stage manager. I guess they've worked together before."

"Maybe he's the reason she never got married," the woman said, revealing either that she had a bad memory or that she'd never read the gossip sheets back in the day.

"Good a guess as any," I said, and Cappy put two fingers in his mouth and let loose a piercing whistle, amplified by the walls of the little dead end, that quieted the crowd instantly.

"We're going in through the front door," he called. "You guys need to get into a sort of line, not more than two or three deep, between here and there, just right along the theater wall, and Jennifer will work her way toward it. She'll sign anything you give her—"

"Except a ransom note," Summers said.

"It's going to take a little while, and she can't stop and talk because we have a *lot* to do in there to make the show tonight as good as you want it to be. So line up quick, okay?"

"The patriarchy," said a woman behind me. "But he's kind of cute for an old fart who's never had a haircut."

The women hauled ass, but it still took probably an hour and a quarter to get Summers through the door to the lobby. She was unfailingly polite as she signed whatever they handed her, often the sleeve from a long-playing record. What impressed me most, though, was the fact that she seemed to be as interested in her fans as they were in her, always leaning toward them as they talked to her, and finding something complimentary to say to almost everyone while maintaining a slow but steady pace. The exception was a man in his late thirties or early forties, one of the few males in the crowd. He was close to the door, which meant he was one of the last fifteen or twenty she talked to before she went in, and she said, "Boy, *you're* outnumbered."

He held out his program. "It's—it's for my wife."

"What's her name, sweetie?"

"Kira."

"Should I sign the program to her or to both of you?"

"She's um, dead," he said.

"Oh, baby," Jennifer said with a quick glance at Cappy, who came a couple of steps closer. "I'm so sorry."

"Well, I just wanted to say thank you. It, ummm, it took her a while to die, and she played your music all the time in the last few months. Said it made her feel better."

Jennifer put a hand on his arm. "Did she have a favorite song? One of mine?"

"It was," he said, and then he swallowed. "It was 'No Return.'"

"*Kira*, right?"

"Yes, ma'am."

"And your name is?"

"Darryl."

"Tell you what, Darryl. Tonight I'll dedicate it to her. To both of you. Would that be okay?" The woman on his left let out a gasp, and the one on the right put a hand on Darryl's other arm.

"It would be, um . . ." he said, and he looked down at his feet.

"Have you got a good seat, sweetheart?"

"I don't know. I haven't looked."

"Cappy," she said, "can you please give Darryl—sorry, I don't know this house. What's the best row?"

"Four," Cappy said.

"Fine. Fourth row, center, for Darryl. I'll be looking for you when the house lights go up." She put a hand on his cheek. "It will take time," she said, "but it *will* get better."

"I know," he said. "I mean, I know that it's supposed to."

"Take it from me, it probably will. How old are you?"

"Thirty-six."

"A terrible time to have to start over," she said, "but you're still young and strong, and you'll do it. It's not like you'll be closing a door on her, sweetie, it's more like she'll be holding one open for you." She gave a quick little sniff and patted his hand. "You've been a lucky man," she said. "Not everybody gets to love like that."

She touched Darryl's arm again, and while Cappy was fanning a bunch of tickets to choose one, she moved to the next woman in line, whose eyes were so wide I thought she might go over backward.

18

Glo-Boy

"Geez," Cappy said, fiddling with his key chain as the glass door into the lobby closed behind us, some latecomers pressing their faces against it for a glimpse of Jennifer. I checked my watch; the whole thing had taken a little under ninety minutes. "You should be on the road, honey," he said. "Half the people I've taken care of in the past couple years can't draw like that. With one night's notice, we've gone, apparently, from a third of a house to SRO for both shows. Seriously, you should be out there more often."

"Don't want to do it anymore," she said. "I had more than enough of it twenty years ago. And I don't need the money."

"I was there, remember? Times are different now." He locked the door we'd come in through, did a little finger-wave to the people who looked like they were trying to breathe through the glass, jammed the keys into his hip pocket, and headed for the door between the lobby and the seats. "Like I've told you half a dozen times, these days nobody cares whether you sleep with girls or boys or Chippendale furniture. That's old news. And obviously, your audience has been holding its breath, waiting to see you again."

"It hurt *Shelley*," she said, gesturing for me to go through ahead of Cappy and her. "You didn't get to see it because I canceled everything, but it pretty much broke my life in half, and it was *worse* for her. It wrecked her relationship with her family.

They were such bluenoses, country clubs and Junior League and Republican fundraisers, and all of a sudden their daughter is on the cover of the shit sheets with headlines like *Jennifer's Secret Love* and, the one that hurt most, *Is This Woman Mr. Jennifer Summers?* with the butchest picture of me in history, looking like a long-haul trucker who specializes in cigars."

Cappy said, "But you're not still—"

"No, of *course* we're not. Still together, if that was what you were about to say, not for decades now. I haven't seen her in years. But, you know, it's not really over for me, not *inside*, it's not, and I can't think of any good reason to open it all up again. I'm just not someone who lives to get onto a stage. The way I do it now, sort of popping up every now and then, suits me fine. And you know what? It's probably kept all those lovely people out there from getting sick of me. If I want to hear myself, I can play my records. Which I don't." She looked back at Cappy, who had stopped walking to focus on the stage, where four scruffy-looking, overweight musicians were unplugging and backing away from their equipment as the roadies swarmed over it to clear the space for the next act. "Who are they?" Jennifer asked, watching the band head offstage in the direction of the dressing rooms.

"Interesting timing," Cappy said. "That's Poison Roses, one of the first mainstream gay bands, not that there have been many. You probably remember their first semi-hit. It was an all-male version of the old Smokey Robinson tune, 'My Guy.' The LP came out on Valentine's day, which I'm sure caused some stomach cramps at the label, but it sold enough to get them signed for two more. They're pretty damn good, if you ask me. They toured the big cities, but no one was going to book them into, say, Tulsa, not in 1984."

"'Left-Handed Heart'?" Jennifer said. "I remember that, I loved it, it was *terrific*. I assume those are their rehearsal clothes. If they're not, I'm going to be severely disappointed."

"Oh, yeah. They'll be dressed like a West Village senior prom. They'll look great."

"But see," she said, "it wasn't the same for women as it was for men, and when has it ever been? You had all these guys like David Bowie, bravely sort of putting one toe into the ring, saying, 'Ahhhh, but I'm *bisexual*,' like that made all the difference. People thought, 'Oh, well, he schtups girls, *too*,' and that kept him on the safe side of the line, kept him in the gold-record club. It was even hip, you know; I mean I knew some *straight* guys who tried to edge into the spotlight. And there were jokes, pretty much good-natured, like Woody Allen on *The Tonight Show*, saying that the best thing about being bisexual was that it doubled your chance of getting a date on Saturday night.

"But *lesbians*—well, there was sort of a veil over that back then, probably because it locked men out and they hated it. Anyway, that's enough of that. You know, I've got a nice house and money in the bank. I've got a couple of good dogs and some time-tested friends. I keep my piano in tune and make up a song every now and then. I might even make another album someday, if I can arouse myself from my pastoral torpor. That's from *Tom Jones*—see, I've even got time to read. Life is so good it worries me."

Cappy sat on the arm of the seat at the end of the row and looked at the stage. "But you're here."

"Well," she said, "you know. Lionel."

"Do I *ever* know Lionel. The gift that keeps on subtracting, as they used to say in some commercial. I'm all in favor of vengeance, you know. Spices things up."

"I think I'm going to have to disappoint you."

He said, "I would have bet a hundred bucks this was coming."

She turned to me. "Cappy knows all about this, but you're new, and it would be rude to leave you out. It was a chance to take a swipe at Lionel that brought me back, blinking into the light, to do these shows after a few years off. A chance to push my way into his act tonight, to be the one person on the stage who doesn't have to kiss his enormous ass." To Cappy, she said, "You know how he sputters when he's pissed off?"

"I've seen it and heard it in cities large and small—okay, mostly small—during the past twelve weeks. It's been the most dependable thing on the whole tour."

"Well, when we talked about this, you and I, what got my attention was the opportunity to muscle my way into his set, make him sputter, shove all these years of resentment up his big ugly nose."

"His big ugly *broken* nose," Cappy said.

"Oh, no," she said. "What happened?"

"In the darkness fate moved its heavy hand. When we were changing the marquee this morning, one of the letters in your name, the first *E* in *Jennifer*, in fact, somehow, ummm, came loose and collided with his nose."

"Is it really broken?"

"The letter?"

"The nose, you nitwit. Is it broken?"

"So our tour doctor seems to feel, although I'm not sure I'd want him treating me for anything more critical than hoof and mouth disease."

"An *E* from my *name*?" She started to laugh, then cupped both hands over her mouth and said, "That's terrible. Even if it's funny, it's terrible. Is he here?"

Cappy said, "Last I heard he was in the number one dressing room, bellowing like Lear on the heath and enjoying all the attention."

"You know," she said, and then she stopped and watched the action on the stage. "I've been thinking about this since I got up this morning. He hired me when nobody else would. The first twenty, thirty times I was ever on a stage—as a professional, I mean—it was with him. Until then, I didn't know where stage right was."

"He stole your *song*," Cappy said.

"And if he hadn't, no one ever would have heard it. I had a box of them, *two* boxes of them, and zero ideas about what to do with them, how to get them to anyone who could make anything *happen*. So Lionel bags one, and I get to walk into *his* record label, demo in hand, demand to see someone who actually mattered, and walk out with a contract. Without Lionel, I'd probably be sitting in some piano bar in Poughkeepsie, singing old Billy Joel songs and waiting for people to drop change in the glass. Crossing out one day after another on the calendar and living the old life of quiet desperation."

"You're too good for that," Cappy said.

"Yeah? You've been in this business since they invented the treble clef. Are you telling me you don't know a fucking army of talented people who wound up dog-sitting? Putting on little-theater musicals that no one except the cast members' families will go to see? I mean, bless those people, may they all be happy, but would I trade places with them? No. So can you take me to him?"

Two guys had just rolled a piano stage center and one of them called out, "Where do you want this, Cappy?"

"Let's ask the lady who's going to play it."

"Hi," Jennifer called. "This is just to set the place, okay? My own piano is coming in a bit and you can just set it on the same marks. Let's come another three, four feet downstage and about four feet to your right, thanks. A little more, a little more to the right—that's it. And could you please angle the keyboard upstage about twenty degrees so the audience isn't just staring at my nose, which is the only thing that sticks out farther than my hair when I'm looking at the keys. Thanks, that's good. Okay, mark it where it is. Cappy, you know about my lighting, right?"

"Yeah, sure. Standard spots, cross-lit while you're at the keyboard with a couple of soft spots from your left, which is to say downstage, just for fill. We have a black backdrop, so the folks out here won't see anything behind you, just you and the darkness. We've set a couple of soft lights stage right that we could monkey with, see if you like them, but I think they're just complications, and every complication has its own little set of problems."

"Agreed," she said. "Junk them."

"But the way you want it, it said in your contract, is you want to come on before the lights, right? Then a spot from the booth hits you and, bang, there you are. *That*, we gotta set. Now."

"You bet," she said.

"Hey, Stan," he called. "Come stand five or six feet upstage of the piano and a yard or so stage right." Stan did as he was directed, and Cappy called out, "Hit him with the spot." To Jennifer, he said, "About there?"

"A couple more steps downstage. Okay, Stan? I've got a nice dress and I'd like to give them a chance to look at it. After that I might as well be a hand puppet, just stuck at the piano until I go to the guitar." She watched as Stan moved. "There, yeah, that's about perfect. Got a Glo-Boy?"

"Sure do, Miss Summers."

"Jenny," she said. "Miss Summers is for opposing attorneys. Put it right there, please."

I said to Cappy, "A Glo-Boy?"

"A mark. Little adhesive X, it sucks up the light from everyone else's turn and glows in the dark. If she's going to come on while the lights are out and then get hit by a follow spot, both she and the folks in the booth need to know exactly where she'll be."

"Hard enough to look like a star," Jennifer Summers said, "without chasing the light all over the stage."

Stan, who hadn't moved, said, "So is here okay?"

Summers glanced at Cappy, who shrugged. "Looks good to me," she said.

"April," Stan called, looking up and past us. "Hit me here with the Super Trouper and mark it."

A blaze of light struck the stage, almost bright enough to be heard, panned over to Stan, and stopped, leaving him squinting up at it.

Feeling like an idiot, I said, "Super Trouper?"

"Follow spot," Cappy said. "Very bright, tight focus. That ABBA song is about one. Singers *love* their follow spots."

"This is all of it, right?" Stan called, lifting a hand to shield his eyes from the light. "Going once, going twice—"

"You got it," Jennifer said. "Thanks, guys. Oh, yeah," she said, raising her voice, "and up in the booth—what was it again, April?"

"April it was and still is," the woman in the booth called. "Love your music, Ms. Summers."

"Then make me beautiful," Jennifer shouted. "Within reason, anyway." To Cappy she said, "My piano ought to be here in half an hour, forty-five minutes. It will *not* need tuning, so don't let anybody get near it except to roll it, *very* carefully, onto those marks and to make sure it fits, then take it off again for the other acts. When it's backstage it should be covered. I've got my guitar, too, out in the car. Don't need any more lighting, except—hey, April, up in lighting? Listen, when I finish at the piano I'll stand and do a bow or two, not milking it, and then I want the Trouper on again, right where I stopped the first time. About half as bright. I'll take the guitar over to the mike that I'm *sure* will be there by then—"

Cappy said, "It'll be two, three feet downstage, closer to the people—"

"No, leave it upstage, right on my first mark. That way, after a song or two, I'll pick up the mike and move closer to them. I'll probably say something like, 'Let's get a little cozier.' April, you need to be ready to follow me when you hear that. Do you know the Kurt Weill song 'My Ship'?"

"My mother's favorite song."

"I am *so* old, but she has great taste. Well, a couple of lines in, I'll break it off and say that thing about getting cozier and I'll stop playing guitar and continue the song a cappella as I pick up the mike and move it, pretty far downstage. You need to keep the Trouper on me. When I stop, that'll be it. I won't move again. After I've done a few more lines with the guitar, I want every other light in this place slowly taken to black. I want the last four songs to feel like we're in a coffeehouse, really intimate."

"You can call for more or less light if you want it," April said.

Cappy said, "What's the last song? We sort of need that."

"It'll be 'The Face in Yesterday's Mirror,' most people remember that one, and then, when they're shouting for more, please God, I'll close it with 'Three Strikes.' Leave 'em with the hit, right?"

"Any encores?"

"If they're *really* rabid about it, I'll come back and do the greatest song in the world, even if I didn't write it, 'The First Time Ever I Saw Your Face,' a cappella. It'll be right where I was standing before, I'll find the first mark, the one with the Glo-Boy. Just have the spot up there, April, okay?"

"You got it."

"Good," Jennifer said. "Cappy, can you take me to Lionel?"

"If he throws something at you, I'm not to blame."

"Anybody who's worked with Lionel," she said, "has learned to duck."

We'd just reached the steps up to the stage, Cappy leading the way while I brought up the rear, when I became aware that someone was behind me. I turned and said, "Hi, Nigel. How was lunch?"

"Had a grand old time. Your daughter is a miracle. They sloped off to Lavender's to pick over some old dresses."

"Thanks for the help with Lionel this morning."

"I've wanted a go at him for weeks. That's Summers, innit?"

"It is." We were at the top of the steps. He seemed to be hesitating, and I wanted to see what would happen when Lionel saw Jennifer, so I said, "Anything I can do for you?"

"No. Maybe. You're sort of—you're sort of a *detective*, aren't you?"

"In the loosest possible sense. Why?"

"Nothing. Maybe we can talk later."

We were walking once again, trailing Jennifer and Cappy, and something on the stage floor snagged my eye, glinting up at me like a dropped coin. Before I could give it any attention, Nigel said, "So, then, later," and yawned at me. "Sorry, mate, not sleeping much. Just grab me."

"Get some rest. When you want to talk, track me down. I'll be here somewhere." I was watching Cappy and Jennifer as they went toward the dressing rooms.

He nodded and said, "Later, then."

I broke into a trot to catch up with Cappy and Jennifer. I hadn't yet explored the dressing rooms, but I knew there was a single row of four of them stage left, and that there was a corridor behind them so the dressing-room doors could open and close during a performance without leaking light onto the stage. The corridor was a dead end, open only on the upstage side, away from the audience, so I had to follow Cappy and Jennifer practically all the way to the alley before we made the right into the dressing rooms. As I caught up, Cappy was saying, "Normally you'd be in number one, which is the star spot. It's got a rug and everything, but Lionel gets it—"

"Because of the Pussycats," she said. "This way, he not only gets the star dressing room, but he also gets to watch the Pussycats get dressed. When I was in the show, I put on my costume in the hotel and wore a raincoat over it to go to and from the theater. Used to really piss him off, although he never called me on it, other than occasional references to the day's weather report."

"He really is Lionel all the way through," Cappy said. He stopped at the first door in the corridor. "Ready?"

"Hold it." She crossed herself and stepped in front of him. "Here goes."

She knocked three times, and a man bellowed "GO AWAY!"

She whispered to Cappy, "Does this thing have a lock?"

"I have no idea," Cappy said. "What the hell, give it a try. I'll be right behind you, so if he throws something heavy, don't duck."

"How gallant," Summers said. She looked at the door handle for a moment, and then she said, "Don't go away for at least a couple of minutes, okay? Stay out here."

"Tell you what," he said. "Changed my mind. You stand over there, just out of range of anything that's thrown, and *I'll* knock and yank it open, all right?"

"Now I feel guilty."

"I can do my end of the show tonight with a black eye and you can't."

"At least put your hand over your face." She took two steps to the left. "Okay."

Cappy knocked loudly, said, "Don't shoot," and pulled the door open.

"I told you—" Lionel bellowed, coming toward him with a balled-up fist. He had enough white gauze over his nose and above his right eye to gift-wrap a volleyball. Three young women were pressed against the walls as though they expected gunfire, although one of them was laughing. Lionel kept coming, his right fist balled up, and then Jennifer stepped into the doorway and one of the girls gasped.

Lionel froze. Jennifer said, "Hi, sweetheart."

Lionel said, in a grunt straight out of a samurai movie, "Uuhh."

"Oh, my God, *look* at these beautiful girls. What an *eye* you have. One amazing group after another." She took a step into the room. "And I'm so *sorry* about your nose."

"I'll just bet you are." Behind Lionel, the Pussycats—one Asian, one Black, and one who was blonder than Denmark— had crowded together to look at Jennifer.

"You *listen* to me," Lionel said, but she stepped the rest of the way into the room, opened her arms, and said, "I need a hug. I'm *so* worried about going on with you." She spread her arms and Lionel reached up without thinking and wiped his nose, then doubled over, making an *MMMMmmmmmmmfffff* sound. Jennifer led him over to a chair, saying, "Poor baby, poor baby." When she had him sitting, she squatted down in front of him with one hand touching his cheek and said to the Pussycats in one long breath, "Hi, I'm Jennifer, who has a spare costume I can borrow? And I'm going to need your help with the routines because I'm pretty rusty, so please be patient with me and my old bones." She grabbed a quick breath as though she was

afraid Lionel might horn in. "I don't want to look like a clown."
With her free hand she reached behind her and did a little swim-
fin motion that meant *bye-bye* in any language. Cappy gave me
upraised eyebrows and quietly eased the door shut as Jennifer
said, "And, Lionel, *you'll* help, too, right, even with that poor
nose? I know what a trouper you—"

Once the door was closed, Cappy punched me on the arm,
hard enough to make me take an unplanned side step, and said,
"That's my girl. In ten minutes he'll be getting everyone onstage
so he can catch her up on the new steps."

19
Mind Map

So: Cappy was buzzing around backstage, crossing out items on his checklist, keeping an eye out for Jennifer's piano, and probably soothing bruised egos; Rina was at Lavender's house, pawing through old clothes; the Four Mugs were out for a late lunch, probably sneering at their food and at one another; and I was momentarily at loose ends. I stood more or less downstage center, where Hamlet and Richard III go to deliver their more socko soliloquies, and I tried to come up with something that would be both low-risk and high-profit. And then, as if he were standing beside me, I heard the voice of my late burglar mentor, Herbie, say, "*Mind map.*"

One of the things Herbie hammered into us, especially as rookies, was the absolute necessity, the moment you went into a place, of mentally mapping several ways *out* of it. "The first few times you'll be excited," he'd said over and over, "you'll be nervous, you'll be eager to get to the good stuff, you'll be pumping adrenaline, so let me impress upon you one more time: if ever you break into a place that has the Hope Diamond in it—not that any of you look that lucky to me—the Hope Diamond will be *the second most important thing* in the house." Then he'd raised his arms like an orchestra conductor and said, "And the *first* most important thing would be?" and in unison, just to show him we were *good* bad boys and girls, we'd chanted, "*Multiple exits.*"

"And you get those how?"

"*A mind map,*" we'd say.

"*A mind map,*" he'd echo, tapping his temple. "And what's the *other* reason you want to explore the place for exits or, if it comes to that, hiding places?" And he would cup his hand to his ear and we'd say, "*To make sure we're alone.*"

"The big three: you're alone, you know how to get out, and, in a pinch, you know where to hide, preferably *several* places to hide. Burn it into your memories. If you don't make this a habit, sooner rather than later I'll be visiting you in jail, if I'm not too pissed off."

So here I was, already pretty far in, and the best you could say about my mind map was that it was in irregular bits and pieces, with areas marked *terra incognita.* I'd seen the stage, the main entrance, the dressing rooms, the seating area, and a few bits of the second floor of the office building, but there were also areas that, for all I knew, were inhabited by penguins. With time on my hands and a relatively empty head on my shoulders, I decided I'd been remiss up to now by not having done at least a token sweep. I turned around and went back to the corridor that led to the dressing rooms—skipping the one in which Jennifer and Lionel were navigating their reunion and the one in which Poison Roses seemed to be arguing over their set—and knocked on both of the other doors, opening them when there was no response to find two cramped, empty, charmless, uncarpeted rooms that reeked of mothballs, which I thought had long been eliminated from everything except memory. The walls had last been painted, from the look of them, during the Korean War, and had been enlivened by graffiti executed in many media, from eyebrow pencil, greasepaint, and indelible Sharpie to, it seemed, stage blood. I *hoped* it was stage blood. What had been written was an upgrade from most graffiti: IONESCO IS A FRAUD was scrawled over one wall; another said LIFE HAS NO FOURTH ACT. No one seemed to have felt compelled to observe that there was no business like show business.

On one wall of each room hung a full-length mirror that would serve for a last-moment costume check—and, I thought, an unkind reminder to our musicians just how many decades separated them from the eager young hopefuls they'd first seen in mirrors like these. It seemed unfair to me at that moment that people change but mirrors remain smug and ageless.

Except for a probably permanent smell of feet and mothballs, and some tidy dry-cleaning bundles that had to be the evening's costumes, that was it. No trapdoors, no secret tunnels, probably no phantom of the opera lurking in the sewers below. I went back out onto the dim, empty stage, its walls now hosting the setups for five bands—instruments, microphones, bottles of medium-priced water—and, stage center, more or less, the soon-to-be-banished stand-in piano. I strolled much of the circumference, saw nothing that caught my eye, and went to stand beside the piano, where I had a good view of the house.

Whatever time it was outside, it was permanent dusk in here; a theater is as blind to the phases of a day as a casino. I mentally broke the stage into quadrants and, starting stage left, where the dressing rooms were, I began to pace it off, doing parallel passes from wall to wall, not looking for much of anything. Within a few moments I'd found the "Don Giovanni" trapdoor, about five feet by five feet, with its edges covered by multiple layers of fibrous tape that looked almost impossible to tear. There were no cuts in it anywhere, as far as I could see. Straightening up, I found myself looking across the stage to the area, downstage right, where Boomboom had his fatal encounter with the wall of Dorothy's house. I registered something missing: the killer flat, which had been propped up against the wall over there, was gone. And then I remembered that the cops had been here. They'd undoubtedly taken it. Too bad it didn't have the original, partly sliced, rope around it.

Back at center stage, I did a slow 360. Nothing different from earlier in the day except the piano and the bands' setups. I faced the orderly rows of seats in the house again, which looked bigger than I'd remembered, and then I realized that someone had turned on a low-wattage row of dirty neon tubes to reveal the outline of the seats in the balcony. One seat seemed to have something thrown over its back, a piece of deep red cloth that could have been a jacket. I made a mental note to check it out although, in my experience, nothing that conspicuous is ever a clue.

I lowered my eyes and, for the first time, considered the big empty room as a single space, a space with a function. Dowdy as it was, it was brilliantly designed, not really a surprise for a floor plan that had been improved over and over by great minds since the middle of the fifth century BC, when Oedipus Rex plucked out his eyes for the first time, in broad daylight on the outdoor stage of the Theater of Dionysus in Athens. In the centuries since, with occasional interruptions for little things like wars, Dark Ages, Puritans, and TV, people had continued to perform plays, and the spaces in which they were acted had been refined according to the demands of the material and the advantages of the technologies of the day. And here was the end result, circa 1945 or so, despite all the wear and tear of careless use: a public room built specifically for things to be seen and heard in it. It was a faded, sagging, cut-rate approximation of an ideal, but even so, its objective had been to let absolutely everyone see and hear absolutely everything. And still, when a man was murdered downstage right, not one person had seen what set into motion the falling wall that killed him. And then I realized where the best seat in the entire house was, and I cupped my hands to my mouth and called, "Hey, up in the light booth. April, right?"

A moment, and then, "Right. You were with Jennifer, weren't you?"

"Actually, I was with Cappy."

"That's okay, we like Cappy, too, don't we, Phil?"

"He hired us," Phil said. I could sort of make out April's silhouette in the booth, but Phil was out of sight.

I said, "Where's my Super Trouper?"

"You gotta earn it," April said. "Even in the cheesiest show-biz movies, nobody gets a follow spot in the first reel."

I said, "I could do my version of the king from *Hamilton*. I sing all the parts. People have thrown parties just to hear my English accent."

"That's okay, we'll accept your word. Look downstage to your left, maybe a thirty-degree angle. See that shiny little *X* on the floor?"

"Sure. Oh, yeah, it's Jennifer's, whatchamacallit."

"Mark. Go stand on it."

"*Duffer*," I said. "An old pro like me? So here I am. Light me up."

"Try not to scream," April said, and then she blinded me.

It was so bright, so *concentrated*, I could almost feel it hit my chest. I found myself with both hands shielding my eyes, backing up rapidly, as though I could outrun light, the fastest thing in the universe. Mercifully, either April or Phil killed the Trouper. I stood there, looking at an infinite black bloom with big purple amoebas pulsating in it. April said, "You're not sup-posed to *look* at it."

"You should have told me."

"An old pro like you? We didn't want to insult you."

"Well, I can't see, but I can still hear. You guys with the the-ater or the tour?"

"Neither, really," April said. "We're freelance. If we were with the tour we wouldn't be having tech rehearsals."

"So Cappy hired you."

"Not bad for someone who's just been blinded."

"You do all sorts of shows?"

"Anything that needs light."

"Who's more of a pain, musicians or actors?"

"By musicians, I assume you mean pop music. Not classical."

"I do."

"Musicians are the worst. They expect us to follow them wherever the hell they go. Actors set their blocking—their movement—in rehearsal, and once they learn where the lights will be, there's a sort of cast-wide contest to drift just a little closer to the hot spots and stay there as long as possible. We don't have to do anything. An experienced actor can find the brightest spot on a stage wearing a blindfold, but those bright spots pretty much stay put as long as that set is in use. Musicians, on the other hand, want us to follow them around, and some band members have it in their contracts that the Trouper is on them for a certain song, when it might be on someone else for the next one. Our lighting cue sheets for this thing look like they were used to teach baby triplets how to scribble."

"Last night—"

"Don't even talk about it."

"The spotlight—"

"Yeah, it was on that poor doofus. Were you here?"

"In the audience."

"You might have noticed that the guitarist kept looking up at us and waving his arm."

"Not sure."

"He must have done it eight, ten times. I guess he figured if we killed the light, the drummer would get the message."

"But you didn't."

"That was the drummer's big solo. That light was *his*, contractually speaking."

"Did you notice anything else?"

"Like *what*? I mean, that was pretty attention-getting, and my job was to make sure people could see it. The only thing I can tell you, his drum set felt like it was an acre wide. Problem is, you want to keep the light tight on the guy who owns it, but a very small change in direction up here is pretty big by the time it hits the stage—I mean, look at this."

The Super Trouper bloomed on the stage about eight feet from me. "Now look at *this*." It jumped two feet in my direction. "I only moved it a couple inches. It's like a bullet, you know? If I point a gun straight at your heart from up here—don't take this personally—all I have to do is angle the gun half an inch away, and I'll miss you by two, three feet." The light went out.

"You guys can see the whole stage—"

"Yeah, but, I mean, if what you're getting at is, did I see anything except the drummer from up here, the answer is no. The inch or two I had to move the Trouper to keep that poor guy dead center in it—poor choice of words—well, that required one hundred percent of my attention. Tell you the truth, when the house or whatever it was hit him, for about half a second there, I was trying to figure out how to get the light *underneath* it so we could still see him. So, yeah, I had the perfect place to see what happened, but I was only focused on a few inches. A gang of Cossacks could have ridden their horses across the stage, driving peasants in front of them, and I wouldn't have noticed."

Below her, in what must have been the balcony, something moved. I said, "Did you know there's someone in the balcony?"

"Sure. Cleaning crew. They're making it all nice for tonight. Obviously been a while since they used it, because they gave us paper masks to wear for the dust. Apparently the last time anybody sat there was *Hello, Dolly!* three years ago."

"Starring who?"

"No idea, Cher's sister's babysitter or someone. Don't know if you've picked up on the vibe, but there are houses for people on the way up and houses for people on the way down."

"Well, listen, if you think of anything unusual, anything out of the ordinary, wave me down and tell me about it, okay?"

She said, "We already had the cops here."

"Yeah, but the cops want to know who did it. I want to know who might do it next. And to whom."

"Eeeeeek," she said. "Well, if we see anything, I mean, other than what we're supposed to be seeing, we'll make a note for you."

"Thanks, guys." I heard a door close, followed by a burst of laughter, and turned to see Lionel and the Pussycats—all five of them—emerging from the little hallway to the dressing rooms.

The thick white bandage over Lionel's nose had been painted a deep red and then spotted with white polka dots in what might have been nail polish, and Jennifer was compressed into a Pussycat outfit that looked like it had been sewed on her, complete with whiskers and little kitty paws. She was taller than the others, so Lionel must have been getting a little sensitive about his height. The group was coming straight at me without so much as a glance, professionals who owned the stage, so I got out of their way and headed for the top of the stairway stage left. I was about to take the first step down when I remembered the thing that had gleamed at me when Nigel was saying he wanted to talk to me later. I turned around and crossed the stage, looking at the floor, and there it was.

A Glo-Boy.

Somebody's mark.

For a moment, I didn't hear any of the noise the Pussycats were making. I was doing a mental replay of what happened the previous evening, and I realized that I knew exactly what I would see when I looked up, *straight* up—and there it was, directly above me: the precise point in the elevated catwalk from which Dorothy's wall had fallen on Boomboom. To make sure, I looked down again and saw the irregular scratches in the stage floor and the large brownish remnant of the blood stain, which had been scrubbed by someone with no expertise. Nothing bleeds like a head wound.

We'd been thinking about Boomboom, Cappy and I, trying to figure out why anyone would want to drop that thing on him. But it had fallen on somebody's *mark*.

I went down to the lip of the stage and called, "April?"

"Yeah? We gotta get working here."

"Did Boomboom have a Glo-Boy in this spot?"

"Hold on," April shouted. Lionel was looking at me with no special fondness, and I raised a one-minute index finger and smiled at him. He did not melt or swoon. Behind him Jenny and the other Pussycats were pushing the piano offstage, leaving the chalk marks for its feet. I was turning to look at the Glo-Boy again when April replied, "No. The stage crew set him up. You know, they have a sort of schematic, a little map, that the bands give them."

"Right, I remember. But there's a mark here. Whose is it?"

"Umm—gimme forty-five minutes. When we're done here I'll go back through the prompt book."

"Fine." I was pretty sure I already knew whose mark it had been, and if I'd guessed correctly, it changed—or, at least, complicated—things considerably. At the same time, it answered a couple of questions I'd been asking myself about what Dressler had told me and which among the four little bears might have gone to see him. I tucked it away for the moment, consigning it to the part of my mind I sometimes think of as the dryer, a chamber that lets things tumble around and bump into each other while I ignore them. From time to time, when I go check on them, I find that they've assumed a new configuration, and very occasionally, if I look at it just right, new questions—or even an answer or two—will emerge from the disorder. That may not sound like much to you, but it's what I've got. I went down the stairs into the audience area, and returned to my mental map.

Ways to get out: obviously, there were the two aisles through which the audience entered, and one emergency exit, a fire door, to my left. Just for the hell of it, I slipped between two rows of seats and gave the door a push and, since that got me nowhere, a pull. It was not only locked, it seemed to be *rusted* locked. Anyone who wanted to leave would either have to go back up an aisle or scramble up one of the little stairways to the stage— where any fire was most likely to start—and then out into the alley. In other words, the place was a potential barbecue.

As I walked toward the doors to the lobby, I glimpsed movement on the balcony and looked up in time to see a big Hispanic guy expertly toss the red garment at the wall at the balcony's edge, where it hung just as he'd intended it to. It was, I could see now, definitely a jacket, a little threadbare on one elbow, but a rich, deep color that suggested it had begun its life in a very good shop. I thought I might have seen it before. Some laughter broke out above me, from the sound booth, just a couple of seconds before it was blotted out by the first burst of music from Lionel Lyon and the newly expanded Pussycats.

Up on the balcony, there were now four guys at work. Two of them were trundling industrial-strength vacuum cleaners into position at the ends of the topmost rows of seats, and others were stripping off the seat covers—probably, I thought, to haul them to a nearby laundromat. It was pretty damn dusty, but the way the guys were going at it, I thought, one way or another that balcony would probably be less sneeze-inducing by the time the paying customers settled in.

I was nattering, not a good sign. And I knew *why* I was nattering: somewhere in the part of my brain that does threat assessment, an alarm bell was ringing its head off. The sight of that Glo-Boy brought home even more vividly that something *personal* had gone awry here, that whatever was happening was more targeted, less random, than the death of some poor old musician. It was closer to home than that, and I had a sudden impulse to even the odds. I took out my phone and dialed Debbie Halstead.

Before I met Debbie, a friend had described her—accurately, as it turned out—as cuter than Hello Kitty and more lethal than a black mamba: five feet, three inches of friendly, cheerful death. Unlike most professional killers, for whom the job is best done from a sanitary distance, and *to* someone who has no *idea* that was his last breath, Debbie enjoyed the flash of realization that seized her victim just an instant before she did it *her* way, an up-close-and-personal bullet through the ear. Some carpers said she wasn't actually a very good shot, but I figured it was just Debbie being Debbie.

"Hey," she said, as chipper as a kindergarten teacher. "Haven't heard from you in a while. If you want a date, I'm taken at the moment, although that could change if he doesn't behave." She wasn't kidding, either; it's impossible to imagine Debbie feeling enough for anyone to put up with any kind of nonsense at *all.* We're friends, in a manner of speaking, I suppose; even though she is, in her own personal way, batshit crazy, I think we're close enough that if someone hired her to take me out, she'd probably charge extra to overcome her reluctance.

"Nope," I said. "I'm afraid it's a professional call. How do you feel about theater?"

"You mean, with real, in-person actors walking around saying stuff?"

"That's what I mean."

"I'm more into TV 'cause I can change the channel, but what the hell, since it's you. Do I have to get dressed up?"

"No. We'll be backstage." A little tornado of dust drifted down around me, and I sneezed.

"Gesundheit. One gun or two?"

"Since when do you carry more than one?" I headed for the lobby, which at least had doors between me and the dust.

"I don't," she said, "but some people like the illusion that they've got options."

"One you and one gun has always been enough. Are you working now, or are you loose?"

"Loose as a goose who was just dealt a deuce."

"Here's where I am," I said, and gave her the address.

"Just barge in, waving my hardware?"

"No. We're going for subtlety. Park as close as you can, and call me."

"Will do. Do I have time to do my hair?"

"Depends on what you want to do to it. Hour, hour and a half should be fine."

"Don't turn off your phone." She hung up, but she said goodbye first. If I didn't know better, I'd think she liked me.

The lobby was still the lobby. Through the glass doors I saw a pretty good-sized group of women out there, probably hoping for another glimpse of Jennifer. I watched long enough to see that at least two women were hawking tickets, probably marked up by 100 percent. That made it official: we'd sold out.

The popcorn machine was back in place, full of unpopped kernels, but still cold. It looked like the refreshments behind the counter had been restocked, too, and the sight made me realize that this was the first legit house I'd ever been in that sold refreshments. Must, I thought, double as a movie theater from time to time.

Four stairways led upward—two, I presumed, to the balcony seats and the others to the restrooms. I climbed up to the balcony and watched the guys—there were still four of them now—strip off the top layer of the upholstery to bare some seriously ratty-looking padding, which was promptly attacked by the men with the vacuums.

As I descended into the breathable atmosphere of the lobby I spotted—to the right of the refreshments bar—the open door to what had to be a basement, from which two more guys emerged, carrying bundles of seat covers in big transparent bags. When they were gone, I took a quick trip down the stairs to do a survey of the space, a vast, dark, damp expanse of concentrated dread that ran, as far as I could see, the entire length of the building. The weight of the structure above was borne on six surprisingly slender pillars on which someone decades earlier had painted flowers, now faded but preserving a kind of ghostlike delicacy, a message from a less utilitarian past.

The pale flowers eased some, but not all, of the anxiety I felt. They couldn't, for example, expunge an appalling smell, rich in rodent piss, or the creepiness of water stains on the walls and floor from some time in the past when the huge space had been ankle deep in some kind of liquid. All sorts of junk—furniture, rolled-up canvas backdrops, alternative sets of curtains, stacks of books that were probably props, a couple of antiquated Vespa scooters that probably had an interesting tale to tell, but not to me—and, almost all the way at the far end, the trapdoor up to the stage. I forced myself to move very quickly to the trapdoor and make sure it was secured, which it was, by an iron latch a quarter of an inch thick. That mission accomplished, I practically sprinted out of there, slowing only to dodge a couple of guys headed fearlessly down for more seat covers.

One of the two flights of stairs in the lobby took me to the men's room. Like men's rooms everywhere, it was as functional as a Kleenex and as charmless as a subway station. Still, at least I could check it off on my mental map. The stairs on the opposite side of the lobby took me, unsurprisingly, to the ladies' room, where I knocked, listened, knocked again, cracked the door, called out, and listened yet another time before I went in. As I expected, it was a different world.

Consistent with the convention of the thirties and forties—when women's rooms were seen as places frequented by a gender who were believed to have better taste and more delicate sensibilities than men—it was an extravaganza that looked like it had escaped from one of the palaces in *The Arabian Nights*. The walls were gold-flecked mirrors from floor to ceiling, and the floor itself was a gorgeous mahogany parquet, punctuated with hand-painted tiles representing half a dozen kinds of leaves and flowers that might have been done by the person who tried in vain to reduce the threat quotient of the basement. Pillars of something hand-painted to look like marble pretended to hold up the roof. It was nice enough to make me wish I had to use it.

Fortunately, I didn't, because when I opened the door to leave, two women in black leather were gazing up at me. The taller of the two, who had hair of that absolute black that's available only chemically and eye makeup that looked like it would have to be removed with a jackhammer, was chewing, at triple-speed, on what I hoped was gum, and the gum somehow made the whole thing *work*. She said, "I hope you didn't do anything standing up in there."

"You guys are in the Razorettes, right?"

"Omigod, a *fan*," the taller one said. "A lot of our male fans seem to hang out in ladies' rooms."

"Well," I said, stepping aside and holding the door for them. "Allow me."

"Sure," the taller one said, and she surprised me by raising an eyebrow. It made her look speculative. "Long as you don't *follow us in.*"

Letting the door swing closed behind me, I said, "I promise."

"Just out of curiosity, since you were in my restroom, so to speak, and I haven't seen you before, who the hell are you with?"

The shorter one said, "Whom."

"Fuck off, Giselle," the taller one said. "The question stands, sonny."

"I'm with Cappy, and also with Jennifer."

"Jennifer's cool," the taller one said, "even if it's all kind of sweet and hazy, the open heart glimpsed through the mist and all that, and Cappy's the best. Okay, you pass. You got a name?"

I said, "You're really going to town on that gum."

She looked at my mouth for a second, and I felt something shift. "Yeah, well, I quit smoking."

"*Vera,*" the short one—Giselle—said between her teeth, "I really—"

"Quitting can be tough," I said to Vera. "When?"

"February six, 1983."

"Wow," I said, "me, too."

She unleashed a smile that turned on and off like a light, and said, "Get *outta* here."

I shook my head. "Amazing. Same day and *everything.* What time?"

She checked her watch. "Three twenty-two P.M."

"Well, well, *well,*" I said, glancing at my own watch. "It's that time for *me,* too." We looked at each other, and the other girl fidgeted. I said, "It must be fate."

"Absolutely," Vera said. "But still, we've *got* to stop meeting like this."

I said, "Then it's probably a good thing there's only one bathroom left."

"*Vera*," said Giselle. "I've only got one costume."

"This is an emergency," Vera said to me. "If you could give us girls a moment or two alone . . ."

"Of course," I said. I pushed the door open again and stood aside to let them pass, and the shorter girl practically knocked me over to get in.

Following her in and holding the door open, Vera said, "You could be dangerous. A poor girl, alone on the road and all."

I laughed out loud, and then she laughed. "I knew it," she said, "too good to be true. You wanna watch it. I'm tough, but Giselle in there is young and impressionable. Maybe I'll see you later. After the show or something."

"Fate, she is a funny thing," I said in what I thought might be a French accent. "But I have ze girlfriend."

"But of *course* you do," she said. "Oh, well, I've still got my gum." And she let the door swing closed behind her.

Halfway down the stairs to the lobby I felt a sharp pang of guilt about Ronnie, and then I thought, *Now I know how Lavender felt*, and I went back to my mind map.

20
Music on Wheels

For all the much-vaunted glamour of the theater—that ever-changing kaleidoscope of the human spirit—I had been in bus stations that were more evocative than the Lafayette. The place was showing its age in all the worst and dingiest ways; it had a cultural case of shiny elbows.

When I pushed open the door to the office building I got a grunt—of acknowledgment, I assumed—from Bluto, who was doing sit-ups in front of the stairway with his legs up on the fourth step. He was really, *really* good at it, and it obviously absorbed 100 percent of his attention, so he didn't even say "Hey" when I started looking around the place.

The chair I thought of as *Lavender's throne* was empty, as was virtually the entire ground floor, the rest of which I discovered when I pushed open the door in the wall opposite the entrance. A dim, paralytically uninteresting hallway led me to one ajar door: a small office that stank of cigarettes and had a bunch of phones in it, obviously newly installed. One was ringing and the others were silent, a couple of them blinking in impatience to deliver their messages. Of the other three ground-level offices, two were dusty and dark, piled any old way with much-abused furniture that had probably been shoved in from other rooms and left to do whatever furniture does when no one is looking. The last office contained bits and pieces of slightly better furniture, much of it piled up in front of an assortment of banged-up soft luggage, uniformly beyond its sell-by date, and most of it too bargain-basement to make even *my* fingers itch. A fifth door opened into a restroom that had been cleaned really, really well sometime during the Great Depression. At the far end of the corridor was a door labeled EXIT, and, as dull as the floor was, it felt like a come-on. Still. I turned around and went back into the lobby.

I had to step over Bluto to get to the stairs, but he didn't even lose count when I transited his chest. The office I was interested in was the one to the right of the stairway—the biggest, judging from the space between the hallway doors, and the only one I hadn't gotten any kind of look at. I didn't get a look at it this time, either; it was aggressively secured by three heavy brass padlocks, all of them fastened to pristine, shiny hardware that couldn't have been in place longer than a few days. The hardware and the locks were formidable, but a lock is only as good as the walls and doors into which it's set, and the plaster up here was so porous and the wood so termite-riddled that I probably could have pulled the hardware out with my bare hands. Few people are more vulnerable than those who think they've got everything nailed down. Much as I wanted to go in, I figured Yoshi and the boys would be back any moment, so I headed down the hall, kicking myself for the time I'd spent focusing on anything but that door; my palms were literally wet at the prospect of going in.

Without the friendly fragrance of the popcorn, the hallway looked darker and narrower than before, more like the perfect setting for a trap. That notion might have been a telegram from my subconscious because at pretty much that precise moment I heard the voices of the thug contingent echoing up the stairs. More accurately, I heard Yoshi yelling at Bluto to get the hell out of the way and go *do* something or he'd be back, flat on his ass and begging for quarters, at Muscle Beach. I did the burglar two-step, silently on the balls of my feet, to Cappy's office, eased the door open, backed in as I looked down the hall, and shut the door soundlessly behind me. Then I turned to see him at his desk, leaning back in his chair, which had been returned, along with the desk, to its usual place. His expression was on the distant side of neutral; it would have been a stretch to call it friendly. I felt a chilly little drip of doubt skitter down my spine.

"The boys back?" he said. He had his cap back on.

"I guess. Long lunch." I went to one of the four folding chairs, still in their schoolroom row, turned it around, and straddled it. For the next few minutes, I wanted him in sight.

"You gave them a lot to talk about," he said.

"I get the feeling they're not long on discussion. It's more like Yoshi says *do this* and they compete to see who can do it fastest."

"Don't underrate them. They're all capable of making an independent decision to blow someone away."

"How far back do you go with them?"

He sat back and regarded me, tossing in a slow, not very warm moment. "Not with *them*, just Yoshi. I did a tour for him, back when I was starting out."

"Guess that went okay."

He leaned forward and brought the front legs of the chair down with a surprising *bang*. Or maybe it was just my nerves.

"It was a nightmare. He hadn't been at it long, and neither had I. I made a lot of mistakes he didn't notice, but that wasn't the problem. The *problem* was the headliner, the top-billed band, Arsenic, the biggest bunch of shits I ever worked with, *including* Lionel. Halfway through the tour I told Yoshi it was either them or me."

"And?"

"And it was me, obviously. I was on a plane home in less than three hours. In the meantime, Yoshi, who for all his calm, buttoned-down style, has never been aces on impulse control, went to the hotel and punched Eddie Boorman, the lead singer, on the nose. Eddie bailed and took the band, assholes one and all, with him. Left Yoshi to make hundreds of thousands of dollars' worth of refunds and try to figure out what to do with all the venues we'd committed to play. An hour before I landed in LA, Yoshi was leaving messages for me to come back to what was left of the tour, all was forgiven."

"Did you?"

"Nope. I had a kind of mentor, Bud Egan, he was like the Bill Graham of Los Angeles, and Bud said, 'Never, *ever* go back once you walk. It'll mark you for life. They need to know you'll actually blow them off if you have to, 'cause if they *don't* know that, halfway through the tour you'll be out there parking cars at the venue, just doing whatever the hell they tell you to do.' So I *didn't* go back, and the tour tanked and Yoshi lost a fortune. A week later I was on the road, running one of Bud's tours. Three fucking art-rock bands: Fleur de Lis, November Rain, and Proust's Ballpoint. Opener was—you ready for this?"

"At this point," I said, "I should be ready for anything."

"It was Jennifer. Her first tour. Three more or less established bands and her, so you can imagine what kind of treatment she got, *plus* being the only chick in the lineup. So she was the opener, the new kid, got the worst twenty minutes of the evening, while everybody's filing in, arguing over their seats, saying hi to each other, and lighting up. *Terrible* spot. But Jenny's first single was just out, the tune she grabbed back from Lionel, and that record absolutely sizzled, went up the charts like a skyrocket; there hadn't been a really good, fresh chick since Joni. The thing went platinum while we were on the road. Two-thirds of the way through, we canned Proust's Ballpoint, paid them off and sent them home, gave Jennifer an hour as opener. You can imagine how the guys in the other bands felt but, you know, showbiz is for grownups. In the end, she even got to come back out for the closer; we made the assholes in Fleur de Lis bring her back for a final song with them. One of hers, no less, a cappella. The lead guy in Fleur de Lis apologized for bad behavior by doing the arrangement, which was great." He settled back in his chair, which creaked alarmingly. "Damn," he said, glaring down at it. "Now I gotta figure out all over again which one of these things is mine."

I said, "Do you know why that flat fell on Boomboom?" The question sounded pathetically dishonest to me: we both knew it hadn't been intended for Boomboom.

He gave me ten full, slow seconds of silent assessment that felt longer, and then he made the safe choice. "No idea, Jack."

I looked straight at him, and he didn't shift or avert his eyes or drop to his knees, crying, "I confess." Finally, he said, "I saw what you saw. And I saw the second rope, too, the one the cops took. In fact, I'm the one who pointed out to you that there *was* a second rope. You think I'm in some kind of conspiracy?"

"In the course of my career," I said, "I've occasionally found myself on the wrong side. I mean, from the burglary victim's perspective, I'm *always* on the wrong side, but occasionally I do chores for other people—like now, for example—and sometimes the situation isn't what it seems to be, or it's much *worse* than it seems to be, and once in a while, it's actually aimed at *me*, maybe to position me to take a fall, to make sure I have a certain bag in my hand, exactly where I shouldn't be when someone comes looking for it. When I realize that I'm in that situation, I bail."

He put his elbow on the desk, blew some hair away from his face, and rested his chin on his palm. "Bail how?"

"Depends on how bad it is. Sometimes I just back off, disappear. Sometimes I intentionally fuck up whatever they're trying to do, sit back, and watch them stumble all over each other, trying to handle it as it falls apart. Once in a great while, I kill someone."

He sat back in the chair. "Dangerous thing to tell somebody you don't know very well."

"I'm taking a chance," I said. "Anyway, it's just your word against mine, and you're in rock and roll."

He laughed, although it sounded like a courtesy. "They're a

bunch of shits, but I'm used to that. I've worked for better and worse. You know what I'm saying? This isn't where you go to meet a better class of people."

"So," I said, "you don't have any ideas. Or none you're eager to share."

He was shaking his head before I finished talking. "Whatever's happening, Yoshi's driving it. I think he told you a lot in your little chat. He wants to be the young gun who brings the old guy down."

"Right. You got any ideas about that?"

"Two," he said. "First, it sounds dangerous, and second, it sort of puts you right in the line of fire."

"We think alike," I said.

He got up, put his arms in the air, and stretched. "I don't mean to be unhelpful," he said, "but I gotta think about old Number One, and I really can't see how this is going to turn around and take a slice out of me."

I got up, too. "Sometimes people get bitten in dogfights," I said. "Hurts like hell, but it was probably nothing personal to the dog."

I had no sooner shut Cappy's door behind me than I heard the door to the office the guys were in open and close. I slipped into the popcorn room before whoever it was came into sight. I counted to ten slowly and eased the door open an inch or two to see Gold walking away from me toward the rear of the building, moving like a man who definitely would not welcome an interruption. I was grateful for the existence of the popcorn room; if I'd ducked back into Cappy's office, he might have interpreted it as fear, which is not an attractive quality in someone whose side you might be considering taking; and besides, I was happy with my exit line.

The notion of walking past the room with the other guys in it had nothing to recommend it, and as I stood there, fidgeting and wishing the popcorn machine hadn't been moved, I suddenly remembered the first time I was up here, when Bluto, instead of turning around and going back the way we'd come, had headed straight on down the hall. I peeked out, saw no one, and did a sort of high-speed tiptoe, following Bluto's imaginary footprints. At the end of the hall I came to an unlocked door on the right that took me down a short corridor to an absolutely lovely sign, a masterpiece of concision, that said EXIT. A flight of stairs later, I was out in the glum dud-November daylight, which was beginning to fade now. The stairs had taken me to a narrow alley between the building and the wall that defined one end of the driveway. It was a really, really *nice* narrow little alley, and I had it all to myself. I was surprised at how good that felt.

And then, with no noticeable transition, I found myself thinking, for at least the tenth time in the hours since I'd seen it, about the length of rope that had disappeared and been replaced with a phony. Leaning against the wall of the building, I closed my eyes and let everything float around. This is the aspect of my reasoning that I think of as the *rinse cycle*. It's gentler and slower than the dryer but occasionally a nice, clean thought will emerge.

Two ways of severing the rope. Why switch? Which was first? Was it done by one person or two? And why the hell hadn't I looked at it a lot more closely?

Well, okay, because I hadn't foreseen that the first length of rope would disappear, even though, in retrospect, that was as inevitable as sales tax; it was, after all, a murder weapon, and the way it had been severed—at least, partially—was a big, fat, glow-in-the-dark indication of premeditation. I closed my eyes and did my best to bring it back. Some people have a memory for faces. I have a memory for *objects*, developed and refined over decades of doing fast once-overs in dark houses to make sure I don't spend half an hour pawing through a box of costume jewelry while Herbie's Hope Diamond languishes, gleaming and feeling neglected, in another room. Or studying a so-so antique samovar when a painting worth tens of thousands is hanging on the wall just above it. Herbie's MO was engraved in my memory: do a quick but thorough once-over and then go back for the plums, starting with the best.

Of *course*, I knew why it had been cut in the two ways it had.

And then I realized that I was thinking, *Rina would love to know that thing about the fast once-over*, and it completely derailed me. I found myself face-to-face with the fact that it had felt *good* to have someone so interested, listening so intently, as I talked about my—well, my line of work. To be specific, it had felt good that it was my *daughter* who was listening. Instantly, I saw Kathy's face, horrified at the betrayal. This would require a *lot* of further thought, at some hypothetical future time. And, until I had resolved things, it would require that I go back to conversational dodgeball with Rina, which would be much more difficult now that I had opened the magic jar and let the blabbering genie out.

All right, the rope. Whoever it was *started* with the fraying: labor-intensive as it undoubtedly was, the fraying stood a chance of being attributed to some kind of natural wear. But the knife? Obviously not.

A raucous burst of laughter ping-ponged back and forth in the alley, which almost certainly meant that the big door to the stage was open. I peered around the building's corner and saw a bright blue truck that had a huge treble clef painted on its side, above the words MUSIC ON WHEELS. Two beefy, laughing guys were going in, carefully shepherding a beautifully polished piano that was itself up on wheels. Jennifer's instrument had arrived. That prompted a look at my watch: to my surprise, it was after four. The next concert was less than three and a half hours off, and a little less than three hours from now they would start letting people in.

I realized that I was vaguely *worried* about those people, worried about the musicians on the stage. And that overrode my instinctive desire to stay out of sight for a while, which had been based on the conviction that I'd blown it when I made the quartet meet with me. Until then I'd just been some guy, sent by a more powerful guy, with God-only-knew how much or how little power of my own; just an unknown entity lurking on the other side of the stage, avoiding confrontations and *looking* at things. And now they thought they knew me better, and, in fact, that was probably *good*: familiarity may not always breed contempt, but it often does have the effect of reducing anxiety; the person we talk to is almost always less threatening than the person we've imagined. Maybe I hadn't blown it at all.

So there I was, newly revealed as a negligible threat, a schlub in over his head. Couldn't have been better if I'd done it on purpose.

As I turned my back on the fading gray daylight and stepped into the even dimmer cave of the stage, I heard the whisper of slippers on a gritty floor and, just barely audible, someone doing something pretty fancy to a guitar. Center stage, two of the Pussycats were working on a step sequence while Lionel, looking like a bear on tiptoes, did it in perfect unison with them, backward, so that his feet were a mirror image of theirs. The women were absolutely fixated on his feet. Lionel had an enormous yellow beach towel draped over his shoulders, and the portion of his face that could be seen over the decorated bandage was polished with sweat.

The guys with the piano had angled to their right to avoid the dance practice, and one of them had just called Jennifer's name. I saw her sitting on a folding chair downstage right, not far from where the fatal wall had come to rest. She seemed to be running through a chord sequence on her guitar, the same three or four over and over, a sort of riff, and I realized that she was probably writing something. She was apparently deaf to the sounds of the dance rehearsal and the voices of the piano guys, even though they were calling her name. Her total absorption reminded me of the time I'd probably come closest to being caught in the act.

Long, *long* ago I had gone into a nice house, high in the Pacific Palisades, that I'd been promised would be empty. It was a slightly unusual job for me because it was midday, and I was much more accustomed to working in the dark. The house was a sprawling, fever-yellow California one-story from the early fifties, what I think of as *earthquake architecture*. It boasted a rambling, spacious floor plan, large high-ceiling rooms with big, bright paintings on the walls, and a pervasive smell of turpentine in the air, which was no surprise since the place belonged to the very successful female artist who'd done the paintings. I'd accepted an assignment—something I rarely do—to steal something specific: a quilt by Grandma Moses. Most people who remember Grandma Moses at all probably don't know that she made quilts, but the fact is that, while she drew and did watercolors early in her life, she didn't begin to paint seriously until she was well into her seventies, when arthritis made quilting almost impossible, and her sister gave her a set of paints. Her quilts are much rarer than her paintings—not surprising since she turned out something like 15,000 canvases—and most of the surviving quilts are in terrible condition. Well-preserved quilts are rare, and the one in the house had been represented as especially fine.

You have to move carefully in a *dark* house for the obvious reason that you have no idea where things are: you might be just a few feet away from a step down or a footstool or a roller skate or something else that could bring you down in a moment of unplanned, panicky slapstick that's both embarrassing and dangerously noisy. But that day the light was streaming through the windows and the owner was supposed to be out sketching landscapes in the hills above Calabasas, so I got careless; looking up at a picture on the wall, I walked into a little end table. I caught it before it fell, but there was nothing I could do about the two books on it, and I had to stand there, absolutely still, counting my breaths until my heart had gone from *prestissimo* to a little slower than *presto*. When it had, and no one had materialized brandishing a shotgun, I had walked the rest of the way across the room on the balls of my feet and opened the door—quietly, out of force of habit—to the room that I'd been told was her studio, which, at least theoretically, was where the quilt would be.

And there it was, doing a quilt version of *nya nya nya*: gleaming smugly at me from a couch on the far side of the room. And there *she* was, between me and it, with her back turned, bent forward so her nose was no more than a couple of inches from the canvas, doing something very delicate with the tip of a fine brush. Holding my breath, I eased the door shut behind me and tiptoed out of the house, although I probably could have tap danced and sung "Swanee" without attracting her attention. It was my first experience of a working artist's total absorption, and now I was seeing it again, in Jennifer Summers. As far as she was concerned, she was completely alone on a crowded, kinetic stage. Since I was the person closest to her, I crossed until I was just a couple of feet from her and said, "Ms. Summers?"

I could almost hear a suction-cup sound as she pulled her attention away from the guitar and looked up at me as though I were a new and not entirely welcome form of life. I said, "Sorry to interrupt you, but your piano has arrived."

She looked toward the door and then back at me. "Please," she said. "It's *Jennifer*. You're very nice. That's unusual in this business."

I said, "Some people inspire niceness. Some people, I'd just as soon strike a match on."

"Well, thank you for putting me in the former category." She got up and leaned the guitar, *very* carefully, against the wall. "Sure enough," she said, looking past the rehearsing dancers, "it's my baby, safe and sound. See you later."

I turned around to look out over the audience area. I could hear Jennifer greeting the movers and the gritty sound of the women's slippers over the floor, as well as a sort of rhythm track that I identified as Lionel's labored breathing. The place might be a dump, I thought, but the acoustics were aces.

Which says a lot for how quietly some people can walk,

because the first indication I had that someone was behind me was when he kicked me, hard, on the back of my right leg.

My knee buckled and I nearly went down, but I did a little stutter-step that kept me upright, and when I turned I saw, backing away from me in a crab's scuttle, Sparks. His nose was swathed in white bandages like a cheap copy of Lionel's, and both his eyes were encircled by dark, raccoon-like bruise patterns. The cursed briefcase hung from a strap over his left shoulder.

"Typical," I said. "On tiptoe, from behind. Gee, I hope your nose isn't broken. In more than three or four places, anyway."

"You and me," he said, and his voice was shaking. "You and me."

I said, "What should I wear? Some people like me in blue."

"Something you can bleed on, asshole."

"Not to be rude," I said, "but you're one of the dullest fucking people I've ever met. It's okay to have a one-track mind, but not when it passes through the same drab, crappy hundred yards of scenery over and over again. What's with the briefcase, looking for a schoolgirl to threaten?"

"We'll see how smart you are," he said, his voice shaking. He literally shoved the briefcase at me. It rattled.

I said, "Have you heard from Captain Marvel's lawyers about that logo yet? Can't be long now."

"Just count down," he said. "Because I've been told you're not off-limits anymore."

"That's funny," I said. "I just got the same message about you. Now get the hell away from me before I shoot you with your own gun." I turned my back on him, putting my hand on my gun; the one I'd taken from him was, as far as I knew, shoved to the back of Cappy's desk drawer. On the off chance I was wrong, I kept my fingers wrapped around the familiar and oddly friendly shape until I heard him scuff away over the gritty floor, muttering. I fought the urge to crane around at him. Then I went toward the stairs that led down to the seats, steadying my breath and wondering where the hell Debbie Halstead was. I'd gone down a couple of steps, still listening for the sound of Sparks slipping up behind me, when I realized there was something in front of me, something red.

A *familiar* red; I'd seen it twice, not so long ago, first thrown over a seat up in the upper level, and a little later, hanging over the balcony's edge as the guys swapped seat covers and kicked up dust. I said, "I was wondering whose that was."

"Whose *what* was?" Nigel said. "Oh. You mean me jacket." And, to my surprise, he blushed.

I said, "Dusty up there," but he was looking past me. I didn't want to give Sparks the satisfaction of seeing me turn around, so I said, "Is he coming back?"

"No. He just kicked the piano those men are bringing in, and now he's heading for the door."

"Imagine," I said, "having a soul so shriveled you'd kick a piano. Tell me when he's gone."

"Gone," he said. "But before he went through the door he gave you a look that could freeze a kipper in a heartbeat. Not a bloke I'd like to have mad at *me*."

I said, "Can I come the rest of the way down, or are you going to propose to me?"

"Of course," he said, backing away. "It *is* a bit *Romeo and Juliet*, isn't it?"

I said, "You wanted to talk to me."

"I did. I still do. I think I might be happier if we weren't out here in broad daylight, so to speak."

"Tell me where."

He looked around as much as he could without turning his head. "Give me five minutes and meet me in the loo."

I said, "The men's?"

He regarded me for a moment and said, "Am I making a false assumption about you? I can't be. I've met your daughter."

"No," I said. "It's just that the women's is nicer."

"I know. They all are. But I think we should stick to tradition if it's all the same with you. We Brits are a conservative lot, in public, anyway."

"Another theater explorer," I said. "Have you been in the basement?"

"For as long as I could stand it. See you in a couple." He turned away, but over his shoulder he said, "Try to be alone, right?" He went up the aisle toward the lobby, and I took a seat and phoned Cappy. When he answered, I said I was doing a complete once-over of the building and asked him to meet me out front and let me in through the lobby.

"You've done that," he said. "When we met Jennifer—"

"Humor me," I said. "I was distracted that time."

"What about those metal detectors?"

I said, "Yikes. I'll tell you when you meet me."

I went back up onto the stage as Yoshi and Prince came in from the alley. Their heads were close together, and they seemed to be a bit heated, but they saw me coming and angled away from me, toward center stage, where the piano guys were nudging the instrument into position as Jennifer watched. Then the follow spot that had almost blinded me snapped on, and the guys looked at the splash of light on the floor and centered the piano in it as Jennifer offered minor corrections and waved thanks to the folks up in the booth. Lionel was back to being Lionel again, grumbling as he led the Pussycats farther downstage, toward the stage's apron. I had a sudden vision of him stepping back into thin air and falling straight into the orchestra pit, as the notoriously difficult choreographer Jerome Robbins once did. His browbeaten cast watched without a peep of warning as he backed away and backed away, ranting at them, until he stepped off the edge of the floor into nothing.

Just to be irritating, I waved at Yoshi and Prince and called, "Hi, guys." Neither of them looked at me. I gave them a cheery military salute and went through the door into the alley with the back of my neck prickling. Stepping out, I nearly bumped into Cappy, who was approaching at a brisk trot.

He said, "Are you telling me that you forgot about the metal detectors?"

"Heaven forfend. A mere detail."

"You're full of shit," he said, but without much malice behind it.

"I am," I said, "but that doesn't necessarily mean we won't have the metal detectors."

"Believe it when I see it. Hey, we just went one hundred percent full for tomorrow."

I said, "I suppose that's good news."

"Little extra in my pocket," he said as we rounded the corner. There were still women in line, getting the bad news one at a time at the ticket window. "Jesus, Charlie," Cappy said to the guy in the window, "just put up the fucking Sold Out sign, would you? You looking for a date?"

The guy in the window said, "Uuhhhh," and Cappy began to flip through his enormous collection of keys. "I'm not quite sure what you can see coming in this way that you couldn't have seen by just walking up the aisle, but it would be rude for me to act like I don't think you know what you're doing."

"Jennifer's nice."

"Yeah." He located the key he wanted. "I would've married her if she hadn't been, as they used to say, left-handed. Or, hell, if she'd said yes." He pulled the door open. "Here you go, scout. See if there's anything you can do about the metal detectors, even this late in the game." Then he looked over my shoulder at the street, and said, "What the hell?" Yanking his key free, he charged toward the excavation, where some teenagers had gathered. I caught the door with my foot as he ran toward them, flapping his arms and streaming the kind of language the kids probably never expected from someone Cappy's age.

The door locked itself behind me with an authoritative double click, which, given my frame of mind, I heard as one possible escape route being sealed off. I glanced around for a second and found no one looking at me through the glass, and then I climbed the stairway on the right side of the lobby. When I got up there I was a little relieved to see Nigel sitting beside the door, his back against the wall and his knees drawn up with the red jacket draped over them.

I nodded toward the restroom and said, "Empty?" and when he nodded, I said, "This is *much* better than going inside. I have no idea why anyone thinks those white disinfectant things they put in the urinals smell better than piss."

"Mmmm," he said, and his tone told me that my opening had not completely engaged his interest. I decided to let him take charge, and sat opposite him on a carpet that smelled almost as dusty as the balcony seats. It was chilly up here.

"I love theaters," he said, as though resuming a conversation. He was looking at the carpeting between his feet. "Doesn't matter whether they're big or small, fancy or basic. I even like—I *especially* like—ones like this place, the old ones that have been shut down for a while, closing in all the magic, the sound and the fury, the cornballs and the geniuses alike. Letting it get all jumbled up together, letting it *bubble* for a while. The older, the better. Not that this place is old by *English* standards, but it's got some wear on it. People who have been dead for decades walked on the boards, said their words, and tried their best to create some kind of world for the audience. You know, it's kind of a miracle that someone can come in here one evening, when they might have just been grocery shopping or dealing with a motorcar that didn't want to start, or fighting with their mate, or talking to their grandkids on the phone, and four, five minutes after the lights go down they're in, I don't know—Venice, with a Jewish merchant who is not being well treated by the Christians all around him, despite their high-minded mouthing about the quality of mercy. And you know, to a certain extent all the people sitting in the dark—even the ones who didn't want to come, the ones whose kids are acting up or who are having trouble meeting the mortgage payment or are worried about a lump in their breast—in a few minutes *they're* there, too, most of them. And maybe, in spite of their worries or the deficiencies of the actors and directors and the wretched cardboard sets, like that wall that landed on poor Boomboom—in *spite* of all of that, some tiny insight, some act of compassion, some perfect phrase, *lodges itself* in their heart and stays there for years to come, maybe all their lives; it changes something about the way they see the world. They don't even remember where they got it. But they're *better* for it. A theater can be a hospital for the soul."

I said, "You've given this some thought."

"Only thing I ever wanted to be was an actor. Started when I was seven. My mum had me modeling, and a picture of me ended up on some milk cartons. I was lucky. That turned into film work and some theater, too, and I made a little money. Good for me, good for Mum and Dad because they were barely scraping by: two jobs, three kids, no savings. When I was sixteen, a manager saw me in a play and decided I looked like a rock star. Had to have been my looks, since he'd never heard me sing, but I said okay, why not, and six months later we had the number four record over there and cracked the top twenty over here. And we went on selling for almost five years."

"But you never went back to acting?"

"I was a curiosity by then. People *knew* me. For a legit director, I mean, a *theater* director, the moment I walked onto the stage, the world of the play, it crumbled in tiny pieces, and look, there was a *rock star* up there. No matter what I did, I wasn't the character I was supposed to be."

"Sorry to hear it."

"Well, it wasn't on a tragic scale. I wasn't working in the mines or mopping up toxic waste. I saw what a wretched job, a job he hated, did to my dad. By contrast, I was on permanent vacation. It's not like I've had a tragic life, it's just that all the good stuff was in act one and we've had a thirty-year anticlimax."

"Lavender still thinks of you."

"She's quite a girl," he said. "When you're on the road, the faces all blur, but I still remember her."

"You said you had something to tell me."

"And I do, but it's a bit squeamish for me. Makes me look like Ebenezer Scrooge, hoarding every tuppence that passes into my hands, just stacking them up in some locked room so I can go in and *breathe* on all of it. You see, this tour is *it* for me. After this, I'm never going to squeeze into those black leather pants again. So I'm being a bit *frugal* this time around, looking for ways to stretch the paycheck a bit. Cappy and I had a little talk—you're not going to tell him about this, are you?"

"Well," I said, "only if it suddenly seems important."

He nodded. "That's reassuring, actually. Everybody in this business says, 'But of course, dear boy, your secret is my secret,' and then they sell it to the nearest customer. We're splitting the money, Cappy and I are, that was budgeted for my hotel room. He puts it on the books as *spent* and then we split however much it is we're saving: ninety, a hundred, hundred and ten dollars per night over the length of the tour. I get almost five thousand dollars out of it, straight into my pocket, not a penny in tax, and I sleep in the theaters. He tells the theater people that he's leaving someone to stay overnight to look after our things, and I find myself someplace cozy and just curl up. As I said, I love theaters. Had some amazing dreams while we've been on the road."

"But this isn't about your dreams. This is about something you saw, isn't it?"

"Not much dust on you, is there?" He leaned back against the wall a couple of times as though he was trying to bounce off it, and I willed myself to shut up. He was working his way toward it.

"I'm trusting you with this because of your daughter—how you are with your daughter and the way she talks about you. Our first night here—that was two nights ago, we got here late in the afternoon—I woke up because I *heard* something. I was in the balcony's front row because the higher you go—in the balcony, I mean—the more of the seat is visible from down below. And it was my first night here, a little spooky, like they all are the first night—and something made a noise. I opened my eyes just as the onstage work lights went on, and I saw *him*—that awful freak with the briefcase—climbing the ladder stage right." He inhaled deeply, blew it out, and said, "So he got up there and went on his hands and knees and started sawing at something, not really sawing but using the side of whatever it was to rub at the rope. Swearing up a storm."

"He was fraying it," I said.

"Certainly my impression. After a while, he said, excuse the language, *Fuck this*, and took something out of his pocket."

"Jackknife?"

"Looked like it," he said. "How do you know?"

"I saw the rope. After it came down."

"But," he said, "he changed his mind. Started to take a swipe with it, then let rip with a bunch of words that made the earlier stuff sound like the way you'd talk to a platoon of Girl Guides."

I said, "Really. And then?"

"He went back to work with the whatever it was."

"Did you tell anyone?"

"I was going to, but first thing the next morning he came in with all four of the bosses, and they were laughing to beat the band. *Everybody* works for them, the bosses, I mean. Even Cappy. Like I said, I wouldn't be telling *you* now if it weren't for your daughter."

"Well," I said, "if it's any comfort, I don't believe that Cappy has anything to do with it. I don't think he's that good an actor."

"Still." Nigel made a clucking noise. "Look who pays his salary."

"I'm thinking about that," I said. "All the time." I got up. "Thanks for letting me know."

Looking up at me, he wrapped his arms around his upraised knees, like an insecure twelve-year-old. He lowered his gaze to the carpet and said, "Say hi to Rina for me. Say hi to Lavender."

22

An Unaggressive Beige

Halfway down the stairs to the lobby, I stopped to call Dressler about the metal detectors. Tuffy answered, and in the background, I could hear extremely melodic instrumental music—*Scheherazade*, by Rimsky-Korsakov. "Nice tune," I said. "Are you soothing a savage beast?"

"Are we ever. Tell me what you want before he asks who it is. You don't want to talk to him, believe me."

"Well, this may seem a little abrupt, but I need a couple of metal detectors, the ones people walk through."

"Anything else?"

I said, "You've got them?"

"Guys in Detroit sent four of them to him a few years ago, one for each door into the house, but he wouldn't let us install them. Said he'd never been that frightened and he didn't want anyone to think he ever *would* be. They're in the basement."

"Can you get two of them over here?"

"When?"

"ASAP."

"I'll have to send somebody. He's not going to let either of us escape to take them to you. I know, I'll send Granny, you know Granny?"

"Not sure I've had the pleasure. Can she lift one of those things?"

"*He*, and he could lift Rhode Island. Last name is Smith, like the apple, you know Granny Smith? Someone gave him the nickname and it stuck. Babe and I can get them into his truck, but he'll need some help getting them out, somebody pretty strong."

I said, "I know just the guy."

"Where you been?" Cappy said. He sounded interested.

"Out and about. The metal detectors will be here in an hour or so. Can you tell Bluto he's got to help bring them in?"

"Who?"

"You know, the walking biceps who's usually downstairs. Let him put all that muscle to work instead of just flexing it at people."

"He's using it right now, standing guard over that damn hole out front, where I chased the kids away. The guys who work over there didn't quit last night until we were wrapping it up here, even *with* what happened to Boomboom and all. So they left a lock undone, which, of course, sent out a siren call to every suicidal teenager within ten square miles. I called the transit office, and they're sending someone to close it up, but, you know, this is the weekend and blah blah blah. So yeah, he can help you, I mean he'll be right there, standing next to the hole, until the guy shows to lock everything up."

"Do you know how to set up the detectors?"

"Plug them in and set the sensitivity to the point where they're not set off by every bobby pin, tooth filling, and Saint Christopher medal within ten feet. I can probably handle it."

"Good," I said, heading for the door. "I have no mechanical skills at all. So I'll let you know when they arrive."

"Mister useful."

I put a hand on the knob, a little spark of anger running through me. "We aim to please."

His chair creaked, and I fought a slightly panicky impulse to turn around. He said, "How's your boss feeling?"

"He's screaming at people," I said, "even people he likes. Not a good sign."

"Long as it's not at me."

Pulling the door open and turning to face him, I said, "When you've been as high up as he's been for as *long* as he's been, we all sort of look alike. A bee stings him, he's likely to take out the whole hive. Good idea not to do anything that might piss him off."

He nodded and said, "I'm used to that. I'm *surrounded* by people I don't want to piss off."

"Well," I said, on the way out of the room, "you wanted to be in show business."

I had no sooner closed the door than I regretted having let my uncertainty about him show. I had no idea how deeply, if at all, he was involved in anything that had brought Dressler to life so suddenly, but at that moment, extending trust to anyone felt like walking blindfolded on a diving board without knowing how long it was, how high it was, and whether there was any water in the pool. I was probably being unfair, but fairness was pretty far down the list of things I was worried about.

Just for the hell of it, and to avoid any potentially unpleasant meetings in the hall, I went down the stairs to the exit at the back of the building and out into the familiar charms of my narrow alley. So, okay: the reason the rope had been severed in two ways undoubtedly came down to good old-fashioned impatience. But then I realized that no one would have intentionally *left* it so close to being cut all the way through; what was to keep it from just falling on the head of someone like poor old Boomboom? Nothing. So . . .

So let's say someone—okay, *Sparks*, no reason to pussyfoot about it—*was* up there, shredding away at the rope, using I had no idea what, some sort of shredder—a slow, boring, and potentially conspicuous process. If I were the one who was doing it, I wouldn't want to be up there on the night of the crime for any longer than absolutely necessary, so let's say he gave himself a running start on the previous night as Nigel looked on, shredding it, say, 80 percent of the way through. Then, before the first show started, he could have climbed back up, cut a little more, and then waited for the victim, figuring he could get through the bit that was left with a couple of swipes, and let it drop. He could then scramble the length of the catwalk on hands and knees and get back down the ladder on the much darker stage left side, while the whole world was looking in the opposite direction, at the brightly lighted victim and the chaos that surrounded him, downstage right.

And then suppose he was up there, slicing away at it, and just as he was a couple of hacks from being finished, the victim suddenly got pissed about something, cut short his time onstage, waved goodbye to the crowd, and stalked off the stage.

As, in fact, I had *seen* him do.

What could Sparks do then?

Well, nothing. There was no way to unshred or uncut the rope and make it safe again, so he probably crossed his fingers that it would hold for a while, and climbed back down. And then he watched all that work go up in smoke as the very next person to inhabit that part of the stage slammed away at the world's biggest drum set for what must have felt like a week, and then *turned on a goddamn machine* that made the entire stage vibrate, and way overhead the half-shredded half strands of rope kissed each other goodbye and parted company, and the flat fell exactly as it was supposed to fall and wiped out a poor schmuck whose only sins were hogging the spotlight a couple of minutes too long and punching the ON button for some kind of demonic drum amplifier.

And the guy Sparks wanted to kill, or injure, or terrify, is still walking around, boring everybody to tears with his memories of some high school teacher who changed his life by handing him a violin.

If I were the shredder, I'd be livid. If I were the shredder, I'd know *exactly* who was to blame: the intended victim, for cutting short his own turn on the stage, and the drummer, for being a goddamn drummer.

So I knew who did it and I certainly knew who had given the *order* to do it, and I was pretty sure I knew why. What to do about it, if anything, was another question.

I was back on the stage, thinking about going up the aisle and making sure the basement door was still unlocked, when someone touched me on the shoulder, sending me eight inches straight up.

"I'm flattered," Debbie Halstead said. "I've been practicing moving quietly, and a launch like that tells me I'm not wasting my time."

"Well, it's definitely working. And it's good to—no, I take that back, it's actually an enormous relief to see you. And you look perfect."

She tugged at her innocuous olive-green blouse, which topped an equally innocuous knee-length belted skirt in unaggressive beige, above a clunky pair of what my mother would have described as *sensible shoes*. "This is one of my two junior-high-school getups," she said. "This is the teacher the boys never think about boinking. The other one is more eye-catching, but I figured invisible was better."

"Perfect."

"Harmless as a pack of Life Savers," she said. She looked past me, squinting, and then her eyes widened and she grabbed my shirt, plus a little bit of skin, in one fist. "Oh my God, is that Jennifer *Summers*?"

"It is." I pried her fingers open. "You like her?"

"Are you kidding? I've loved her since I was ten."

"You want to meet her?"

She opened her mouth, closed it, opened it again, and said, "I can't, I mean, I wouldn't dare."

"*You*? You're *afraid* to meet—"

"What if she's a jerk? She helped me grow up and then she got me through two broken hearts."

I said, "You've had a broken heart?"

"Like I said, two of them. Well, the same heart, but two breaks. Why *wouldn't* I get my heart broken? I'm a girl, right?"

"No, I mean, yes," I said. "Or, rather, I mean, *no*, no reason at all. Forget it. Sorry I said—"

"Glad to know I rattled you a little. The guys are both dead now, but that doesn't mean I didn't, you know, soak my pillow with tears over them."

"You cried over them, uhh, before or after they, uhhh—?"

"*Before*, of course, when the flame was still burning. You think I could waste somebody I love? I mean, come on, I'm not a *machine*."

"But then, after . . ."

"Oh, well, *after*, I mean, *sure*. At that point, they were just irritants, and embarrassing irritants at that. Women are held to a higher standard than men. It's hard enough for some people to take me seriously as it is, without them thinking that some minor-league wannabe Romeo can come along and do a wheelie on my heart and then just drive merrily away, honking his horn at the next idiot while I'm going through boxes of Kleenex like some twelve-year-old. Wrong image *entirely*. Not good for business."

"I can see that."

"Wow," she said, staring at Jennifer. "She looks really good. Maybe I *won't* mind getting older. A *little* older, anyway. So, who we gonna shoot?"

"Maybe no one, maybe a couple of guys. You sure you don't want to meet her?"

"No, I'd probably just drool on her. Only one or two?"

"If I had my way there'd be four, but I don't actually remember the last time I had my way."

"Self-pity is *so* attractive in a man."

"Let's take a look around. Can't hurt, and it might give you some ideas." I led her toward the stairs down to the seats. "Come on, we'll start at one end of the place and work our way through. There's a building out back, too."

"I saw it when I came up the driveway. Anyplace sound-proof?" We were going down the stairs.

"Won't matter in a couple of hours, when the music starts."

She turned and lifted her chin at Jennifer. "Is she going to sing?"

"She's the headliner."

"That means she goes, like, last, right?"

"You got it."

"Well, let's get it over with so I can listen."

"Jesus," she said, "this is *fabulous*, right out of *Phantom of the Opera*."

We were in the basement. I'd shown her the two bathrooms, the balcony, and the popcorn machine. Then I'd opened the basement door and stepped aside. Debbie immediately found the light switch and then almost fell down the stairs in her enthusiasm. "It's *perfect*. It's the kind of place I used to dream about when I was a kid who was starting to think about my line of work. This was what I always imagined as the scene of the crime, and what did I get? Parking lots, office buildings, a *men's room*, no style at *all*. This is like, a . . . a little girl's *dream*."

"Speaking of which," I said, "I have to make a phone call. You look around, indulge yourself. If you want to test your silencer, close the door and shoot something, check out the acoustics. See you in a minute or two."

She turned off two of the four light switches to enhance the ambiance or something, and I went back into the lobby and closed the door behind me. It was getting dark out, but Bluto was out there, standing guard over the hole in the street. He'd found a couple of chunks of concrete and was working on his biceps. A few passersby, including a couple of girls in their late teens, had stopped to watch the show.

"Hey," Rina said. "You won't *believe* the stuff I've got. And the things for Ronnie, her knees are going to melt. This place is like a clothes museum."

"Good," I said. "Do you trust her?"

"Do I—of *course* I do."

"Well, tell her to take you home." Behind me, I heard a muf-fled sound, like someone forcefully closing a book, so Debbie's silencer was aces.

"Home? You mean it's not a secret any—"

"Not from her."

"We're *hungry*," Rina said. "She knows this great little Thai place that's just—"

"Fine, fine, eat something. But call me within ninety minutes or so to tell me where you are and that you're going—"

"—home, right, got it, will do. Bye."

I couldn't think of a time when she'd hung up on me before, although, being a teenager, she must have. I glared at the phone long enough to overcome my desire to throw it across the lobby, and then I looked up to see, through the deepening dusk, Bluto making his biceps explode for the teenagers, who were now tak-ing turns photographing each other squeezing his flexed arm. Their hands looked *tiny*. Bluto was clearly in heaven.

An icy little ripple of worry about Rina laid claim to my spine. She was, as people say, at an impressionable age, and Lavender, no matter how much I liked her, was probably not the ideal role model. My concern about Rina did a graceful sidestep to let me focus on my dread about how Kathy would react when she learned about all this. We were going to have to find some way, Rina and I, to sanitize it before the three of us settled in to catch up.

An extremely distinctive truck painted in horizontal stripes of red, white, and blue, and with what looked like a tommy gun on the center of its hood, eased its way to the curb, barely missing the big excavation mound, and a guy I sort of recognized got out. Bluto had broken away from his admirers, practically bristling at the opportunity to actually *guard* something, and had taken a couple of reflexive steps to shoo the intruding truck away. But then he stopped cold, his lower jaw limp with astonishment as the truck's door opened and the driver unfolded himself, one anatomical wonder at a time. Fully revealed, he made Bluto look like the *before* dweeb in the vintage bodybuilding ads—the skinny wimp at the beach in whose face all the buffed dudes were kicking sand while his soon-to-be-ex-girlfriend gazed adoringly up at them. As I pulled out my phone again, the new guy took a better look at Bluto, and you could almost hear the bond between them snap into place; here were two men with literally everything in common. The new guy stopped, nodded approval, pointed to his own shoulders to indicate the muscles that, according to Rina, made Bluto's head look so weensy, and then flashed an upraised thumb. Even the thumb looked like it had muscles. Bluto practically dropped to one knee.

When Cappy answered, I said, "Your metal detectors are here." I crossed the lobby and went through the door into the basement, eyed a path through the junk that would take me to Debbie without taking me through any spider webs, and then closed the door and turned off one of the remaining light switches, sinking the place into the kind of gloom that, in a movie, usually precedes the first sighting of a clawed hand.

"Let's just sit tight for a bit," I said, feeling my way. "No point in getting everybody curious yet."

23
You Have to Aim in Front of Them

"I ever tell you how I got started?" Debbie said.

We were on very shaky folding chairs in the approximate center of the basement, which offered an ever-dimmer pile of *stuff* in all directions, and I was staring in thinly masked horror at a jumble of furniture about ten feet from us that looked like it had adorned a sitcom in the 1980s, and beneath which something unarguably large had just scuttled. It was too ratlike to be anything but a rat.

I said, "How do you feel about rats?"

"They're fast," she said, "and you have to aim in front of them so they actually *run into* the slug. It's an interesting problem. I wasted a lot of perfectly good bullets before I figured it out. I can get about three in five now. You want to hear my story?"

"Not really, but thanks for asking. There's one under that chair over there."

"Probably not. They're too smart to stay where you saw them go. He could be behind us by now."

I said, "Ahh."

"I can't *believe* you, mister big burglar, going all dampie-pants like that over a *rat*."

"I am dampie-pants. I have an entirely reasonable dislike for rats."

"*Dislike*? You almost jumped up and stood on your chair. You did everything except say *eeek*."

"It's aesthetic," I said.

"So," she said, settling back to a creak of disapproval from her own chair, "you're *really* not interested in my story? Girl like me doesn't get many chances to tell it."

"Can't imagine why."

"Damn," she said. She patted the pocket that had the gun in it and said, "There's your rat again. Or maybe it's a bigger one. My *God*, it's got a cigar." When I didn't rise to the bait, she sighed and said, "Okay, present tense. Why am I here?"

"In case someone behind me needs shooting."

"Yeah, like I couldn't beat you to someone who was in front of you while you get your gun caught on your zipper or something. Who's our client?"

"Irwin Dressler."

"Ohmigod," she said, one hand over her heart. "You *know* him?"

"Yes."

"Can I meet him?"

"That's entirely up to him."

"Well," she said, "Irwin *Dressler*? Let's get cracking."

I heard a noise from the lobby and said, "Wait here for a minute." By the time I was standing, she was up with her gun in her hand. When I had cracked the door and peered out, I saw Cappy on the other side of the lobby with his back to me, pouring popcorn kernels into the popper. I waved Debbie back, stepped into the lobby, eased the door closed behind me, and said, "Free, or for sale?"

"Jesus," he said, whirling around. "Don't *do* that."

"That kind of reaction," I said, "some people might say *guilty conscience*."

"That kind of sneaking up on a guy," he said, "some people might say *burglar*."

I said, "Well, I just wanted to tell you that I admire the way you grab a chore and *bang*, perform it. No terse orders, no dispatching inferiors. You just get out and do it."

"I haven't got a lot of inferiors," he said. "What are *you* up to?"

"Just, you know, getting the lay of the land. So, a couple of hours and change before the curtain goes up."

"Little less than that now," he said. "Two more glittering nights of show business, and then I can kiss this bunch of antiques goodbye and go count my money." He regarded me for a moment. "So. You getting what you want?"

"My cup runneth over."

"Must not be much of a cup."

I said, "The best way to avoid disappointment is to have modest expectations. You think Sparks is still mad at me?"

"I'd say that's a safe bet. He hasn't got a forgiving nature." He leaned down and hit a switch. "Popcorn coming up."

"Where is he?"

Cappy straightened up and took a couple of steps away from the machine. He looked at me for a good ten or fifteen seconds.

I said, "Sooner or later, unless I've badly misjudged you, I've got to take a chance on you. And, maybe, vice versa."

"Yeah," he said. "Problem is not knowing what comes with either vice or versa, isn't it? Which door leads to the million dollars and which leads to the shot in the head? It's a powerful argument for making careful decisions and, probably, slow ones, not just responding to people's charm and going off half-cocked, you should forgive the mention of a firearm. The *temptation* is just to hang there noncommittally, the last ornament to get put on the Christmas tree, and hope that nobody comes along and breaks you just because it looks like it might be fun. You getting what you need?"

I said, "What do I need?"

He looked down and used a kind of paddle to stir the popcorn kernels. "That's the question, isn't it? Well, hell, you got me the metal detectors and that's something, although I'm only going to use one because I think two would blow out the power in the lobby. Most of the people who we—or, more precisely, *you*—probably need to worry about are already here. But I have to admit that it demonstrated an impressive level of pull, and it's hard not to respect pull, or at least factor it into the equation of the moment." He hung the paddle on the side of the machine and looked at me. "He's in dressing room three, putting ice on his face, and I have no idea who told you that. But if something really horrible should happen to him, I'll know who to thank."

The first thing we heard when I pulled open the door into the theater was something vaguely boogie-woogie being played on the piano, a good strong left-handed rhythm and some bright scampering around on the high keys, and then the stage lights went on, and I saw it was Jennifer. Debbie grabbed my sleeve, and said, "Let's take a break."

"Can't," I said. "We know where he is now, and we don't know where he'll be later, so—" but then Jennifer stopped playing and called up to the booth, "Look okay?"

"Looks great," April called down from the lighting booth.

"Good enough for rock and roll, right?" Jennifer said, and then she looked down at the guitar she had just picked up and started to strum.

I had to grab Debbie's elbow and pull her to the steps that took us up to the stage and past Jennifer, who nodded at us without losing a word of the lyric. I towed Debbie all the way upstage until we were practically at the big door to the alley and we could see down the little corridor of dressing rooms. I whispered, "There," pointing to a door partway down that bore a hand-scrawled sign that said DO NOT FUCKING DISTERB. I led her to it and then I stepped aside, gave her an *After you, Alphonse* bow and mimed knocking. I could feel my heart banging against my shirt, so I wasn't quite as steady as I would have liked to have been, despite the reassuring weight of the gun in my hand. Debbie's own gun had materialized to sit so comfortably in her grip that it could have been a surgical implant. She stepped up to the door and put her ear to it, and then she took a step back, winked at me, raised the gun to chest-level, and used her free hand, her left, to knock.

"Yeah? Leave me the fuck *alone*." He sounded like someone who'd been trying to blow his nose since the summer solstice.

"They sent me with some ice," she said, sounding about twelve. "Mr. Perlman did?"

"Fuck him *and* his ice."

"And some *pills*?" she said.

"Well, you know how to open a fucking door, don't you?"

"I can work it out." She waved me away so I wouldn't be in his line of sight and said, "Coming in." She used her left hand to turn the knob and push the door open a few inches so she could peek through the crack, waving with her gun hand to drive me a few more steps back, and she said, "Oh, you poor boy. I'm not sure that nose will ever straighten up."

"Who the fuck cares what you're not sure about? Where's the pills?"

"Well," she said, opening the door the rest of the way and pointing her gun at him. "I lied about the pills." Then she said, "No, no, no, *no*. Keep them where I can see them."

"Where *we* can see them," I said, following her into the door-way. "Wow, you're going downhill *fast*."

He was scrabbling at his open briefcase, but Debbie crossed the little room in one long leap and shoved it away with her right foot, and then she leaned over and used the barrel of her gun to tap the bridge of his nose, provoking a clear, unwavering soprano response. I came into the room, feeling safe as milk, and closed the door to keep the sound in.

"*Damn*, you're dumb," she said as he cupped both hands over his face and rocked back and forth, demonstrating a sur-prisingly melodic whimper.

"That's his favorite sound," I said, grabbing a corner of his briefcase and pulling it toward me. "But only when somebody else is making it."

"Okay," Debbie said, touching the barrel of her gun dead-center on the top of his head. "Now, *listen*. Just so you can't claim we didn't tell you, the pink thing on the end of this gun is a highly effective silencer. It's about as noisy as a dart hitting the board, and just so we're clear, I'm really enthusiastic about the notion of shooting you. And you might as well settle in because we're here and we're not leaving until Junior has whatever he wants, and one more peep out of you and I'll break your nose again." She looked at me. "Am I butting in?"

"No, no," I said. "Carry on."

"So," she said to him, "we're here to—" She glanced at me for a moment. "*Why* are we here?"

"We're here to tell him that his services are no longer needed. We're here to tell him that we're going to walk him out to his car, assuming he has one, and that he should get it started, pull it away from the curb, and then keep driving until the climate changes. We're here to tell him that the next time we see him he'll have about a twentieth of a second to appreciate how effective your silencer is, and from that point on he'll be a piece of furniture that absolutely everyone wants to get rid of."

"Clear to me," Debbie said. "Although I can't speak for him."

"Don't waste your time on him," I said as I unzipped the bag with its awful Captain Marvel logo. "He doesn't get any smarter than that. Just your basic square-root IQ, barely capable of opening and closing doors in the right order. Ahhhhh, *here* we are."

And accompanied by a moan of protest from Sparks, I pulled it out. I was looking at it when I heard Debbie say, "What the hell is that, the wheel of fortune?"

"Yeah," I said, "if all your possible futures are terrible." I turned it over in my hands. Somehow, it was both heavier and lighter than I'd anticipated. It was ice-cold to the touch, which was kind of counterintuitive, considering what it had been built to do. The surface was a dull matte gray when I'd been expecting it to be demonically shiny, polished to mirror the damage it was created to do. I'd heard its effect described in meticulous detail, but I hadn't imagined how stupid-looking it would be. Probably his victims' most shameful memory of their encounter with Sparks was how completely they had yielded everything they had out of fear for something as crude-looking, as *amateurish*, as this.

"Damn," I said, "this is pathetic."

"You'd be fucking surprised," Sparks said, and Debbie jammed the gun into his mouth, pushing hard enough this time to provoke a groan of pain.

"Actually," I said, "you're the one who's going to be surprised. I don't suppose you remember a guy named Leadfoot Perkins? Car thief?"

"Mmmfff," Sparks said around the gun, and then he swallowed loudly enough to identify the muffled word, which had probably been a denial, as a lie.

"Well," I said, "he remembered *you*." I took another look at the thing in my hand, hefting a couple of times, still trying to adjust to how *light* it was.

It was, as Leadfoot had said, a dull metal disk, about the size of a medium pizza and a couple of inches thick, with that plagiarized logo scrawled in blood-red something or other on both sides. Bristling from its edges were a bunch of mismatched little plug-like things, some slightly bigger than others. They were the business ends of automobile cigarette lighters.

I said to him, "Leadfoot eventually killed himself."

I looked Sparks in the eyes and tried to hold his gaze, but he couldn't look away from the thing in my hands as I pushed one of the little plugs and then another. A few seconds later, one of them popped partway out with a sharp, lethal-sounding *click*, and Sparks leaned back against the wall hard enough to bang his head, and his eyes rolled up to the ceiling. He was emitting a wordless soprano vowel, and I said to Debbie, "Shut him up."

"Are those—" she said, stretching out to grab a handful of cotton wipes, probably for removing makeup, from the shelf in front of the mirror and stuffing them into his mouth alongside the bloody rag. "I mean, are those things—"

"They are," I said. The tip of the one I'd pulled out was a dull red glow. Of course, it doesn't take a whole *lot* of heat to make a man scream. "Fourteen of them, I think. My friend, the one I called Leadfoot, made it through five of them before saying what he didn't want to say. Then he said it, and he *still* got two more of them."

Even with the cloth in his mouth, Sparks was emitting the high shrill of a manic teakettle. He straightened his legs to kick at me, but Debbie tapped his nose again with her gun barrel, and he stopped moving, although the muffled voice scaled up a couple of notes.

"Wow," she said, glancing back at the device, "that's fucking *evil*, and I mean that as a compliment."

"Let's see," I said, pushing another one of the plugs in. It went in about half an inch and stopped, then clicked into place. The act took me back to my teenage years, driving around in my terrible little car and smoking one cigarette after another. "See," I said, "here's the drill. We wait until the lighter pops out—as it's just about to do—and then we pull it out and admire his handiwork." It popped, and I drew it out and showed her the glowing tip. "See," I said, "he's removed the little metal sheath that originally surrounded the heating element, which was there to make sure you didn't accidentally touch it to your lip or your nose instead of your cigarette, since you were, at least theoretically, focused on your driving. That means that you can apply it quite easily to the subject's bare skin"—I touched the cigarette lighter to Sparks's arm, and he launched himself a good ten inches straight up, a dog-whistle-high shriek finding its way around the cloths stuffed in his mouth. He was kicking his legs wildly, and it was, I supposed, a tribute to the intensity of his pain that he didn't even seem to notice when Debbie put the barrel of her gun to his forehead and pushed, hard enough to make his head bang against the wall behind him. She wiggled it side to side, saying, "Calm down or die, calm down or die," and after a few kinetic seconds, he subsided. A soft whimper forced its way through the rags, but it was barely audible.

I said to him, "Just for the record, because I'm not comfortable with assumptions, tell me who you actually wanted to kill when you cut through that rope. I already know the answer, so if you tell me a lie, you'll regret it immediately."

The next lighter popped out. To Debbie, I said, "Pull out the muzzle, please," and she snagged the cloth and tugged it out of his mouth, but he was already shouting something that turned into "*not kill, not kill, not kill*," so fast it was a single word.

"Fine, not kill. And *who*?" I asked, but Debbie reached across me and pulled out the lighter that had just stuck its head up.

"Damn," she said, looking at the red glow at the lighter's tip. "*You* thought this up?" She touched it to his arm, and he went airborne again, emitting a sound as thin and high as a squeaking door. "That is truly *awful*," she said. "Makes me feel like a Campfire Girl. On the other hand, you're lucky that my friend here seems to want you alive because I have to tell you, left to my own resources, I'd kill you just for the endorphin rush."

Sparks's squeal settled into a broken whimper.

"Oh, well," she said to me, "who knows where we'll be six months from now? But whatever happens, we'll always have this dressing room."

As Sparks gabbled away, I said to her, "It's a shame I'm in a relationship." I leaned toward him. He stank of terror. "Sparks. Pay attention. Who were you trying to get?"

He said, "Oscar, Oscar, *Oscar*. But not kill. Just . . . warn."

I pushed the lighter back in and said, "Warn him about what?"

"Talking, they thought he was talking to somebody, I don't know who, they didn't tell me who. Honest, I swear, *really really really*."

"I could play with this thing all day," I said, "but I can't think of anything else to ask you at the moment, and someone is going to want this room pretty soon. *Plus*, I've got a couple of other clocks ticking, so here's what I need from you if you don't want to take your last few breaths through a couple of feet of dirt out there in that hole they're digging for the whatever it is—you know the hole I mean?"

He said, "*Yesyesyesyes.*"

"Although, I have to tell you," I said, "if we take you out to the subway excavation, and if they ever finish it and get it running, you'd probably be the first person to arrive in Santa Monica. Are you *listening*? Don't talk, just lift your eyebrows if you are."

His eyebrows shot practically to his hairline.

"Okay, here we are. Calm down, clear your mind, and *think* about this before you answer me, and maybe you'll spare yourself a world of pain. What's the thing Yoshi least wants me to know?"

He said, "Ummmmmmm."

"Give the man an answer," Debbie said, "or I'll make sure you're conscious and cuffed hands to feet when I put you in the bottom of the hole and start to fill it up. And then, if we meet in the afterlife and we're on speaking terms, you can tell me how long it took to die. Got it?"

He said, "Yesyesyes."

"So," Debbie said. "Tell the nice man what your boss doesn't want him to know."

Sparks looked from me to her and back again, and then he licked his lips, cleared his throat, and said, "He paid me off."

I waited a moment and said, "Congratulations, I guess. As they say in the Book of Luke, the servant is worthy of his hire, but I'm not sure why you think I might want to know that."

"With all due respect," Debbie said, "I think you may be missing the point."

"I'm sorry," I said. "I just keep thinking about shooting him."

Debbie said to Sparks, "They paid you off? Are they pulling out? Leaving?"

"Tonight," Sparks said.

"Well," I said. "That changes *everything.*"

Part Three

The Reckoning

"I really *was* a Girl Scout," Debbie said, opening her big purse. "I wanted to be a Boy Scout, but, you know, the patriarchy and all that. Anyway," she said, feeling around in the bag, "I started to look for ways to be *prepared*, even though I was a girl. I mean, who needs to be prepared more than a girl? For a while, when I was in junior high, *being prepared* meant carrying a big purse to hide all the makeup my parents wouldn't let me wear to school, and all the stuff to get it off on the way home. At school I was a painted teen, a hopeful hussy. At home I was as chaste as Quaker Oats. *Here* we are." She brought up a tangle of cord and a pair of handcuffs. "For pushy dates," she said. "But *after* junior high, *being prepared* stood for other things, which modesty prevents me from disclosing."

I said, "Aaawww, come on."

"Not a chance. Although, as a bonus from being a Girl Scout, I learned to tie some killer knots." To Sparks, who had been standing beside one of the basement's painted pillars and staring at the gun I was pointing at him, she said, "So we lied about letting you go home, but you're still alive, and we're going to try to keep it that way, although I think it would be a bit much for you to expect to be comfortable, too. Turn your back to the pretty pillar, say goodbye to all the nice painted flowers, and put your hands behind you. Come on, come *on*, you know what I want, back pressed against the pillar, arms extended back with your wrists together on my side of the pillar. *There* we are," she said, and I heard a decisively metallic *click*. "Okay, just stay there, not that you have much of a choice." To me, she said, "Can I have your chair?"

I said, "I kind of like this chair."

"Do you plan to sit in it for the rest of the day?"

"I have a feeling I'm losing control of the situation. Why can't you give him *your* chair?"

"I was going to give it to *you*, but fine. Bring it here so he can sit on it."

"Oh, hell," I said. "He can have mine. It's more than he deserves, though."

She shoved the chair I had claimed until it was right behind Sparks's left knee and said, "Lean your shoulders back and scoot your butt as far as possible from the pillar and the—just a second. Okay," she said. "Sit."

He did, looking so surprised when he hit the seat that I thought he'd half expected her to yank it out from under him. Then he said, "My arms hurt."

"They'll get numb pretty quick," Debbie said. She stepped in front of him and said, "Spread your legs," and then she kicked the chair, which slid over the floor until it was jammed against the pillar. Backing up, she surveyed her work. "That should be better. You're lucky we're not feeding you to the rats. Open wide."

To my surprise, he did, and she jammed the stained rag and the cotton puffs back into it. Then she fumbled around in her purse, which appeared to have an infinite capacity, and brought up a gaily colored scarf. She went behind him, stretched the scarf over his mouth, and knotted it tightly on the other side of the pillar. "This is the Trucker's Hitch," she announced, "a gift of the Girl Scouts. As the name implies, it's so slip-proof you can tow a car with it." When she was finished, she went around to face him, and then she leaned down and said, "Here's the deal. You'll notice that we haven't killed you. But that decision is reversible at any time. That hole outside is all yours if you do anything, and I mean anything at *all*, to attract attention, and that especially means that when we come back in here, we expect that gag to be in your mouth. Nod if we're clear."

He nodded. I said, "This may be gilding the lily, but why don't you tie his ankles to the legs of the chair?"

"Oh my God," she said, "a *collaborator*. I'll give you this, Junior, you know how to show a girl a good time. But I'm out of rope. Anyway, those handcuffs are there to stay."

I looked at my watch: coming up on seven. The sounds of the audience's arrival had grown. Through the closed basement door I heard a woman laugh and realized that the voices I could hear were mostly female. The customers sounded cheerful and expectant, and the popcorn smelled great.

"Want some popcorn?" I asked.

She said, "Aren't we on any kind of a clock at *all*?"

"We are, but it's a fairly leisurely one at the moment. They won't arrive until a little after eight."

"They," she said.

"Yup, they. Or them, if you prefer."

"And in the meantime, we just cower in our cave?"

"I wouldn't put it that way. I mean, we have popcorn. I know, why don't you go check his gag?"

"Oh, *well*," she said. "That'll certainly fill the time."

"Do it slowly. See, this is one of the differences between a burglar and a hit-person. A hit-person runs on adrenaline. A burglar wants as little adrenaline as possible."

"How mundane," she said.

"Well," I said, "unlike a hit-person, we have a fairly normal life expectancy, so we need to reserve our resources." I headed toward the door. "Gotta make a couple of phone calls."

"And I can't hear them?"

"At some point in the not too distant future we're going to have to leave this asshole in here, and in the event someone might find him, I don't want him to hear what I'm about to say. Anything else?"

"Popcorn sounds good," she said, and then she picked up Sparks's machine. She said, "This *is* kind of a temptation."

"Well, resist it. Even *with* the gag he'll make too much noise."

I went to the door, cracked it open a couple of inches, and looked out: two women for every man. I had a feeling the male bands weren't going to have much of a night, but I was happy for Vera and the Razorettes and for Jennifer. And, I thought, for the Pussycats, even in spite of Lionel.

"Excuse me," I said as I opened the door directly in front of a woman who was heading for the popcorn.

"No damage," she said. "But I'm ahead of you in line."

"All yours," I said. I pulled the door closed behind me, went across the lobby and into a very dark and fairly drizzly night. Poor Bluto was still standing guard, damp but muscular, beside the hole. He'd moved on to deep knee bends.

Rina didn't answer, and I'd already left one message on her voicemail. More than one was undignified, but I was mad enough to risk losing face, so I said, "I am not amused at not having heard from you. When you pick this thing up, you call me, and I mean instantly." I disconnected with the lack of satisfaction that always accompanies a futile gesture and called Ronnie, who said she hadn't heard from Rina and sounded a little cranky about it. Then, acting on a sudden ripple of doubt provoked by the ever-present question *What else could go wrong?* I called Dressler.

"You're not going to believe this," Tuffy said, "but it's been so long since he started his car that the battery is dead."

"Well, take *your* car. Take Babe's."

"He won't ride in them. Says they project the wrong image. Says image is very important right now."

"Who am I to argue, but they're not going to get here for fucking ever."

"Got a limo coming, big as an ocean liner, he says. Oughta be here in an hour or so."

"Why so damn long?"

"He had to borrow it from somebody. So it'll have private plates and all, doesn't look like a rental. He says it's important, the kind of car, so no rental plates. But the guy who owns it was out in it and they had to take him home and then wash the car."

I said, "Jesus. Does it have a flower vase they can fill?"

"I'll ask."

"You know," I said, "they probably won't even see it. They'll be upstairs."

"Would you like to explain that to him? I'd be happy to take him the phone."

"Skip it."

"So who should I say called? He's going to want to know—"

"Tell him it was the Auto Club, calling to say he might want to check his damn battery once in a while."

"I think not," Tuffy said, and hung up.

I stood there, persuading myself that I was calm until I realized that I was shifting my weight from one leg to another with no purpose at all. Every few seconds a gust of cold air hit me as another audience member pushed his or her—well, *mostly* her—way in. Two uniformed kids I hadn't seen before, one boy and one girl, maybe eighteen or nineteen, were checking tickets and directing the customers to the right section, although most of them headed for the popcorn line.

Overhead, a bell chimed a couple of times and the lobby lights dimmed to let the audience know that magic time, or what would pass for it tonight, was fast approaching. I checked my watch; if that had been the ten-minute bell, they were starting almost half an hour early, and I had a sudden chilly vision of Dressler pulling up in his fancy car ten minutes after the thugs had made a graceful exit.

Cappy, doing a nifty bit of broken-field running through the paying customers, came into the lobby via the left-hand aisle. He had a huge bag of already-popped popcorn, which he poured into the heated tub at the side of the machine. Spotting me, he called, "This is the end of it. Have to get some more for tomorrow."

Feeling a slight pang about his assumption that I'd be there tomorrow, I said, "Show's starting early, isn't it?"

"Ninety percent full. Everyone else will miss a few minutes of Corner Pocket's set, but that's actually a mercy. We should charge them extra 'cause they didn't have to hear it."

I looked at my watch and said, "Anything from the metal detectors?"

He was looking at my watch, too, and I could almost hear the question gathering itself in his head, but he chose to answer my question instead of asking one of his own. "It was about what you'd expect from a Jennifer Summers crowd. A lot of pings, mostly hair clips and barrettes, a few deadly nail files, about fifty pieces of metal jewelry, and a large spatula. And from the original fan base, the ones who reserved before we put Jennifer's name up, a great many heavy key chains and half a dozen reasonably small knives. Only one gun, and he said he'd forgotten he had it."

"A spatula?"

"Don't ask. The usher, the girl in the uniform over there, said, 'You planning to flip anybody with this?' and got what will probably be the biggest laugh of the night."

"You should put her onstage."

"I think the show is funny enough already. Be interesting to see how the early ticket-buyers, whose taste does not run, shall we say, to nuance, will feel about Jenny." He looked over my shoulder. "Who have we here?"

I said, "Gender?"

"On the fair side of the fence."

"Rating on the make-me-crazy scale?"

"Wouldn't dream of answering such a Neanderthal question."

"Oh, come on," Debbie said behind me. "I'm interested in hearing it, too. When we girls get together, that's all we talk about, how guys rate us."

I said, "Where's the baby?"

"Asleep," she said. "Or at least quiet."

"So," Cappy said, "you guys, uhh, you guys are—"

"No, no, no, *no*," Debbie said, flicking my left ear with her index finger as she came up beside me. "Or, as the French would say, *Mais non.*"

"*Sounds* like them," Cappy said. "So, who you are is . . ."

"I'm Debbie," she said, showing what looked like every tooth she'd ever possessed. "And *you* are?"

He caught my eye for a tenth of a second, and there was a question behind the glance. "Cappy."

"Oh," she said, her eyes widening. She did everything but knot her hands in front of her heart. "You're the one who's in *charge* of everything. Junior talks about you all the time. But all that responsibility . . . all these *people*—I'd pictured a much older man."

Cappy said, "He does? You did?" And as I stood there, marveling at her technique—give her a couple minutes more and he'd probably help her steady the gun as she aimed it at his ear—a microphone emitted a saw-your-head-in-half shriek, and as it died away we heard a little polite applause, and Cappy looked at his watch and said, "To the minute."

"It's *starting*?" Debbie said, sounding like someone who's just had Christmas explained to her for the very first time. "So early?" Her eyes went to mine so briefly I would have missed it if I'd blinked. "Can we go watch?"

"For what it's worth," Cappy said, but then he smiled at her. "Come on up." He jogged to the stairway on the left. I followed Debbie, who was following Cappy, exhaling a buoyant string of wide-eyed drivel about how *exciting* it all was. At the switchback halfway up, he paused and said to her, "What you're about to see are the cheapest seats in the house, but they're my favorites because you can see *everything*, including a lot of the audience. I've always thought that the audience was a big part of a show. You don't want an audience, go watch it on a fucking DVD."

"I couldn't agree more," Debbie said. "The audience is *so* important."

I was about half amused and half creeped out; I was seeing a sort of practice session, and Cappy didn't have a chance.

"You're getting a special audience," he said, and I wished I had a pie to push in his face. "This is a more interesting bunch than we've been drawing, because of—I'm sorry, do you know Jennifer Summers?"

Giving him eyes that looked like big soup spoons that were longing to be filled with something sweet, she said, "She's one of my all-time favorites."

"Me, too," Cappy said. "Hey, Junior, where you been *keep-ing* this girl? So, okay, let's go." He turned and started up the stairs again, and Debbie followed, but not until she'd given me a raised eyebrow and batted her lashes at me. At the same time, and that's hard to do.

We pushed through the swinging doors. From the top step of the balcony we looked down over the backs of hundreds of heads toward the stage, where, to my surprise, Oscar Fiddles wasn't in his place. Instead, standing on the same fatal Glo-Boy, was the mummified radio DJ who'd been handling the band introduc-tions from offstage. His opening line was the one with which he'd started his show for decades: "Boys and girls, *lend me your EARS*," and then he waited for applause long enough to make it painfully apparent that there wouldn't be any. A woman shouted out, "*Jennifer*."

"I know, I know," he said, with a toothy grin, profoundly insincere, even from this far away. "Let's get the show on the road."

Someone started a rhythmic clap, which spread throughout the house.

"*Boy*, does he have this coming," Cappy said.

The DJ, whose name I'd long managed to forget, plowed on. "Bear with me for a second, boys and girls, for a little perspective: what you're about to see—"

Some guy who sounded like he gargled with small rocks called out, "When?" and some people in the audience laughed.

"He's dead," Cappy said. "When they laugh, it's over."

As if on cue, a different male shouted, "Change the station," but to no avail: the DJ said, "Now, now, boys and girls, I need about one minute of your time. This is the thirty-eighth of thirty-nine shows for this here tour—thirteen weeks on the road, three shows in each town, so you're seeing the last appearance of tonight's lineup."

Someone threw a paper plane at him, probably torn from the program and folded in a lap, and the plane got a warm round of applause. He sidestepped it and said, "And what a lineup it is, three great bands and the first appearance anywhere in more than ten years—"

The clapping had been enhanced with stamping. Enough of it was coming from the balcony that I could feel the floor vibrate. Three or four new paper planes were launched at the stage.

"Jesus," Cappy said. "This place is too old for all that stamping." He turned away, apparently with the objective of racing down to the stage and strangling the DJ, as the stamping scaled up and a few people started to chant, "Jennifer, Jennifer, Jennifer."

Planes were coming from all over the place. "What you're seeing," I said to Debbie, "is years of passive loathing taking wing at last."

"The one and only," the DJ said, obviously scanning the orchestra section for more guided missiles, "and I'm as eager to hear her as you are, but *first* . . ." A small fleet of paper airplanes dive-bombed him, and Debbie elbowed me and pointed to four women in the balcony's second row who were folding so fast their hands were blurs. Cappy, who had paused and turned back to the stage, spotted them and laughed out loud.

"And she'll be up here soon," the DJ said, just barely sidestepping a little beauty with a bomber's tapering wings. "But, not to be cut short by a rude minority—"

The house was shaking from the stomps. Cappy said, "I knew

he was a mistake. That damn Yoshi." At that point, we saw a large paper bag that had obviously been weighted with something float up from the fourth or fifth row, miss the DJ, hit the stage floor, and explode into a fountain of popcorn. Retreating backward toward the wings stage right, the DJ said, "This isn't the spirit of rock and roll, people."

"The hell, it's not," Cappy said, but as he pushed the door open to get downstairs, April, up in the lighting booth, took charge, killing the DJ's spotlight and bringing up a couple of new ones that were aimed at the curtain in center stage. Someone hit a loud chord on an electric guitar, and the DJ, not to be forgotten, stepped about four inches onstage in the dark and shouted into his mike, "Okay, boys and girls, let's rock it and sock it with *Corner Pocket*."

The curtain lifted, the music got much louder, and a sudden outpouring of light revealed four somewhat overweight men, well past middle age, who looked like they saw daylight once or twice a year, probably by mistake, and were longtime participants in a receding-hairline contest. I said to Cappy, "Haven't seen *them* around."

"They like hotels. To be more accurate, they hate everything *except* hotels. And heroin. I'd heard they were a problem but I had no idea they were the touring representatives of the living dead. You know the dope tom-tom?"

"Not really."

"Well, it works." For the second time he pushed open the door to the stairs, but this time he held it for us. "Swear to God, every time we checked into a hotel there'd be guys with paper bags in their laps, waiting in the parking lot or, if we had a lobby, in the lobby. I finally had to tell Eddie—that's the guitarist, he's the main guy in the band—I had to tell him to find a coffee shop and make his buys there. From then on, first thing we saw in every town was all these guys laying rubber, trying to get to McDonald's or whatever it was that night. None of those bums have a penny of their salary left. It was advanced to them one town at a time."

Following him down the stairs, Debbie said, "How are they going to get home?"

"They live, if that's what you want to call it, here in LA. I'll probably wind up floating them their cab fare. And it'll be worth it. They get no sympathy from me. I know people like to romanticize it, make it into some kind of twenty-first-century *La Bohème*, but bottom line, most dopers are trash. They'd steal your last nickel if you had a starving kid to feed, so fuck 'em. Excuse me, miss."

"Debbie," Debbie said.

"So, Debbie," he said as the door closed behind us, "what do you do?"

Debbie said, demurely, "I shoot people."

"Yeah?" he said, going down the stairs. "Far out. You get much demand for that?"

"As much as I can handle," Debbie said. "And it's not seasonal."

I said, "Is Oscar okay?"

Cappy had stopped a few steps from the bottom to look up at Debbie, and it seemed to take him a moment to process my question. "Sure," he finally said to me, starting back down. "He just wasn't eager to open the show for some reason. He's probably either huddled in some dark corner or up in the guys' office, where all the cash is, wishing he had a rearview mirror to see his friends in. The guys like to go up there and try to smell the money through the suitcases." He opened the door, catching it with one hand for us, and then hurried past us to the popcorn machine. Down here, even muted by the theater's walls, the band sounded just as crappy as it had from the balcony.

The three of us stood around the popcorn machine as if it were a warm fire on a cold evening. Cappy looked at it, his mouth pulled to one side. "You think I should send someone for more popcorn for the break between acts?"

I said, "Won't do much for the bottom line."

"No," he said, "but it might put them in a better mood for Jenny."

"She'll make her own mood," Debbie said.

"If I ever do another big tour," Cappy said, "it'll be all women."

Debbie found a stray kernel in the tub and popped it into her mouth. "We're just as bad, but different."

"I'd settle for different. So, how do you make a living shooting people? I mean, is there a career path?"

"Same as anything else. You just do the best you can every time. You give it the old college try, and eventually you get a reputation. Among certain people, I mean. And, of course, it can't always be shooting." She was shaking her head like someone mildly exasperated by a stupid question. "See, that's the trickiest problem; if you're in this business and you want to make a success of it, you're going to need to do a certain number of jobs and you don't want to leave any tells: not always a gun, not always a .32, not always through the ear, not always close enough for powder burns." She shook her head at the folly of it all. "Cops are really good at comparing details, if nothing else, and if you don't change things around some, you might just as well autograph the hit's forehead. But still, you want the people who might *hire* you to recognize your work. So it's tricky."

Cappy said, "So how do you do it?"

"Uh-uh," she said. "A girl's got to have *some* secrets."

"Would you do me?"

She was running her index finger around the vat and licking salt off it. "Of *course* not."

"Well," he said, "that's sort of a relief."

She was shaking her head. "It's below stupid to pop people you know. The very first thing the cops do is look for what they call, in that peculiar cop poetry, *known associates*. You do *not* want to be a known associate."

"So," he said brightly, "why are you here?"

Debbie glanced at me for no longer than the average blink and said, "You know, it's a rare group of people that doesn't include someone who needs killing."

25

It's Nice to Know That No One Feels a Sense of Urgency

"He's nice," Debbie said, not putting much into it. We were pushing through the front doors and into the cold drizzle, leaving behind us yet another drum solo. "Can we trust him?" She stopped, and I almost walked into her back. "What's he *doing*?" she asked, nodding toward a very wet Bluto. "He was there when I *got* here. Is this some sort of bodybuilding ritual, lifting wet rocks in the rain?"

I was busy punching up my phone, so I didn't answer her. Bluto *was* looking the worse for wear, and she splashed across the sidewalk toward him. When Babe answered, I said, "Get it into gear. I'm ninety percent sure they're leaving early."

"How early?"

"I don't know, but they started the show half an hour ahead of schedule. If they really want to get out of here, they could do it pretty much anytime."

"Right," he said. "But the car's not here—"

"Well, *get* it there. Take a fucking bus if you have to."

"Listen," he said, and his tone reminded me that, cakes and aprons notwithstanding, both he and Tuffy had taken out a significant number of hard cases in their pre-domestic careers. "We're going to do everything we can. We'll call you when we're around the corner. If they try to leave, stall them."

"Right," I said. "I'll engage them in conversation, ask them about the Dodgers, start a rhyme circle."

"Checking on the car now," he said, and hung up.

"Well," I said, "it's nice to know that no one feels a sense of urgency."

Coming back from a short chat with Bluto, Debbie said, "He wants a cup of coffee. And a date."

"Probably wants to bench-press you."

"I'll get him some at that restaurant. That way, I can change into some dry clothes, too. Unless you have some other use for me."

"Me?" I said. "What possible use could I—"

"Yeah, yeah, yeah. Anyone ever tell you that you were wound too tight? Who were you talking to?"

"One of Dressler's guys. I'm worried they'll be late."

"They? Do you mean *Irwin Dressler* is actually *coming*? *Here*? Is this your way of, of, of telling me *Irwin Dressler* is coming?"

"If he ever gets here."

She said, "I *definitely* have to change. I can't meet Irwin Dressler in *these* rags."

"He's not coming to—"

"How long until he's—"

"That's what I was just *talking* about."

"Well, the clothes are in the car, like always. You know, sometimes you want to go into a building as one person and come out as—"

"Don't change. Just get Mr. Universe over there some coffee if he's touched your heart, and then come into the stage area."

"You're so masterful. But you can go chase your tail if you think I'm going to meet Irwin Dressler looking like a street girl who can't afford an umbrella. To *be* successful you need to *look* successful."

"Fine," I said. "Get the guy some coffee, do your makeup, buy some shoes, but get back as soon as you can. Time is fleeting, and it won't stop just because Irwin Dressler isn't here."

As she angled away toward the restaurant and/or her car, I reluctantly stepped out from under the marquee and into the dud-November damp. Heading toward the stage door, I managed to avoid most of the drizzle by staying so close to the building that my left shoulder was brushing the wall, but when I was finally back inside I found that what I had actually accomplished was a wet left shoulder.

It was dark in there; virtually all the lights from the booth were concentrated center stage, on one of the worst-sounding bands I'd ever heard in my life—it sounded like each of them was playing in a different time zone. Their backdrop featured a logo of crossed pool cues that ended in high heels, taking the design into a rarely explored area of bad taste. When my eyes had adjusted and I could yank them away from the logo, the first person I saw—because his silver hair reflected what little light there was—was Oscar Fiddles. He was only about twenty feet from me, but he seemed to be absorbed entirely in a painstaking study of the floor.

I went over and stood next to him, breathing in a scent that was sweeter than baby powder. My feet had to be in his line of vision, but he was obviously elsewhere, so I cleared my throat. Then I cleared it again. He pulled his gaze away from the floor and looked at me, and when he did, his eyes doubled in size and he took a quick backward step that carried him right into a collision with the wall. The wall won, prompting a little stagger-step bounce forward. I put a hand on his shoulder to steady him, but he ducked beneath it, stepped back against the wall again, licked his lips, and said, "Hi."

"Hi, yourself," I said, and he looked nervous enough that I decided to wait him out.

He cleared his throat a couple times, nodded toward center stage, and said, "This is a terrible band."

"I wouldn't argue with you."

"They were Yoshi's, these guys," he said, getting his conversational feet under him. "His terrible taste. You wouldn't know it now, to look at him—how piss-elegant he is, what a sprauncy little nobleman—but he had a thing for noise. Not music so much, just noise."

I made a bet with myself that he was one of those guys who can't just let a conversation die out, and I won. He said, "What a disappointment."

"What's a disappointment?"

He shook his head. "The music, the bands, the whole damn thing. The tour. I had such hopes for it, my *last* great hope, probably, old as I am. See," he said bitterly, "that should have tipped me off right then. I mean, I *should* know by now, as long as I've been alive, that it wouldn't pan out."

"Why not?" I said, just to keep him talking. "It might have."

"Nope. People always want to make something wonderful, but we almost never quite do. This thing—this tour, the way it turned out—it isn't what *any* of us really had in mind." He was looking at the floor again, blinking rapidly. "It's like a cosmic joke. People, the way we're made, we can imagine almost anything, and we can imagine it as *perfect*, but we can't make it *real*, can't make it live up to our hopes. It's God's mean side showing itself. He made us that way on purpose, to amuse him. You know what's the greatest book ever written?"

"No," I said, "what?"

"*Frankenstein*. Because that's what it's all about. You got this guy, brilliant guy, he's a *doctor*, got his own lab, lives in a *palace*, no less. Studies his whole life, *invents* things, all he wants to do is make the perfect man, and he tries, and tries, puts his life into it, what does he get? Eight feet tall with bolts in the neck. Guy can barely grunt. Children run screaming. What kind of mean shit is that? That's God's sense of humor, that's what."

I said, "That explains a lot. Diet Coke, for example. First class on American Airlines."

"I'm serious."

I said, "I can hear that you are, and I'm sorry. Sorry that— that things didn't work out better."

"Aaaahh," he said, packing quite a lot into it.

I figured, *roll the dice*, and said, "Why did you guys start so early tonight?"

"*I* don't know," he said. "Yoshi's got a bug up his ass. Well, I guess we all do. We want this thing to be over. I mean—I mean, *you* look at us—what are you, thirty-five?"

"Pretty close."

"I still got it," he said. "I've always been able to do that. But, you know, you get to be our age, I mean the age of the guys and me, and it's like every day is a week, it's like those old movies where they wanna show you it's been a while, so a bunch of pages get ripped off a calendar. Getting close to the end, so we're, you know, sorta packing our bags."

"But you've got a show tomorrow."

"Well, yeah, sure. Tomorrow."

The band ended whatever it had been attempting to play, and the lights went down. A couple of the band members started to shout, but the main curtain dropped fast enough to make a noise when it hit the stage. Fiddles said, "About time."

I said, "Sounds like you guys are in a hurry."

If Oscar had been a gambler he would have been everyone's favorite poker opponent. He widened his eyes, opened his mouth, closed it, took a step back. "Well, I mean, come on, we've got, uhhhh, Jennifer Summers tonight, right? I mean, can't give *her* a short set. Lookit the crowd, they're mostly chicks, right?" He nodded to confirm the predominant gender of the crowd. "I mean, those guys, that band, who cares? Anyway, now they can get home and shoot up earlier."

"Doesn't sound like the band agrees with you." There was some junior-high style shoving onstage between the band's guitarist and two stagehands who had materialized to clear the playing area. The other band members seemed to be taking it more philosophically.

"Buncha jerks. They're lucky they're not out sweeping the street. They should be *glad* they got cut off. Now they can get home and . . . I already said that." He took another step back, bringing himself up against the wall, and said, "Nice chatting with you. We didn't really get time to, um, uhhh—my, my, *my*." He ran his fingers through the coils of silver hair and patted it into shape. "And who's *this*?"

I didn't even have to turn around. "Her? She's my cousin."

"Lulu," Debbie said. She had a plastic dry-cleaning package slung over her left shoulder, which, I couldn't help noticing, kept her gun hand free.

"And you certainly *are* a lulu," Oscar said, literally going on tiptoe.

"Oh, you big *flirt*." Debbie poked him in the ribs, prompting a high giggle and a half-hearted slap at her hand. "What a beautiful head of hair."

He fluffed it again. "I'm Oscar."

"But of *course*, you are. Junior's been talking about you."

"Yeah?" I got a dubious glance.

"Sure. He says you're the only one who really loves the music."

Oscar seemed to think about it for a moment. "And he's right. For the other guys, most of them, anyway, it's just an item on the balance sheet and a chance to get away from their wives. None of them has music in his soul the way I do. So, you're his, uhhh, *cousin*, right? I gotta say, you got the looks in the family."

"Oh," she said, poking him again, "*you* should talk, with that beautiful halo of hair. My mother always says the really dangerous ones are the devils who look like angels."

"Once upon a time, maybe," he said, so happy he was practically emitting light. "Once upon a time."

"Banked fires are the warmest of all," Debbie said as I tried to keep my jaw from dropping, "and they *last* the longest, too." She gave me a quick glance and said to him, "I hate to go when we've just met, but we've got to check up on the baby."

"Sorry, Oscar," I said, as Oscar said, "The *baby*?"

As Debbie towed me toward the door, I called back over

my shoulder, "So, how long do you think the show will last tonight?"

He started to say something, closed his mouth, and started over. "As long as Jennifer wants it to."

Behind me as we emerged into the apparently permanent drizzle, the DJ said, "Coming right up, boys and girls, *the Razorettes*," and I heard some enthusiastic female cheers.

"I remember them, sort of," Debbie said. "They were really pissed off, right?"

The drizzle had added *cold* to its list of modifiers, so we were staying close to the stage wall, giving me a wet right shoulder to go with the left. I said, "At everything."

"Well, good for them, why be selective? That's what show business needs, some really heavily armed women." She glanced over at me. "You seem kind of distracted. Did I interrupt something I shouldn't have?"

"No. I was just confirming my instinct that if any of these guys can be turned against the others, it's Oscar. And he's got a reason. Problem is, no matter *what* I do, it'll be a bust if I can't find a way to hurry Dressler along. He could wind up pulling into the driveway in a fucking chariot drawn by giant tarantulas, but he's not going to be happy if the guys he needs to talk to are halfway to Xanadu with his money. I can tell you, neither of us wants to be within twenty miles of him if that happens."

We reached the end of the driveway, where there was no wall to cower beside, and Debbie broke into a jog to get under the marquee. It had started to come down pretty good, so I followed suit. Bluto was still out there, holding the hot cup of coffee to his cheek as though it were the Holy Grail. I said, "They shouldn't just leave him there like that."

"Softy," she said. "Men are such marshmallows. He speaks English, right? Dressler, I mean. You *could* tell him to get the lead out. Are you *frightened* of him?"

"Of *course*, I'm frightened of him. I mean, he's nice to me, he trusts me, to some extent, anyway, but he's Irwin—"

She was reaching back to hold the door for me. "He trust you or not?"

"I just *said*, to some extent."

"So he trusts you and you speak the same language. What's the fucking *problem*?"

Struck by the simplicity of the question, I stopped, but she'd already let go of the door, and it essentially knocked me the rest of the way into the lobby. She was filling a bag with popcorn, which was frothing out of the machine, making a noise like an elves' gunfight, so Cappy had been wrong and there had been more upstairs. I said, "Right. You go check on the baby."

"Forget it," she said, "I'm not missing this." She held out the bag of popcorn, which I waved off, and then she leaned against the refreshments stand as I punched up the number.

When Tuffy answered, I said, "Is your car there?"

"I'll call you when—"

"Then put him on, and don't argue with me. I either talk to him now or I'm out of here and you guys can play it by ear, if you ever actually get here."

He didn't say anything. I listened to some nice guitar shredding by the Razorettes, who were opening with a bang, and then Dressler came on the line and said, "*What?*"

I said, "Please forgive my tone, but the way things are going, you're going to arrive at an empty theater. I mean, there will probably still be a show and an audience, and I could leave a few standing-room tickets at the door if you'd like me to, but I'm pretty sure that's *all* you're going to find if you guys don't locate an accelerator and push it to the fucking floor. Let me say this one more time: I'm ninety percent sure *they are getting ready to leave.*"

The pause was probably no more than five or six seconds, but I found myself holding the phone away from my ear as though it might explode. Then he said, "Noted, and thank you for insisting. The car is maybe fifteen minutes from the house, and we'll be waiting outside for it. It should take another twenty-five minutes to get there. Do me a favor and don't leave."

A *favor*? I said, "Done."

"We'll call you when we're a couple of blocks away. I've looked at aerial pictures of the place, so I know the layout. Is the driveway empty?"

"It was about a few minutes ago."

"I'll call when we're two minutes away. Please meet me in the driveway."

"Will do."

He said, "I know you will. And I'm grateful." He disconnected.

I said to Debbie, "He's *grateful*? He said *please*?"

"As he should be. Come on, let's go check on the baby."

26

Such a Doily

We waited a moment to make sure no one was coming into the lobby from either the theater or the bathrooms and then slipped through the basement door, flipped on the lights, and went down the steps. He was still there, but not for lack of trying: he'd managed to move, chair and all, about halfway around the pillar, and he gave us a stricken look as the lights came up.

"Wow," Debbie said to him. "Do that eight or ten times more and you'll turn into butter. And *look* at your nose, not that you *can* look at your nose, but take it from me, it's *enormous*. You might think about keeping it that way, it hides some of your face."

I said, "I almost feel sorry for him."

"You're such a doily." By the time she got to the bottom of the steps, Sparks was already trying to sidestep the chair around so he could put the pillar between himself and Debbie. "Just relax," she said. "It's not worth the effort to hurt you. Junior, are you wearing a belt?"

I said cautiously, "Yeah." The basement seemed to have gotten colder. Above me, the ceiling was vibrating along with the Razorettes' thumping bass line, and a fine miasma of old dust was sifting down onto Sparks. And, apparently, me, since I sneezed.

"Well, give it to me. Your belt. And gesundheit."

I said, "My pants are too big."

"Your problem. You were right about tying his legs, does that make you happy? Look, I'm taking mine off, you can take yours off."

I said, "A girl said that to me in ninth grade, and being a dimwit, I believed her. Scarred me for life. Turned my back to be a gentleman, and she kept hers on, and I can still hear her laugh."

"Come on, come on. I've got mine in my hand, okay?"

I said, "I hate this." But I took it off. My pants felt like I'd lost thirty pounds. I said, "If these fall down and I trip on them, you'd better fucking defend me."

"Try keeping them up." She was crouching in front of Sparks, who was whimpering. She put her belt around his ankle and the leg of the chair and tugged it tight as he tried to kick her with the other foot. She pulled a pin from her hair and stuck it into his kicking leg, and even through the junk in his mouth he emitted an interesting, completely genderless *yeeep*. "Hand me my purse," she said.

"Sure," I said. "Hand you your purse. It's so nice to have a *function*." I gave it to her, and from it she plucked a long, gleaming, metallic thing that looked like serious business, even from a few feet away. She looped my belt around his free leg and the chair leg nearest it, and pulled it tight enough to add an octave to his upper range. Then she pushed the sharp thing through my belt to make a new hole, and cinched the belt tight. She gave it a second look, poked a hole in her own belt, and pulled *it* tight. "Don't worry about the pain," she said to him. "They'll go numb in no time."

I said, "What *is* that thing?"

"It's a crochet needle, silly," she said, finishing with the second leg. "I customized it. It's amazing what you can do with a whetstone." She dropped the needle back in her bag. To Sparks, she said, "You going to be good?"

He said something that was all vowels, since he couldn't close his mouth, and she said, "Attaboy." To me, she said, "Now what?"

"Well," I said, "in a little bit, as much as I don't want to, I think we need to be out in the rain. The only way for them to leave, and the only way for Dressler to arrive, is via the driveway, and that's where he wants to meet us. I suppose we could stay up against the stage wall, but that's not much better."

"And me in my change of clothes."

"Don't worry, you'll look great wet. I think we're okay for a few minutes, maybe even thirty. I'm pretty sure they're not going anywhere until the last acts, which in this case are Jennifer and the Pussycats, are on the stage and the audience is really settled in. From that point on, I figure, they'll feel confident that the evening won't crash and burn, and they can make their exit. What they'll do, I think, is hurry things along until then, and while she's on the stage they'll feel free to disappear. Absolutely everybody, including the stagehands, will be watching that show. And Dressler is going to call before he arrives."

"Can you get me that big chair?" She pointed to a perilously sloping armchair, missing two legs, that had been shoved into the pile of stuff the rat had run under.

"It's pretty dusty," I said.

"So call *Consumer Reports*. Can you get it for me, or not?"

"Sure, sure. I live to move dusty, rat-infested furniture around."

"Push it so it faces me, okay?" I held my breath against what I visualized as an explosion of dust and mystery filth and was surprised to find it pretty clean. I towed it over to her, and she turned her folding chair to face the big one so she could use it as a footrest. When she was all settled in, she leaned back and closed her eyes. "Call me about three minutes before you need me."

In less than a minute, she was asleep, looking as defenseless as a slumbering angel. Gazing down at her, I felt an uneasy mixture of affection and fear. She *liked* me, whatever that meant to her.

Well, there was nothing to do here and I didn't want to wake her, so I went back into the lobby, took out my phone, and called my wayward daughter.

And got voicemail. The fatherly message I left this time would not have been endorsed by *Parents* magazine and would have required some bleeping to be heard on so-called reality TV. When I disconnected I was angry, worried, and somewhat ashamed. I don't talk to her like that.

I was in no state of mind to watch somebody sleep. So, just for the hell of it, I went into the theater, where the band was totally cranking, and I slowly walked the right-hand aisle all the way down to the stage, and then turned around and came back up, looking for I had no idea who. And whoever it was, he or she wasn't there, although one woman gave me a double thumbs-up, apparently in celebration of the music. And that seemed to be a unanimous reaction; I saw about a dozen fans, all male, up and irritating the people behind them by dancing and waving their arms, ignoring a relatively steady flow of paper airplanes aimed directly at them. When I turned back around, the woman who had given me the thumbs-up was launching her own plane at the dancers, and the band surprised me by kicking it up even further. I made a note to download all their albums when this was over.

Back in the lobby, I found myself fighting a sudden wave of apprehension about Rina. Up until now, I'd figured she'd been just as fascinated with Lavender as I'd been, but that conviction was getting thinner with every minute I didn't hear from her. I called Ronnie, who answered with a somewhat brusque, "She hasn't called me, and I've been calling her, too. The first time I called, she said she was having a great time with someone named Jasmine or something—"

"Lavender."

"Right. They were eating and she had a big surprise for me—"

"Clothes," I said.

"I guess. She sounded enthralled with Lavender."

"She's pretty interesting. How long ago was that?"

"Forty-five minutes, at a guess. So there's no point in talking to me, it would probably be better if we stayed off our phones, just in case."

"You're right."

"Are you in any kind of danger?"

"I don't think so."

She said, "Try that one again."

"No," I said, "none at all."

"That's a relief," she said. "I'll call you if I hear anything." She hung up.

I looked at my watch. It had been all of fourteen minutes since I'd tiptoed out of the basement to avoid disturbing the slumber of my lethal sidekick. And that made it about eighteen minutes since I'd chatted with Dressler.

The only constructive thing I could think of doing was to make sure the guys were where they were supposed to be.

It took a minute and a half, including a second or two to wave in what I hoped was a reassuring manner at Bluto—who had apparently been forgotten—to hike around to the stage entrance and look inside. Oscar had pulled up stakes, and the representative thug of the moment was Eddie Prince, who was hulking downstage right with his hands shoved into his hip pockets, the immemorial pose of high school tough guys. He was projecting menace, very skillfully, in the direction of the band onstage and Vera, the woman I'd chatted with, was giving him attitude so solid it seemed to have an actual weight.

I was wondering what the beef was until movement in the vicinity of the dressing room caught my attention, and I saw Lionel lumber into sight, followed by the Pussycats, including Jennifer, who was laughing with one of the other women as though they'd known each other for decades. So the second act of the night, the Razorettes, was, like the first, going to get an early hook, leaving Lionel and the Pussycats, who might also be cut short to give Jennifer the longest possible set before the curtain went down for good on the evening and, if I was right, on the tour.

And if I *was* right, by the evening's end, the four musketeers would be long gone, taking with them the gross receipts—which, I suddenly realized, would include tomorrow's box office take, too, since it had been a sellout since midday.

Clean sweep.

But how *soon* would they leave?

At that moment, the band finished a number and the lights went dim. I could hear the furious protest from the women on the stage as Prince, menacing even in the dim work lights, lumbered toward them, pulling something, possibly a blackjack, from his pocket.

I entertained a brief fantasy of going over there and decking him, but prudence and practicality raised their boring heads, so instead I turned back into the wet night and ran for the door to the office buildings realizing I'd already put another couple of minutes behind me.

At a trot, I told myself, I could hardly get much wetter by the time I got there, but by the time I *did* get there I had water dripping down my face. I pulled the door open onto a Bluto-free lobby. Lavender's empty chair fired a pang of anxiety at me that hit me right in the heart, almost making me yank out my phone again. *But*, I thought, *if she's not going to answer, she's not going to answer*. Fighting the fear that she might not be *able* to answer, I turned to the business at hand. Herbie had repeatedly stressed the wisdom of dealing with the things we might be able to deal with rather than wasting energy on fretting over the things that were out of reach, and that seemed like the thing to do.

Herbie's Lesson Number Three, repeated literally hundreds of times, was *Don't take anything for granted*. Even though I was 90 percent sure that everything I was interested in was happening on the second floor, I checked out the first level before going upstairs.

I had never, so far as I remembered, worn a watch that ticked, but I kept thinking I could hear the one on my wrist. I actually slapped it as the door to the downstairs offices closed behind me.

It took all of one minute to open every door on that floor and look behind it—*never* forget to check behind the door you just opened—and do a quick memory check. Whoever used the phone last had traded the folding chair that had been there for a wheeled one that looked like an improvement. Other than that, it was exactly the way I'd memorized it.

I wanted to go upstairs, but I needed a better fix on Dressler's ETA. I pulled out my phone.

When he picked up, he didn't greet me. Instead, he called out, "How much longer, Pete?" and Pete said, "Eleven to twelve minutes, depending on the rain. More if we hit a snarl."

Dressler said, and it wasn't a question, "You heard."

"I did. Do me a favor and—"

"Don't interrupt me. I'm in a killing mood, and I can get indiscriminate. You'll be outside when we arrive."

"Sure," I said, "if—"

"If nothing. Be there. You know where they are?"

"Sure. I mean last time I—"

"*Know where they are.*"

He hung up.

I stood there, looking at my phone as though it had just tried to bite off my ear. That was my first exposure to the person most people had in mind when they said *Irwin Dressler*.

Front stairs or back? The back was, as the poet says, the road less traveled, but it would require me to pass Cappy's office, and I literally didn't have a second to spare for him. I hit speed dial for Debbie, and she said, "Now?"

"A few minutes. Are you ready to go?"

"I'm always ready to go. Just got to put on my new shoes. Where and when?"

"I'll be there in three minutes. If I don't show up, flag Dressler's car when it arrives and tell him they've got me. I'll either be okay or I won't."

"You're breaking my heart." She hung up.

So maybe she *didn't* have a crush on me.

I went back into the lobby and took the stairs in speedy tip-toe mode, essential when you see red flashing lights bouncing off the window of a house you shouldn't, strictly speaking, be in. Made it to the top soundlessly and without an encounter and tiptoed across the hall to the big office, where I put my ear to the door.

A burst of male laughter, the kind I associate with dirty jokes. No way to count the mirthful, but it could easily have been three, or even four if Prince was back, but my guess was that the rule of the moment was to keep one of them in the stage area, in case a band mutinied or the place caught fire, while the other three warmed their hands in the glow of an expected happy ending. For a moment I asked myself what was to prevent three of them from deserting the fourth, allowing them each a slightly heavier bag of loot, but then I decided that it felt wrong, that the only one of them the others would lock out without much fear of reprisal was Oscar, and he was in there.

My watch, while it doesn't have an alarm, does have—or I *imagine* that it has—a way of squeezing my wrist when my awareness of time falters, especially when there's very good reason to be paying attention to every second, much less minute. I backed away, still listening, and then speed-tiptoed down the stairs, across the lobby, and into the increasingly ambitious drizzle, which was getting perilously close to saying the hell with it and calling itself rain.

If Dressler was on the fast track, time was getting short. I ducked into the stage door and grabbed my phone just as it rang.

"Getting there," Dressler said. Then, not to me, he called, "How much longer?"

"Six, seven minutes," someone—neither Babe nor Tuffy—said, and Dressler said, "You heard?"

I said I'd heard.

"You strapped?"

"I am," I said, "and I've got someone with me who's armed, too."

"Anyone I know?"

"No."

"Get rid of him."

It was risky enough to say no to Dressler without also correcting his pronouns. I said, "No. This is someone I trust, someone with serious skills."

"Your evaluation is noted. We'll see." He hung up.

I inhaled about a gallon of damp, cold air, hitched my pants up, and ran for the front of the building.

27
You Going to Shoot Them or Lure Them onto the Rocks?

"Ready to go," Debbie said. She was not only awake and alert, but also transformed from head to foot, and she'd turned on two more of the basement's overhead lights, presumably to verify details. The basement looked terrible, but she was a revelation. Gone was the frumpy junior-high-school teacher and in her place was the sleek seductress who in a 1940s movie would ceaselessly crisscross the Atlantic on an ocean liner, picking out millionaires, plucking a foot-thick wad of their excess cash, and leaving them happier than they'd been before the boat sailed.

I said, "Jesus, you going to shoot them or lure them onto the rocks?"

"My God, a compliment." She smoothed the front of her dress, a shiny little number in beige silk that looked like what you'd hope to be wearing when you finally win an Oscar. "Are we ready?"

"If we're not," I said, "we're late." I tugged at my pants, which were sagging a little more now that they'd gotten wet. "That dress is going to get wet."

"I'll live with it," she said, giving a final tug at the silk over her hips. It had already looked good, but now it somehow looked better.

I smiled at her and said, "How's the baby?"

Baby said, "Mmmmmmfffffff."

"Who cares?" she said. "Let's go, let's get out there."

I followed her through the basement door, across the empty lobby, then outside, where I saw that half an inch of slop had accumulated on the driveway, making it clear that the rain had increased to an almost malicious extent. I could actually hear it now, so the drops were both more plentiful and bigger.

"Look at that poor clown," Debbie said, lifting her chin in Bluto's direction. "This is like cruelty to animals."

"I actually see it as a good sign, at least for the rest of us. What it suggests to me is that the guys are nervous enough to get sloppy, forget details. I'll take any little edge I can and look for a way to sharpen it."

"You're nervous," she said. "You don't usually chatter."

"Jesus," I said, looking past her. "That poor old—holy shit." I started to run, and the rain, suddenly much colder, slapped me in the face. I'd been so busy talking to Debbie and thinking about the rain and looking for whatever giant car they would arrive in, that I'd actually been looking *past* the foursome of Dressler and three other guys, two of whom were Babe and Tuffy, as they slogged down the sidewalk toward us. I ran into the rain and got to them just as they turned into the driveway. Up close, I slowed to take in the third guy, who was worth multiple glances. He was big enough to hollow out and use as a storage room, and he had a hairline so low he could have combed his eyebrows into it. His tiny, almost colorless eyes huddled close to a nose that looked like it was borrowed from a crash test dummy. The overall effect actually stopped me a few steps short of Dressler.

"Don't waste time asking about the car," Dressler said. He was talking to me but looking past me, obviously at Debbie, who had followed me. "We already know we're not in it. And you would be?"

I said, "This is Debbie—"

"Halstead," Dressler said, nodding. "Sure, sure, I know about you. You did Mickey Engel, for which many people from sea to shining sea often drop to one knee and say *thank you*."

"Ohmigod," Debbie said with a hand splayed over her heart. "You've, um . . . you know my *work*? And I'm just, um, I mean, this is such—I never thought I'd—"

"Yeah, yeah, yeah," Dressler said. "I know how you feel. There are times I look in the mirror and say, *I can't believe it's you.*" He glanced at me and said, "Maybe we could get the little lady under that thing over there?" He lifted his chin toward the marquee.

"Sure," I said, "but we can't go in that way, we've got to—"

"The secret of success—anyway, one of the secrets of success," he said, walking past me, "is to consider things one at a time. You think Edison could have invented the light bulb if he'd been thinking about searchlights and movie premieres?" Once we'd followed him out of the rain, he turned to me. "So. An overview."

"Two buildings," I said. "Theater here and two-story office back there. Gotta go outside to get from one to the other. Theater's obviously in use right now—" I was interrupted by a burst of cheering and a loud, showy, deceptively difficult guitar run that echoed down the alley, so Lionel and the Pussycats were knocking them dead. "One of the guys was in there a few minutes ago—"

Dressler shook his head, and some raindrops took a dive from his hair for his shoulders. "*One of the guys?*" he said. "*In there? A few minutes ago?* Not helpful. Which guy? In where? How *many* minutes?"

"Right," I said. "In the theater, backstage. Prince. Maybe twelve, fourteen minutes ago. Hold on." I sidestepped him and jogged up the alley to the open door. It took me a moment to spot Prince because he'd pulled up a chair. Not many people exude menace sitting in a chair, but he managed it.

I went back. "Prince," I said, "and he's still there."

Babe and Tuffy were already sheltering up against the wall, but to the big guy the rain might as well have been a special effect. Dressler waved him in and then used the same hand to make a little circle that meant *hurry it up*.

"He's sitting," I said. "So I think he's going to be there for a while."

Dressler said, "Let's change his plans. Turk, go get him. No fuss."

"Sitting downstage right," I said to Turk. "I think he's actually watching the band. It's got some nice-looking women in it. Do you need me to point him out?"

"Nope," Turk said in a voice that had been dredged from the bottom of the sea around the time the first books in the Old Testament were written. "I seen him arredy." He squared, or perhaps cubed, his shoulders and splashed his way into the alley, throwing off malice in all directions, like handfuls of black glitter.

Dressler said, "And the others?"

"In the office building at the end of the driveway, the one you can't see right now. They're in an office on the second floor. That's where the money is, I'm pretty sure." I did a revision on the fly: "Or, at least, that's where the suitcases are that are supposed to be holding the money."

Dressler turned around and walked back out into the rain, angling left to go up the alley with Debbie about three steps behind him, close enough to be holding his coattails. She was flanked by Babe and Tuffy, who were wearing identical black suits and white ties that might have been created for a revival of *Guys and Dolls*.

"No, no, *no*," I said, "no, really, I'm fine, don't wait for me." As I stepped out from under the marquee, the rain doubled in volume, hitting the asphalt with a sound like a giant piece of paper being crumpled. I sidestepped a new but ambitious puddle that was laying claim to the bottom of the driveway. "Seriously," I said to their receding backs, "don't let *me* slow you down."

Over his shoulder, Dressler called, "Which office?" He reached the stage door and stopped there, not even sidling up to the wall to get out of the blossoming downpour. Debbie was standing beside him, soaking wet and loving every moment. Babe and Tuffy flanked them, dripping in unison, apparently not wanting to suggest that anyone lacked the sense to come in out of the rain.

When I reached the stage, I claimed a relatively dry area beside the open door and said, "Right up front. Second story, on the right."

"The one," he said, shaking his head wearily, "with that big fat *window* in it?"

"No," I said, with a surge of irritation. "That's the hallway. The window in that room looks out to our right."

"My apologies," Dressler said, startling me. Beside him, Debbie had her mouth open in apparent shock. "I'm wound a little tight here. And you think all three of them are in there."

"That's how it's been since the audience arrived: one on the stage and three in that room."

"What's downstairs?"

"No one. Empty offices."

He pursed his lips. "How long since you looked?" Debbie was hanging on his every word.

"Less than twenty minutes."

"Anyone else on that floor? The second one?"

"One guy. In an office more than halfway down the hall. He's a hired hand, the tour supervisor, keeps the musicians in line."

"Dangerous?"

I said, "I've been asking myself about that. He's an old hand, and I think his loyalties are more with the musicians than they are with the bosses. But he's no creampuff."

"Okay, okay, but if you're wrong, *you* shoot him." He looked around, seeming startled by what he saw. "It's *raining*."

Debbie said, "Let's get you out of the wet," and to my astonishment she took his arm and led him into the shelter of the wall. "We can't let you catch a cold."

"Not yet," he said. "Not until these fuckers are powder."

Debbie let go of his arm.

We heard a rising swell of applause from the stage, complete with some whistles of approval for, probably, the Pussycats. The noise seemed to push Turk through the door and into the rain. He had Prince literally by the ear, looking like a giant schoolboy who'd been caught writing something nasty on the whiteboard. Prince looked at Dressler, winced, and said, "Oh."

"You were expecting maybe the Salvation Army?" Dressler said. "Eddie. Do you want to get at least *some* of the money you guys were planning to steal?"

Prince seemed to examine the question for a catch and then said, "Yes?" as though he wasn't sure it was the right answer.

"And do you want to live to spend it?"

"*Yes*," Prince said. There was a moment of silence, which he filled by saying, "Please."

I said, "Is the door to the upstairs office locked?"

"Yes."

"Do you have a key?"

"Only Yoshi has—" At the sight of Dressler's upraised hand, he cut off the words and swallowed.

I looked over at Dressler, who gave me a little rolling gesture that meant *keep going*, and I turned back to Turk. "Was he armed?"

Turk lifted the hem of his dripping shirt to show me a beautiful little Rohrbaugh R9 Stealth Elite, worth roughly $1200. I said to Prince, "And the others? Are they strapped?"

Prince was looking at the gun like he was saying goodbye to the love of his life. "Not Fiddles," he said. "The others, though, sure."

"I'm extending you an opportunity, Eddie," Dressler said, leaning toward Prince. "This is your one and only chance to be on the winning side. Are you paying attention?"

"Oh, yes," Prince said fervently. "Yes, yes, yes."

A huge round of applause rolled up from the audience and pushed its way into the rain, and a woman began to sing.

"Listen, you got a hand," Dressler said. "They approve." To Turk, he said, "Give him his gun back."

Turk stared at him for a second but Dressler snapped his fingers and said, "I'm tired of being wet. Do what I tell you."

Turk said, "Pop the clip?"

"Of course not," Dressler said. "He's with *us* now." He stopped talking for a moment, doing a good imitation of someone who was listening to the music. Then, as I surreptitiously pulled my own gun and Prince shoved his back into a holster beneath his shirt, Dressler said to him, "Eddie? Eddie, are you listening to me?"

Prince looked startled at the possibility that he might *not* be. "*Yes*, yes, sir."

"Well, good." Dressler indicated Debbie and said, "This is Miss Halstead. Miss Halstead has taken out . . ." He glanced at Debbie.

Debbie said, "Seventeen."

"Out of how many tries?"

"Seventeen."

"Seventeen so far," Dressler said, "and I think she's shaving it. Shooting you will be her primary assignment when we're in that room up there, so you'll want to avoid ambiguity."

Prince blinked and said, "Sir?"

"Doing something she might possibly mistake, or even *start* to mistake, for something I wouldn't like. That could include clearing your throat all of a sudden. At that point she will shoot you in the testicles. Is that clear? Any nuances that you might have missed?"

"No, sir." He wiped his face, and for a second I thought he was sweating, but then I realized that the rain was gaining in confidence.

In the brief, waterlogged silence that followed Dressler's threat, the guitar ended a brief little run, the woman began to sing again, and I realized it was Jennifer, so old Lionel had rearranged the act. Her voice was pure and sweet and rich and, in the low notes, warm enough to make me feel like I could dry my clothes by standing in the open door. For just a moment, everything was all right.

"Girl's got a nice voice," Dressler said. He nodded. "Sings good. Sounds a little like Kitty Kallen."

28

What You Always Do Is Exactly What We Want

Most of us kept one hand on the theater wall, as though we were afraid the saturated ground might dissolve beneath our feet. Dressler was in front with me behind him, and the others followed in a semi-orderly straggle. When we ran out of wall, we froze for a few seconds, and then Dressler hissed to me, "Make sure there's no one downstairs and then do *exactly* what I told you." And then, a little louder, to the group, "*All* of you, do exactly what I say. Whisper *yes*."

Everyone whispered *yes*, and Dressler turned, touched my shoulder, and looked into my eyes. It wasn't the easiest gaze to meet; I felt like every failure of my life was blinking at him. Then he shook his head and said, "*Go*, Junior."

I covered the distance in fourteen long, splashy steps, landing on my toes to make less noise, and then I stopped and put my ear to the door. I listened for a shaky count of ten, opened it a crack, put one eye to it, and slowly opened it wide enough to make sure no one was standing behind it. I was listening so hard that the rain sounded like a monsoon. When I'd scanned the room to my satisfaction and nothing jumped out and shouted *boo* or shot me in the face, I said my usual pre-danger prayer, *Lord, I apologize for anything I might have done recently that pissed you off*, and then I pushed the door the rest of the way, until it touched the wall. I turned toward Dressler's collection of thugs, held up my palm, the classic *stay where you are* gesture, stepped all the way into the lobby, and eased the door closed. Then I held my breath for a long minute and waited for something to kill me. When nothing did, I latched the door and stood without breathing for long enough to ascertain that no one was walking around over my head. I heard some male voices engaging in a somewhat heated but indecipherable discussion. They sounded occupied, which made me feel a little bit less likely to be heard, so I speed-walked across the lobby to the door that opened into the first-story office space and lifted it on its hinges to eliminate any squeak. There it all was, dull but unchanged: phones still blinking, rooms still empty except for old furniture, the stack of beat-up suitcases still, far as I could tell, intact. By the time I'd finished my tour, I'd been in the building for almost two minutes, and it felt like a geologic age. I was pulling open the door that would take me back into the lobby when the door on the floor above me opened and, a moment later, closed.

My heart was doing its best to batter its way through my ribs as I hung suspended, one foot in the lobby and the other in the hallway to the empty offices, agonizing over what I'd do if the person who was moving around up there had been ordered to come downstairs—possibly to go to relieve Prince on the stage, as he had relieved Fiddles. How could I not have *thought* of this? The second he opened the front door he'd see everyone, with Dressler front and center. I had just stepped into the front room to paste myself to the wall beside the stairs—figuring that it would be a tactical advantage to have my gun in his ear—when the person above me began to walk *away*, toward the back of the building and, possibly, Cappy's office. I had just lost the sound of his footsteps when I heard a door squeak open and sigh closed. Burglars who don't want their career cut short learn to *remember* squeaking doors, and the door to Cappy's office was as noiseless as a sunset. That left the popcorn room, mostly empty now, and the back door—but that was by far the longest way around to get to the stage, and who takes the long way when it's raining?

The only other door up there led to the bathroom. A slow count of thirty later, something got flushed, and with a surge of horror I envisioned Dressler and his crew, still lined up like bowling pins along the theater wall as whoever it was walked back from the john and, you know, just decided to check out the old rain through the window at the end of the hall. I had a lunatic notion that I could wave them away, back them into the theater, but I was too late. The footsteps went back toward me, then over my head and then toward the front of the building. With that big fat window right in front of him.

I figured a little noise was the less dangerous risk, and I ran on tiptoe to the front door and pulled it open to try to wave them in as fast as possible.

And saw no one.

The increasingly chilly rain, the dark sky, the open stage door, a truck splashing by in the street. All of it as uninhabited as an old drive-in theater.

Above me, the door closed. I got rid of a gallon of air.

And someone whispered, "And so?"

I went straight up, maybe a foot or more. When I landed, Dressler was soothingly patting my shoulder with one hand and saying, "*Shhhhhhhhhh*," as he used the other hand to reach past me and stop the door, which was ambling toward me at a lei-surely pace, undoubtedly lonely for its latch. "You're still alive," he whispered.

"Ask me in a minute." My heart was pounding like Boom-boom's big drum amplifier, the one that had brought Dorothy's wall slicing through the air and started this whole thing. When I was finished massaging my chest, an action that seemed to amuse him, he whispered, "We're coming in, yes? And don't tell us to be quiet."

I mimed zipping my lips and took over the task of holding the door for them. Dressler had lined them all up practically touch-ing the external wall; whoever looked out the upstairs window, if anyone had, would have had to put his head right through the glass and peer straight down to spot them. They were emphatically soaked, and they gave out the dank, chilly smell of wet socks.

"You just stay next to me," he whispered to me as the others filed in, looking wet. "Everyone has an assignment. I got two killers, Turk and your girl, to watch Yoshi because he's got the most to lose, although he doesn't know the half of it yet. So that leaves Babe, Tuffy, and Prince over there to manage the others. Assuming that Prince doesn't change sides." He was already whispering, but at that point he leaned toward me and said into my ear, "You keep an eye on Prince, okay?"

For a supposedly lethal force, Dressler's army looked like leftovers at a picnic. Babe and Tuffy's once-dapper, once-crisp white suits were saturated and shapeless and dripping so heavily that the two of them looked like melting snowmen. The giant, Turk, had brown hair dye streaking his face, and his shoes made a squelching sound when he walked. Debbie, on the other hand, looked like she'd bought a dress that was specifically designed to be worn underwater and she had just come from a pleasant game of pinochle with some mermaids. She had an anticipatory gleam in her eye, and it was hard to imagine a group of men anywhere, no matter how occupied or genteel, who wouldn't have sneaked at least one appreciative glance. Prince was no wetter than everyone else, but he was the only one in the group who looked terrified.

Dressler turned toward the door to the downstairs offices and raised his eyebrows inquiringly, and I gave him a thumbs-up. He held my gaze a little longer, and I could see the thoughts tumbling around: Take my word that things were the way I'd described them? Send someone in to check? Go himself? After what felt like a full minute, although it was probably just a few seconds, he sighed, nodded, and gestured us all into a tight, damp-smelling circle, incongruously spiced by a breath of lily of the valley, courtesy of Debbie.

In a barely audible whisper, he said, "Does anybody *not* know his"—he nodded at Debbie—"or her assignment? Don't do it wrong when we get up there; I'm giving you a chance to clarify right now. Anybody?"

Nobody spoke up.

Dressler met everyone's eyes for a moment and said, "That's a small room, right, Eddie? And shhhh." Eddie whispered, "Right," and sort of hung there like a marionette who knew more strings were due to get yanked but wasn't sure which ones they would be.

"The *room*, Eddie." The whisper had turned into a hiss. "Small room or big room? Who's probably up there? Where are they usually in the room?"

"The other three," Prince said, sounding like someone who's on the lookout for a trick question. "They move *around*," he said.

"Ssshhhh," Dressler said, and drove it home by putting his index finger to his lips. "Which part of the room are they *usually* in?"

"The back wall," Prince said. "'Cause that's where the suitcases are."

"Good, so that's another question answered. Are they flush with—sorry, sorry, are the suitcases *pushed right up against* the wall or are they a few feet in front of it? And what else is in the room?"

"Ummm. Up against the wall. Like touching it, even. There's a couple of desks that Yoshi pushed off to the side—"

Dressler, who had his eyes closed, said, sounding weary, "*Which* side?"

"Right," Prince said. He paused and said, "And left."

Debbie rolled her eyes with such conviction I could almost hear them.

Dressler gave Prince an encouraging smile. "Big enough to hide behind?"

"For Oscar, maybe. The rest of us, we'd stick out."

"How many chairs, and where?"

"Four, but they move around. Mostly, they're at the end of the room opposite the door 'cause nobody wants to be the one who's farthest from the money."

"Nothing else?" Dressler waited, sighed, and said, "A window, for example?"

"We got one of those. On the right. Over there." He demonstrated. "Just one."

"Extra weapons?"

"Nope. We're all strapped, but nothing special. Oh, yeah, we got a watercooler. Yoshi found it in the room where the popcorn used to be. He says nobody drinks enough water, Yoshi does. We're all pissing like elephants."

I had the feeling he was enjoying the attention, and it didn't take an imaginative leap to understand that his opinion was rarely asked.

Dressler picked up on it, too, because he said, "You're doing great, Eddie. Anything we don't know? That could be important, I mean."

"Well," Prince said in all sincerity, "Yoshi wouldn't want you to know this, but he's got a second gun."

"Really," Dressler said, pal to pal. "Doesn't surprise me at all. Where does he carry it?"

"Middle of his back, where his belly button would be if it went all the way through. A few inches higher than his belt. Makes it hard for him to be comfortable in a chair."

"I'll bet it does." Dressler was looking at Debbie. "Anything more?"

"Yeah, he acts like he's right-handed but he's really, you know, two-handed. Ambidextrous. Can even sign his name with both of them."

"Think of that." Dressler was talking to Prince but still looking at Debbie. He said, "Is there a password?"

"A . . ."

"*Eddie*," Dressler said through his teeth. "What do you say when you knock?"

"Ummmm," Prince said, "sometimes I say, *It's me*?"

"And then do you have to wait for someone to open the door?"

"Only if it's locked."

"Is it usually locked?"

Prince paused as though he thought it might be a trick question. "Sure. Some of the time, I mean. It's got all that money—"

Dressler closed his eyes for a moment and then said, "Do you have the keys?"

"No. Uhhhh, Yoshi's got them."

"Right," Dressler said, "and sorry. At my age we forget things. Okay, here's what you're going to do. You're going up to the door and you're going to knock and then call out, 'It's me,' and then you're going to turn the knob. And if it's locked, you'll wait a few seconds and knock again. Okay?"

"Sure," Prince said. "That's what I always do. I mean, sometimes it's not locked when the guys are in it, but when it's locked, I—"

"Good, Eddie, good." Dressler actually patted his arm. "I thought that might be the case. It will be easier to remember if you just do what you always do: knock, tell them who you are, and try to turn the doorknob. What you always do is exactly what we want." He looked around at the circle. We were jammed shoulder to shoulder to be able to hear, and we smelled like a room with a bad leak in the ceiling.

"Okay," Dressler said. "Listen up. First on the stairs, Eddie, followed by Junior and me. Then Debbie and Turk, and then the rest of you. Just bunch up tight. The basic idea is, you shoot any-body who goes for a gun." He stopped a moment and then said, "Eddie. Most doors, from outside, they open on the left." Prince was watching Dressler's lips with his mouth open. "From *inside* the room," Dressler said, stifling a sigh, "the doorknob is usu-ally on the right. From outside, it's on the left. Is that the way it is upstairs?"

Prince squeezed his eyes closed, and Dressler said, "Never mind. Not a word, not a sound, not a sneeze. Are we clear?"

We were, apparently, clear.

"Let's go," Dressler whispered, "and God—keep an eye on all of us."

29
Kneecap

Just before Dressler opened the door to the stairs, I hissed, "The next-to-last stair at the top. Step over it. It squeaks."

"Listen to him," Dressler said.

"And I'm going to hold the door up there open for everybody," I said, "because the hinge squeaks when it closes."

"No," Dressler said. "We're not screwing around with the order in which we arrive. One of the last group—you, Babe—you go up right next to Junior and hold the door for the rest of us. But don't let go of it until Prince here has *knocked on the door to the room they're in*, and then get to us with your gun in your hand. When that door opens I want a lot of guns pointing in it. All of you," he said, "guns out *now*. And Babe, you hold this door down here until we're all in, and you ease it shut. Got it?"

"Go last," Babe said. "Ease it shut."

"See?" Dressler asked the group at large. "See how to do it? I don't need to ask if he's clear on what I want. People just don't get the kind of *training* we used to get. There's a million ways to get killed and most of them are stupid, but no matter how dumb they are, there's no way to live through any of them." He gave us a long look, and then he said, "Good luck, everybody. Remember Yoshi's surprise gun. Let's go."

As Babe came forward and pulled the door open, there was

an explosion of cheering and applause from the stage, loud even here, and Dressler said, "Must be for that lady. Sings like they used to, with a melody and everything." He looked around. "Applause doesn't last forever, let's use it." And he motioned Prince to start up the stairs.

Except for Dressler himself snagging the toe of one shoe on a stair halfway up and having to throw out an arm to keep from going down on one knee—an event that prompted a forest of outstretched hands that were hurriedly pulled back—we got up there surprisingly silently, still buffered by the applause, which was on the fade by the time Babe eased the door closed behind us. In the new silence, we all regarded each other. Everyone had a gun out except for Dressler and Prince, who, looking like his feelings were hurt, had put his into Babe's outstretched hand. With that formality taken care of, all of us except Dressler, Prince, and Debbie plastered ourselves to the wall on either side of the door, and Dressler waved Prince into knocking position. Through the door we could hear an energetic conversation, clearly heated, although the words were difficult to catch. Debbie positioned herself on Prince's immediate right; sure enough, the door opened on the left. Dressler was a few feet behind Debbie, where he wouldn't be visible until he chose to be. Then, after a long, breath-holding moment, Prince got the nod from Dressler and knocked three times.

Someone called out, "Yeah?"

"It's me," Prince said. It was a little shaky, but I doubted anyone inside the room would notice. Debbie was close enough behind him to be putting final touches on the tailoring of his jacket.

Someone who sounded like Yoshi said, "Why the hell aren't you—no, no, come in, stupid. Jesus *Christ*."

Instantly, everyone was more or less standing at attention on one side of the door or the other. Prince closed his eyes and said, "Coming in," and turned the doorknob. Before I could even blink, Debbie had a foot against his butt, and when she shoved, he stumbled into the room, windmilled his arms, got tangled in a chair, and went down. Before he'd hit the floor, Debbie was standing in the doorway, gun in hand, saying, "Think twice or die, *think twice or die*. Hands out in front of you, *all* of you, fingers spread, and that goes for you, too, asshole." Her gun was on Yoshi. "And *keep* them that way." Over her shoulder, she said, with a certain amount of glee in her voice, "Boys? It's safe to come *in* now."

I went in right behind Debbie with the giant, Turk, behind me, all of us checking the hands of the other men in the room, and when we were satisfied we stepped aside to let most of the others enter. Yoshi and Gold and Oscar were standing, as ordered, at the far end of the room. The chair behind Yoshi was lying on its side, so he'd jumped up and kicked it away. I'd followed Debbie into the room as fast as I could, just in case one of them was dumb enough to go for her, but they all had the stunned, frozen expression of someone who has looked away from a movie screen just as the monster first lumbers into sight and starts eating the supporting cast. Yoshi's shirttail was out, so he might have been on the verge of going for his backup piece. Just as Prince had said, there were four folding chairs all cattywampus at the far end of the room and a tidy line of big, expensive-looking suitcases behind them, right against the wall. There were five of them, all the identical make and color, and, being a crook, I immediately wondered whether whoever chose them had been contemplating the old switcheroo with at least a couple of them. Crooks are such cynics.

"You," I said to Yoshi. "I want your hands on top of your head and your fingers interlaced. Same for all of you, okay?"

As he complied, Yoshi said to Prince, "You dumb son of a bitch."

I said, "Shut up," just because I wanted to, and I heard Prince take a short, sharp breath, just barely on the contained side of a gasp. I looked back to see Babe and Tuffy drip their way in, their matching guns in hand, and then I heard a noise like someone hocking a gob of phlegm, and a bit of the wall about three inches from Yoshi's head turned into a cloud of powder, another testimonial to Debbie's silencer. Then Jack Gold let out a long, low moan, and I turned to see Dressler come into the room. He had slicked down his thinning hair and straightened his clothes as much as possible. The resulting look could be summed up as damp but dapper.

"Yoshi," he said softly, "I am very disappointed in you."

The wall behind the three of them was white, but not as white as Yoshi's face. He said, "Listen, I can—"

"Yeah, yeah, I'm sure you can." Dressler looked around the room: the chairs, the suitcases, the desks jammed up against the walls, the watercooler. "So prosaic," he said. "So fucking *banal*. The three of you—sorry, the *four* of you, don't think I've forgotten about you, Eddie—the four of you: add up all your brains, and on a good day you'd come up with a halfwit. The bunch of you, stuck in this ugly little room, planning to take me down."

"Irwin—" Yoshi's voice sounded like it had been peeled, like he didn't have enough breath to support it. "It's not what—"

Dressler said, "Enough," and though he hadn't raised his voice, Yoshi took what looked like an involuntarily step backward, coming up against the suitcase directly behind him and knocking it into the wall with a hollow *thunk*.

"Doesn't sound so full to me," Dressler said. "You guys did all this, the tour, the betrayal, all of it, for *small money*? Such a disappointment, all of you."

At the word *betrayal*, Yoshi closed his eyes for a long moment. "All of you," Dressler said again, "*all* of you, but lemme tell you, it's mostly *you*, Yoshi, and lemme also tell you how I know that. It's a little something you never heard anything about." He looked around the room for a moment and said, "Oscar. Get me that chair. Yoshi's not going to need it. Tuffy, you get their guns."

"Yes, sir," Fiddles said. He extended both hands to move the chair. When he was just a few steps from Yoshi, he yanked his hands back as though the chair were redhot. "Uhhh, Yoshi, could you move a little?"

I was surprised that the look Yoshi gave Fiddles didn't literally open a wound. Yoshi took a side step away from the chair and waited, staring a scorch mark into the section of floor just in front of his feet, as Oscar carried the chair to Dressler, turned it around to face the back wall, and put it down. Then he reached out to move it a little, but Dressler said, "*Enough*. Oscar, just fucking subside. I've been using chairs for a long time, you know?" He turned the chair around so the back faced the others, and straddled it. It was a very uncharacteristic pose for a man whose body language usually bordered on the formal.

He waited until Tuffy had possession of all the guns, including Yoshi's extra. "*Why* am I disappointed, you might ask? Well, first, of course, this is how you repay my friendship? You come to me, you ask, I give, right? Not a whole lot. But not lunch money, either. I figure, you know, we're *partners* now. But then what? You don't call, you don't write, you're ducking *my* calls like a teenager with a new girlfriend, and even when you come to LA, nobody's knocking on my door saying hi, how are you, thanks for everything and here's your free tickets, seats way down center, and maybe—just maybe—a limo. 'Cause I gotta tell you, that girl who's singing now, I'd hold still for her for eight, nine songs, maybe longer. Not dreck, like most of the acts you guys worked with. Sounds like—a little like—"

"Like Kitty Kallen," I said.

He looked at me long enough to make me swallow, and then he said, "It's a good thing for you that I like you. *And* it's a good thing for you that you're going to do me a favor tonight. A big one."

I had a sudden desire to go to the bathroom. I said, "I am?"

"Sshhhhh," he said. "I'm talking to Yoshi."

Yoshi was examining the air in front of him with the kind of concentration I always figured astronomers reserve for a potential footprint on the surface of Mars. It wasn't hot in the room, but little beads of sweat gleamed on his forehead.

He opened his mouth, but Dressler held up a hand, and Yoshi did a good imitation of someone swallowing his tongue. "This is going to take a minute or two, so make yourself comfortable. Oh, sorry, I forgot I took your chair. So just stand there. It won't kill you. Maybe."

He shifted his weight on the chair and glanced at the ceiling like someone who was organizing his thoughts, although I knew he usually organized his thoughts three or four days in advance. "See, I always say, it's what you don't know that'll kill you, and here's what you don't know. Okay? Seven, eight months ago, I said to myself, *enough with the airplanes*. Enough with the airports and the crap food and being all folded up in those seats with your knees in your teeth, and all the times you think you're gonna die. *Enough* already. And you know what? I'm getting a little *tired*—see, you were *right* about that, about maybe the job *was* getting a little too big for me. Maybe. And I'm thinking, stop with the planes, and forget San Francisco and Seattle, forget Portland, which is nickels and dimes, but Frisco and Seattle, they both pay pretty good. So I was thinking, get someone *younger*."

Across the room, I heard Yoshi swallow. Dressler said, "Sorry. You were going to say something?"

No one moved. I could hear my heart in both ears.

"Up to you," Dressler said. "Although God knows in your position, *I'd* be talking a mile a minute by now." Jack Gold, who hadn't moved a muscle since jumping up when we pushed into the room, cleared his throat, and Dressler said, "I haven't forgotten about you, Jack, but I'm talking mainly to Yoshi here because I know about a couple phone calls he placed."

Yoshi said, "Just fucking shoot me."

"Young people," Dressler said. "All the *time* they got in front of them, or *might* have in front of them, and still it's always hurry, hurry, hurry. So, it's a funny thing, I'm on the phone three, four weeks ago with Artie in Detroit—we've got a couple of Arties, but you know which one I mean, don't you, Yoshi?

And I'm telling him about maybe I'll be cutting back, and I just tossed out two, three names, guys who might step in, and when I stop, Artie doesn't say anything. Well, you know, Artie doesn't stop talking very often, so naturally my ears go up, I wonder did I offend him or something."

Yoshi said, "I don't have to listen to this," and took a step forward.

"But you *do*. Stop walking, right now."

"Or what," Yoshi said. "You gonna bore me to death? You gonna shoot me or not?"

"Not me, no," Dressler said. He glanced at Debbie. "Darling?"

"I'm not your fucking darling," Yoshi said, and then we all heard the doorknob behind us turn, and heads began to swivel around, and Yoshi grabbed the distraction to break into a sprint toward the corridor. He got to take three long, fast steps before Debbie blew his right kneecap off.

The impressive silencer muted the sound of the shot, but it couldn't do much to mute Yoshi, who went down as though the floor had been snatched out from under him, writhing around and emitting the piercing falsetto scream of a banshee, a sound that made both Dressler and me cover our ears.

In the tone she might have used to describe the view from her favorite vacation spot, Debbie raised her voice to be heard over the screams and said to Dressler, "See, the knee is a good spot because you know he's not going to die unless you decide to let him bleed out, and even that would be fifty-fifty because of, you know, the clotting factor, *plus* it hurts like hell, so you know he's not going to get up and stroll off anytime soon. Or maybe anytime, depending on which bits the bullet took with it."

"But it's a small target," Dressler said, "and he was moving. Very impressive."

"What can I say?" Debbie said. "You know the old thing about how you get to Carnegie Hall?"

"Practice, practice," Dressler said, nodding.

Yoshi's co-plotters were frozen at the far end of the room. Fiddles had his hands over his ears and the other two had theirs clamped over their mouths. If one of them had covered his eyes, they would have looked like the see-no-evil monkeys. I decided not to share the likeness.

Standing in the half-open door, Cappy cleared his throat. "Well," he said, "I don't want to, um, intrude, so I'll just—"

"No, no, no, no," Dressler said, holding up a hand. "No intrusion, none at all. Yoshi, shut up or she'll do the other one." To Cappy, he said, "What's the problem?"

"It's, it's, it's nothing. I just, um . . ." He blinked a couple of times, trying not to look down at Yoshi. "I just wanted you to know, to let *all* of you know, that the, uhhh, the Pussycats, Lionel and the Pussycats? They ran a little over because they were having so much fun, and Jenny just figured, ummm, no need to stop everything and close the curtains and make everybody wait around for the announcement and all that, so she just went over to the piano and started her set. Means we'll probably finish minutes early. I mean, if anybody cares."

Yoshi emitted a yip of pain. He had both hands wrapped around his shattered knee and he was bleeding impressively.

"*Jenny*," Dressler said, "she's the one with the voice?"

"Umm, yes, sir."

"Good, good, well thank you. We'll be finished in here pretty quick, maybe I'll get one of her records later. Tell me I can trust you, and that I don't need to make you wait here until we leave."

"No, sir," Cappy said, glancing at me. "I've got plenty to do." Dressler said, "Junior?"

"He's okay," I said. "He keeps this thing running."

"I know, I know," Dressler said, "the show must go on and so forth. What I never heard was why."

Cappy surprised me by saying, "Because we don't let people down. Those people in the seats tonight, they're here because even though we may not be the nicest guys in the world, we can give them something that makes them feel young again, and because they heard about it and figured out how to get tickets and paid and maybe made a *date* out of it, some of them. Even if it was with their husband or wife. And because they drove in the rain and because they waited in line, and probably a few of them paid for babysitters, maybe for their grandkids, 'cause we got a lot of kids being raised by their grandparents now, and because on the shows I run, we *don't stiff the audience*."

Dressler said, "If you ever want to do something different, call me."

"Sometimes I hate my job," Cappy said, "but I'll never do anything else." He looked down at Yoshi. "Is he going to bleed to death?"

"No," Dressler said. "He's clotting already, and in a few minutes he'll have a doctor looking at him, making that *tsk tsk tsk* sound some of them make, the one that convinces you that you're already dying."

"A few minutes?" Cappy said.

"Beginning when you leave. You want the clock to start ticking, go away."

"I'm gone," Cappy said, and he was. Through the open door came a tidal wave of applause and whistles, so enthusiastic it could have been an uprising.

"Wish I could sit back and listen to her," Dressler said. "So, just to finish up with you, Yoshi. Even though you already know some of what I'm going to say, I'll tell you that you didn't need to end this thing flat on your back with a knee no doctor in the world can fix one hundred percent. You coulda been running the Northwest. Woulda been a nice place to be, you know? If you did good, bigger pieces would begin to land in your lap and there woulda been more guys working under you so you could build up a good, dependable loyalty base. Which you would have needed when the old lion decided to step aside for good *on his own terms* so he could start to take naps, maybe catch up on his reading. You would have been right there standing in line, maybe number one.

"So that'll give you something to think about when you're limping around in Dinwiddie, Virginia, eating at McDonald's and looking for a car to steal. See, the thing *about* an old lion is that, when some greedy *young* lion decides to shove him to one side and grab the best seat at the table, the old lion is *waiting* for him. He's already finished off a couple of young ones and left them somewhere for the birds to eat. I mean, how in *hell* do you think he got to be an old lion in the first place?"

Yoshi's eyes were squeezed shut. I could hear him swallow.

"But like most people who secretly believe nobody else is real, you got it wrong. So you cheated yourself out of a promotion, but that's the least of your problems. Soon as you can travel—say, forty-eight hours from now—you want to be in one of the places where we don't do business. I'd leave the country if *I* was you, but if you stay in the States, you need to be someplace that's not on our map. Some smaller town in the South, like Dinwiddie, maybe, or maybe someplace in the corn states, which I hear are very entertaining if you have a long attention span. But you're going to need to heal quick and hit the road quick because in seventy-two hours, Artie—the *other* Artie—is going to put out a Black Letter with your name and picture on it, and it's worth fifteen K to the person who turns you into a spot on the carpet. If it's a team of two, they get ten each. We got guys, as I'm sure you know, who'd take out their mom and *her* mom for fifteen grand. On her birthday, no less. Hey, grunt or something to tell me you understand. I'd hate, or at least I'd mildly dislike, knowing you got killed just because I wasn't clear about things."

Yoshi said, "Fuck you."

"Such impoverished wit," Dressler said. He got up and went to the back wall, keeping his shoes out of the blood. "Which one of these suitcases has the most money in it?"

Yoshi said nothing, but Gold cleared his throat and said, "Second from the left probably has the most. Is that right, Yoshi?"

"Fucking idiot," Yoshi said through clenched teeth.

"You're sure of that?" Dressler asked. "I'm asking both of you: You're *sure* that if I took that one and another one home and popped them open, the second one from the left, the one you chose, would have more money in it than the other one?"

Gold said, "Supposed to be."

Yoshi said, "I'm dying."

"If I'd wanted you dead, you'd be dead by now. Press your hand on it, it'll hurt like hell but it'll slow down the bleeding. So let's open that case, okay?"

Yoshi said, "Do whatever the fuck you want."

"Junior," Dressler said. "Can you pop those locks?"

I said, "Well, sure, but, but I actually think—"

"Don't think, *open*. Tuffy, can you prop that door open? I want to hear the lady sing."

I said again, "I *really* think—"

"The suitcase," Dressler said. "*Now*."

Tuffy must have gotten the door, because I heard, to my amazement, the first verse of "Stormy Weather."

"It's *music*," Dressler said. Then he said, "Oscar. Come here."

I had pulled out the suitcase Gold had indicated and carried it to the desk that was closest to Dressler. I went to work on the lock as Fiddles crossed the room, avoiding the pool of Yoshi's blood by the widest possible margin. By the time my all-in-one jackknife was making the lock nervous, Fiddles was standing obediently in front of Dressler, carefully not blocking his view of the suitcase. If he'd had a forelock, he would have tugged it like some aging serf in the presence of the local baron. Over the music from the stage I could hear Yoshi breathing. It sounded the way I imagined Sparks's rasp had sounded as he sawed away at the rope on that catwalk.

"You and me," Dressler said to Fiddles. "We need some time to talk. Come tomorrow at two in the afternoon, got it?"

"Got it."

The lock was a little trickier than I'd thought, and there was a second lock behind it.

"And you, Gold. You come at three. Prince, you at four."

"Yes, sir."

"Bring something to put money in, all of you. I'm not giving away my paper bags. I have to fight Babe and Tuffy to keep the ones they bring home from the store."

It took a couple of long, silent moments before the lock gave up, and I could feel Dressler's eyes on me every second I was at it. His gaze had a chilly weight to it; it felt like the opposite of sunlight, like *cold* was somehow streaming through a window and making my hands numb and clumsy. It was, to say the least, a distraction. But then the second lock gave up the fight, and I took a look inside, tilted the suitcase toward Dressler, and said, "Gee, I hope everybody's hungry."

I don't know whether he'd been expecting anything other than money, but if he was it probably wasn't *menus*—hundreds of them—plus paper plates, paper napkins, and stationery, all pilfered, I assumed, from the hotels in which they had bunked. There were some newspapers, too, folded flat and jammed into the case to create a plausible weight.

On the floor, Yoshi laughed. It wasn't a very convincing laugh, but I had to admire the purity of his malice.

Dressler said, "Another one, do another one."

"Give me a minute," I said. "If you want to open all of these, we'll take them up to your house—"

"I hear a *but*," Dressler said. "But what?"

"But these were meant to be stolen," I said. "They were *designed* to be stolen. With the double locks, no one who managed to get into this room alone for a few minutes would have stayed in here, wasting the time it would take to get the damn things open. What he would have done, he'd have grabbed as many suitcases as he could handle and then he would have hit the road."

"Or she," Debbie said.

"Or she. So," I said to Dressler, "like I tried to say before, give me a damn minute, would you?"

Without waiting for a reply, I left the room, turned right, and jogged down the corridor toward the stairway at the rear of the building, and when I got down to the first floor, I went into the room with the cheap, beat-up old luggage in it. Sure enough, the first one I picked up—a battered canvas carry-on bag—had a bright, shiny new lock. I also grabbed a couple of old suitcases, both of them gratifyingly heavy, and lugged them up the stairs.

When I came in, Dressler glanced at the suitcases and said, "The old bait and switch. You're too smart to be breaking into houses."

"We all do what we love," I said, "if we're lucky. There are more downstairs." The lock was a little touchy but when I got it off and unzipped the bag, we were rewarded by orderly rubber-banded stacks of cash, some of it new enough to give me a brief wrinkle of worry, but when I flipped through a couple of the bundles everything looked reassuringly spendable; at least, there were no duplicate serial numbers. Under each rubber band someone had slipped a piece of cardboard, like the shirt stiffeners used by good dry cleaners. Written on each, with a thick black marker, was the purported total of the stack.

"This is thoughtful," Dressler said to Yoshi. To Gold, he said, "Jack. Make yourself useful. Pull any two of the stacks with the rubber bands—not in the top two or three layers—and tell me whether the count agrees with the number on the cardboard. And I mean agrees one hundred percent, got it? And put it *all* back when you're done, or your cut tomorrow will be just enough to cover the gas you'll use getting home from my place." He pulled a phone from his pocket and punched in a bunch of numbers without taking his eyes off of Yoshi.

"You," he said, inclining his head in my direction, "go get the rest of those. And you, sweetie," he said to Debbie, "shoot anyone who does something I might not approve of." He got up and turned his back on the rest of us. "Harvey," he said into the phone, "got a customer for you, bullet through the knee. If we're lucky it's a clean in and out. I know, I *know* the odds, but the guy's right here and I want to cheer him up. Since he's obviously not walking, you're going to need the meat wagon, but I got some guys who can tote him around for you, on this end, anyway." He looked at Yoshi with absolutely no interest, as though he were something Dressler had decided not to pack. "I want him to be able to walk when it's over, but I don't care if he can dance. We're on Wilshire, more or less midtown." He rattled off the address. "How long?" He said to Yoshi, "Can you live another twenty minutes?"

Yoshi said, "Fuck you."

"Yup, he's got lots of piss and vinegar," Dressler said into the phone. "He's only got one knee, but piss and vinegar all over the place." He glanced at me. "Why are you still here?"

I said, "Gimme ten minutes," and when I closed the door he was demanding to know what was so important, but I figured he was too distracted to stay pissed off. I took the front stairs two at a time and ran out into the rain—now really pelting down—and around to the front of the theater and into the lobby, where I found Bluto shivering and dripping water on the second step of the stairs that led to the men's room.

He looked at me and said, "Don't tell them you saw me inside."

"I wouldn't dream of it. When was the last time you got paid?"

He looked at me with total concentration, and I could almost see the calendar pages flipping in his head. "Two days?"

"And you get how much a day?"

Another pause, and I said, "Forget it. Here." I pulled out one of the bundles from the suitcase and peeled off ten hundreds. "Extra because you had a bad-weather clause in your contract." I handed it to him. "You can go home now. There's been a change of management."

He said, "Nobody's mad at me?" He hadn't even looked at the money.

"How could anybody be mad at you? You're probably the nicest person in the whole fucking place."

He got up, water still dripping from his hair, and folded the money, uncounted, into his sopping front pocket. His shoes made a little squelching sound as he rose. He cleared his throat a couple of times, and I realized he was blushing. "I'm sorry about your tire," he said. "Yoshi made me do it."

"Don't worry about it. Feels like a million years ago, and I needed a new set of tires anyway. Listen, probably tomorrow Cappy will be in charge of everything, so why don't you call him in the morning, see whether he needs some help? But for now, go home, okay?" And I turned and opened the door to the basement.

30

Foxtrot

I began to dial Rina's number before the basement door had swung fully closed behind me, but a glance at Sparks dictated an immediate change of priorities. Tied to the pillar in part by Debbie's scarf, he had somehow managed to work his way to his left, probably a quarter of an inch at a time, until he'd made it about a third of the way around the pillar, at which point the chair's legs snagged on something and he'd toppled sideways, chair and all, leaving his weight supported only by the scarf around his neck.

He was motionless. His torso was twisted tortuously, cork-screwed out of alignment when the chair got stuck and fell over. The pose was so lifeless that I was queasy about even taking a closer look, and when I did, his face was white enough to sug-gest heaven, seen from above. The cumulative impact was so discouraging that I immediately turned away and began to look for a carpet big enough to roll him up in so that no one would spot the body before I came back in the morning.

Then I jumped a foot into the air, propelled by a tiny all-consonants sound that he probably thought was a scream but that suggested the last two or three ratchets of a windup toy, so airless I immediately thought, *This is what it sounds like when a fish sneezes.* As much as I loathed him, it was, on the whole, good news that he was alive; strictly speaking, I would have been an accessory to murder, and I have an almost superstitious aversion to committing crimes that are above my rank, so to speak, and which probably call for a whole new set of skills for covering one's tracks. I paused for a moment, looking for an alternative to saving his life but failing to come up with anything. Also, he *had* just spared me from having to deal with a large, awkward, rapidly stiffening human cold cut, so I took out the little multiblade everything-knife. It was having a busy night. My hands were shaky enough that I sliced through the scarf and nicked his neck, but he was too busy sucking in air to lodge a complaint. Abandoning my misgivings, I cut everything in sight until he was sitting on the icy concrete floor, still pasty-faced and shivering with what looked like a combination of cold and terror. I put away the knife and pulled out my gun, and then I leaned down to show it to him. He didn't scream or wet his pants or beseech heaven for deliverance, but he nodded once, and I went to the chair Debbie had occupied and sat, training the gun on him. Then I said, "Hurry it up with the recovery. I need your full attention, in, like, three seconds."

While he released a little string of coughs without much air behind them, I checked my watch. I needed to be back in that room with Dressler and his hapless coconspirators. I was about to hurry him when he suddenly drew a breath so long and so deep that I half expected him to explode.

"Are you with me?" I said. "Nod if you understand."

He swallowed loudly, maybe milking it just a little, and then nodded. His nose, which had been a shambles before, had now swollen to a point where I figured he could probably see it with both eyes.

"Good," I said. "Now listen to me because there won't be any reruns. Here's the first thing. You're fired. The guys who hired you are no longer in charge; in fact, one of them is a few minutes away from being hauled to a hospital. Nobody wants to see you. If they owe you money, go home and phone them tomorrow, if you've got a number. They'll probably hang up on you, but you'll have the satisfaction of having given it the old college try. Do *not* come back. The next time either my associate or I see you, we will gut-shoot you and watch you die. With all the friends you've made here, I could probably sell tickets. Do you understand all this?"

"Yes."

He was *sulking*, his lower lip protruding so far that for a second I visualized grabbing it with both hands, stretching it back over the top of his head, and watching him suffocate. Reluctantly, I put the thought aside and said, "Second."

I waited until he looked up at me.

"Second, someone saw you late Thursday night, up in the catwalk, rubbing away at the rope that held up the house that landed on poor old Boomboom. Who told you to do it, and why? And if you don't answer me, the person who saw you will be talking to the cops by nine tomorrow morning."

"They made me do it," he said.

"Yes, I can imagine what a gaping hole it must have torn in your conscience. Who made you do it, and why?" I checked my watch. By now, Dressler had probably sent someone to find me.

"Yoshi."

"Why?"

"He thought that Fiddles had been spying on them for somebody. But, see, it was supposed to come down when Fiddles was onstage, standing up. It would have missed him by a foot or two, just scared the shit out of him. Only reason that asshole drummer got killed was 'cause he was *lying down*. But it was just s'posed to scare Oscar, tell him that, you know, it could get serious if he kept ratting on them."

"Where's your car?"

"Around the corner," he said, and swallowed. "On, ummmm, on Norton."

"Here's your Christmas present. Go get into it and never come back."

He said, "But—"

"Or die right now." I pointed my gun at his head. "Personally, I'm neutral about it."

He got to his hands and knees. "I want my machine."

"I'm not making myself clear. Get going *right now* or I'll blow your left kneecap off. You can ask Yoshi upstairs what it feels like. Out of here by the count of five. One . . ."

"My briefcase. It's got my keys."

I pulled the vile device out of the bag, rifled through the other stuff, and came up with his wallet and his keys. I tossed them onto the floor, just a couple of feet from him. "That's it," I said. "That's what you get. Get up now and get going or I'll just shoot you and wonder later what to do with the leftovers. *Move.*"

As if to express appreciation of my plan, the audience over our heads erupted into applause, shrill whistles, cries of "All *right*," and some vigorous foot-stamping.

He got up, looking pretty shaky, and said, "I don't know if I can drive."

"Well," I said, "it's either drive or get shot in the head. Or, I'll tell you what. You want to go upstairs with me right now and say hi to Irwin Dressler?"

Dressler's name has a way of galvanizing people, and it didn't fail this time. With a minimum of fumbling and a few aggrieved sighs, he retrieved the keys and the wallet and then leaned on the chair to get his feet under him. I heard something over the continuing crowd noise and realized he was mumbling, and suddenly I remembered that Leadfoot Perkins said that Sparks had mumbled when he was using the machine, that Leadfoot could hear it over his own screams.

The memory made my gun hand itch. But when I shoved it into my pocket, I realized that he was up and on the way out. I followed him toward the door. When he reached it, I stretched an arm past him to grasp the knob and said, "One more thing before you leave this room. You've met my friend, and you need to know I've got a whole *cloud* of people like her I can put on your ass, and if I *ever* hear you've built another of those things, you'll be dead within ninety minutes. Is that clear?"

I opened the door, and he scuttled into the lobby, but I got in between him and the door to the street. I opened the door to a chilly blast of sodden air and said, "Have I made myself clear?"

He said, "Yeah, yeah, yeah," and brushed past me, turning right, toward Norton. As much as I needed to get upstairs, I watched him go until the rain swallowed him up. And then I ran out into the cold and the wet, splashing toward the office building.

31

I Haven't Turned into a Rhododendron

I made it to the door into the lobby in about ten seconds, but that was enough to soak me, and once I got over the reflexive surge of irritation, I took a deep breath and thanked the rain. It had centered me, literally cooled me down, and probably made me less likely to shoot the next person who looked at me wrong.

Voices, relatively calm, were coming from the room upstairs, and as the lobby door closed behind me, I caught sight of a flash of light coming through the last couple of inches before the latch engaged. I put my hand on my gun and pushed the door open just far enough to let me squint through the crack. The vehicle had lights going in all directions, but the rain was so heavy it still took me a moment to recognize it as a sort of ambulance, an enormous SUV spangled with lights and with the huge intertwined snakes of a caduceus splashed on one side. As I wondered for the hundredth time what mythical fighting snakes have to do with medicine, the thing came to a stop and flashed its headlights, and I pulled the door open, waved my arms for attention, and pointed upstairs. The driver hit his brights for a second, which I read as *message received*.

I let the door swing closed, sprinted into the corridor between the downstairs offices, grabbed the remaining suitcases, and snatched up a little carry-on that I was briefly tempted to kick into a corner and come back for later. Then, encumbered as I was, I took the back stairs two at a time. By the time I shouldered my way into the second-floor hallway, I saw a couple of people, one of whom was Debbie, milling around at the other end of the corridor, outside the room the four plotters had been sharing, and I heard Dressler's voice, dispassionate as ever, calling for the people in the office to get the hell out of the way so the two guys coming up the stairs with the stretcher wouldn't have to do broken-field running to get to Yoshi.

More applause drifted over from the theater, and I could just barely hear the opening chords of Jennifer's indelible first hit, "Three Strikes." Debbie saw me, and said, "Where the hell have you been?"

"Tending to the baby," I said. "Tell you later." I followed the stretcher-bearers into the room, and Dressler looked over at me and said, "Now is better than never but I was getting ready to send out a search party." It wasn't a joke.

"Sorry," I said. "There was a situation downstairs, but it's over."

"Good," he said, paying me the tribute of not asking for an explanation. "Glad to have you on hand. Don't put that stuff down, we're going to carry all of it downstairs. I've had enough of this place. Tuffy, you take one of the new ones and open it and tell me yes or no. So," he said to the three guys in front of the far wall, "you all know what time you're coming?"

They said, more or less in unison, "Yes, sir."

"Well, I think you'll be happy with the payoff, especially considering what it might have been. You'll get a good piece of your share, minus what I pocket to compensate myself for all this tsuris. You can spend a while counting it when you get home, throw it up in the air and let it snow down on you."

"Like Scrooge McDuck," Oscar said, and then, when no one responded, he added, "sort of."

Tuffy looked in the small bag, which he had simply ripped open since he lacked my experience with locks, and said, "Money."

Dressler nodded, "Good, good." To the white-uniformed stretcher-bearers, he said, "Don't drop him. He's a jerk, but I think he hurts enough already." He watched critically as they eased Yoshi onto the stretcher, then he glanced at Gold, Prince, and Oscar and said, "You guys just stay up here for at least fifteen minutes. Then you can do what you want, watch the rest of the show, go home, I don't care." To me, he said, "Where's the pretty one?"

"Outside in the hall, waiting for us," I said. "She anticipates things."

"She's an unexpected dividend," he said. "I'll have work for her." He took one last look around the room. "Babe, Tuffy," he said. "Bring all that ugly luggage with you. And you, Turk, you get the decoys. They're probably empty, but they're nice bags. Since I'll still be taking airplanes, paying calls on people to prove that I haven't turned into a rhododendron, maybe I can use them. They'll all go in the trunk of the car with the other stuff."

I said, "Must be some car."

"You just wait and see," Dressler said. "It's worth it, I guarantee."

He was already on the phone as we went down the stairs. "Come around now, okay? We're on the way out. Just go to the marquee and—what? The *marquee*, the, um—"

"The place in front where the roof juts out," I said, and got a look that could have soured a gallon of milk on the other side of a thick wall. We stepped through the door, leading our badly matched parade into the rain.

"Where the fucking *entrance* is," Dressler said, turning up his collar. "I know, I *know* there's a big hole there. Pull to the curb just *past* the hole. Jesus," he said to me. "Maybe I should drive the car, too." He turned, looked over his shoulder, and said, "Sweetie? Sweetie, can you come up here for a minute?"

I said, "You never call *me* sweetie."

"Count your blessings," he said. "And I need to talk to you about your—"

Debbie inserted herself between Dressler and me with an ease that was almost symbolic. "Ah," he said. "*There* you are. I want you to take Babe or Tuffy, your choice, and you and him go around the corner and in front of the theater, check for anybody who looks like he might want to kill me, and then come back and tell me it's all okay out there."

"But what if they shoot *us*?" Debbie said, and I realized with a tiny jolt of something that felt like jealousy that she was *teasing* him. *I* never teased him.

"Then we'll hear the shots and when they die down we'll come out blazing away and you, you'll have flowers on top of your casket like you wouldn't believe. And every major crook in California following you all the way up the hill, making like they knew you."

Debbie said, "Will they cry?"

"Anyone doesn't cry, *poof*," Dressler said. "The *poof* means a bullet in the base of the skull, and I say *poof* out loud like that because I can't snap my fingers in the rain."

"I'd like to be buried in yellow," she said. "Black makes me look sallow."

"And so you shall, my dear, yellow as a Frito. But in the meantime it's raining, and I don't know about you, but rain gets *me* wet."

"Got it," she said.

"Good. Tuffy, give Junior that bag of money and go out front with Miss America here, let us know if it's clear."

"Sure thing," Tuffy said, and to Debbie, he said, "ladies first."

"*Now* you're polite." She took the gun out of her purse, checked it automatically, and walked briskly to the end of the driveway, making the turn at the end just as Tuffy caught up with her. Then he was out of sight, too.

I tucked the bag under my left arm and pulled out my phone, and Dressler said, "I want you to know that you've disappointed me."

I said, "I didn't think I'd had an opportunity." I started to punch the numbers, but he put his hand over the phone. I held my hand back and said, "Getting in between a man and his phone can be—"

He kept his hand where it was. "You don't need to make that call."

I said, "Excuse me? I *do* need to—"

"I'm telling you that you don't," he said, shaking his head. "No credit to *you*, though. You're blessed and you treat it like it's nothing, like it's a pocketful of change."

I said, "This is beginning to sound personal, and while I have enormous respect and even affection for you, there are only a few people who are allowed to get personal with me, and you're not one of them."

"And who are they?"

"This is not what I—"

He took his hand off the phone and gave me a look that practically froze the rain that was pelting my forehead. He said again, "Who are they?"

"Obviously," I said, "my wife or partner, whatever she is, my former wife—" Something drove past on the street, golden as a sunset, longer than Baja California, and so beaded with water it looked like they'd skipped the paint and gone straight to an inch of wax. It had more antennae than the average radio station. I said, "Is that us?"

"It is. Your wife and who else?"

"My *first* wife, my mother—are you going to try to sell me insurance?"

He was considerably shorter than I was, but he managed to look down at me, and he shook his head. "Where's your daughter?" he said, and for a moment my heart sank so sharply that I thought I might pass out.

I said, "What are you—don't fuck around with me, I don't care who you—"

"Yes, you do. And you should."

I started to say something, but what came out was, "Is my daughter in that car?"

"No thanks to you."

I said, seeing bright spots, "You just hold it *right there*."

"No thanks to you," he said again. "Wandering around in the fucking rain, not even a raincoat, outside a *rock and roll concert*. Do you know what kind of people—"

"*Is she in the car?*"

He stepped back, and I realized I'd taken a couple of quick steps in his direction, and he said, "Like I said, no thanks to you."

"I've been phoning her since *lunchtime*. She wasn't alone, she was with—"

"She still is," Dressler said. Then he startled me by reaching up and patting my shoulder. "You're a good boy," he said, "overall, I mean. Not the world's best father, maybe, but a good boy. So you're telling me that you knew Rina was with—with . . ."

"Lavender," I said. "And I don't have to tell—"

"Right, *Lavender*. Such a name. And that was all right with you?"

"Was it *all right*—" I started to turn toward the giant vehicle, but he grabbed my arm. Generally speaking, Dressler didn't grab people.

"So you think she's . . ." His voice tapered off and he lowered his eyes until he was looking at my chest. "You think she's, umm, all right?"

"*Lavender?*" I said.

"You think she's all right?"

"I think she's a terrific human being," I said. "Meeting her was the best thing to come out of this whole nightmare. Do you think I'd trust Rina with—"

"I'm glad to hear it," he said. Then he started to say something and swallowed.

"Come *on*," Debbie shouted, waving us toward her. "The palace has arrived."

The rain doubled in volume, to a degree that felt almost personal, and the others hurried past us toward the shelter of the giant whatever-it-was, but Dressler didn't seem to notice. "Wait," he said, even though I hadn't moved. "So you think she's okay?"

I said, "I think she's solid gold."

There was a long pause, and then he said, "She seems nice."

I waited, but that was apparently it. The rain increased. Just to move things along, I said, "Yeah, like I said, I think she's twenty-four carat."

He said, "Don't laugh at me."

"Last thing on my mind."

"Do you think . . ." He swallowed. "Your daughter's friend . . ."

"Lavender," I said.

"I haven't forgotten. So, *Lavender*, do you think, ummm, do you think she can foxtrot?"

Whatever I was about to say vanished from my mind, as though the rain had dissolved it. I said, "I think she can probably do the Texas two-step on one foot."

"Yes," he said. "That's what I think." Then he said, "Let's have a party."

"A party."

"All of us. At my house. Now. You and your daughter—we can send the car for your wife—plus the boys, your friend Debbie, and ummm, Miss, umm, Miss Lavender. Do you think she'd like that?"

I said, "I can't actually *speak* for her, of course, but I'll bet you a thousand dollars right now that she'll jump at it."

"Well," he said. He was oblivious of the rain running down his face.

I said, "Well."

He threw an arm around my shoulder. Since he'd completely forgotten the gun in his hand, its barrel scraped my chin as he pulled me in the direction of the biggest luxury vehicle in the world, half limousine, half school bus, six rows of very wide seats. Rina waved at me, a bit tentatively, from the second row. Next to her, Lavender serenely watched our advance.

"Hurry *up*," Dressler said, picking up the pace. "Get it moving, you're a young man, get the lead out. What are we *waiting* for?"